HEAD LAND

Ten Years of the Edge Hill Short Story Prize

HEAD LAND

Ten Years of the Edge Hill Short Story Prize

Edited by Rodge Glass

First published September 2016
Freight Books & Edge Hill University Press
49-53 Virginia Street
Glasgow, G1 1TS
www.freightbooks.co.uk

A CIP catalogue reference for this book is available from the British Library.

ISBN 978-1-910449-38-7
eISBN 978-1-908754-82-0

Typeset by Freight in Plantin
Printed and bound in Poland

the publisher acknowledges investment from
Creative Scotland toward the publication of this book

Edge Hill
University

An Anthology is a Joint Effort

Contents

Introduction

A Brief Look at the Landscape

by Rodge Glass

Times have changed.

In the 21st century, the short story world is organised. It's joined up. It fights for its space and fights well. It's sure to be seen. No longer can lovers of the form complain about being marginalised, overlooked, maligned – no more sad-faced complaints, please, about being seen as a 'poor cousin' to the novel by readers and reviewers alike; or lamenting attitudes on the European side of the Atlantic when it comes to the shorter form. We don't need book festivals to punctuate their schedules any more with panels on 'the state of the short story', hand-wringing about 'what is to be done?' I don't say this because I believe the common view in the writing community is that the form is in rude health. On the contrary, you still hear those complaints. But because I think that *should* be the common view. I believe the short story form in the UK and Ireland in particular *is* in rude health right now, and to say otherwise is to ignore many factors that have changed the game in the last decade. Yes, writers will tell you that publishers receive the news of their latest collection with an 'ah yes, very nice, but how is that novel coming along?' Yes, advances for short story collections remain, in most cases, small change, and it's a battle for short stories to find shelf space in book shops. But that's not the whole story.

The truth is, there has been a significant sea change which shouldn't be ignored. If you are now a young short story writer looking to make your mark, there are an abundance of opportunities out there, and it's easier than ever in our super-connected online communities to find each other, give and receive advice, make recommendations and share links to this or that competition. And they are myriad. There are now more short story prizes than ever before too, some life-changing in terms of money, opportunity and reputation – I'm thinking particularly of the £30,000

Sunday Times Short Story Award for a single story, won by Kevin Barry in 2012 (featured here), whose debut collection, *There Are Little Kingdoms*, was published as recently as 2007 by an Irish independent, The Stinging Fly Press, on a small print run. Less than a decade later, Barry is now one of the most revered authors at work in the form, with an international reputation. Then there's the £15,000 BBC National Short Story Award, which Jon McGregor (featured here) was runner-up in twice, which our own 2013 winner Sarah Hall won in the same year for her story 'Mrs Fox', and which is tied to annual publications by the groundbreaking short story-exclusive pioneers, Comma Press of Manchester. (And Comma have two representatives in this book.) Until recently there was also the Frank O'Connor International Short Story Award, won by Carys Davies in 2015, another prominent, distinctive voice who features in *Head Land*. (Are you seeing a pattern yet?)

In terms of publications there's also the recent high-profile history of the short story, Philip Hensher's exquisite and exhaustive two-volume anthology *The Penguin Book of the British Short Story*, spanning the earliest niche magazines and going right up to the present day. Hensher includes less than twenty living writers in his vast selection. Four of those also feature here – Adam Marek, the master of the artifice short story, is one of them. If you survey the landscape of short story for just a little while, you'll start to notice who many of those making the pace are. Where Hensher's excellent overview aims to take in the whole history of the form from Dickens and Defoe right through the 20th Century and up to the present day, our book aims to give a snapshot of the contemporary short story, zooming in on what it does in the now.

An argument sometimes put forward by doom-mongers is that our greatest prose writers don't make their name in the form; they treat it like a hobby. Part-time. An indulgence. That couldn't be more wrong. There are several of the UK's finest prose writers who have chosen to specialise in short fiction, and have remained with heavyweight publishers while doing their best work. It's often said that major publishers don't sign short stories. So it's interesting, I think, that both Jonathan Cape and Faber & Faber are so well represented in this anthology. Helen Simpson, for example, is a Cape writer who has worked exclusively in the short story, and been widely celebrated for it. (And yes, she features here too.) Ali Smith is a true short story specialist, an expert in both the experimental and the accessible. A.L. Kennedy also has never left the short form behind – though known partly as a novelist, she has published seven collections of stories, which is hardly a part-time contribution. Sure, not everyone can win the Windham-Campbell prize recently awarded to Tessa Hadley (featured here, of course), or the worldwide Dylan Thomas Prize won by Rachel Trezise (you guessed it). And anyway, prizes aren't everything. Art is not judged ultimately by who won what. Prizes, like all shorthand, can be reductive too. But for the short story, prizes occupy a crucial place in the literary landscape. They offer hope. They help writers keep going. To keep writing hard and clear about what hurts – and to resist commercial imperatives. These imperatives are increasingly resisted by independent publishers too. Freight Books, our partner for this, our first ever Edge Hill University Press book, published several first class collections and several story anthologies in 2015, notably from Janice Galloway and Lara Williams; they also run the bold *Gutter* magazine. Nicholas Royle of Salt Publishing edits the superb *Best British Short Stories* series which celebrates names known and unknown, often uncovering real gems – including writers who have also featured on our own shortlists over the last decade. Royle, of course, is also a fine short story writer – and yes, he's featured here too. The truth is, in the world of the short story, opportunities are many and restrictions are few. If you're good enough, the chances are you will make your mark eventually. It's not perfect. But not many worlds are that meritocratic.

At the same time as all this, there is an explosion in interest in the form from students in our universities. Creative Writing courses are popping up all over the nations of England, Scotland, Wales and Ireland, both the North and the Republic too. There are more readers and writers than ever. In terms of academic attention, there's more of that too, with many of the leading lights in the form now working within academia, crossing over between creative and critical work and back again. Hensher, Hadley, McGregor and many others find reasons to work in universities, often passing on enthusiasm for the short story form to the next generation. I'm writing this in the week that the European Network for Short Fiction Research is holding its latest conference, bringing together critics and short story practitioners at our own Edge Hill campus in a field which is growing and evolving with speed. There's no shortage of interest, or lack of quality either.

In this introduction, this cheerleading list, I feel I've hardly scratched the surface of the current literary landscape. I've not mentioned the many fora, websites, live literature nights, courses and the like which show time and again the appetite for the form. I've not mentioned the continuing strength of short fiction in Ireland, who contribute giants like Colm Tóibín and Claire Keegan to these pages as well as exciting newcomers like Madeleine D'Arcy. I've not covered the extraordinary strength in depth in Scotland, another powerful and distinct tradition represented here by the likes of John Burnside and Kirsty Gunn, amongst others. Why, you might wonder, am I mentioning all this – aside from because it gives me an excuse to namecheck some of the writers in this anthology? And to show that it's not just me who thinks they're worth celebrating? Because I believe that the Edge Hill Prize is a part of the short story's success story over the last ten years. That culture change. That shift from the margins, inwards. And I think this book is a small part of that too. *Head Land* exists to celebrate the contribution our Prize has made, give it a home between covers and, most importantly, to return people to the work itself.

Despite the many others listed above, the Edge Hill Short Story Prize remains what it was ten years ago: the only UK & Ireland prize for a single-authored collection that exists. We also run a parallel prize for our MA students, represented in *Head Land* by Carys Bray, a previous winner of that award and now a successful prose writer in her own right. There's a third award too, The Reader's Prize, awarded by the students themselves to their favourite of each year's shortlist. Much of the credit for the existence of all these must go to Ailsa Cox, the world's first Professor of Short Fiction, who has been running the Prize since its inception. When the Creative Writing team came up with the idea of setting up an in-University Press, it seemed natural for the Short Story Prize to be the subject of our first publication, and we're grateful to Ailsa for giving us her blessing. Happily, this coincided with the 10th anniversary of the Prize. Once the first project was decided, my co-director James Byrne and I set about appointing students to the various roles – and since then, those students have been getting on with the business of publishing. My own contribution here has been minimal. The credit goes to the interns. They have selected and sifted the stories, engaged with the authors, organised the events and pushed for the publicity. Which was the whole point in the first place. To empower students, so they can get meaningful experience in the publishing world, and prove they can do a great job when given the opportunity.

And so, finally, to *Head Land*. But why this name? Well, there is no overarching theme in this book, no crowbarring of these stories into some forced stylistic approach or trend. I've read too many introductions where editors seek to find unity where there is little. No, when putting the book together we simply invited a selection of writers who have won or been shortlisted for the Prize over the last decade – some of our favourites, some we felt should be recognised – and asked those writers to donate a single story from their nominated collection to this anthology. Which means that what holds the stories together is quality, not content. In some cases, writers chose the particular stories themselves. Their favourites. Ones they felt represented their work in the short story form best. In some cases, writers liked the idea of our press team making the selection. Which they were happy to do.

As with any collection of voices, there is diversity here, it's hard to summarise without being reductive, and I don't want to single out any particular story either. What's important is to hear each writer's voice, to observe the place they occupy in the landscape. Because that's what a great short story writer is – someone who occupies a unique space on the page. Who can be mistaken for no one else. Whose sentences can only be their own. So, *Head Land* it is then. We hope you like it. If you like it, tell others about it, about this form, these writers. Search out their other books and also those featured on our shortlists who don't appear here – this is not a Best Of, after all – just a selection. A taster. A sample. And most of all, a celebration.

Rodge Glass, Reader in Literary Fiction, Co-Director of Edge Hill University Press

Colm Tóibín

A Priest in the Family

She watched the sky darken, threatening rain.

'There's no light at all these days,' she said. 'It's been the darkest winter. I hate the rain or the cold, but I don't mind it at all when there's no light.'

Father Greenwood sighed and glanced at the window.

'Most people hate the winter,' he said.

She could think of nothing more to say and hoped that he might go now. Instead, he reached down and pulled up one of his grey socks, then waited for a moment before he inspected the other and then pulled that up too.

'Have you seen Frank lately?' he asked.

'Once or twice since Christmas,' she said, 'he has too much parish work to come and visit me very much, and maybe that's the way it should be. It would be terrible if it was the other way around, if he saw his mother more than his parishioners. He prays for me, I know that, and I would pray for him too if I believed in prayer, but I'm not sure I do. But we've talked about that, you know all that.'

'Your whole life's a prayer, Molly,' Father Greenwood said and laughed warmly.

She shook her head in disbelief.

'Years ago all the old women spent their lives praying. Now, we get our hair done and play bridge and go to Dublin on the free travel, and we say what we like. But I've to be careful what to say in front of Frank, he's very holy. He got that from his father. It's nice having a son a priest who's very holy. He's one of the old school. But I can say what I like to you.'

'There are many ways of being holy,' Father Greenwood said.

'In my time there was only one,' she replied.

When he had gone she got the *RTE Guide* and opened it for the evening's television listings; she began to set the video to record *Glenroe*. She worked slowly, concentrating. In the morning, when *The Irish Times* had been read, she would put her feet up and watch this latest episode. Now in the hour she had to spare before she went out to play bridge, she sat at the dining room table and flicked through the newspaper, examining headlines and photographs, but reading nothing, and not even thinking, letting the time pass easily.

It was only when she went to fetch her coat in the small room off the kitchen that she noticed Father Greenwood's car still in front of the house; as she peered out, she could see him sitting in the driver's seat.

Her first thought was that he was blocking her car and she would have to ask him to move. Later, that first thought would stay with her as a strange and innocent way of keeping all other thoughts at a distance; it was something which almost made her smile when she remembered it.

He opened the car door as soon as she appeared with her coat held distractedly over her arm.

'Is there something wrong? Is it one of the girls?' she asked.

'No,' he said, 'no, there's not.'

He moved towards her, preparing to make his way back into the house. She wished in the second they locked eyes that she could escape now to an evening of cards and company, get by him quickly and walk to the bridge club at the hotel, if she had to. Anything, she thought, to stop him saying whatever it was he had come to say.

'Oh, it's not the boys! Oh, don't say it's the boys have had an accident and you're afraid to tell me!' she said.

He shook his head with certainty.

'No, Molly, not at all, no accident.'

As he reached her he caught her hand as though she would need his support nonetheless.

'I know you have to go and play bridge,' he said.

She believed then that it could not be anything urgent or important. If she could still play bridge then clearly no one was dead or injured.

'I have a few minutes,' she said.

'Maybe I can come back another time. We can talk more,' he said.

'Are you in any trouble?' she asked.

He looked at her as though the question puzzled him.

'No,' he said.

She put her coat down on a chair in the hallway.

'No,' he said again, his voice quieter.

'Then we'll leave it for another time,' she said calmly and smiled as best she could. She watched him hesitate, and she became even more determined that she would go immediately. She picked up her coat and made sure the keys were in the pocket.

'If it can wait, then it can wait,' she said.

He turned away from her, walking out of the hallway towards his car.

'Right you be,' he said. 'Enjoy your night. I hope I didn't alarm you.'

She was already moving away from him, her car keys in her hand, having closed the front door firmly behind her.

The next day, when she had finished her lunch, she took her umbrella and her rain coat and walked to the library on the Back Road. It would be quiet, she knew, and Miriam the new girl would have time for her, she hoped. There was already a molly@hotmail.com, Miriam had told her on her last visit to learn how to use the library computer, so for her first email address she would need to add something to the word 'Molly' to make it original, with a number maybe, hers alone.

'Can I be Molly80?' she had asked.

'Are you 80, Mrs O'Neill?'

'Not yet, but it won't be long.'

'Well, you don't look it.'

Her fingers had stiffened with age, but her typing was as accurate and fast as when she was twenty.

'If I could just type, I'd be fine,' she said as Miriam moved an office chair close to the computer and sat beside her, 'but that mouse will be the end of me. It doesn't do what I want it to do at all. And my grandsons, the two oldest ones who know all about computers, they laughed when I called it a rat. They can make it do whatever they want. I hate having to click. It was much simpler in my day. Just typing. No clicking.'

'Oh when you're sending emails and getting them, you will see the value of it,' Miriam said.

'Yes, I told them I was going to send them an email as soon as I could. I'll have to think of what to put into it.'

She turned her head when she heard voices and saw two women from the town returning books to the library. They were studying her with a fierce curiosity.

'Look at you Molly. You've gone all modern,' one of them said.

'You have to keep up with what's going on,' she said.

'You never liked missing anything, Molly. You'll get all the news from that now.'

She turned and began to practise opening her Hotmail account, as Miriam went to attend to the women, and she did not turn again as she heard them browsing among the stacks of books, speaking to one another in hushed voices.

Later, when she felt she had used enough of Miriam's patience, she walked towards the cathedral and down Main Street into Irish Street. She greeted people she met on the street by name, people she had known all of her life, the children of her contemporaries, many of them grown middle-aged themselves, and even their children, all familiar to her. There was no need to stop and talk to them. She knew all about them, she thought, and they about her. When news spread widely that she was learning how to use the computer in the library, one or two of them would ask her how it was going, but for the moment she would be allowed to pass with a warm, brisk greeting.

Her sister-in-law sat in the front room of her house with the fire lighting. Molly tapped on the window and then waited while Jane fumbled with the automatic system.

'Push now!' she could hear her voice through the intercom.

She pushed the door firmly and, having closed it behind her, let herself into Jane's sitting room.

'I look forward to Monday,' Jane said, 'when you come down. It's lovely to see you.'

'It's cold outside, Jane,' she said, 'but it's nice and warm in here, thank God.'

It would be easier, more relaxing somehow, she thought, if one of them made tea, but Jane was too frail to move very much and too proud to want her sister-in-law in her kitchen. They sat opposite each other as Jane tended the fire almost absent-mindedly. There was, she thought, nothing to say, and yet there would never be a moment's silence between them.

'How was the bridge?' Jane asked.

'I'm getting worse at it,' Molly replied, 'but I'm not as bad as some of them.'

'Oh, you were always a great card player,' Jane said.

'But for bridge you have to remember all the rules and the right bids and I'm too old, but I enjoy it, and then I enjoy when it's over.'

'It's a wonder the girls don't play,' Jane said.

'When you have young children, you've enough to think about. They never have a minute.'

Jane nodded distantly and looked into the fire.

'They're very good, the girls,' she said. 'I love it when they come down to see me.'

'You know, Jane,' Molly replied, 'I like seeing them and all that, but I wouldn't care if they didn't visit from one end of the week to the next. I'm one of those mothers who prefers her grandchildren to her children.'

'Oh, now,' Jane replied.

'It's true, Jane. I would go mad if a week went by and my lovely grandsons didn't come down on a Wednesday for their tea, and I'm always raging when their mothers come to collect them. I always want to keep the boys.'

'They're nice when they are at that age,' Jane said. 'And it's so handy that they live so close together and they get on so well.'

'Has Frank been here?' Molly asked.

Jane looked up at her, almost alarmed. For a moment a pained expression came on her face.

'Oh Lord no,' she said.

'I haven't seen him much since Christmas either,' Molly said, 'but you usually know more about him. You read the parish newsletter. He gave up sending it to me.'

Jane bowed her head, as though searching for something on the floor.

'I must tell him to call in to you,' Molly said. 'I don't mind him neglecting his mother, but neglecting his aunt, and she the holiest one in the family...'

'Oh, don't now!' Jane said.

'I will, Jane, I'll write him a note. There's no point in ringing him. You only get the machine. I hate talking into those machines.'

She studied Jane across the room, aware now that all the time her sister-in-law spent alone in this house was changing her face, making her responses slower, her jaw set. Her eyes had lost their kind glow.

'I keep telling you,' she said, as she stood up to go, 'that you should get a video machine. It would be great company. I could bring you down videos.'

She noticed Jane taking a rosary beads from a small purse and wondered if this were being done deliberately as a way of showing that she had more important things to consider.

'Think about it anyway,' she said.

'I will, Molly, I'll think about that,' Jane replied.

Darkness was falling as she approached her bungalow, but she could easily make out Father Greenwood's car parked again in front of her car. She realised that he would have seen her in one of the mirrors just as soon as she saw him, so there would be no point in turning back. If I were not a widow, she thought, he would not do this to me. He would telephone first, minding his manners.

Father Greenwood got out of the car as she approached.

'Now, Father Greenwood, come in,' she said. 'I have the key here in my hand.' She brandished the key as though it were a foreign object.

She had put the heating system on a timer so the radiators were already warm. She touched the radiator in the hallway for a moment and thought of taking him into the sitting room, but realised then that the kitchen would be easier. She could stand up and make herself busy if she did not want to sit listening to him. In the sitting room, she would be trapped with him.

'Molly, you must think it strange my coming back like this,' Father Greenwood said. He sat down at the kitchen table.

She did not answer. She sat down opposite him and unbuttoned her coat. It struck her for a moment that it was the anniversary of Maurice's death and that he had come to be with her in case she needed his support and sympathy, but then remembered just as quickly that Maurice had died in the summer and that he had been dead for years and no one paid any attention to his anniversary. She could think of nothing else as she stood up and took her coat off and draped it over the armchair in the corner. Father Greenwood, she noticed, had his hands joined in front of him at the table as though ready for prayer. Whatever this was, she thought, she would make sure that he never came to her house unannounced again.

'Molly, Frank asked me—'

'Is there something wrong with Frank?' she interrupted.

Father Greenwood smiled at her weakly.

'He's in trouble,' he said.

Immediately she knew what that meant, and then thought no, her first reaction to everything else had been wrong, so maybe this too, maybe, she thought, maybe it was not what had immediately come into her mind.

'Is it…?'

'There's going to be a court case, Molly.'

'Abuse?' She said the word which was daily in the newspapers and on the television, as pictures appeared of priests with their anoraks over their heads, so that no one would recognize them, being led from courthouses in handcuffs.

'Abuse?' she asked again.

Father Greenwood's hands were shaking. He nodded.

'It's bad, Molly.'

'In the parish?' she asked.

'No,' he said, 'in the school. It was a good while ago. It was when he was teaching.'

Their eyes were locked in a sudden fierce hostility.

'Does anyone else know this?' she asked.

'I came down to tell you yesterday but I didn't have the heart.'

She held her breath for a moment and then decided she should stand up, push her chair back without caring whether it fell over, not moving her eyes from her visitor's face for one second.

'Does anyone else know this? Can you answer a straight question?'

'It's known about all right, Molly,' Father Greenwood said gently.

'Do the girls know?'

'They do, Molly.'

'Does Aunt Jane know?'

'The girls told her last week.'

'Does the whole town know?'

'It's being talked about all right,' Father Greenwood said. His tone was resigned, almost forgiving. 'Would you like me to make you a cup of tea?' he added.

'I would not, thank you.'

He sighed.

'There will be a court hearing before the end of the month. They tried to have it postponed, but it looks like it will be Thursday week.'

'And where is Frank?'

'He's still in his parish, but he's not going out much, as you can imagine.'

'He abused young boys?' she asked.

'Teenagers,' he replied.

'And they're now grown up? Is that right?' she asked.

'He'll need all…'

'Don't tell me what he'll need,' she interrupted.

'It's going to be very hard for you,' he said, 'and that's killing him.'

She held the back of the chair with her hands.

'The whole town knows? Is that right? The only person who hasn't known is the old woman? You've all made a fool out of me!'

'It was hard to tell you, Molly. The girls tried a while ago and I tried yesterday.'

'And them all whispering about me!' she said. 'And Jane with her rosary beads!'

'I'd say people will be very kind,' he said.

'Well, you don't know them, then,' she replied.

He left her only when she insisted that he go. She checked the newspaper for the evening television and made her tea as though it were an ordinary Monday and she could take her ease. She put less milk than usual into the scalding tea and made herself drink it, proving to herself that she could do anything now, face anything. When a car pulled up outside, she knew that it would be the girls, her daughters. The priest would clearly have alerted them and they would want to come now, when the news was raw, and they could arrive together so that neither of them would have to deal with her alone.

Normally, they walked around the side of the house and let themselves in the kitchen door, but she moved quickly along the short corridor towards the front door and turned on the light in the porch and opened the door. She stood watching them as they came towards her, her shoulders back.

'Come in,' she said, 'from the cold.'

In the hallway, they remained for a second uneasily, unsure which room they should go into.

'The kitchen,' she said drily and led the way, glad that she had left her glasses on top of the open newspaper on the table so that it would be clear to them that she had been occupied when they came.

'I was just going to do the crossword,' she said.

'Are you all right?' Eileen asked.

She stared at her daughter blankly.

'It's nice to see the two of you together,' she said. 'Are the boys well?'

'They're fine,' Eileen said.

'Tell them I'm nearly ready to take messages from them on an email,' she said. 'Miriam said one more lesson and I'll be away.'

'Was Father Greenwood not here?' Eileen asked.

Margaret had begun to cry and was fumbling in her handbag looking for tissues. Eileen handed her a tissue from her pocket.

'Oh yes, today and yesterday,' Molly said. 'So I have all the news.'

It struck her then that her grandsons would have to live with this too, their uncle on the television and in the newspapers, their uncle the paedophile priest. At least they did not have his surname, and at least Frank's parish was miles away. Margaret went to the bathroom.

'Don't ask me if I want tea, Eileen. I don't want tea,' Molly said.

'I don't know what to say,' Eileen replied. 'It's the worst thing.'

'Have you told the boys?' she asked Eileen who had moved across the kitchen and was sitting in the armchair.

'I had to tell them and so did Margaret because we were afraid they'd hear in school.'

'And were you not afraid I'd hear?'

'No one would say it to you,' Eileen said.

'You didn't have the courage, either of you,' she said.

'I still can't believe it,' Eileen said. 'And he's going to be named and everything.'

'Of course he's going to be named,' Molly said.

'No, we hoped he wouldn't be. The victims will ask that he be named. And he's pleading guilty. So we thought he mightn't be named.'

'Is that right?' Molly asked.

Margaret came back into the room. Molly noticed her taking a colour brochure from her handbag. She put it on the kitchen table.

'We spoke to Nancy Brophy,' Eileen said, 'and she said that she would go with you if you wanted to go to the Canaries. The weather would be lovely. We looked at prices and everything. It would be cheap enough, and we'd pay the flight and the package and everything. We thought you'd like to go.'

Nancy Brophy was her best friend.

'Did you now?' Molly asked drily. 'Well, that's lovely, I'll look at that.'

'I mean when the case is on. It'll be all over the papers,' Eileen continued.

'It was good of you to think of it anyway. And Nancy too,' Molly said and smiled. 'You're all very thoughtful.'

'Would you like me to make you a cup of tea?' Margaret asked.

'No, Margaret, she wouldn't,' Eileen said.

'It's the boys you both should be worrying about,' Molly said.

'No, no,' Eileen replied. 'We asked them if anything had ever happened. I mean if Frank...'

'What?' Molly asked.

'Had interfered with them,' Margaret said. She had dried her eyes now and she looked at her mother bravely. 'Well, he hasn't.'

'Did you ask Frank as well?' Molly enquired.

'Yes, we did. It all happened twenty years ago. There was nothing since he says,' Eileen said.

'But it wasn't just a single episode,' Margaret added. 'And I read that you can never tell.'

'Well, you'll have to look after the boys,' Molly said.

'Would you like Father Greenwood to come back and see you again?' Eileen asked.

'I would not!' Molly said.

'We were wondering...' Margaret began.

'Yes?'

'If you'd like to come and stay with one of us for a while,' Margaret continued.

'What would I do in your house, Margaret?' she asked. 'And sure Eileen has no room.'

'Or even if you wanted to go to Dublin,' Eileen said.

Molly went to the window and looked out at the night. They had left the parking lights on in the car.

'Girls, you've left the lights on in the car and the battery'll be run down and one of your poor husbands will have to come and bail you out,' she said.

'I'll go out and turn them off,' Eileen said.

'I'm going out myself,' Molly said. 'So we can all go.'

'You're going out?' Eileen asked.

'I am, Eileen,' she said.

Her daughters looked at each other, puzzled.

'But you usually don't go out on a Monday night,' Eileen said.

'Well, I won't be able to go out until you move the car, because you're blocking the drive. So you'll have to go first. But it was nice to see you, and I'll enjoy looking at the brochure. I've never been in the Canaries.'

She saw them signalling to each other that they could go.

The town during the next week seemed almost new to her. Nothing was as familiar as she had once supposed. She was unsure what a glance or a greeting disguised, and she was careful, once she had left her own house, never to turn too sharply or look too closely in case she saw them whispering about her. A few times, when people stopped briefly to talk to her, she was unsure if they knew about her son's disgrace, or if they too had become so skilled at the plain language of small talk that they could conceal every thought from her, every sign, as she could from them.

She made clear to her daughters that she did not wish to go on any holidays or change her routine. She played bridge on Tuesday night and Sunday night as usual. On Thursday she went to the gramophone society, and on Wednesday, after school, she was visited, as always, by her four grandsons, who watched videos with her, and ate fish fingers and chips and ice cream, and did part of their homework until one of their mothers came to collect them. On Saturday she saw friends, other widows in the town, calling on them, as she could use the car. Her time was full, and often, in the week after she had received the news of what was coming, she found that she had forgotten briefly what it was, but never for long.

Nancy Brophy asked her if she was sure she did not want to go to the Canary Islands.

'No, I'm going on as normal,' Molly said.

'You'll have to talk about it, the girls say you'll have to talk about it.'

'Are they ringing you?'

'They are,' Nancy said.

'It's the children they should be worrying about,' Molly said.

'Well, everyone is worried about you.'

'I know. They look at me wondering how to get by me quickly enough in case I might bite them, or I don't know what. The only person who came up to me at the bridge club was Betty Farrell, who took my arm and asked me, with them all watching, to phone her or send word or call around to her house if I needed anything. She looked like she meant it.'

'Some people are very good,' Nancy said. 'The girls are very good, Eileen and Margaret. And you'll be glad now to have them so close.'

'Oh, they have their own lives now,' Molly said.

They sat for a while without speaking.

'Well, it's an awful shock the whole thing,' Nancy continued eventually. 'That's all I'll say. The whole town is shocked. Frank was the last person you would expect...You must be in a terrible state about it, Molly.'

'As long as it's the winter I can manage,' Molly said. 'I sleep late in the mornings and I'm kept busy. It's the summer I dread. I'm not like those people who suffer from that disorder when there's no light. I dread the long summer days when I wake with the dawn and think the blackest thoughts. Oh, the blackest thoughts! But I'll be all right until then.'

'Oh, Lord I must remember that,' Nancy said. 'I never knew that about you. Maybe we'll go away then.'

'Would you do something for me, Nancy?' Molly said, standing up, preparing to leave.

'I would, of course, Molly.'

'Would you ask people to talk to me about it, I mean people who know me? I mean, not to be afraid to mention it.'

'I will, Molly. I'll do that.'

As they parted, Molly noticed that Nancy was close to tears.

Two days before the trial, as she was walking back to her house with the morning newspaper, Frank's car drew alongside her and stopped. She noticed a pile of parish newsletters on the back seat. She got into the passenger seat without looking at him.

'You're out early,' he said.

'I'm just up,' Molly replied. 'I go out and get the paper before I do anything. It's a bit of exercise.'

When they reached the house, he parked the car and they both walked into the kitchen.

'You've had your breakfast, I'd say,' she said.

'I have,' he replied. He was not wearing his priest's collar.

'Well, you can look at the paper now while I make toast and a cup of tea.'

He sat on the armchair in the corner and she could hear him fold and unfold the pages of the newspaper as she moved around the kitchen. When the toast and tea were ready, she set them out on the table, with a cup and saucer for each of them.

'Father Greenwood said he was down,' Frank said.

'He was,' she replied.

'He says you're a lesson to everyone of your age, out every night.'

'Well, as you know, I keep myself busy.'

'That's good.'

She realised that she had forgotten to put some butter on the table. She went to the fridge to fetch some.

'The girls are in and out to see you?' he asked.

'If I need them, I know where they are,' she said.

He watched her spreading the butter on the toast.

'We thought you might go away for a bit of a holiday,' he said.

She reached over for the marmalade and said nothing.

'Do you know, it would spare you,' he added.

'So the girls said,' she replied.

She did not want the silence between them to linger, yet everything she thought of saying seemed unnecessary. She wished he would go.

'I'm sorry I didn't come in and tell you myself what was happening,' he said.

'Well, you're here now, and it's nice to see you,' she replied.

'I think it's going to be…' He didn't finish, merely lowered his head. She did not drink the tea or eat the toast.

'There might be a lot of detail in the papers,' he said. 'I just wanted to warn you myself about that.'

'Don't worry about me at all, Frank,' she said.

She tried to smile in case he looked up.

'It's been bad,' he said and shook his head.

She wondered if they would let him say Mass when he was in prison, or have his vestments and his prayer books.

'We'll do the best we can for you, Frank,' she said.

'What do you mean?' he asked.

When he lifted his head and took her in with a glance, he had the face of a small boy.

'I mean, whatever we can do, we will do, and none of us will be going away. I'll be here.'

'Are you sure you don't want to go away?' he asked in a half-whisper.

'I am certain, Frank.'

He did not move. She put her hand on the cup but the tea had gone cold. He sighed and then stood up.

'I wanted to come in anyway and see you,' he said.

'I'm glad you did,' she said.

She did not stand up from her chair until she heard him starting the car in the drive. She went to the window and watched him reversing and turning the car, careful as always not to drive on her lawn. She stood at the window as he drove away; she stayed there until the sound of his car had died down in the distance.

Nicholas Royle

The Rainbow

In the days before the rainbow came and stayed, no one really understood what rainbows were or how they were formed. People knew enough so that when rain fell and the sun shone they would look out of the window or go outside. But once there, they didn't know which way to look. Towards the sun or away from it? It didn't seem to matter how many rainbows they saw, they always forgot which way to look the next time. It was as if it were the least significant detail. As soon as their random gaze fastened on the arc of the spectrum, all other considerations melted away and they became children again, lost to wonder.

The Rainbow of the Buttes-Chaumont changed all that.

There was nothing unusual about the rainbow when it appeared to the residents of the 19th and 20th *arrondissements* on a sunny, squally afternoon in early June. Or there was nothing about it that appeared unusual. It did in fact turn out to be the most unusual rainbow there had ever been, because when the rain stopped and the sun continued to shine it didn't go away. It wasn't immediately returned to whichever great warehouse rainbows get stored in when not in use.

The rain stopped around five pm and a few of those people who were out and about expressed mild surprise when the rainbow failed to fade. Half an hour later, with the sun glittering in the puddles scattered around the many paths of the parc des Buttes-Chaumont – and for that matter the streets of the *quartier*, cobbled thoroughfares and paved walkways alike – and glancing brightly off the surface of the ornamental lake, the rainbow still had not faded. People, more people than usual, made their way to the top of the artificial hill and the grand pagoda that crouched there with its views of Montmartre and the Sacré-Coeur and the north-east suburbs of Paris – and now the rainbow. Its mid-point seemed to be almost directly overhead. It occurred to some that it was the first time they had been able to stand underneath a rainbow rather than have no choice but to view it from afar.

Naturally, I joined those people making their way to the park. I first noticed the rainbow as I was leaving a *boulangerie* on the avenue Secrétan with a demi-baguette that I had purchased to have with my dinner that night. At this point it had already stopped raining, but I was aware that rainbows can sometimes linger while rain is continuing to fall in invisible showers. My apartment lay between the *boulangerie* and the rainbow in any case, opposite the library of the 19th arrondissement, so I walked in that direction. A demi-baguette was all I needed since I would be eating alone.

I approached my building with my key in my hand and stopped when I reached the street door. I looked up at the rainbow shimmering through the trees and, instead of unlocking the door, carried on walking towards the park. Why bother sticking to a schedule when you're the only one who will be affected by its being altered? I no longer had to worry about Gilles expecting me back. I could do exactly as I pleased. We neither of us had to worry about the other any more. Those days were over. Now I could please myself. I crossed the road and entered the park. All around me, neck muscles strained to allow people to look up at the rainbow. The ambient level of conversation was higher and more excited than normal. Strangers smiled at each other, even exchanged remarks. *Why hasn't the rainbow faded? What's going on?* Along with everyone else, I made my way up to the pagoda on top of the hill. I had to queue when I got near the top, but for once nobody seemed to mind waiting. Instead they chatted freely with one another. Having got over their awe and astonishment in a surprisingly short time, people became very relaxed with the idea of a rainbow that wasn't going away.

I stood at the top for ten minutes or so and no one jostled me to make me give up my place. Being that much closer to the rainbow, although still some distance away, altered the perspective. Now it was a little like standing underneath the Tour Eiffel and following the curving perspectives with a giddy eye. It was quite a big rainbow, starting close to Notre-Dame des Buttes-Chaumont on rue de Meaux and finishing somewhere near place des Fêtes. Eventually, feeling lighter than I had on my way up the hill, I made my way back down the path in order to head home and cook dinner. Witnessing a miracle may be a moving experience, but it doesn't preclude eating. Or drinking. Without making any special effort I would probably have got through a bottle of Beaujolais.

Halfway down the hill, just before my path turned to the right, on the stone bridge ahead of me, I saw Gilles. He was standing alone, looking up at the underside of the rainbow. My breathing became shallow and my mouth turned into a desert as I thought about going over to him and seeing if he would acknowledge me, but I knew that it would finally shatter my fragile heart if, among all these strangers who were swapping confidences and even touching each other on the arm as if to verify they were still alive, he turned away – as he had every right to do.

I walked away before he could look down and see me, and returned home.

The apartment had been cramped when the two of us had shared it, but it was a sad, abandoned palace without him. The fridge had always been too full of his little bottles of German beer, but now my dried-up bits of cheese rattled around in it. With his CDs by Michel Petrucciani and Erroll Garner constantly playing, there had never been a moment of true peace, but now the endless silence threatened to drive me mad.

I tore bits off my demi-baguette and chewed them as I stirred a white sauce for my pasta. I opened a bottle of Beaujolais and drank half of it before I had even sat down.

The rainbow was all over the TV news. The politicians spluttered and made pompous pronouncements that should have been cut to spare them their blushes. The Church made much out of the fact that the northern end of the rainbow dangled tantalisingly above their outlet on rue de Meaux. Local residents and businesses had turned the place des Fêtes into a street party, presided over by the colourful shadow of the rainbow's southern end.

The science correspondents searched in vain for rational explanations, the meteorologists had their heads in the clouds. Best of all, as ever, were the vox pops. *It's just beautiful, it makes me so happy,* sighed a young girl with rainbow hair, dancing away from the reporter's microphone.

I slept badly that night, although there was nothing new in that. I had slept badly every night since Gilles had gone. It wasn't that the bed was too big without him, but that it was too cold and the wrong shape. I woke up thinking it must be morning, but it was dark outside and when I checked my watch I saw it was only 1 am. Rather than spend an hour or two trying to get back to sleep, I decided to get up and put on some clothes.

The night air was surprisingly warm, like an angora cardigan draped about my bare shoulders. The traffic was light, enabling one to hear the gentle percussions of a thousand footfalls as more and more people flocked to the Parc des Buttes-Chaumont. I fell in step with them. No one spoke, but their silence was inclusive rather than alienating. Everyone belonged. In the night sky the colours of the rainbow were different. The shades were subtly altered and considerably muted. Standing beneath it, you imagined you felt its microscopic moulting pixels falling on your upturned face like a shower of glitter, but it was just a light breeze feathering the tiny stiffened hairs on the back of your neck. I went back to the apartment and slept like a baby for the first time in a week.

The next morning it was almost impossible to move from the apartment into the street for the outside broadcast vans, their huge wheels up on the kerbstones, a rainbow-hued gallimaufry of cables snaking across the pavement. Short-bearded men in fleecy tops and baseball caps muttered busily into mobile phones as they strove to forge order out of chaos. Other men stooped under the weight of broadcast-standard video cameras. Still others hefted bright lights and fluffy mikes. A hundred reporters rattled off their pieces to a hundred cameras, all of them standing with their backs to the rainbow. Rank upon rank of photographers sought out the best angle, their tripods an aluminium forest. Inevitably, a handful of photographers started snapping the snappers, their picture editors having told them to come back with something different for once.

Policemen stood about, hands on hips, clearly unsure what role to play, content for the time being just to gawp at the rainbow. Overhead, helicopters weaved in and out of the great arc itself, their buzzing a constant drone that became almost unnoticeable. But then, from one of the aircraft, dangled a man on a thin wire. Lowered to the rainbow, he could be seen from the ground actually to touch it. A collective gasp went up from down below. He turned and waved at the crowd, then returned to his close inspection of the rainbow. Signalling to his pilot, who maintained his stationary position, he carefully moved to straddle the rainbow. Then, taking something from a tool belt around his waist, he appeared to cut into the rainbow and remove a small section, no bigger than an ice cream wafer. Giving a further signal to the hovering machine, he was winched clear. The crowd burst into applause. A thousand camera lenses glinted in the sunshine.

Need I mention that not a drop of rain had fallen since the night before?

I somehow managed to worm my way through the crowds to the gates and so into the park. In tiny pockets between the massed spectators, jugglers juggled and unicyclists unicycled. Fire-eaters ate fire, but they did it more or less for fire-eating's sake, since everyone around them was looking up at the sky with fixed, beatific smiles upon their faces.

I waded through to a slightly less crowded corner of the park, where a few enterprising characters had set up little stalls selling rainbow-coloured fruit lollies, rainbow-dyed T-shirts, rainbow-patterned yo-yos and rainbow stickers, transfers and temporary tattoos. Since I had not had any breakfast, I handed over ten francs for a rainbow lollipop and headed for one of the gates on the south side of the park. Glancing up at the lambent hues visible through the trees, I meandered vaguely in the direction of place des Fêtes, which I ultimately approached, with a wry smile, by way of rue des Solitaires.

Place des Fêtes had been turned into an open-air trade fair. The square was a riot of candy-striped awnings and trestle tables, individual covered booths and open-plan consultation platforms representing everything from merchants selling genuine broken-off pieces of rainbow to New Age gurus promoting their own ten-step plan to transforming your life with the rainbow's help. A handful of white youths in black bomber jackets glared sullenly at a stall set up by the Rainbow Alliance, which described itself as a broad-based, non-party political group formed with the sole purpose of crushing the National Front once and for all. I added my signature to a long list of names scrawled on rainbow-printed paper, then thought about wandering over to the commercial stalls on the far side of the square.

Some people you recognise from a split second's blurred view from behind, others you can stare at for half a minute and still not be quite sure. Gilles belonged to the former group. I spotted his back, moving through the crowd in front of me. The tiny whorl of hair on the back of his neck confirmed his identity when I got closer, but really I hadn't needed that confirmation – I would know him anywhere, even now. Perhaps especially now.

Once I had accommodated the sudden lump in my throat, I decided to follow him. He slipped easily through the crowd, pausing occasionally to look up at the end of the rainbow, which glowed and shimmered like a mellow firework. Fittingly, a fire engine stood nearby, its ladder extension reaching up to the underside of a patch of orange. A fireman stood guard on the appliance itself at the bottom of the ladder. A couple of very tall cranes had been erected, like the ones used to get bird's-eye views of football stadia. From the relative safety of the pod at the top of each crane, officially sanctioned research scientists and rainbow data collectors worked at the colourface itself.

I looked down at Gilles and felt my heart loosen. He had been gone a week, no more. I had spoken to no one about it. There was, after all, no one who could console me. Nor could anyone bring him back to me. Somehow it felt longer than a week and yet at the same time I couldn't believe seven days had passed since he had last been by my side. I had thought I had loved other men until I met Gilles and I realised I had never even looked beneath the surface of being with another person.

He hadn't changed. There was still that irritating tuft of hair that stood up from his crown – irritating to him, rather than to me. If he'd gone off with someone else, there would perhaps have been pressure to get a haircut. I got close enough to see that there was a stain on the sleeve of his shirt that had been there before. Tomato juice from the last Bloody Mary he had made for me after our last night getting drunk together. If he were still alive, he would no doubt have visited a launderette in the meantime.

I followed him to the stalls across the square, where his gaze ranged over the various gaudy chunks of rainbow. I watched his hand move from one to the other, hesitating then moving on. He withdrew his hand for a moment and I thought he was going to turn around and see me, but then he reached out and picked up a piece that graduated from indigo to violet.

A curious thing happened. As I watched over his shoulder, the piece of rainbow in his hand became less distinct. It seemed to dissolve. I began to feel light-headed and had to look away.

I became aware of a general murmur around me. A murmur of consternation and, increasingly, dismay.

I looked up. The rainbow was fading. Its subtle dismantling had begun.

When I looked back to where Gilles had been, he had disappeared into the crowd.

Neil Gaiman

The Flints of Memory Lane

I like things to be story-shaped.

Reality, however, is not story-shaped, and the eruptions of the odd into our lives are not story-shaped either. They do not end in entirely satisfactory ways. Recounting the strange is like telling one's dreams: one can communicate the events of a dream, but not the emotional content, the way that a dream can colour one's entire day.

There were places I believed to be haunted, as a child, abandoned houses and places that scared me. My solution was to avoid them: and so, while my sisters had wholly satisfactory tales of strange figures glimpsed in the windows of empty houses, I had none. I still don't.

This is my ghost story, and an unsatisfactory thing it is too.

I was fifteen.

We lived in a new house, built in the garden of our old house. I still missed the old house: it had been a big old manor house. We had lived in half of it. The people who lived in the other half had sold it to property developers, so my father sold our half-a-house to them as well.

This was in Sussex, in a town that was crossed by the zero meridian: I lived in the eastern hemisphere, and went to school in the western hemisphere.

The old house had been a treasure trove of strange things: lumps of glittering marble and glass bulbs filled with liquid mercury, doors that opened onto brick walls; forgotten toys; things old and things forgotten.

My own house – a Victorian brick edifice in the middle of America – is, I am told, haunted. There are few people who will spend the night here alone any more – my assistant tells of her nights on her own here: of the porcelain-jester music box that spontaneously began to play in the night, of her utter conviction that someone was watching her. Other people have complained of similar things, following nights alone.

I have never had any unsettling experiences here, but then, I have never spent a night here alone. And I am not entirely sure that I would wish to.

'There is no ghost when I am here,' I said once, when asked if my house was haunted.

'Perhaps it is you who haunt it, then,' someone suggested, but truly I doubt it. If we have a ghost here, it is a fearful creature, more afraid of us than we are of it.

But I was telling of our old house, which was sold and knocked down (and I could not bear to see it empty, could not stand to see it being torn apart and bulldozed: my heart was in that house, and even now, at night, before I sleep, I hear the wind sighing through the rowan tree outside my bedroom window, twenty-five years ago.) So we moved into a new house, built, as I said, in the garden of the old one, and some years went by.

Then, the house was halfway down a winding flint road, surrounded by field and trees, in the middle of nowhere. Now, I am certain, were I to go back, I would find the flint road paved, the fields an endless housing estate. But I do not go back.

I was fifteen, skinny and gawky and wanting desperately to be cool. It was night, in autumn.

Outside our house was a lamp-post, installed when the house was built, as out of place in the lampless countryside as the lamp-post in the Narnia stories. It was a sodium light, which burned yellow, and washed out all other colours, turning everything yellow and black.

She was not my girlfriend (my girlfriend lived in Croydon, where I went to school, a grey-eyed blonde of unimaginable beauty who was, as she often complained to me, puzzled, never able to figure out why she was going out with me), but she was a friend, and she lived about a ten-minute walk away from me, beyond the fields, in the older part of the town.

I was going to walk over to her house, to play records, and sit, and talk.

I walked out of our house, ran down the grass slope to the drive, and stopped, dead, in front of a woman, standing beneath the street-lamp, staring up at the house.

She was dressed like a gypsy queen in a stage play, or a Moorish princess. She was handsome, not beautiful. She has no colours, in my memory, save only shades of yellow and black.

And, startled to find myself standing opposite someone where I had expected no one, I said, 'Hello.'

The woman said nothing. She looked at me.

'Are you looking for anyone?' I said, or something of the sort, and again she said nothing.

And still she looked at me, this unlikely woman, in the middle of nowhere, dressed like something from a dream, and still she said nothing at all. She began to smile, though, and it was not a nice smile.

And suddenly I found myself scared: utterly profoundly scared, like a character in a dream, and I walked away, down the drive, heart thudding in my chest, and around the corner.

I stood there, out of sight of the house, for a moment, and then I looked back, and there was no one standing in the lamplight.

I was fifty paces from the house, but I could not, would not, turn around and go back. I was too scared. Instead I ran up the dark, tree-lined flint lane and into the old town, and up another road and down the road to my friend's house, and got there speechless, breathless, jabbering and scared, as if all the hounds of hell had chased me there.

I told her my story, and we phoned my parents, who told me there was no one standing under the street-lamp, and agreed, a little reluctantly, to come and drive me home, as I would not walk home that night.

And that is all there is to my story. I wish there was more: I wish I could tell you about the gypsy encampment that was burned down on that site two hundred years earlier – or anything that would give some sense of closure to the story, anything that would make it story-shaped – but there was no such encampment.

So, like all eruptions of the odd and strange into my world, the event sits there, unexplained. It is not story-shaped.

And, in memory, all I have is the yellow-black of her smile, and a shadow of the fear that followed.

Tamar Yellin

An Italian Child

I have an Italian child.

High in the hills west of Florence, off the road to Viareggio, next to the chapel of San Stefano, in a villa hung with jasmine and a pergola of roses where they eat in summer: that is where my son lives. A villa with large dark rooms, green shutters, a view of olive trees and the distant Apennines; a garden with fir trees and rabbit hutches and a barking dog. In the morning the cockerel crows at dawn, all day the voices call him, Jacopo, Jacopo, he crosses the field on his long brown legs; he rides the tractor with Umberto and collects small red plums in a basket for the noon meal. He is dark, he is thin, he does not resemble me: he has a sensitive mouth. His eyes are accustomed to the sun, his long eyebrow touches his temple. My boy will be seven tomorrow; this is all I know.

Mrs Webster places the fax on my table and says: You'll have to do this one by teatime. It's urgent. That is how she speaks to me. She says the minimum, as though, if she allowed herself to say more, we might be drawn into the rapids of conversation.

We're well suited. I don't want to talk. Later, we will take tea at our desks, eat a ginger biscuit each, pore over our translations. Sometimes, on the telephone, I hear her speak French. It is incongruous, like drinking cold claret.

The number seven bus rides past my window in a sluice of rain, and another twenty minutes have gone by. They will be taking their siesta now at San Stefano. The high bedrooms with their enormous wardrobes, their great laundry presses, stand dark and still behind the closed shutters. He lies, a check of sunlight on his cheek, in a sea of tangled sheets and toys. His limbs are like sticks: I have seen the photographs.

I know what the afternoons are like at San Stefano, how Maria always rises first, makes English tea because she likes it that way, sweeps a few leaves from under the pergola. While I, who never learnt how to sleep in the daytime, spent the hours thumbing books in the study, gilded editions of Hardy and James with their light signature, E. Matteotti. Under the pergola, holding her teacup in both hands, Maria told me: There are two people in Emanuella, a princess and a peasant. Sometimes she likes to be a princess, sometimes she plays at being a peasant.

Yes, I said, but me she expects always to be a prince.

Well, I know my own daughter, she said, and you know your wife. But how to keep her satisfied, that's always the question. We had many conversations there, among the roses, while Emanuella was sleeping.

And later when the others emerged, one by one, from the darkened bedrooms, Umberto carrying a disarranged *La Stampa*, Emanuella winding her hair into a knot, we sat aside, Maria and I, in our collusion, the taste of secrets still in our mouths. And I watched my wife a little guiltily as she reached into the cupboard for the water jug, knowing I had talked of private things she would resent, the intimacies, problems of our marriage.

Mrs Webster is sipping her PG Tips now, eating her biscuit with an intense, abstracted look. Her husband, I believe, is a professor of semiotics. Perhaps his obsession with symbols has driven her to silence. Perhaps they communicate with each other by looks and signs, by semaphore.

Only once did she notice the photograph standing in a corner of my desk. It's my son, I told her. Oh, really? And on an impulse, forgetting herself, she picked it up. He doesn't look like you, she said. No, I agreed, he doesn't. He always looked Italian, like his mother.

Another bus passes and the next but one, the five-fifty, will be mine. This summer we haven't had a summer. It has rained, I think, every weekend, with sunshine only on alternate Mondays. You are a different person in the heat. Your body frees itself. You become aware of your shoulders particularly, as the bravest, most sensuous part of yourself.

In San Stefano we were different people. Strangers. Seven summers visiting, we never made love in San Stefano.

Jacopo was conceived in an English winter, in front of a two-bar electric heater, in a third-floor flat off the Kilburn High Road, in complete happiness. We dreamed of impossible lifestyles: six months here and six months there, if it was a boy we would call him Jacopo, if a girl Francesca. We ate granary bread and hard pale English tomatoes; she wore my lumpy sweater. Circling her knees with her long, foreign hands, she talked authoritatively of dual culture, of the privilege of bilingualism.

For you and me it is different, she said, one of us will always be a stranger. But he will be at home in both places. He will be truly English, truly Italian.

(Christmas, Roehampton, my mother's house: Emanuella turning over the pudding on her plate and murmuring, mortified: I can't eat this! My incomprehension, as I settled back in my usual chair, of the way she perched rigidly, like a typist, on the edge of hers. My barely concealed irritation.)

He won't be English or Italian, I answered. He will be ours. We will be his homeland.

(Easter, Lucca, the cathedral: in front of the Holy Cross she lit a taper, pulled her shawl over her head and genuflected. Done for my benefit, to remind me how easily she could fall out of my arms and back into belief. Her profile, pale and still as a saint's, said: These are the things which are mine and not yours. Now you are the exile.)

Jacopo, Mrs Webster repeats. That's a lovely name. But no one could pronounce it, and the children laughed. They're calling me Pinocchio, he cried, they say I've got a long nose. I stroked his smooth hair (dark: Emanuella's hair, not mine) and thought, We should only give our children ordinary names. We should not afflict them with beautiful names which will be made ridiculous.

'In rapidly changing markets, flexibility is essential and a streamlined decision-making process allows fund managers to respond positively and quickly to events. Furthermore—' I glance at my watch. One day they will have computer programs to do what I do. I always wanted to translate great literature. But how many people are privileged to do that? One or two, perhaps, in a generation. Sometimes, at home, I still dip into I Promessi Sposi.

I wonder what tomes Mrs Webster has explored in the original French. Some Molière, maybe; a bit of Racine. The standard texts she probably still keeps from her student days. It is difficult to imagine her tackling anything more racy, through her half-glasses.

They say, of course, that something is always lost in translation. That may be true; but something else is gained. I love the strangeness in translated English: the spareness or lushness which breathes through it, spareness, perhaps, if it is from the Italian; lushness if it is from the Spanish. English grows, for once, exotic, sprouting fruit you'd never find in a Surrey garden.

Conversation is a different matter. It is easier to tell lies in a foreign language. Which is surely why so many people pray in Latin.

Day is darkening prematurely, the air intensifying for another flush of rain. My husband is meeting me, Mrs Webster says; would you lock up? She has her umbrella at the ready, the coat with the orange check which she wears summer and winter. She has already lost the bit of tan with which she returned from two weeks in Provence.

And so she rushes off. We have never spoken about it, but she knows I have nobody to rush for. English fashion, she avoids asking personal questions: nothing is any of her business. Even when she picked up the photograph and was dying to know, she politely refrained from inquiring about the boy's mother.

Emanuella always accused me of not talking enough. So like a man, she said. Getting words out of you is like getting blood out of a stone. But so far as I remember we were always talking: it was the language which let us down. And then, in San Stefano, it was the body language. Maria noticed. She doesn't address you, she said. She doesn't look at you. Something is wrong. As if we could attempt to cover the miles of frozen waste between us by handing over the spaghetti. And so I had to tell Maria, you are right: we cannot communicate.

I double-lock the blue door with its faded brass fittings and step out into the rain (a true Englishman never forgets his umbrella, and I raise mine like a black ensign). Ms. Matteotti, you were always so intense: an overdose of literature and politics had killed your sense of humour. When you frowned your whole face aged a generation.

You certainly did not remember your umbrella that day you ran out into the Kilburn High Road, wanting to be free, tears and mascara and hair streaming down your face, your dark dress clinging. Thrusting me off as though I were the warden of some institution you had escaped;

while all I could think of was Jacopo, abandoned in the flat, and the fear that you might dash under the next bus. Don't touch me! you shrieked, playing both peasant and princess at the same time, the rain trickling into your Cartier shoes, and I thought, stupidly, I don't suppose we are going to the party now; I will have to telephone and make our excuses.

I step back as the number seven slooshes in to the stop, carefully close the wings of my umbrella and climb aboard. The interior of the bus smells like the changing room at the squash courts, but for a moment, seated safely here, I feel an intense rightness, almost happiness.

How easily one can slip into the habit of being alone again, of eating toast at midnight, wearing socks in bed, putting off tedious errands until tomorrow. We can manage without each other, after all. I knew that when you clutched at Jacopo, your hair dripping, and flung the towel back as though I could give you nothing else worth having.

My place is small, and faces north: beneath my window a graveyard stretches to a belt of trees; it makes a sort of garden. Rain casts itself against the windows like a sad relentless comforter.

I plug the kettle in and reach for a tin of soup. At San Stefano now they will be bringing dinner under the pergola, setting plain white plates on the flowered oilcloth, a jug, a basket of bread. Voices come from the kitchen, Italian fragments, *Ma no, e poi, capito*, the dog pads in and out on slow paws, following the dishes with its hopeful muzzle; a slow trail of smoke rises to the stars. Jacopo is playing with his cousin: the two boys circle the house like greyhounds. Hidden in the barn is his birthday bicycle.

They say the Tuscans are descended from the Etruscans, that they have even identified a Tuscan gene. How would it be, I wonder, if my Jacopo looked like me, if, among the dark-haired and almond-eyed children there was one fair flabby child called Jack who couldn't stand the sun? How would his mother feel when she looked at him? Would she always remember, would she love him in the same way? But he is not flabby and fair, he is dark and thin as a spider: his aunt breaks a piece of bread in her jewelled fingers and says, But have you felt his arms? There is nothing there, not even any muscle.

I carry my tray of soup to the lounge and without more ado switch on the television, the colour and noise of which throw an instant blanket over loneliness. These are the things one does not admit to: that one cannot live without the television, that it stays on all the time, that it is a wrench to turn it off, last thing at night, and suffer the equally instant silence and darkness. I will watch anything except game shows: news, hospital dramas, comedy thrillers, hospital-comedy-drama thrillers with topical themes, anything to dull the brain and ward off solitude. It is nearly two years, and when two years are up we will be made official, stamped void, our decade together acknowledged a legal error.

Maria writes to me that she is well and happy, and maybe hopes I will derive some selfless pleasure from the knowledge. Sometimes, perhaps, she thinks of me, with the nostalgia of complete detachment. I am glad she is well; I'm not surprised she is happy. Who can blame her, everyone said when they heard she had gone back, isn't it very lovely there, and after all, it is the place where she belongs. I wanted to answer that we belong together, that a husband and wife should be their own country, that one should not abandon the other. But I did not say so, for these notions of loyalty are not popular. The kingdom of love is not a fascist state, even under the rule of marriage. All citizens retain the right of free passage, and may, if they so wish, revoke their citizenship.

I have an Italian child. A child who has forgotten his English, who speaks only Italian. A child who if he wrote me letters would begin 'Mio caro papa', but he never writes. He is running in the garden now at San Stefano, catching fireflies; it is late and he should be in bed. The fireflies hang in the darkness like Christmas lights; the jasmine whose flowers, they say, are the holy stars which fell at the birth of Christ, stands heavy with scent near where the adults talk. My grandmother used to say that once you have children you are never alone in the world, there is something of them in you, of you in them: you have thrown in your lot with existence, planted your stake in the future. Somewhere at San Stefano my flesh and blood is running under the stars. He catches the languid fireflies and traps them beneath a jar in the kitchen. When he comes down in the morning there will be money.

Claire Keegan

Close to the Water's Edge

Tonight he is out on the balcony, his dark tan stunning against the white of his dress shirt. Five days have passed since he left Cambridge to spend time with his mother on the Texas coast. Up here, the wind is strong. The plastic leaves of the tall, potted plants beat against the sliding glass. He does not care for the penthouse with its open–mouthed swordfish on the walls, the blue tiles and all the mirrors that make it impossible to do even the simplest thing without it being reflected.

Early in the mornings, the porters erect wooden loungers and stake blue parasols on the private strip of sand. As the morning heats up, the residents come out to lie almost naked in the sun. They bring paperbacks, towels and reach into their coolers for Diet Coke and Coppertone. He lies in the shade and watches the procession of young men with washboard bellies walking the strand. They are college kids his own age who stay at the motels closer to the strip.

Towards midday, when the heat becomes unbearable, he swims out to the sandbar, a good half-mile from the shore. He can see it now, the strip of angry waves breaking in the shallows. Now the tide is advancing, erasing the white, well-trodden sands. It's ten years since the ban on DDT came into place and the brown pelicans are back. They look prehistoric gliding over the water, scooping their prey with their huge bills, their high, plummeting dives. A jogger stays on the hard sand close to the water's edge, his shadow at his side.

Inside, his mother is arguing with his stepfather, the Republican who owns this complex. He is a man of humble origins who made his money out of exports and real estate. After his parents divorced, his mother said people have no control over who they fall in love with, and a few months later she married the millionaire. Now he can hear them talking, their enraged whispers gathering speed on the slope of their argument. It is an old story.

'I'm warning you, Richard, don't bring it up!'

'Who brought it up? Who?'

'It's his birthday, for Christ's sake!'

'Who said anything?'

The young man looks down. At the hot tub, a mother braces herself and enters the bubbling water. Screams from racing children pierce the night. He feels the same trepidation he always feels at these family occasions, and wonders why he came back here when he could be in Cambridge in his T-shirt and jeans, playing chess on the computer, drinking Australian beer. He takes the cufflinks from his pocket, a gift his grandmother gave him shortly before she died. They are gold-plated cufflinks whose gold is slowly wearing off revealing the steel underneath.

When his grandmother first married, she begged her husband to take her to the ocean. They were country people, pig farmers from Tennessee. His grandmother said she had never laid eyes on the Atlantic. She said if she saw the ocean, she could settle down. It wasn't something she could explain but each time she asked her husband, his response was the same.

'Who'll take care of things round here?'

'We could ask the neighbours—'

'What neighbours? That's our livelihood out there, Marcie. You know that.'

Months passed, she grew heavy with child and finally gave up asking to see the ocean. Then, one Sunday, her husband shook her awake.

'Pack a bag, Marcie,' he said. 'We're going to the coast.'

It wasn't yet light when they got into the car. They drove all that day, across the hills of Tennessee towards the coast. The landscape changed from green, hilly farmland to dry plains with tall palms and pampas grass. The sun was going down when they arrived. She got out and gasped at the bald sun sinking down into the ocean. The Atlantic looked green. The coast seemed a lonely place with the stink of seaweed and the gulls fighting for leftovers in the sand.

Then her husband took out his pocket watch.

'One hour, Marcie. I'll give you one hour,' he said. 'If you're not back by then, you can find your own way home.'

She walked for half an hour with her bare feet in the frothy edge of the sea, then turned back along the cliff path and watched her husband, at five minutes past the appointed hour, slam the car door and turn the ignition. Just as he was taking off, she jumped into the road and stopped the car. Then she climbed in and spent the rest of her life with a man who would have gone home without her.

His twenty-first birthday is marked by a dinner at Leonardo's, the fancy seafood restaurant overlooking the water. His mother, dressed in a white pants suit with a rhinestone belt, joins him on the balcony.

'I'm so proud of you, honey.'

'Mom,' he says and lets her embrace him.

His mother, a small woman with a hot temper, likes to go marketing. She drinks a glass of fresh grapefruit juice with vodka before she goes and makes out a list on the counter. Olive oil, artichoke hearts, balsamic vinegar, veal. All the things she could never afford. She avoids the aisle of toilet paper and dog food, goes straight to the deli and points to the monkfish, the prosciutto, the organic cheese. Once, she bought a ten-ounce jar of beluga caviar and ate it with her fingers in the parking lot.

'I'm so proud of you,' she says now, staring at his throat. She puts her glass down and reaches out to knot his tie. 'There,' she says, standing back to look at him again, 'How many mothers can look at their sons and say, "My boy's going to Harvard University"? I'm a pig-farmer's daughter from Tennessee and my boy is going to Harvard. When I'm low, I always remember that, and it cheers me up no end.'

She takes a sip from her glass. Her nails are painted a hard and shiny red.

'It's no big deal, Mom.'

She looks out at the water and down at the strand. He never really knows what's going through her mind.

'You play your cards right and this could all be yours someday.' She gestures to the complex. The gesture is reflected, from different angles, in the mirrored room behind her. 'You wonder why I married him but I was thinking of you, all along.'

'Mom, I don't—' her son begins but just then the millionaire comes out with a lighted cigar and blows a mouthful of smoke into the night. He's a plain man with an Italian suit and the whitest teeth money can buy.

'You all ready? I could eat a small child,' he says.

They take the elevator to the ground floor where a porter opens the front door. Another man, in a gold-braided uniform, brings round the car. The millionaire tips him and gets in behind the driver's seat even though the restaurant is less than a ten-minute walk along the strand.

When they reach Leonardo's, the owner greets them, shakes his stepfather's hand. There's a palm tree growing in the middle of the restaurant with a parrot chained to one of its branches. They are escorted to a table under the chandelier. Yellow light spills over the white cloth and cello music is coming out of the walls. A basket of bread is laid out, butter, a selection of shellfish on a wooden board. His stepfather reaches for an oyster, loosens it with his knife and swallows it. His mother picks up a fat shrimp as the maître d', a thin man with dark brown skin, appears.

'How may I help you this evening?'

His stepfather orders the wine and tells him to bring out the champagne.

'Did you hear about this guy Clinton? Says if he's elected President he's gonna let queers into the military,' he says. 'What do you think of that, Harvard?'

'Richard!' his mother says.

'It's OK, Mom. Well, I don't think the tradition of—'

'What's next? Lesbians coaching the swim team, running for the Senate?'

'Richard!'

'What kind of defence would that be? A bunch of queers! We didn't win two World Wars that way. I don't know what this country is turning into.'

Smells of horseradish and dill spill out from the kitchen. A lobster has got loose in the tank but the waiter dips a net into the water and snaps a thick elastic band around his claws.

'No more politics,' his mother says. 'It's my boy's night. He got a 3.75 grade point average last semester. Now what do you think of that, Richard?'

'3.75? Not bad.'

'Not bad? Well, I should say not! He's top of his class!'

'Mom.'

'No, I won't be hushed up this time! He's top of the class, and he's twenty-one years old today! A grown man. Let's have a toast.'

'Now there's an idea,' says the millionaire. He pours champagne into the flutes. The glasses fizz up but he waits for the contents to settle.

'Here's to the brightest young man in the whole state of Texas,' he says.

They are smiling now, suddenly at ease. There is a chance that this dinner will not be like the others.

'...and to not having queers in the military!'

The mother's smile capsizes. 'Goddamn, Richard!'

She raises her hands. As her hands move, her son realises how beautiful her diamonds are.

'What's the matter? It's just a little joke,' her husband says. 'Doesn't anybody round here know how to take a joke any more?'

The waiter arrives with a steel tray, and the entrées. Turbot for the lady, salmon for the young man and a lobster.

The millionaire ties the bib around his neck, takes the pincers and breaks open the lobster's claw.

'There must be some fine women up there at Harvard,' he says, picking out the meat. 'Some real knockouts.'

'They accept us on the basis of intelligence, not looks.'

'Even so. The best and the brightest. How come you never bring a girl down?'

At this point, he could say something. He composes a retort, decides to speak, then looks at his mother and hesitates. His mother's eyes are pleading for his silence.

'They must be all around you like flies,' says the millionaire, 'a young man like you. Why, when I was your age I had a different woman every weekend.'

'These olives!' the mother says. 'Taste these olives!'

The millionaire puts his head down and concentrates on his food. The young man flakes a piece of salmon off the bone. His mother stares at the parrot in the tree.

'Is there anything else you need?' she smiles the old, apologetic smile.

'No, Mom,' he says, 'I'm fine. This is good.'

After their plates are taken away and the waiter has brushed the crumbs off the cloth, the maître d' comes back and whispers into his stepfather's ear. The chandelier is doused and a lighted cake is carried from the kitchen by a nervous, Mexican waiter singing 'Happy Birthday'. It is a pink cake, the pinkest cake he has ever seen, like a cake you'd have at the christening party for twin girls.

The millionaire is grinning.

'Make a wish, honey!' his mother cries.

The young man closes his eyes, and when his eyes are closed he realises he does not know what to wish for. It is the unhappiest moment of the day so far but he blows hard, extinguishing the candles.

The millionaire takes the knife and carves the cake into uneven pieces, like a pie chart. The young man stuffs a piece in his mouth and licks the frosting. The millionaire reaches for his mother's hand, clasps her jewelled fingers.

'Happy birthday, son,' she says, and kisses her husband on the mouth.

The young man stands up and hears himself thanking them for a pleasant birthday. The lights come back on and then he hears his mother calling his name, the waiter saying, 'good evening, sir,' at the door. He is crossing the highway now, finding a space between the speeding cars. The other college kids are out on the promenade. He stands for a moment and watches a bungee jumper throwing herself into mid-air, screaming. She dangles for a while above the ground until a man comes over and takes her harness off.

Down at the deserted beach, the tide has reclaimed the strand. The water is black, the night wind streaking white frills across the surface. He loosens the knot at his throat and walks on, towards the pier. There, yachts with roped-in sails stand trembling on the water.

His grandmother, with whom he lived while his parents broke up, is dead now. Not a day has passed when he has not felt her absence. She said if she'd had her life to live again, she would never have climbed back into that car. She'd have stayed behind and turned into a streetwalker sooner than go home. Nine children, she bore him. When he asked what made her climb back in, she said, 'Those where the times I lived in. That's what I believed. I thought I didn't have a choice.' His grandmother is dead but he is twenty-one years old, inhabiting space on the earth, getting As at Harvard, walking on a beach without any time constriction in the moonlight.

He kicks off his shoes and walks in his bare feet, along the strand. The white waves at the sandbar are clearly visible in the darkness but they do not seem so angry as in the day. There is the smell of cigar smoke on his clothes. He puts the cufflinks safely in his pants pocket, strips naked, and leaves his clothes further up the strand. When he wades into the big, white-fringed waves, the water is cold. He swims out, feeling clean again.

He does not have to stay here. He can call the airline, change his flight, go back to Cambridge.

By the time he reaches the sandbar, he is tired. The water is colder, the waves angrier, now that it is night but he can rest here, as always, before the return swim to the shore. He lowers his feet to feel the sand. A thick wave thrashes over his head, knocking him back into the deep water. He swallows water, goes further out to find the shallow place but he cannot feel the bottom. He never meant to drink all that champagne. He never meant to go swimming in the first place. All he wanted was a happy birthday. He struggles for the longest time, goes under water, believing it will be easier if he comes up only for air. Panic strikes him and then time passes and the panic changes into something peaceful. Why are opposites always so close? It's like those beautiful, high notes on the violin, just a hair's breadth away from a screech. He gives up and feels himself coming to the surface. He floats till he feels able to go on then slowly fights his way back to the shore. It is a long way off but the lights of the complex are clear against the sky and getting closer.

When he reaches the shallow water, he crawls up onto the beach and collapses on the sand. He is breathing hard and looking around but the tide has taken his clothes. He imagines the first species that crawled out of the sea, the amount of courage that took. He lies there until his breath comes back then makes his way back to the pier where the boats are. Further off, a couple is walking a dog. He goes along the yachts looking at the decks until he sees a yellow T-shirt hanging over a rope. He puts it on but it's too short to cover his privates so he puts one leg into the arm hole and awkwardly ties the cloth to cover himself.

When he gets back to the complex, the porter opens the door. In the lobby, he presses the button and waits for the elevator. When the elevator comes, it's full of well-dressed people. A woman in a red dress looks at him and smiles. He gets in and presses 25. The elevator's walls are mirrored and his reflection is a slightly sunburned man who is shivering. When he reaches the door he hesitates and tells himself his mother will open it. He presses the button and hears the electronic bell ringing inside. Nothing happens. Maybe they are still at the restaurant. Maybe they are in a bar somewhere. Maybe the porter will open the door for him. He is wondering if he can call down to reception when the millionaire opens the door and looks at him.

'Well!' he says 'What have we got here?'

He looks at the yellow T-shirt tied like a diaper at his waist.

'You have a good time?' he says. 'You finally got your hook in the water?'

The young man dodges past him and runs down the hall. Several versions of himself run down the hall alongside him.

'Your mother's losing her mind over you!'

He gets into the shower, stands under the hot water, realising he almost drowned. He stands there for a long time, gets out and wraps himself in a dressing gown. Then he looks up a number in the directory and lifts the phone.

'Hello,' says a woman's voice. 'Delta Airlines. May I help you?'

For a moment, he cannot answer. His mother has walked into the room and is standing there with a glass in her hand. He thinks about her mother who, after coming all that way, and with only an hour to spend, would not get into the water, even though she was a strong river swimmer. When he'd asked her why, she'd said she had no idea how deep it was.

'May I help you?' the voice asks again.

Chris Beckett

Monsters

'This is Dirk Johns, our leading novelist,' said the poet's mother, 'and this is Lucille, who makes wonderful little landscapes out of clay…'

'Oh, just decorative,' protested the novelist's tiny, bird-like wife, 'purely decorative and nothing more.'

'And this is Angelica Meadows, the painter. You perhaps caught her recent exhibition in the Metropolis, Mr Clancy? I believe it received very good notices.'

'I believe I did hear something…' I lied, shaking hands with a very attractive young woman with lively, merry eyes. 'I'm afraid I spend so little time in the Metropolis these days.'

'And this,' went on the poet's mother, 'is the composer, Ulrika Bennett. We expect great things of her.'

No, I thought, looking into Ulrika Bennett's cavernous eyes, great music will never come from you. You are too intense. You lack the necessary playfulness.

And then there was Ulrika's husband, 'the ceramicist', and then an angry little dramatist, and then a man who uncannily resembled a tortoise, complete with wrinkled neck, bald head and tiny pursed little mouth.

'Well,' I said, 'I'm honoured'.

The tortoise was, it seemed, 'our foremost conductor and the director of our national conservatory.'

'The honour is ours, Mr Clancy,' he said. 'We have all read your extraordinary books, even out here.'

'William!' called the poet's mother, 'Let us lead the way to dinner!'

The poet turned from a conversation with the painter Angelica. He had wonderfully innocent blue eyes, which had the odd quality that, while they seemed terribly naked and vulnerable, they were simultaneously completely opaque.

'Yes, of course, mother.'

He pushed her wheelchair through into the panelled dining room and the guests took their seats. I was given the head of the table. William sat at the opposite end, his mother by his side. Servants brought in the soup.

'William and I are trying hard,' announced the poet's mother to the whole company, 'to persuade Mr Clancy that there is more to our little colony than cattle ranches.'

'Indeed,' I said soothingly, 'there is clearly also a thriving cultural life which I would very much like to hear more about.'

Well, they needed no second bidding. *Remarkable* things were being achieved under the circumstances, I was told, for the arts were struggling by with an *appalling* lack of support. Apart from the poet's mother, Lady Henry, who was of course *wonderful,* there was not a single serious patron of the fine arts to be found in the whole of Flain. Everyone present did their heroic best, of course, but not one of them had achieved the recognition that their talents deserved…

And so on. I had heard it many times before, in many more provincial outposts than I cared to remember. I made my usual sympathetic noises.

It was as the dessert was being served that I became aware of the poet's blue eyes upon me.

'Tell me honestly, Mr Clancy,' he asked – and at once his mother was listening intently, as if she feared he would need rescuing from himself – 'had you heard of even one of us here in this room, before you knew you were coming to Flain?'

I hadn't, honestly, and from what little I had seen of their outmoded and derivative efforts, it was not surprising. (Let us face it, even in the Metropolis, for every hundred who fancy themselves as artists, there is only one who has anything interesting to say. It is just that in the Metropolis, even one per cent is still a good many gifted and interesting people.)

But before I could frame a suitably tactful reply, William's mother had intervened.

'Really, William, how rude!'

'Rude?' His face was innocence itself. 'Was that rude? I do apologise. Then let me ask you another question instead, Mr Clancy. What in particular were you hoping to see on your visit here? Please don't feel you *have* to mention our artistic efforts.'

'Well I'm interested in every aspect of course,' I replied. 'But I don't deny that I'd like to learn more about the fire horses.'

There was a noticeable drop of temperature in the room and everyone's eyes turned to Lady Henry, watching for her reaction.

'Fire horses,' sighed the novelist, Johns. 'Of course. The first thing every Metropolitan wants to see. Yet surely you must have them in zoos there?'

I shrugged.

'Of course, but then we have *everything* in the Metropolis, everything remotely interesting that has ever existed anywhere. I travel to see things in context. And fire horses *are* Flain to the outside world, the thing which makes Flain unique. It was wonderful when I first disembarked here to see boys with their young fire horses playing in the streets.'

'How I wish the brutes had been wiped out by the first colonists,' said the poet's mother. 'Your curiosity is perfectly understandable, Mr Clancy, but this country will not progress until we are known for something other than one particularly ugly and ferocious animal.'

'Yes,' I said, soothingly, 'I *do* see that it must be irritating when one's homeland always conjures up the same one thing in the minds of outsiders.'

'It *is* irritating to think that our country is known only for its monsters,' said Lady Henry, 'but unfortunately it is more than just irritating. How will we ever develop anything approaching a mature and serious cultural life as long as the educated and uneducated alike spend all their free time yelling their heads off in horse races and horse fights, and a man's worth is measured in equestrian skill? I do not blame you for your curiosity, Mr Clancy, but how we *long* for visitors who come with something other than fire horses in mind.'

'Hear, hear,' said several of them, but the poet smiled and said nothing.

'Well, I'll have to see what I can do about that,' I said.

But of course in reality I knew that my Metropolitan readers would not be any more interested than I was in the arch theatricals at the Flain Opera or the third-rate canvasses in the National Gallery of Flain, straining querulously for profundity and importance. 'The Arts' are an urban thing, after all, and no one does urban things better than the Metropolis itself.

'I hardly like to mention it,' I said in a humble voice, which I hoped would be disarming, 'but the other thing for which Flain is famous is of course the game of sky-ball.'

The poet's mother gave a snort of distaste.

'Ritualised thuggery!' she exclaimed. 'And so tedious. I can't abide the game myself. I honestly think I would rather watch paint drying on a wall. I really do. At least it would be restful.'

But Angelica the painter took a different view.

'Oh I *love* sky-ball!' she declared. 'There's a big game tomorrow – the Horsemen and the Rockets. William and I should take you there, Mr Clancy. You'll have a wonderful time!'

William smiled.

'Good idea, Angie. I'd be very glad to take you, Mr Clancy, if you'd like to go.'

'But Mr Clancy is to visit the Academy tomorrow,' protested his mother. 'Professor Hark himself has agreed to show him round. We really cannot…'

'I do *so* appreciate the trouble you've gone to,' I purred, 'but if it is at *all* possible to put Professor Hark off, I would very much like to see the Horsemen and the Rockets.'

For, even back in the Metropolis, I had heard of the Horsemen and the Rockets.

'Well, of course,' said Lady Henry, 'if you want to go to the game we must take you. You know best what you need to see. I will talk to Professor Hark. No, a sky-ball game will be… an experience for me.'

'But good lord, Lady Henry,' I protested, 'there's no need for you to come if you don't want. I'm sure William and Miss Meadows and I can…'

Polite murmurs of support came from the distinguished guests, but Lady Henry was resolved:

'Don't be ridiculous, Mr Clancy, of course I will come. We must sample every aspect of life, must we not? Not just those we find congenial.' She summoned up a brave smile. 'No, I am sure it will be *great fun.*'

So we set off in the Henrys' car the next morning, Lady Henry riding up in front next to the elderly chauffeur (the seat had been removed to accommodate her wheelchair) while William and myself reclined on red leather in the back. We picked up Angelica on the way and she squeezed in between us, warm and alive and smelling of freshly-mowed grass.

'I do hope you don't support the Rockets, Lady Henry,' she exclaimed, 'because I must warn you I'm an absolutely *rabid* fan of the Horsemen!'

Lady Henry gave a breathless, incredulous laugh.

'I can assure you I really have no idea about "supporting" anyone, Angelica, but I'm absolutely determined to have fun!' cried the poet's mother bravely.

She grew braver and braver by the minute. In fact, as the stadium itself came into view and we began to pass the supporters converging on the ground, Lady Henry's braveness became so intense that I feared it might blow out the windows of the car.

'What a good idea this was, Mr Clancy! What fun! The colours are very striking don't you think in this light, Angelica? Red, blue. Almost luminous. One thinks of those rather jolly little things that you paint on glass.'

'Which are the Horsemen and which are the Rockets?' I asked.

'The Horsemen wear red,' William began, 'because their emblem is a...'

'Here, Buttle,' interrupted Lady Henry, 'pull over here and let me speak to this man.'

A steward was directing the crowds to the various gates and Lady Henry waylaid him:

'I say, could you arrange some balcony seats for us please... I will need someone to carry me up the stairs... And our hamper too... No, no reservations... I *do* hope you are not going to have to be bureaucratic about this, as I am a personal friend of the mayor... and this is Mr Clancy from the Metropolis, the distinguished writer... Thank you so much... Here is something for your trouble... You are doing a stalwart job I can see.'

I glanced at William. I could see he was angry and embarrassed, though Angelica seemed just to be amused.

'There,' said Lady Henry with satisfaction. 'Drive on Buttle, thank you. Now if you drop us off just here I believe these are the young men now who are going to help us up the stairs.'

With one steward unpacking our substantial picnic hamper for us, another sent off to find her a blanket and a third dispatched to search for aspirin (for she said she had a migraine coming on), Lady Henry settled into her seat and surveyed the scene.

'Of course, I have absolutely no idea of the rules, William. Just tell me what on earth these young men are going to be trying to do.'

'To begin with the Rockets will be trying to get to the top, Mother,' said William, 'and the Horsemen will be trying to get to the bottom. After each goal they reverse the direction of play. The main thing is...'

At this point the game itself began, to a great bellow from the crowd.

'The main thing is, Mother...' William began again patiently.

But the old lady made an exasperated gesture.

'Oh, this is all much too complicated for me. I'm just going to concentrate on the spectacle of the thing I think. The spectacle. And it is all rather jolly I have to admit. Rather your sort of thing Angelica isn't it? Red and blue painted-on glass. The sort of cheerful, uncomplicated thing that you do so well.'

Then a huge roar of emotion rose around us like a tidal wave, preventing further conversation. A goal had been narrowly averted. Angelica leapt to her feet.

'Come *on* you reds!' she bellowed like a bull.

William watched her with a small, pained, wistful smile which I could not properly read, but did not join in. Lady Henry winced and looked away.

'I quite liked your last show Angelica,' she said, as soon as the painter sat down in the next lull, 'but if you will forgive me for being frank, I am starting to feel that you need to stretch yourself artistically a little more if your work is not in the end to become a bit repetitive and predictable.'

'Let's just watch the game, shall we, Mother?' said William.

Six massive pylons were arranged in a hexagon around the arena and between them were stretched at high tension a series of horizontal nets, one above another every two metres, ascending to fifty metres up. Each net was punctured by a number of round openings through which the players could drop, jump or climb, but these openings were staggered so that a player could not drop down more than one layer at a time.

All the same, if no one stopped them, the specialist players called 'rollers' could move from top to bottom with incredible speed, dropping through one hole, rolling sideways into the next, swinging beneath a net to the one after, dropping and rolling again... the ball all the while clutched under one arm, and the crowd roaring its delight or dismay. 'Bouncers', who specialised in upward dashes, used the nets as trampolines to move with almost the same breathtaking velocity as the rollers, even though they had to work against gravity instead of with it.

But of course neither bouncers nor rollers got a clear run. While these high-speed vertical dashes were taking place through the nets, other players were swarming up or down to positions ahead of the opposing team's rollers or bouncers in order to block them off. Pitched battles took place at the various levels, with players bouncing from the nets under their feet to launch ferocious tackles, or swinging from the nets over their heads to deliver flying kicks. It was like football, but in three dimensions and without constraints. Eight players were taken off injured during the match.

'Do you play sky-ball at all, William?' I asked in the car on the way back.

William was about to answer when his mother broke in.

'I always insisted that he should be excused from the game,' she said, turning her head towards us with difficulty. 'William never showed the slightest inclination towards it, and it seemed to me absurd that a sensitive child should be put through it.'

'Oh but my brothers loved it,' exclaimed Angelica. 'Michael must have broken every bone in his body at one time or another, but it never put him off. He couldn't wait to get back into the game.'

We turned into the drive of Angelica's home. In front of her family's large and comfortable farmhouse, William got out of the car to let her out and say goodbye. A short exchange took place between them which I couldn't hear. I wasn't sure if they were arranging an assignation or conducting a muted row.

'Do you know, William,' said Lady Henry, when he had rejoined us and we were heading back down the drive, 'I'm beginning to have second thoughts about Angelica. I am not sure she is *quite* one of us, if you know what I mean. I can't help feeling that Angelica the artist is really a very secondary part of her nature and that underneath is a pretty average country girl of the huntin' and shootin' variety. Don't you agree?'

But the poet declined to answer.

'There are some fire horses for you, Clancy,' he merely said, as we passed a paddock with a couple of yearling beasts in it, feeding at a manger in the far corner.

'I gather boys in Flain are given baby fire horses to grow up with?' I said.

'It's traditional, yes,' William said.

'And were you given one?'

We had left the estate of Angelica's family and were back on the empty open road. William looked out of the window at the wide fields.

'Yes. My Uncle John gave me one when I was six.'

'Did you learn to ride? I've seen boys in the street with their small fire horses and they seem quite dangerous.'

'No, I never learned. And yes, they are dangerous. In fact Uncle John himself died in a riding accident only a few years after he gave me the horse.'

'Oh, I'm sorry.'

'Don't be, Mr Clancy,' said William's mother, once again straining to turn round and look at me. 'Don't be sorry at all. My brother was a foolish and immature young man who liked to show off with fire horses and fast cars because he wanted to impress a certain kind of silly young woman. The accident was *entirely* his own fault.'

I glanced at William. But he was still looking out of the window and I couldn't see his face.

'What would have been tragic, though,' went on Lady Henry, 'would be if I had allowed my brother to persuade William to ride – and *William* had had an accident. After all William is now Flain's foremost poet and it was obvious even at that age that he was quite exceptionally gifted. Imagine if all that had been thrown away because some stupid animal had flung him off its back and broke his neck?'

Some minutes later William, with an obvious effort, turned towards me.

'Ah here we are. Almost home. Do you know I think I must have nodded off a while there, I do apologise. A whisky Clancy perhaps, before we change for dinner?'

Two days before my departure from Flain, Lady Henry received some bad news about her northern estates. It had come to light somehow that her steward up there had been embezzling funds over many years. Lady Henry was in a state of distraction that night, torn between competing desires. For whatever reason, she seemed to hate the idea of leaving William and myself to our own devices, but she also found it intolerable not being at the helm to manage the crisis in the north. In the end it was the latter anxiety that won out. The following morning, after a great flurry of preparation that had every servant in the house running around like agitated ants, she set off in the car with Buttle.

William and I took our coffee out onto the stone terrace which overlooked the park and watched the car winding along the drive, out through the gate and on into the world beyond. It was a bright, fresh, softly gilded morning, on the cusp between summer and autumn.

William sighed contentedly.

'Peace!' he exclaimed.

I smiled.

'Mother has arranged for us to visit that sculptor's workshop this morning,' he then said. 'Do I take it you actually want to go?'

I laughed. 'To be quite honest, no. Not in the slightest.'

'Well, thank God for that. I think I will scream if we have to traipse round many more of Mother's artistic hangers-on.'

We poured more coffee and settled back comfortably in our chairs. A family of deer had emerged from the woods to the left to feed on the wide lawns along the drive and we watched them for some minutes in companionable silence.

Then he suddenly turned the full blueness of his gaze upon me.

'Have you read many of my poems, Clancy?'

'Yes, all of them,' I told him quite truthfully. 'All your published ones at least.'

I do my research. When I decided to accept the invitation from William's mother to visit them, I had hunted down and looked through all six of William's slim little collections, full of veiled agonised coded allusions to his mother's catastrophic accident while pregnant with William, his father's shotgun suicide a week before his birth. (Why do we feel the need to wear our wounds as badges?)

'And, tell me quite honestly,' William probed. 'What did you think of them?'

I hesitated.

'You write very well,' I said. 'And you also have things to say. I suppose what I sometimes felt, though, was that there was a big difference between what you really *wanted* to say and what you actually were able to express in those verses. I had the feeling of something – contained... something contained at an intolerably high pressure, but which you were only able to squeeze out through a tiny little hole.'

William laughed. 'Constipated! That's the word you're looking for.'

On the contrary, it was precisely the word I was trying to avoid!

I laughed with him. 'Well no, not exactly, but...'

'Constipated!' His laugh didn't seem bitter. It appeared that he was genuinely entertained. 'That is really very good, Clancy. Constipated is exactly right.'

Then, quite suddenly, he stood up.

'Do you fancy a short walk, Clancy? There's something I'd very much like to show you.'

The place he took me to was on the outer edges of their park. The woods here had been neglected and were clogged up by creepers and by dead trees left to lie and rot where they had fallen. Here, in a damp little valley full of stinging nettles, stood a very large brick outbuilding which could have been a warehouse or a mill. There were big double doors at one end, bolted and padlocked, but William led me to an iron staircase like a fire escape to one side of the building. At a height equivalent to the second storey of a normal house, this staircase led through a small door into the dark interior. Cautioning me to be silent, William unlocked it.

It was too dark inside to see anything at first, but I gathered from the acoustics that the inside of the building was a single space. We seemed to be standing on a gallery that ran round the sides of it. William motioned to me to squat down beside him, so only our heads were above the balustrade.

Almost as soon as we entered I heard the animal snorting and snuffling and tearing at its food. Now, as my eyes adapted, I made it out down there on the far side of the great bare stable. It must have been nearly the height of an elephant, with shoulders and haunches bulging with muscle. It was pulling with its teeth at the leg and haunches of an ox that had been hacked from a carcass and dumped into its manger.

'He hasn't noticed us yet,' whispered William. 'He wasn't looking in our direction when we came in.'

'I take it this is the same horse that your uncle gave you?' I asked him, also in a whisper.

William nodded.

'But you never rode him?'

'No.'

'And *will* you ever ride him?'

William gave a little incredulous snort. The sound made the fire horse lift its head and sniff suspiciously at the air, but after a second or two it returned again to its meat.

'No of course not,' he said, 'even if I knew how to ride a fire horse, which I don't, I couldn't ride this thing now. No one can ride an adult fire horse unless it was broken in as a foal.'

'Yes, I see.'

'I'll tell you something, Clancy. If you or I were to go down and approach him, he would tear us limb from limb. I'm not exaggerating.'

I nodded.

'So why do you keep him?'

It seemed that I had spoken too loudly. The beast lifted its head again and sniffed, but this time it didn't turn back to its food. Growling, it scanned the gallery. Then it let loose an appalling scream of rage.

I have never heard such a sound. Really and truly in all my life and all my travels, I have never heard a living thing shriek like that dreadful fire horse in its echoing prison.

And now it came thundering across the stable. Right beneath us, glaring up at us, it reared up on its hind legs to try and reach us, screaming again and again and again so that I thought my eardrums would burst. The whole building shook with the beating of the animal's hooves on the wall. And then, just as with my hands over my ears I shouted to William that I wanted to leave, the brute suddenly emitted a bolt of lightning from its mouth that momentarily illuminated that entire cavernous space with the brilliance of daylight.

William's face was radiant, but I had had enough. I made my own way back to the door and out into the open. Those decaying woods outside had seemed sour and gloomy before, but compared to the dark stable of the fire horse they now seemed almost cheerful. I went down the steps and, making myself comfortable on a fallen tree, took out my notebook and began to record some thoughts while I waited for the poet to finish whatever it was he felt he needed to do in there. I was surprised and pleased to find my imagination flowing freely. The imprisoned fire horse, it seemed, had provided the catalyst, the injection of venom, that sooner or later I always needed to bring each book of mine to life. Inwardly laughing, I poured out idea after idea while the muffled screams of the tormented monster kept on and on — and from time to time another flash of lightning momentarily illuminated the cracks in the door at the top of the stairs.

After a few minutes William emerged. His face was shining.

'I'll tell you why I don't get rid of him, Clancy,' he declared, speaking rather too loudly, as if he was drunk. 'Because he is what I love best in the whole world! The *only* thing I've ever loved, apart from my Uncle John.'

Behind him the fire horse screamed again and I wondered what William thought he meant by 'love' when he spoke of this animal which he had condemned to solitude and darkness and madness.

'I feel I have fallen in your esteem,' he said on the way back to the house.

There had been a long silence between us as we trudged back from the dank little valley of brambles and stinging nettles and out again into the formal, public parkland of William's and his mother's country seat.

'You are repelled, I think,' William persisted, 'by the idea of my doting on a horse which I have never dared to ride. Isn't that so?'

I couldn't think of anything to say, so he answered for me.

'You are repelled and actually so am I. I am disgusted and ashamed by the spectacle of my weakness. And yet this is the only way I know of making myself feel alive. Do you understand me? You find my work a little constipated and bottled up, you say. But if I didn't go down to the fire horse, shamed and miserable as it makes me feel, I wouldn't be able to write at all.'

I made myself offer a reassuring remark.

'We all have to find our way of harnessing the power of our demons.'

It would have been kinder, and more honest, if I had acknowledged that the encounter with the fire horse had been a catalyst for me also and that for the first time in this visit, my book had begun to flow and come alive. But I couldn't bring myself to make such a close connection between my own experience and his.

That night William slipped out shortly after his mother returned, without goodbyes or explanations.

'I suppose he showed you his blessed horse?' said Lady Henry as she and I sat at supper.

'He did. An extraordinary experience I must say.'

'And I suppose he told you that the horse and his Uncle John were the only things he had ever really loved?'

My surprise must have shown. She nodded.

'It's his standard line. He's used it to good effect with several impressionable young girls. Silly boy. Good lord, Mr Clancy, he doesn't *have* to stay with me if he doesn't want to! We are wealthy people after all! We have more than one house! I have other people to push around!'

She gave a bitter laugh.

'I don't know what kind of monster you think I am Mr Clancy, and I don't suppose it really matters, but I will tell you this. When William was six and his uncle tried to get him to ride, he clung to me so tightly and so desperately that it bruised me, and he begged and pleaded with me to promise that I'd never make him do it. That night he actually wet his bed with fear. Perhaps you think I was weak and I should have made him ride the horse? But, with respect Mr Clancy, remember that you are not a parent yourself, and certainly not the sole parent of an only child.'

Her eyes filled with tears and she dabbed at them angrily with her napkin.

'His father was a violent, arrogant drunk,' she said. 'Far worse than my brother. He was the very worst type of Flainian male. He pushed me down the stairs you know. That was how I ended up like this. He pushed me in a fit of rage and broke my back. It was a miracle that William survived, a complete miracle. And then, when I refused to promise to keep secret the reason for my paralysis, my dear brave husband blew off his own head. I wanted William to be different. I wanted him to be gentle. I didn't want him to glory in strength and danger.'

She gave a small, self-deprecating shrug.

'I do acknowledge that I lack a certain… lightness.'

'Lady Henry, I am sure that—'

But the poet's mother cut me off.

'Now *do* try this wine, Mr Clancy,' she cried brightly, so instantly transformed that I almost wondered whether I had dreamed what had gone before. 'It was *absurdly* expensive and I've been saving it for someone who was capable of appreciating it.'

In the early hours of the morning I heard William come crashing in through the front doors.

'Come and get my boots off!' he bellowed. 'One of you lazy bastards, come down and take off my boots.'

And then I heard him outside the door of my room abusing some servant or other who was patiently helping him along the corridor.

'Watch out, you clumsy oaf! Can't you at least look where you're going?'

He still hadn't emerged when I left in the morning for the Metropolis.

Ali Smith

True Short Story

There were two men in the café at the table next to mine. One was younger, one was older. They could have been father and son, but there was none of that practised diffidence, none of the cloudy anger that there almost always is between fathers and sons. Maybe they were the result of a parental divorce, the father keen to be a father now that his son was properly into his adulthood, the son keen to be a man in front of his father now that his father was opposite him for at least the length of time of a cup of coffee. No. More likely the older man was the kind of family friend who provides a fathership on summer weekends for the small boy of a divorce family; a man who knows his responsibility, and now look, the boy had grown up, the man was an older man, and there was this unsaid understanding between them, etc.

I stopped making them up. It felt a bit wrong to. Instead, I listened to what they were saying. They were talking about literature, which happens to be interesting to me, though it wouldn't interest a lot of people. The younger man was talking about the difference between the novel and the short story. The novel, he was saying, was a flabby old whore.

A flabby old whore! the older man said looking delighted.

She was serviceable, roomy, warm and familiar, the younger was saying, but really a bit used up, really a bit too slack and loose.

Slack and loose! the older said laughing.

Whereas the short story, by comparison, was a nimble goodness, a slim nymph. Because so few people have mastered the short story she was still in very good shape.

Very good shape! The older man was smiling from ear to ear at this. He was presumably old enough to remember years in his life, and not so long ago, when it would have been at least a bit dodgy to talk like this. I idly wondered how many of the books in my house were fuckable and how good they'd be in bed. Then I sighed, and got my mobile out

53

and phoned my friend, with whom I usually go to this café on Friday mornings.

She knows quite a lot about the short story. She'd spent a lot of her life reading them, writing about them, teaching them, even on occasion writing them. She'd read more short stories than most people know (or care) exist. I suppose you could call it a lifelong act of love, though she's not very old, was that morning still in her late thirties. A life-so-far act of love. But already she knew more about the short story and about the people all over the world who write and have written short stories than anyone I've ever met.

She was in hospital, on this particular Friday a couple of years now, because a course of chemotherapy had destroyed every single one of her tiny white cells and after it had she'd picked up an infection in a wisdom tooth.

I waited for the automaton voice of the hospital phone system to tell me all about itself, then to recite robotically back to me the number I'd just called, then to mispronounce my friend's name, which is Kasia, then to tell me exactly how much it was charging me to listen to it tell me all this, and then to tell me how much it would cost to speak to my friend per minute. Then it connected me.

Hi, I said. It's me.

Are you on your mobile? she said. Don't, Ali, it's expensive on this system. I'll call you back.

No worries, I said. It's just a quickie. Listen. Is the short story a goddess and a nymph and is the novel an old whore?

Is what what? she said.

An old whore, kind of a Dickensian one, maybe, I said. Like that prostitute who first teaches David Niven how to have sex in that book.

David Niven? she said.

You know, I said. The prostitute he goes in to in 'The Moon's a Balloon' when he's about fourteen, and she's really sweet and she initiates him and he loses his virginity, and he's still wearing his socks, or maybe that's the prostitute who's still wearing the socks, I can't remember, anyway, she's really sweet to him and then he goes back to see her in later life when she's an old whore and he's an internationally famous movie star, and he brings her a lot of presents because he's such a nice man and never forgets a kindness. And is the short story more like Princess Diana?

The short story like Princess Diana, she said. Right.

I sensed the two men, who were getting ready to leave the café, looking at me curiously. I held up my phone.

I'm just asking my friend what she thinks about your nymph thesis, I said.

Both men looked slightly startled. Then both men left the café without looking back.

I told her about the conversation I'd just overheard.

I was thinking of Diana because she's a bit nymphy, I suppose, I said. I can't think of a goddess who's like a nymph. All the goddesses that come into my head are, like, Kali, or Sheela-Na-Gig. Or Aphrodite, she was pretty tough. All that deer-slaying. Didn't she slay deer?

Why is the short story like a nymph, Kasia said. Sounds like a dirty joke. Ha.

Okay, I said. Come on then. Why is the short story like a nymph?

I'll think about it, she said. It'll give me something to do in here.

Kasia and I have been friends now for just over twenty years, which doesn't feel at all long, though it sounds quite long. 'Long' and 'short' are relative. What was long was every day she was spending in hospital; today was her tenth long day in one of the cancer wards, being injected with a cocktail of antibiotics and waiting for her temperature to come down and her white cell count to go up. When those two tiny personal adjustments happened in the world, then she'd be allowed to go home. Also, there was a lot of sadness round her in the ward. After ten long days the heaviness of that sadness, which might sound bearably small if you're not a person who has to think about it or is being forced by circumstance to address it, but is close to epic if you are, was considerable.

She phoned me back later that afternoon and left a message on the answerphone. I could hear the clanking hospital and the voices of other people in the ward in the recorded air around her voice.

Okay. Listen to this. It depends what you mean by 'nymph'. So, depending. A short story is like a nymph because satyrs want to sleep with it all the time. A short story is like a nymph because both like to live on mountains and in groves and by springs and rivers and in valleys and cool grottoes. A short story is like a nymph because it likes to accompany Artemis on her travels. Not very funny, I know, but I'm working on it.

I heard the phone being hung up. Message received at three forty-three, my answerphone's robot voice said. I called her back and went through the exact echo of the morning's call to the system. She answered and before I could even say hello she said:

Listen! Listen! A short story is like a nymphomaniac because both like to sleep around – or get into lots of anthologies – but neither accepts money for the pleasure.

I laughed out loud.

Unlike the bawdy old whore, the novel, ha ha, she said. And when I was speaking to my father at lunchtime he told me you can fish for trout with a nymph. They're a kind of fishing fly. He says there are people who carry magnifying glasses around with them all the time in case they get the chance to look at real nymphs, so as to be able to copy them even more exactly in the fishing flies they make.

I tell you, I said. The world is full of astounding things.

I know, she said. What do you reckon to the anthology joke?

Six out of ten, I said.

Rubbish then, she said. Okay. I'll try and think of something better.

Maybe there's mileage in the nymphs-at-your-flies thing, I said.

Ha ha, she said. But I'll have to leave the nymph thing this afternoon and get back on the Herceptin trail.

God, I said.

I'm exhausted, she said. We're drafting letters.

When is an anti-cancer drug not an anti-cancer drug? I said.

When people can't afford it, she said. Ha ha.

Lots of love, I said.

You too, she said. Cup of tea?

I'll make us one, I said. Speak soon.

I heard the phone go dead. I put my phone down and went through and switched the kettle on. I watched it reach the boil and the steam came out of the spout. I filled two cups with boiling water and dropped the teabags in. I drank my tea watching the stream rise off the other cup.

This is what Kasia meant by 'Herceptin trail'.

Herceptin is a drug that's been used in breast cancer treatment for a while now. Doctors had, at the point in time that Kasia and I were having conversations in this story, very recently discovered that it really helps some women – those who over-produce the HER2 in the early stages of the disease. When given to a receptive case it can cut the risk of the cancer returning by 50 per cent. Doctors all over the world were excited about it because it amounted to a paradigm shift in breast cancer treatment.

I had never heard of any of this till Kasia told me, and she had never heard of any of it until a small truth, less than two centimetres in size, which a doctor found in April that year in one of her breasts, had meant a paradigm shift in everyday life.

It was not August. In May her doctor had told her about how good Herceptin is, and how she'd definitely be able to have it at the end of the chemotherapy on the NHS. Then at the end of July her doctor was visited by a member of the PCT, which stands for the words Primary, Care and Trust, and is concerned with NHS funding. The PCT member instructed my friend's doctor not to tell any more of the women affected in the hospital's catchment area about the wonders of Herceptin until a group called NICE had approved its cost-effectiveness. At the time, they thought this might take about nine months or maybe a year (by which time it would be too late for my friend and many other women). Though Kasia knew that if she wanted to buy Herceptin on BUPA, right then, for roughly twenty-seven thousand pounds, she could. This kind of thing will be happening to an urgently needed drug right now, somewhere near you.

'Primary'. 'Care'. 'Trust'. 'Nice'.

Here's a short story that most people already think they know about a nymph. (It also happens to be one of the earliest manifestations in literature of what we now call anorexia.)

Echo was an Oread, which is a kind of mountain nymph. She was well known among the nymphs and shepherds not just for her glorious garrulousness but for her ability to save her nymph friends from the wrath of the goddess Juno. For instance, her friends would be lying about on the hillside in the sun and Juno would come round the corner, about to catch them slacking, and Echo, who had a talent for knowing when Juno was to turn up, would leap to her feet and head the goddess off by running up to her and distracting her with stories and talk, talk and stories, until all the slacker nymphs were up and working like they'd never been slacking at all.

When Juno worked out what Echo was doing she was a bit annoyed. She pointed at her with her curse finger and threw off the first suitable curse that came into her head.

From now on, she said, you will be able only to repeat out loud the words you've heard others say just a moment before. Won't you?

Won't you, Echo said.

Her eyes grew large. Her mouth fell open.

That's you sorted, Juno said.

You sordid, Echo said.

Right. I'm off back to the hunt, Juno said.

The cunt, Echo said.

Actually, I'm making up that small rebellion. There is actually no rebelliousness for Echo in Ovid's original version of the story. It seems that after she's robbed of being able to talk on her own terms, and of being able to watch her friends' backs for them, there's nothing left for her – in terms of story – but to fall in love with a boy so in love with himself that he spends all his days bent over a pool of his own desire and eventually pines for near-death (then transforms, instead of dying, from a boy into a little white flower).

Echo pined too. Her weight dropped off her. She became fashionably skinny, then she became nothing but bones, then all that was left of her was a whiny, piny voice which floated bodilessly about, saying over and over exactly the same things that everybody else was saying.

Here, by contrast, is the story of the moment I met my friend Kasia, more than twenty years ago.

I was a postgraduate student at Cambridge and I had lost my voice. I don't mean I'd lost it because I had a cold or a throat infection, I mean that two years of a system of hierarchies so entrenched that girls and women were still a bit of a novelty to it had somehow knocked what voice I had out of me.

So I was sitting at the back of a room not even really listening properly any more, and I heard a voice. It was from somewhere up ahead of me. It was a girl's voice and it was directly asking the person giving the seminar and the chair of the seminar a question about the American writer Carson McCullers.

Because it seems to me that McCullers is obviously very relevant at all levels in this discussion, the voice said.

The person and the chair of the meeting both looked a bit shocked that anyone had said anything out loud. The chair cleared his throat.

I found myself leaning forward. I hadn't heard anyone speak like this with such an open and carefree display of knowledge and forthrightness, for a couple of years. More: earlier that day I had been talking with an undergraduate student who had been unable to find anyone in the whole of the Cambridge University English Department to supervise her dissertation on McCullers. It seemed nobody eligible to teach had read her.

Anyway, I venture to say you'll find McCullers not at all of the same stature, the person giving the paper on Literature After Henry James said.

Well, the thing is, I disagree, the voice said.

I laughed out loud. It was a noise never heard in such a room; heads turned to see who was making such an unlikely noise. The new girl carried on politely asking questions which no one answered. She mentioned, I remember, how McCullers had been fond of a maxim: nothing human is alien to me.

At the end of the seminar I ran after that girl. I stopped her in the street. It was winter. She was wearing a red coat.

She told me her name. I heard myself tell her mine.

Franz Kafka says that the short story is a cage in search of a bird. (Kafka's been dead for more than eighty years, but I can still say Kafka says. That's just one of the ways art deals with our mortality.)

Tzvetan Todorov says that the thing about a short story is that it's so short it doesn't allow us the time to forget that it's only literature and not actually life.

Nadine Gordimer says short stories are absolutely about the present moment, like the brief flash of a number of fireflies here and there in the dark.

Elizabeth Bowen says the short story has the advantage over the novel of a special kind of concentration, and that it creates narrative every time absolutely on its own terms.

Eudora Welty says that short stories often problematize their own best interests and that this is what makes them interesting.

Henry James says that the short story, being so condensed, can give a particularized perspective on both complexity and continuity.

Jorge Luis Borges says that short stories can be the perfect form for novelists too lazy to write anything longer than fifteen pages.

Ernest Hemingway says that short stories are made by their own change and movement, and that even when a story seems static and you can't make out any movement in it at all it is probably changing and moving regardless, just unseen by you.

William Carlos Williams says that the short story, which acts like the flare of a match struck in the dark, is the only real form for describing the briefness, the brokenness and the simultaneous wholeness of people's lives.

Walter Benjamin says that short stories are stronger than the real, lived moment, because they can go on releasing the real, lived moment after the real, lived moment is dead.

Cynthia Ozick says that the difference between a short story and a novel is that the novel is a book whose journey, if it's a good working novel, actually alters a reader, whereas a short story is more like the talismanic gift given to the protagonist of a fairy tale – something complete, powerful, whose power may not yet be understood, which can be held in the hands or tucked into the pocket and taken through the forest on a dark journey.

Grace Paley says that she chose to write only short stories in her life because art is too long and art is too short, and that short stories are, by nature, about life, and that life itself is always found in dialogue and argument.

Alice Munro says that every short story is at least two short stories.

There were two men in the café at the table next to mine. One was younger, one was older. We sat in the same cafe for only a brief amount of time but we disagreed long enough for me to know there was a story in it.

The story was written in discussion with my friend Kasia, and in celebration of her (and all) tireless articulacy – one of the reasons, in this instance, that a lot more people were able to have this particular drug when they needed it.

So when is the short story like a nymph?

When the echo of it answers back.

Jeremy Dyson

Michael

It started with a Valentine's card.

Danny hated Valentine's Day. At seventeen he had yet to receive a card, or indeed to send one. So on 11th February, walking back from college, Danny was surprised to find himself heading into Mathers in the Merrion Centre, facing the temporary lines of hearts and bunnies, the repeating pinks and reds. He reached out and picked up a glossy picture of Pooh Bear. He opened it. 'Roses are red, Eeyore is blue, Honey is sweet, says Winnie-the-Pooh.' He put it down. It seemed juvenile and unappealing. He looked down the row, not knowing what he was searching for. He paused at a smaller card, more expensive. It featured a heart, like most of the others, but it was dark purple, almost blue – as if it was suffocating. There was no message inside. The design was stark and graphic.

Even as he left the shop with the card hidden away in his shoulder bag he didn't know what he was going to do with it, or why he had bought it. This was what he was like. His own actions were mysterious to him. He made himself feel sick.

Dinner was quiet. Or rather he was quiet. His brothers sat on either side, oblivious to him. Had he bought the card to impress them? Because by now he'd decided he was going to post it to himself. Who was it from? He was going to make up a name before he wrote it. He would disguise his handwriting. Carefully. They would see it on Wednesday morning. He would open it, say nothing, put it in his bag, go to college.

He sat in his room with a candle burning, the door bolted. He'd put the fastening on himself two years ago – a bathroom lock he'd bought from Woolworths. He took a fine-tipped Pilot pen from the wooden box on his suitcase. He wrote the card. 'To Daniel, from?, with love...' He adopted a careful, ornamental style – almost like calligraphy. He added a single kiss. He let the ink dry and closed the card, then replicated the hand on the light-brown paper envelope, this time writing his full name

– Daniel MacFadden – followed by his address. He tried to imagine not knowing who he was as he wrote it out. He placed the card inside his bag, laying it flat along the bottom. Tomorrow he would buy a book of stamps.

If Danny had done things in the order that he had planned them then what followed may never have occurred. As it was he didn't post the card. It lay, semi-forgotten, at the bottom of the bag, already a matter of some half-conscious shame. Maybe he had no intention of posting it after all. Another one of his opaque rituals that resisted comprehension. And then, during lunchtime in the common room, Jardine and his crew were playing soccer with a tennis ball, rebounding it off the walls, scoring points when they hit pictures or windows. Danny sat in one corner by the folding doors, an uneaten sandwich in his lap. As he might have expected, the ball came close to him several times. Danny wasn't going to react, even when it flew a few centimetres from his face. He would have succeeded in this aspiration had the ball not landed in his bag. It was Jardine himself who was responsible for the kick.

'Come on Gollum – give it back.' At first Danny didn't even respond. 'Gollum, you dick,' said Jardine, making his way over towards Danny. And as he arrived, Danny remembered the card. Instinctively he pulled the bag – a dirty Adidas holdall – onto his lap and zipped it closed. He should have taken the ball out first, of course, but he didn't.

'Give it back, Pogle,' said Jardine, reaching for it with long arms. He had red hair and the colour of it seemed to blur into the acne on his face. Danny clutched the bag to himself. He couldn't let Jardine get hold of it.

'No,' he heard himself say.

Jardine laughed. Pickering and Whieldon, his cohorts, laughed too.

'Give it to me now, Gollum, or I'll fucking nut you. I'll fucking hurt you.'

'No,' said Danny. There was no courage in this. It was blind self-preservation. Because Jardine would see the card. He tried to resist as the bag was pulled off him.

'I'll fucking kill you with it,' said Jardine, his eyes screwed up, his red face hot. 'You shit insect.' And the bag was pulled from Danny. He heard the Velcro rip. The file folders; the pads; the scratched tin box of compasses and protractors; the light-brown Valentine's card – all were spread over the carpet tiles, the tennis ball rolling unwanted among them.

It was Whieldon who saw the card. Picked it up, together with the ball.

He threw the ball to Jardine but kept the card. Danny shouldn't have said anything, but he heard himself doing so.

'Give it to me.'

Whieldon threw it to Jardine. Jardine read out the address.

'What's this?' he said, wafting it in the air like a fan.

'Give it to me.' Danny heard the envelope tearing. He didn't want to look. He searched his imagination for some kind of reason why the card was there – who he might be posting it on behalf of. A sick grandmother who always used to send him Valentines? It was useless. He didn't even speak as the thing was withdrawn.

'To Daniel – from question mark – with love.' The last word read out by Jardine with humiliating emphasis.

'What?' said Pickering, delighted at his own incredulity.

'To Daniel from question mark with love,' Jardine said again. 'Sending yourself Valentine's cards,' he added loudly for the benefit of the others in the room.

'MacFadden's sending a Valentine's to *himself*,' said Pickering.

'MacFadden, you wanker. You sad fucking wanker.'

Danny couldn't speak. He couldn't move.

'I'm in love with myself,' said Whieldon.

'What the matter with you, you sad fucking shit,' said Jardine.

Later, sitting in Economics, Mr Geldard at the front writing on the whiteboard, while from behind a gentle chorus began, almost inaudible at first, swelling gradually until it filled the room.

'With the record selection, with the mirror reflection, I'll be dancing with myself... I'll be dancing with myself.' Soon the whole class was singing.

'Well there's nothing to prove and there's nothing to lose... I'll be dancing with myself... dancing with—'

Mr Geldard turned around and the class immediately silenced, all eyes flicking down to notepads and laps. All eyes except Danny's, which stared straight ahead and were wet with tears.

He was silent at dinner that night. He wasn't going to speak of what happened. He couldn't have done had he been asked to. Everything burned inside.

'Greg's going to see the Valetta game,' said Lawrence, Danny's eldest brother.

'The jammy fucker,' said Marshall, Danny's younger brother.

'Marshall, if you don't mind,' said his father.

'Yeah, Marshall,' said Lawrence, flicking a pea at him, 'don't be such a foul-mouthed fucker.'

'Lawrence,' said his father.

'Yeah, Lawrence,' said Marshall. 'You bastard.'

Danny's father leaned across and hit Marshall's knuckles with a fork. Lawrence laughed. Danny read the back of the ketchup bottle throughout this exchange, trying to use the list of contents to force the words of the song from his head. Even when he mentally shouted it down the Gen X lyric ran on and on. Without warning Danny stood up.

'Daniel,' said his father.

'Toilet,' said Danny.

His father watched him leave the kitchen.

'You know what Greg's like,' said Lawrence, not responding to Danny's exit. 'With his luck his car'll break down, or they'll get lost on the way or his dad'll die or something.'

'Give me that potato if you're wasting it.'

'Fat pig.'

'Says you.'

'Says you.' The banter faded out as Danny made his way upstairs.

He was relieved to find himself in the bathroom. He shut the door. Felt safety and satisfaction as he slid the bolt and flicked its hexagonal arm downwards. The relief was momentary. The burning returned to his belly. He took off his shirt. He hated looking at himself. He was the wrong shape. His thinness a metaphor for his weakness. All he could discern was a skeleton. There was something repulsive about it. He examined the lines down his arms. Different shades of pink and red depending on what stage of healing they were at. They marked time. A calendar of shame. But he was proud of them too. They were his. They spoke of a certain courage. An identity. He'd already spotted the razor in the hollowed-out soap holder dug into the tiled wall. It was at the back, behind a wodge of wet soap – a cheap yellow and white disposable. The edge of the blade was visible. It winked in the light. He didn't want to think about it, but the idea was there, upon him. A delicious thrill. Something to encounter the song which persisted and bit. There was anger too, and hatred. Some for Jardine and his pack, but more, much more, for himself. Without even being aware of reaching for it he found the razor in his hands, the imperfect steel dotted with dried soap and severed yellow hairs. He picked at the surrounding plastic. It hurt his nails. He remained determined, the sensation dulling, or shouting down the feelings of vileness – a trailer for what was to come. How far could he go? A cold rush of adrenaline. His heart thumping tightly. The blade, free now, its bared base cleaner and lighter than its sullied edge. He wanted to shout as he dug it into his arm, not in pain but with the release of it. The rage and hatred he felt for himself. For everything. Himself was everything. Let it stop. Let it cease. Let it go black and end and hate and fuck them and fuck me.

It was two months before they let him home, he must have cut deeper than he'd intended. There'd been a transfusion. Now he took to riding his bicycle around the suburban estate he lived on.

He wasn't going back to college. Not yet. Not this year. No one was going to make him. There was talk of another place, starting again. He liked the idea. The faintest tremor of interest from him brought gushes of enthusiasm from his parents. His brothers avoided him. No one was comfortable with him straying too far from home. But the bike rides were tolerated. Besides, he didn't want to go much further. At first he'd been nervous just leaving the house, as if there were something dangerous waiting for him outside. He imagined a thick length of pink rubber, one end looped around his leg, the other tied to a post in his bedroom. Tight at first but gradually it slackened and lengthened. The High Ashes where he lived were a thinly spread estate of sixties semis, all of similar proportion and style. Just beyond them was open countryside, some of it smeared with patches of thick messy woodland. Steadily he got to know these roads, the overgrown hedges, the potholed narrow lanes. He would ride back and forth, the mud-scented wind blowing sharp and cold in his face. Sometimes he would observe things. Something about the landscape attracted outsiders, or people who misbehaved. There was evidence of drug use – charred silver paper and ripped-up cigarettes. Abandoned pornography made papier mâché by the rain and dew. Sometimes he dared himself to see how late he would stay out. Not to test his parents, but rather himself. Playing with the edges of fear seemed like a new hobby. It was April and night began to fade in around seven. There was one patch of gravel opposite a field of turnips. The air was laden with their overripe pungency. On the other side of the road was a patch of woodland. It rolled down towards the A61 about half a mile away and extended ahead of him for at least twice that distance. He'd toyed with the idea of exploring it but the pink rubber wouldn't stretch that far. Once he thought he saw something stirring, deep within the unleafed branches. He stood upright on his pedals and moved off at some speed, gravel grinding beneath his wheels.

Without college and college work to occupy him, Danny found himself cycling more and more. He rarely strayed from his adopted route though sometimes he varied the order in which he rode the roads. Inevitably he would return to the same patch of gravel. He would roll up on the bike, holding himself upright with one foot on the ground, staring into the dark mass of branches and bracken. Something kept drawing him back. It was like a dare. And then one day someone else was there. He was perturbed, as soon as he arrived, to see a figure standing, not on the gravel lay-by, but at the edge of the woods themselves. Wearing a long coat, with straight dark shoulder-length hair, their back to the outside world. Danny had to look hard to be sure it wasn't a shadow, or a misperception of tangled branches and overgrown ivy, but then the figure moved. Danny's first inclination was to ride straight off again – until he saw it was a girl of about his own age, or a little older. She stared at him. Right at him. He stared straight back. There was something combative in her gaze which he found himself determined to take on.

'Yeah?' she said.

'What?' said Danny.

'And?' she said.

'And what?' he said.

'Well, go on then.'

'Go on then where?'

'Fuck off,' she said, holding his gaze.

He stood there, his heart thudding. It wasn't fear. He wasn't going to go anywhere.

'What are you doing here?' he said.

'Mind your own business.' She had stepped out of the trees, and onto the edge of the road. Danny lifted his foot off the ground and onto the pedal. He stood upright, pushing downwards, moving the bike back and forth along the gravel.

'What's in the woods?'

'Trees,' she said, holding his stare.

'Fuck off then,' said Daniel, not quite believing that he was saying it. He sat down in his saddle, pushed harder and rolled off the lay-by and onto the tarmac, speeding away from her and back towards the houses of the High Ashes. He was a little way down the lane when he heard her calling to him. He applied the brake, feeling the wheel push against its resistance. He brought the bike to a halt. He looked back over his shoulder. She was still standing there, tall and thin, outlined by the wooded undergrowth behind her.

'What is it?' he said, coming to a rest on her side of the road. He used the opportunity to gain a better view of her face. She was pretty, but pale, as if she were ill. Her dark hair was cut into a long fringe at the front. She pushed it out of her face, hooking it behind her ear.

'I said, "Have you got a light?"' She looked straight at him again, as if there were a challenge in the request.

'Don't smoke,' said Danny. The girl lifted one of her legs and pulled at her shoe – a plain black pump. The sole was coming loose at the front. 'What's your name?' he asked. She answered him but he couldn't quite make out her reply. 'Sorry?' he said.

'Jeanne,' she said. Danny nodded. For some reason he'd thought she'd said something quite different.

They walked for a while, Danny pushing his bike ahead of him. The conversation was intermittent. Danny tried to keep it going.

'Do you know it round here?' he said.

'No.'

'Did you get the bus up – the thirty-six?' He wondered what she'd been doing. She'd walked out of the woods.

'Uh-huh.'

'Were you looking for mushrooms?' he said.

'In April?' She laughed at him, then seeing his expression said, 'Getting away from my boyfriend. He'd come looking for me.' Danny's face must have reacted in some way he wasn't aware of because she added, 'I don't like him. I never liked him.'

'Why don't you finish with him?'

'I have done,' she said, and then, after a brief pause, 'He hates me being with Michael.' They came to a halt by a little grassy bank. It was the girl that decided to sit down. She took off her coat, laying it on the grass behind her. She shuffled backwards, seating herself on it. She was wearing a long black dress. The sleeves were loose, revealing the pale skin of her arms. They looked narrow and delicate. One finger of her hand carried a heavy-looking ring.

'Who's Michael? Your new boyfriend?'

'No,' she said, laughing. She shuffled forward as if trying to get comfortable. 'Don't want another boyfriend.' She reached behind and started digging in one of her coat pockets. She withdrew her cigarettes. She flipped the top of the box revealing a lighter inside. 'I like being on my own. I like being with Michael.' Having lit a cigarette she stretched herself out, leaning back on her arms. There were three scars, hard, calloused lines of dark skin, marring the smooth cream. Cuts. She looked at Danny. Saw that he'd seen. She didn't change her posture, or try to conceal them. She drew on the cigarette and exhaled. He wondered whether to say anything. He thought about revealing his own scars. He did neither.

'You don't say much,' she said.

Danny shrugged.

'What were you doing out here?' she said.

'Nothing, I live here,' said Danny.

'Out here?'

'Over there.' He pointed down the road, towards the distant houses. He watched her smoking and was aware of feeling light-headed – almost feverish. Everything was suddenly very bright. The girl pulled on her cigarette and watched the smoke dissipating into the air.

'Do you ever think about the universe?' she said, shifting her elbows and laying on her back. She stared up at the sky. 'Shall I tell you what I like to do? I lie on my back at night and look up. But I like to imagine that this bit of the planet's facing down. So I'm looking down and down and down, into infinity.' She went quiet and closed her eyes. 'And then I like to imagine falling. And thinking that no matter how long I fell I'd never never never hit the bottom.' Danny looked at her. She turned towards him and started to laugh. She threw her cigarette, still lit, off in the direction of the trees. 'I'm joking,' she said. Then, 'Have you ever had sex?' She sat upright.

Danny shrugged. He felt uncomfortable. 'I've got to get back in a bit,' he said.

'The one thing I like is a good night's sleep. I used to sleep after we had sex. My old boyfriend. I can't get to sleep so easy now.'

Danny nodded.

'Do you want to know what my hobby is?' She was babbling now, as if insane. In his imagination he saw the cuts, marring her skin. 'History,' she continued, answering her own question. Danny suddenly sat up himself.

'What?'

'History.'

'History's my hobby,' he said. His response sounded stupid, parroting her like a child, but it was true.

'I'll bet,' she said.

'I wrote a book about the Napoleonic wars,' he said.

'What do you mean, you wrote a book?'

'It took me three years. I started it when I was fourteen.'

'Do you know what history teaches us?' said the girl. He looked at her, waiting for her answer. 'That someone somewhere is going to set off another atomic bomb.'

Danny didn't respond. But he had had the same thought himself. The girl stood up, shaking out her coat. Again the brightness and the wooziness.

'Do you want to meet up again?' she said as she buttoned herself up.

'Meet up?' He didn't seem capable of speaking without using words she'd just used herself.

'Any time. On Monday.'

'Monday's Easter.'

'I know.' She looked at him intently. She smiled.

'All right,' he said quietly.

'Good. Two o'clock. Same place.'

'Will you be there?' he asked, hearing the foolishness of the question.

'Turn up and see.' She crossed back over the narrow road, back towards the woods. She glanced at him and then walked purposefully into them, as if they were where she lived.

The rest of the weekend Danny cycled about his adopted domain, trying not to pause every five minutes at the patch of gravel where the trees started. He'd filled an old tartan flask from the tap. He stopped at one point and sat on the small grassy bank sipping from it. He watched the branches, thinking he might see her striding out of them at any time. It was cool, cooler than when he'd set out. He pulled his duffel coat around himself. It was new. The material still felt stiff and unfamiliar. Mum had bought it for him when he came out of the hospital. He swigged at the water. It tasted metallic. He wished he'd let the tap run longer, and then he remembered it was a side effect of the tablets they'd put him on. Everything tasted like that. A gust of wind came, picking up a faded foil packet from the side of the road. It skittered around the uneven tarmac in a circular dance before being pulled along into the trees. Danny found himself on his feet. He left his bike where it was, flat against the grass. It would be alright for a few minutes. He'd never once seen anyone else here. Apart from the girl.

He supposed he'd wandered in there hoping to find the footpath – the one she must have taken down to the main road assuming that was where she had gone. He hadn't walked far before exploring any deeper became very difficult. The remains of the bracken snagged his feet. Lines of narrow birch and brambles seemed to thicken with every step. One of the toggles of his coat caught on a spiralling branch of holly. He looked back over his shoulder. He could still see his bike. He had only come ten metres or so and he could get no further. She must have come from a different part of the woods. He looked around, trying to peer through the slatted undergrowth. It was thick and dark and silent. With difficulty he made his way back out into the light.

Danny sat at dinner as he had sat at every other dinner since he had returned home, watching the family around him rather than participating in their banter. Marshall – who had taken up magic as a hobby – was performing a trick with the pepper grinder, wrapping it in a paper serviette.

'You're such a prick, Marsh.'

'Shuddup.'

'I can see it's gone already.'

'Shuddup. Just watch.'

'It's in your lap. You've dropped it in your lap. There's nothing there.'

Danny watched them through a screen of thick Perspex. The only thing that was different now was that there was something with him on his side of the plastic. He was accompanied by the thought of the girl. He saw Lawrence reach across and press the paper serviette flat.

'See – told you.'

'Dad!'

'You're a faker. You're so shit, Marshall.'

Danny felt himself force another smile.

Later they were in the living room, playing Rummikub. Or rather everybody else was. Danny sat back on the sofa, looking on, watching them kneeling round the coffee table in the centre of the room shouting at each other.

'Dad. Tell him. He's putting down more than he's allowed.'

'Ignore him, Father. He knows not of what he speaks.'

'You put down a seven and thought I wouldn't notice.'

'Dan – are you coming to Marshall's magic club show?' Lawrence had turned to Danny, suddenly moving his attention from the game.

'Leave him, Lawrence,' said Marshall. 'Danny. You don't have to go.'

'I think he should go. I think you should go.' Danny, not expecting this direct engagement, shrugged his shoulders.

'Why not? It's your brother's inaugural night. The rest of us have got to suffer.'

'Leave him,' said Dad.

'I just thought he might enjoy it.'

'You can talk,' said Marshall. 'You didn't want to watch an hour ago.'

'I just thought he might want to get out the house. See some life.'

'Lawrence,' said Dad.

'Come on. It'll be a laugh. We can heckle him together.'

'No thanks.' Danny heard himself say it. Hating himself for not wanting to go. Hating Lawrence for asking him.

'Well, great. How's that for family solidarity.'

'Lawrence. Leave him alone.'

Danny stood up from the sofa. He walked towards the door.

'Danny.' Lawrence called to him. 'Danny.' Danny reached the comfort of the corridor outside and headed for the stairs.

When he set out on Monday – the bike friendly beneath him – Danny didn't expect that the girl would be there. But he rode off anyway. He wanted to see her. He'd been trying to picture her almost all the intervening time since they last met. It was the feel of her that he'd been able to recall so clearly. A sharp spike that somehow brought comfort.

It was colder today. A return to winter. The narrow branches swung and swayed. He almost didn't want to dismount. He felt that if someone were to observe him, sitting on the grassy hump in this chilly weather, they would think he was mad, or misbehaving. He stared into the woods. There was a fence at their threshold. Struts of splintered oak, roughly nailed into one another. He supposed this whole area was part of the old golf course – which was now disused, most of it sold off for building development. Only the woods remained wild and untrodden, part of something else. Did anyone own woods, or were they just there, like the sea?

'Hello.'

He turned startled. She was stood at his side.

'I didn't think you were going to come,' he said. She was dressed as she had been before. Her long coat. Her heavy ring.

'Michael wasn't going to let me. I came anyway.'

Danny didn't like this talk of Michael. It made him tighten up. Made her feel further away from him.

'Do you want to meet him?' she said. 'I thought you might like to.'

'Maybe. If you like.' There was a pause in which Danny heard the rush of the wind through the branches. 'I thought… I thought you might want… a walk or something.' He was nervous just being with her. She seemed so much older than him. She pursed her lips, studying him.

'I thought you might want to come with me. To see where we are,' said the girl. 'No one knows you're there.'

Danny nodded again. His heart was fluttering. A tingling inside. The sense of being about to cross some line he had never dared cross before.

'Come on then.'

As he swung his legs over the old fence Danny found himself wondering what her life must be like. Nothing like this. He wanted to ask about it but was frightened that it might anger her, that she might abandon him. He didn't want to be without her. He'd been clinging onto the thought of her for three days.

As the trees and ferns closed around them the tight-headed wooziness returned – a sense that he was somewhere to the left of his mind and body, watching what was happening with a detached eye. The feeling made him panicky and he searched for real physical details to cement himself into reality: the sensation of treading down the overgrown grass stalks; the momentary discomfort when he caught his ankle on an exposed tree root. When he'd tried to walk in here by himself he'd been unable to find a path. The girl knew her route as if it were marked clearly in the uneven ground. There was no indication that Danny could discern of when to turn one way or when to head another yet she seemed to have an unerring instinct about exactly where to go next. The tangled brambles and clumps of dried-up ferns seemed to part for her as she moved.

The further they got into the trees the more Danny's sense of alarm grew. The idea that he wouldn't be able to find his way out of there.

'You know what,' he said. She hadn't spoken a word since they left the road. 'I think I'm going to have to head back.' She continued walking, as if she hadn't heard him. Despite himself Danny carried on walking faster, trying to catch up with her. He didn't want to be left alone in there. 'I said, I think I'm going to head back. I didn't realise it was this far.' She came to an abrupt stop and turned towards him.

'You know what Danny,' she said, 'You've just got to make a choice. You can go back. Or you can come with me. It's completely up to you. You've just got to decide.' She looked at him directly. Danny could hear a rustling high above, the cawing of some great black bird – an unseen crow or rook wrestling with prey. She put one hand on her hip and chewed her lip waiting for his response.

'I'll come with you,' he said, and it started to rain.

The branches above them began to patter. As they walked fronds of ferns and broad-leafed weeds hopped and jerked under the percussion of the raindrops. The air itself seemed to be tinged green. Water ran down Danny's face. Momentarily, he felt submerged.

'Sometimes,' said the girl, her voice only just audible above the rush of falling water, 'sometimes do you wake up and think, How am I going to make it to the other side?'

'What?' said Danny.

'The other side of the day. Have you ever woken up and had that thought?'

It was a common thought for Danny. A regular feeling. 'No,' he said.

'Really. I thought you might have.' She strode onwards, navigating the incline ahead of them without any drop in her pace. The terrain was unexpectedly dramatic. They seemed to be in some kind of gully, a former watercourse perhaps or a glacial path. Any sense of the proximity to the old golf course, now built on, had disappeared.

'But don't you find yourself thinking about the future – and not wanting it? Like something ugly someone's given you.'

'No.'

She turned and smiled at him. 'Yes, you do. I know you do.'

'No, you don't.'

'When I first saw what Michael showed me, I was scared. I don't feel anything now. That's better, isn't it?'

The woods had become quieter now. The occasional birdsong had faded out, without Danny noticing. Maybe the rain had silenced them. Just the trudge of their footsteps and the swish of the vegetation as they passed.

'I never got how my parents saw the world,' said the girl. 'To them it all looked clean and safe and they thought that's how it is.'

'Things are one way underneath,' said Danny. 'How else do you get history?'

She let out a high-pitched laugh, almost like a squawk.

'There's no such thing as history. That's made up too. The made-up things get solidified – that's all.'

'The world is as the world is,' said Danny.

'The world is shit,' she said, coming to rest in a muddy clearing. 'It hurts, Danny, and that's the truth. Isn't it? The world just hurts.'

'It doesn't always,' he said.

'Doesn't it? When didn't it for you?'

'Lots of times,' he said.

'Yeah. Lots of times,' she picked up a stick from the ground and began to bash away at a large fern. Drops of water flew off it, into the damp air. 'I believe you,' she said.

As they descended towards the summit of a small hill Danny spotted something emerging through the branches – the slated roof of a small building. They rose higher and more of it emerged. It stood alone, surrounded by dark trees and foliage. It wasn't until they reached the crest of the slope that Danny became aware of something else, an obstacle between them and the structure – a large expanse of black stagnant water. It filled a portion of the valley beneath them. The ground around the circle of shore nearest them was flat and navigable but it rose abruptly on both sides forming a kind of natural funnel. The escarpments were rocky and knotted with brambles and bracken. They didn't look at all passable.

'Reservoir,' said the girl. 'It fed the golf club.'

'How do we get to there? To the building?' He assumed that was where they were going. She scrambled down the other side of the hill, until she reached the water's edge. She sat down on a small rock, gathering her coat beneath her. It had stopped raining.

'Through there,' she said. He raised his eyes to look at the water. It narrowed at the far end to a small neck only a metre or so wide. Jutting from this area was a rusted metal railing, canted at an odd angle. Wet-looking vegetation coiled around its spokes.

'You're joking,' said Danny. The girl shook her head.

'No,' she said. 'That's the way through. That's the only way through.'

'Well, I might as well head back now.' He thought about his bike, leaning on the mound of grass. The girl laughed.

'Why?'

'I'm not going in there.'

'Why?'

'It's freezing. And dirty. I don't care what's over the other side.'

'It's easy, Danny.'

'I don't care. I'm not going in.'

'I'll go first. I'll show you the way. You only have to follow me.'

'No.' He stayed where he was – halfway down the slope. She stood up, holding his gaze.

'You've come this far,' she said. 'Why wouldn't you go all the way, Danny?'

He stood there shaking his head.

'Michael's waiting.'

'No.'

'Well, he was right. He said you were a coward.'

'What?'

'He said you wouldn't want to come.'

'How does he know? He doesn't know me.'

'Playing it safe. Too fucking safe. You haven't got the guts.'

'No. That's not true.'

'Just too frightened. Too frightened to show them.'

'You don't know. He doesn't know anything. You don't know anything.'

'Well, come in then. Show them. Then they'll understand.'

'No.'

'Come on.'

'No.' Danny turned. Began to head back up the slope. Tried to imagine his way back out of the woods.

'Danny.'

'No.'

'Well, I'm going through. I'll see you,' she said.

He wasn't going to turn around.

'Say goodbye then,' she said. The woods all vivid around him – the greens and browns, the wet earth, the rotting flora. He thought of not seeing her again. He wanted to take one more look, to fix her in his mind. To prove that he hadn't imagined the whole encounter. She was still there, at the edge of the dirty water. 'Well?' she said. Danny shook his head – the smallest movement he could bring about while still answering her question. She raised her eyebrows. He repeated his miniature headshake. Then, without any indication as to what she was doing, she shrugged off her coat. Still looking at him, she reached behind her head and began unbuttoning her dress. She stepped out of it, laying it on the ground. She slipped off her pumps and rolled down her tights. For a moment she stood there, in black underwear – a vision against the skeletal trees behind her. Danny found that he'd turned to face her, his heart skipping. She smiled and reached behind her head again, unhooking her bra. He could see the goose pimples forming on the skin of her arms, her small breasts and nipples hardening in the cold. The thickened red lines of scar tissues around her wrists. He walked towards her. He was in territory he'd never trod before. When he was a couple of metres from her, standing level with her on the shoreline, she took off her pants.

'Come on,' she said.

He began to unlace his boots, sitting down on the dry, decaying leaves to pull them off. He was trying not to think about what would come next. He pulled at his jumper, and then the sweatshirt beneath. He felt the cold air hit his own scars, rawer and more recent than hers. He wanted her to see them, to acknowledge them. He looked at her, angling his arms towards her as he unbuttoned his jeans. Her nakedness felt like a point, digging into him. She smiled at him and he went towards her. He'd kept his own pants on. Before he reached her she turned and walked into the water. He winced at the thought of it.

'What about our clothes?' he asked. She didn't answer.

He watched her beauty, the pale gentle curves, disappearing into the black water. He felt the decision being made somewhere within. He followed her.

At first, up to his ankles, it was almost acceptable, but as he felt the line of cold climb his legs it became more like pain.

'Just do it. Get your shoulders wet, get under.' She was ahead of him, swimming languorously along. The bottom of the pool fell away sharply, and the uncomfortable muddy stone was replaced by a void. Forcing himself, feeling something like exhilaration, he swam after her. The sensation didn't last. The coldness was too much. He thought it would become tolerable, but in fact it became harder to cope with as each second passed. She was at the iron gate, the rusted metalwork slimy and black where it jutted from the water. 'Come on then,' she said. 'Let's do it.' Danny began to panic. He couldn't feel anything beneath him. He pushed his legs around in the water, wanting to sense something, to prove they hadn't gone numb. They might as well have been amputated. There was only an absence – an area in which he had no effect at all. He tried to turn around in the water, but there was something like a current moving him towards the gate. There was the girl ahead of him, her dark hair spread out on the water around her. 'Deep breath,' she said.

'Don't,' said Danny.

She plunged herself under the water. Suddenly he was alone on the surface. 'Don't,' he said again but there was no way she could have heard. He was breathing very fast. Too fast. His head buzzed. Everything seemed very dark. The sense of being alone there was unbearable. In spite of the freezing water biting into him he went under. He didn't want her to leave him there.

At first he didn't think he'd be able to open his eyes. It took two or three goes. When he did, there was just enough light to see. There was a sense of rippling sky above, broken by branches. It seemed lighter from down there. She was ahead of him, near the plunging black lines of the iron grille. There barely seemed enough room to swim through. He would have to turn back. He would have to return to the surface. But she was through, or she seemed to be on the other side. He reached out and touched the iron. Its surface was abrasive, full of tiny jags and splinters. A hand reached out from the other side. Her heavy-ringed hand. It pulled at Danny with some force, dragging him into the grille. He would never get through. His head might, his shoulders even, but not his hips. As he had this thought, she seemed to pull even harder. Something was wrong. Her hand was colder than the surrounding water – a blacker hole in an already black sky. He needed to take another breath. The need was transforming itself into a hurt. He thought he could see her face. He thought he could see her smile. There was nothing pleasant in it – only wickedness. He thought of the last smile he'd seen. His brother Marshall. He thought of the magic show, thought of them laughing. Thought of Lawrence, sitting next to him, squeezing his leg. He pulled back from the grille, using whatever force he could draw on. He stretched up hard, reaching down deep within himself, pulling and pulling and pulling.

He found himself on the side of the shore, curled up tight, hugging his legs. He couldn't remember how he got there. He was shivering, his teeth clicking uncontrollably, every joint tight. He propped himself up on his elbows. He could see the girl on the other side of the gate, or at least what he took to be her hair, pooling across the scum-covered surface of the water.

'Jeanne,' he called out. It was the first time he'd used her name. He waited for her to break the surface. When she didn't he called her name again. He scrambled around until he found his things, trying to dry himself on leaves and desiccated ferns as he searched. Despite the fact that he was still damp he got dressed as hurriedly as he could. He felt that he'd dreamed taking his clothes off. He tried to get as close to the gate as possible. He found a broken branch on the ground. Clinging to the earthy bank at the side of the pool, he poked the branch through the slimy ironwork. A hand broke the surface. It was black. As black as the water. As black as the hair. At first he thought it couldn't be hers. It was swollen and fat-fingered. And then he registered, almost embedded in the purulent tissue, her heavy silver ring. He leaned across the water as far as he dared, pushing the branch. A face broke the water, or the remains of one. Half of it was consumed by a grin where the flesh had gone. The eye sockets were empty too. Only the hair remained as he had seen, thick and dark, trailing down over the exposed bone.

It was three weeks before he told anyone. It made no difference – except to her grieving parents who'd thought she had fled to London, fifteen months earlier. She'd been called Georgia.

Nobody had ever heard of Michael.

A.L. Kennedy

Vanish

It had been her fault, entirely. Dee's fault – the whole bloody evening.

Which, to be truthful, made him slightly glad – it was, after all, three months since she had hurt him a new way. Tonight, in her undoubted absence, she was letting Paul feel reconnected, touched.

He'd bought the tickets for her just before they'd split, intending to give her a treat – an almost-birthday treat – 19th October and a trip to the West End, a fairly pricey dinner first and then off to a show. 19th October meant pretending she was a late Libra instead of an early Scorpio – as if that mattered a toss and would in any way have made her not a car crash as a person. Paul didn't even read horoscopes, she was the one who read horoscopes, he thought they were total shit. Probably, if he checked somewhere, consulted a website, it would be set down as axiomatic that early Scorpios were also total shit. But at that point he'd been trying for her, he'd been keeping the faith and imagining she would come through and turn out to be – *What? Sane? Undamaged? Undamaging?* – he could no longer be bothered to guess.

For the usual reasons, he'd gone the extra mile again, got hold of tickets before the place sold out and reserved them two seats in their future, side by side and near the front without being too close, because that could get scary. This magician bloke was somebody she'd talked about – she'd said he was really good – and there was bugger all she thought was really good on anything like a consistent basis – himself included – and the guy was going to be in London for a limited engagement, which sounded exclusive, sounded right – so everything should have worked out fine.

Everything might have worked out fine.

She could have enjoyed it.

The chances of that happening had been quite high.

But then she'd done a runner, she'd ditched him, and this time it was clearly permanent.

And Dee hadn't even known about the tickets. This leaving a possibility that had swung away now and again from beneath Paul's feet: a trapdoor thought of her being in the theatre anyway: of their meeting in the foyer, on the stairs, in the stalls: his hope and fear interweaving, building up an uneven, uneasy stack.

I didn't see her, though. The whole evening I didn't see her. And I almost did look.

Frankly, I don't believe she'd have got it together enough to have come along. So why would I see her? How could I?

And I did look.

I did, in fact, very much look.

I stared so hard things went all cinematic – felt like I was the one who wasn't really here.

For a while, he'd assumed he would tear both the tickets up – or else ignore them until their relevance had faded.

And then, at the turn of the week, he'd decided he ought to enjoy the whole experience on his own, reclaim it. Naturally, he'd skip the dinner and the effort at romance. There wasn't another woman he could take – a substitute, stand-in, fresh start – it just so happened there was no one new to hand and that kind of thing would, in any case, only hurt him: he wasn't ready for it yet. Nevertheless, he'd been fully persuaded that he should set out for an evening of having fun.

Even if the chances of fun happening had been quite low.

He'd dressed nicely – best suit, a flashy tie which he'd regretted and had taken off almost at once – it was folded in his pocket now. For some reason he had forgotten that nothing made singleness worse than being wellturned out. If he could look good – and he did look pretty good, pretty easily – then his being not on the arm of a lovely escort was down to some deeper problem, an internal flaw.

Kind eyes, decent haircut, reliable mouth – somebody said that once: reliable mouth – but repeatedly bolloxed relationships, year after year. Must be broken where it doesn't show, then – something important about me gone missing, or else never arrived.

Dee – she said that I had a reliable mouth. So that probably doesn't count as true.

The other sodding ticket hadn't helped him: a leftover left with a leftover man, it had been a problem at once, already heavy in his pocket as he'd walked from the underground, wandered up and eyed the posters hung outside the theatre: high monochrome repetitions of the magician's face.

He does have a reliable mouth.

Jesus, though, I don't even know what that would mean, really. Reliable, unreliable…

He has a mouth, that's all. Right where you'd expect. There it is, under his nose and over his chin – a mouth.

And he looks like a twat.

At least I don't do that.

The rhyme had made him smile – something from the Dr Seuss version of his life.

My girl let me down flat.

She is also a twat.

Paul had fingered the ticket and known he couldn't sit beside cold air, a ghost.

Which was why he'd turned up slightly early – this way he'd have some time to make enquiries in the queue.

'Hi. I have a spare ticket – do you want it?'

Clearing his throat and then being more assertive, 'Would you like this?'

Or maybe less assertive, 'Excuse me, would you like this?'

He'd been asking people who didn't have tickets, who wanted tickets, wanted them enough to come down here and wait in the hope of returns and who should have been pleased by an opportunity like this, an act of uncompromised generosity.

'Hi. Oh, you're together – this would be no use then.' These ones had been bastards – a matching pair of self-satisfied bastards – covered with certainty, with the spring of the sex they were going to have tonight. 'No, I'll look for someone by themselves. I wouldn't want to break you up. I'm sorry.'

'Yes, it's a real ticket.'

'Good evening, I just wondered…' He'd noticed he was starting to sweat. 'I have an extra ticket. There's nothing wrong with it. It's for quite a good seat – look.' The bloody thing had warped where he'd been touching it too long. 'That's a good seat.'

People had acted as if he were offering them a snake - which would always sound rude, now he thought about it, rude more than poisonous – *Hi, would you like my snake? I have this snake. Free snake. Free to a good home. Tired old snake seeks any deargodplease home that it can get.*

The best thing was truly, genuinely not to think of anything to do with sex at present. And maybe not ever again.

'Yes, you would be sitting next to me. Sorry.' Talking to women – had he, at any time, known how he should do that? 'Is that a problem? I'm not trying to… We'll forget about it, okay?… No, just forget about it. Really.' That's how you end up with the crazies – by never learning how you ought to reach the normal ones. 'You don't have to pay – I've paid. Sorry, that was me being ironic.'

Not that I expect you to appreciate that, or to find it amusing – but trust me – trust my perhaps reliable mouth, which I am not moving in case it shows you how I think – trust me while I do think, quite loudly, that I am laughing with my brain.

Leastways, maybe not laughing, but there is definitely something going on with me and with my brain. I think it is, perhaps, packing in advance of being gone.

'No, I don't want any money. The ticket's just no use to me… Well, if you want to pay me – then the price is written on it. Forty-five quid… Yes, it *is* a lot, but then it *is* a good seat… Well, twenty quid isn't forty-five quid – that's like… that's like you're… I'd rather you didn't pay me. Either nothing or the price, how would that be…? I'm finding it quite hard to understand why you don't opt for nothing… No, I wouldn't want to do that – it would hurt. *But feel free yourself.*'

He'd never been aware of it before, but he did fairly often grit his teeth.

Then again, he did fairly often have reason to.

'Ticket…? Ticket?'

Eventually someone had tapped Paul on the shoulder – this causing the foyer to ripple, contract, until he'd realised he was looking into an unfamiliar manic smile. The person smiling was slightly Goth-looking but clean, perhaps a student, had said his name was Simon and had asked if he could have the spare seat. Paul released the ticket with a kind of joy, or else at least a kind of satisfaction, because he was working on the principle that if you wanted something you should get it, you absolutely should, no matter who you were or how ridiculous your need. This was the only magic that might ever be worthwhile and should therefore be demonstrated, encouraged to spread and thrive.

Thus far it had only affected Simon, of course: granting him a seat he could not have afforded, even if he'd made it to the head of the returns queue. The excitement of this and his relative proximity to the stage, once they were both seated, made Simon chat a good deal, which Paul had not anticipated.

'This is beyond… this is out of this world, is what this is. I just couldn't get off work, only then I *did*, only then I hadn't got a ticket, but I thought I'd have a go in any case, and *then* the bus broke down – I mean, what would be the probability of *that* particular bus breaking down on the way to this particular theatre? I *had* to *run*. From *Regent's Street*.'

Paul tried to calculate the probability of *his* breaking down while seated in the stalls of this particular theatre.

Simon, it was clear, had an overlarge capacity for joy. 'He's amazing – The Great Man. They call him that – TGM. The initials. Did you know that? TGM. Not just us – his crew, his assistants, everyone *in the business*.'

It was ridiculous and unfair to imagine a person like Simon could unknowingly drain each remaining pleasure from those around him and leave them bereft. 'Do you know his work? Amazing guy. I've seen every show.' Even so, as Simon cast his hands about, shifted and stretched, Paul found himself taking great care that they didn't touch, didn't even brush shoulders, just to be sure that no draining could take place.

'The show before this? – *Mr Splitfoot?* – what a night. You see your first one and you always think he couldn't top it – but then he does. Excels himself. Over and over. *The lesson of excellence.* I had to go to Southport for him last January, can you *believe* it? *Southport*.'

Paul found he *could* believe in Southport but was primarily very happy to allow a new and gentle sliding thing to peel out across his mind and muffle him, make him almost sleepy, something close to sleepy: certainly opened, unsteady and soft. Simon was still talking – Paul could feel that – but the young man was also apparently dropping, further and further: falling with his sound beneath him into the wider and deeper changeable din of individuals fitting themselves to an audience, becoming large, expecting. Their want teased and pressed at Paul's will and he tried to join them in it, to let go.

I don't know, though. I don't know.

The theatre was an old one: gilt and rose-painted mouldings, candle brackets and layered galleries, rattling seats of golden plush and a chandelier there above them, holding up a monstrous threat of light.

I don't know.

Paul could appreciate the beauty of it, obviously – only he'd caught this other sense as well: that every charm was closing on him, folding down into a box, a mechanism already carefully set and working. He could almost hear it tick: cogging round to make him overly substantial, dense. And the ushers – it had seemed there were too many ushers, too many men dressed in black with unusual shoes who paced and watched and loitered casually, stood by the stage and by the entrances, moved with a purpose that made them another part of the elaborate, obscure machinery, of a building that had turned into a game. Paul didn't much like games – they made him lose. He didn't much like anyone who played them.

But it's just a performance. It's magic: that kind of game. If I think something's going on, then it probably might be, but there's no need to fret. It's nothing personal – it's just the magic, not anything wrong.

All of these people, packed in snug: they'd sent the air up to a blood heat and he'd liked that, which surprised him. And maybe this was how the game would work him – making him trapped and then offering release: the hope of joining something strange, the chance to be lost in the mind of a crowd, to evaporate. It had been, in a way, extremely welcoming.

I don't know, though.

Straight ahead had been the tall, naked dark of the stage. It stared at him, prepared.

Everyone else in here understands this. They're going to like it. They want to play.

I might not.

Then his morning fear had tickled unexpectedly in his chest – the creep of it as he would get out of bed and be alone – no one else there, nobody's belongings, only time in the flat and books he didn't read and DVDs of films he never really fancied watching and maybe this would be the way it was from here on in – forever – maybe even with somebody there he was meant to love, trust, be loved by, maybe even then it would stay the same, had always been the same: himself locked somewhere airless, somewhere dead.

This evening is all of the things that she *would like. Not me.*

And he'd sat inside this thing that Dee would like while panic tilted in his neck and signalled a chill to the small of his back. He'd begun to wish hard that the lights would go down before he cried.

And then they did.

Like magic they did.

At the perfect point.

Exactly when another moment's wait would have toppled him, the colours had mellowed, the auditorium was withdrawn, was dimmed to exit signs and its private variety of night.

Evaporate now and nobody would see.

Nobody would stop me.

Or nobody would help.

There was no music.

Just breath – the audience noticing its nerves, stirring, giggling, settling again and holding.

Paul had shut his eyes. He'd inhaled the vaguely sweet and powdery warmth, the taste of attention, of other lives.

All right, then.

He'd tried to concentrate, to push and lift away from the restrictions of his skin, his skull. He was very tired, he'd realised, and had a great desire to be peaceful, uncluttered, unharried – to be not himself.

All right, then.

He'd begun to hear footsteps and, for an instant, they had seemed so natural, so much the start of an answer to soften his current need, that they might have been some internal phenomenon, an oddly convincing idea. Then they grew sharper: the hard, clear snap of leather soles that paced, perhaps climbing closer – yes, there was definitely a suggestion of stone steps winding upwards to the stage and raising an authoritative, measured tread. The sound was just a touch peculiar, amplified, treated.

All right.

Paul had unfolded his arms.

Yes.

He had let his hands rest easy on his lap. He'd blinked.

Yes.

He'd looked clear out into nowhere, into the free and shapeless deep of everything.

Do what you like.

And Paul had grinned as the footfalls halted, the proper pause extended and then the magician had walked out from the wings.

You do just precisely whatever you would like.

And The Great Man had been – *What?*

Sane?

Undamaged?

Undamaging?

'Oh, what did you think, though. Really. I *mean*...' When the final applause was done with, Simon had been not unexcited. 'First half – *fantastic,* but second half? Always a kicker.' He'd clutched at Paul's forearm, shaking it gently. 'What did you *think*? I didn't ask in the interval, I held back – didn't I hold back? – but *how* was that?' Simon had cornered him up at the top of the aisle, turning to peer back into the emptying theatre, the emptied stage. He'd pulled his free hand through his hair, smiling, then shaken his head and laughed. 'Jesus, how *was* that?'

Paul had smiled, too – although he'd also shrugged away from Simon's grip. Then he'd breathed in – tasted deep – tasted something like physics going quite awry, like unexpected possibility. 'It was all right.' He'd thought, for a second, the game might not be over.

'It was—,' Simon had interrupted his outrage and checked Paul's face. 'Oh. Yeah.' He'd grinned. 'It was all right.' He'd seemed to consider for a moment. 'You feel a bit weird, yeah? Bit stunned? Mugged? Fuddled?'

To Paul, it hadn't felt quite appropriate that someone who was barely past teenage, who probably had at least one bad tattoo, and a no-doubt exhaustive regimen of mildly unnerving self-abuse was asking Paul about his personal condition.

Still, a response would do no harm. 'A little – a bit weird. Maybe. Yes. That stuff that he did with the... the dead...' It was sometimes good to make a conversation, join in.

'Then you should come along with me. You'll like this.' Simon had leaned in close enough to prove that his breath smelled of crisps. 'The show after the show.' But he'd also been unmistakably very serious and almost tender. 'Honest. It'll be good.' Simon had padded off without another glance, repeating as he went, 'How was that... How just the bloody hell was that... How *was* that...' He'd expected Paul to follow.

And Paul had.

This isn't a chat-up, though, is it? Even if I was gay, he wouldn't be my taste at all – embarrassed if he'd think he was…

Then again, he's clearly a nutter – so probably I'd fall for him completely.

Walking out of the theatre and round the bend.

Oh, quite exactly round the bend. And maybe here is where I get mugged. Factually, unmagically mugged. He'd be a really useless mugger, though – a lover, not a fighter: young Simon – well, a wanker, not a fighter. But he could have pals – mugger chums. Maybe.

Around one more corner and they'd stopped in a little lane.

This exact and precise little lane – mildly cold and unmistakably damp and faintly piss-and-disinfectant-scented lane – this lane at the back of the theatre where I am currently standing. After all this time. Still standing.

Worries had reeled by, but had left Paul curiously sanguine – unworried, in fact.

Still am – calm as you'd like.

Simon had brought him to see the stage door and the jovially restless cluster of other young men in black drainpipes, or disreputable coats, plus a scatter of slender, underdressed girls and a few motherly types.

'He'll be out in a while,' Simon had murmured as if he were in church. 'It's what he does. He comes and speaks to us.'

Paul had been mainly glad he didn't have to go home yet, but he couldn't help asking, '*What*? Who does?'

'TGM. It's what he does. No photographs, no autographs – says then it isn't friendly – but he'll chat. To everyone. To you. Then it's like you're friends. We're his friends.'

'You're kidding.'

'Why would I be kidding?' Simon had frowned, but then was interrupted by the appearance of two stocky pals – real, non-mugger pals – in what Paul thought must be second-hand suits – or they possibly both enjoyed wearing their dads' clothes. While Paul watched, the three men had shaken hands and fussed in each other's pockets, producing a flurry of small trophies: wallets and house keys, bus passes and condoms and christknewwhat, which they had passed between themselves for a while, deadpan – stealing and passing, returning, then stealing again.

After reclaiming his unlikely handkerchief for the third time, Simon had nodded to indicate Paul, 'This is Paul. He gave me a ticket.'

'You want to watch that.' The more solemn newcomer had tugged at his walrus moustache and extended his arm, 'Hi. My name's Mr Palm.' He winked. 'You can call me Morritt.'

'And I would be Knot. Not Not – and not Knott – a K and one T – Knot. Davenport Knot – it's a family name.' The unmoustachioed Knot had waved politely and inclined towards Simon, 'How many did *you* sneak in? Any? Were you trying? Did you get any? A few? You did try? Was there the offer of a finger ring at any point? A bit of badinage and wordage?' He'd nudged Paul lightly, 'Beyond me to say how fine it is, splaying with words. Word splay. Words play well, don't they? Don't you just love words? Love-me things, love-ly things.' He'd grinned, over-broadly, and then snapped his whole face into neutral, examined his thumb.

Simon had shrugged at Paul, 'They're feeling antisocial. So they're being...'

'Playful.' Morritt had winked again, 'I'm always anti-social. Comes of being a sociopath.'

'Like I said, they're not in the mood for company, so I'll escort them and conduct what I will not at all or in any way describe as a debriefing over there.'

Morritt let his eyes grin but kept his face immobile and seemed to be searching Paul for something – not predatory, but curious, forensically interested.

'Morritt, leave him be.' Simon had patted Paul's shoulder, 'I'll be back in a bit. And –' He grinned like the boy he almost still was, 'Thanks again. Wouldn't have missed it.'

Which is how you end up standing by yourself and waiting. In a lane at night with your feet getting chilled – waiting for no one you'd wanted to meet in the company of strangers. And most of the strangers have headed off home.

All of the motherly women have gone, given up – except for the one with the shopping bag full of papers. Paul knew not to talk to *her* any more – and not to make eye contact, because that would start her off, as well.

'These are letters for TGM. I send them, but I know they don't get through. So I bring him the copies myself. He always smiles at me. He's lovely. He should eat more fruit.'

Paul had already been caught by her twice – once with the letter story and once with the much more complicated crap about there being some kind of grand conspiracy against magicians in general and TGM in particular – because he was so highly skilled – and only she knew how to stop it and TGM was fully aware of this and would one day ask her for her help which she would then graciously give. She was called Lucy.

Didn't want to know her name. Didn't want to know anything about her, or have anything to do with her. Funny, cos she's madder than anyone I've ever met and she does have nice tits. Big, anyway.

And she'd be grateful for the attention.

Sweet Jesus, what am I turning into.

And he glances at his watch to distract himself and it's ten past one and everybody's still here waiting – well, not so many as there were, but definitely some, a small crowd – eight people, counting himself, which he does, because he's people – and Paul has no way of being sure if this is normal – a three-hour wait. He doesn't like to interrupt Simon and his friends to ask them, because they seem to be enjoying themselves, giggling and showing each other cards, coins, little gadgets, and if he steps into that and messes it up for them, then he'll be the boring old bastard who knows nothing and shouldn't be here and he's sure that will make him depressed, so he won't attempt it and then he thinks that maybe the magician is busy and – here it comes as quick as fainting, weakness, shame – the sly, worst possible thought comes ramming in – he imagines that maybe Dee *is* here, maybe she came, maybe she'd talked about the magician because she knew him and maybe they're in there now, in his dressing room – lots of lights and a countertop, mirrors and maybe – why not – a bed – or a table – no, a bed – no, a hard, clinical table – and maybe he's touching her, maybe they're doing it, doing weird stuff, magician stuff, things that take three hours and counting, things that make her think the little bastard's really good, that open her and make her squeal – he has this image of her skin and smears of make-up, stage make-up, of things that appear and disappear.

Except that's mad.

So mad it hurts.

Madder than Lucy.

I have no reasons to believe it, not a one.

Stark, staring Lucy.

Mental.

As stupid as staying here when I ought to just chuck it and head for home.

But I've been here so long that I might as well keep on.

Paul's vaguely nauseous, though – images of clever fingers and slippery skin pitching in at him, so he walks a bit, strolls round, swallows and rubs his eyes, as if this will make the brain behind them sensible.

In a doorway, one of the three remaining girls is sitting and holding a programme and Paul thinks the step beneath her must be dirty and that's not right and she'll be perished and, to distract himself, he goes over and suggests, 'You could have my jacket. Borrow my jacket.'

She has dull blonde hair, 'No, it's okay,' and tiny wrists which manage to make Paul feel she has sometimes considered slashing them.

'You look freezing.' He wants to hold her, finds he is talking as if they have met before, are friends – the way you talk to people when you know how to talk to people.

'No, it's okay.'

She doesn't seem annoyed by him or anything, so he sits down next to her, is quiet for a bit, gives her time, and then, 'Do you like him – the magician?'

'Yeah.'

'And you want him to sign that. Your programme.'

She tucks her feet in nearer to herself, to the backs of her thighs. This will wrinkle her skirt. 'I don't think he's coming to see us tonight. It's late. He wouldn't make us hang around this long. Something must have happened. Guests. Or he's tired. Everyone else has come outside. Not him. He's gone another way.'

Paul sees how she is curled all to the left, beside the wall: trying to keep cosy, and thinks this must be uncomfortable and ineffective. Her blouse is old-fashioned, Laura Ashley, something like that – he can't really tell in the shadow.

'TGM doesn't sign things.' She yawns just enough to put a tremor in her jaw: a sweet, sweet trembling.

'No. I forgot.'

'What did you think?'

'About what?'

'The show.' This makes her begin to smile and he can imagine the same gentle, drowsy expression being there for some person who cares about her, lighting for them in a dawn with pillows and the spread of her hair. She faces him – perhaps studying, perhaps amused, he can't be sure – and asks again, 'What did you think? You haven't been before, have you?

Whatever funny little club we are, you're not really in it yet.'

Paul wants to yawn, to join her in that – because yawns are infectious and he is tired and it would be very easy for him to tremble, 'I thought –' offer her a piece of himself that might seem sweet, and he would – by the way – like to see her hair on a pillow, anyone's hair on his pillow, 'I thought...' But it's too late for that, doesn't matter, and it's fine for him to tell her now what's true – tell her as he would in a first morning when everything is interesting and you want to talk and you feel that you'll never get all that you need of this new woman and who she is and what she might enjoy and there is no pain from anywhere, not yet. 'I thought...' It's additionally fine – it will be absolutely fine, any disclosure – because in the morning this blonde whose name he does not know and will not ask will have forgotten him entirely. He'll be gone. 'I thought he was great.' All gone.

'But?'

'No but.' He smiles to reassure. 'Really. There's no but.' He knows he can hold her hand and she will not take it amiss, so he does, squeezes her fingers, cuddles them, and they sit together in the doorway with the cold of the stone underneath them and he says, 'I thought he was very good at what he does and... it was how he did it. Because of him not being that big, you know? He didn't look like a big man, not tall – and not, not some twat in a campy suit, or a Gandalf beard, or some kind of... I mean he's not a twat – and he was like my size – and ordinary, average – smart but average – and trying so hard to make these things happen, these bonkers things – and they did – he tried hard enough so that they did. I mean, it wasn't easy. Not that I didn't think he'd manage, just that it wasn't easy. He had to *fight*. It's all just fake, I get that – but he had to fight – he took the trouble to make it seem beyond him, impossible – and then he beat it. He won.'

Paul begins again with, 'For people like me...' and then lets it fade. And he won't even attempt, 'And he was – he was like he was *magnificent* – because if you win you're allowed to be magnificent. You should be.' Because he thinks it would send him a little bit weepy – the way he'd got when there'd been that section in the second-half business that used a length of chain. He'd remember the chain: had a strong suspicion he would dream it, because it already had been half-turned to a dream when it was presented, there had been a quality about it that had slipped right in.

'When it lifted, when the chain lifted... It's a trick, I know it's a trick –

but it was right… It was the way that you need it to be.'

She squeezes *his* fingers now. 'Like something coming true.'

It is pleasantly, slightly painful to consider this. 'Yeah.' The word seems damp and fluttery in his throat.

'That's what I come for.' And she pecks his cheek. 'That's why I come. To see that. Because it isn't real anywhere else.' And then she lets him go, because they are nothing to each other, he is nothing to her, 'I think I'll head home now.'

He is nothing to anyone. 'Will you be all right?' His knuckles feeling unnerved, stripped. He has the hands of no one.

'Yes.'

She stands, slightly unsteadily and Paul rises with her and holds her shoulder for a breath. 'It was nice meeting you.'

'And it was nice meeting you.' This before she walks away, aiming for the street and a cab, he guesses. No other options beyond a cab at this time of night. Unless she's walking. Alone. Alone might not be safe.

Paul shouts after her, 'You'll be okay? Do you need somebody with you?' But she half turns, waves her programme at him and shakes her head, keeps on round the corner and back to the usual, old world.

The other girls must have given up too, when he was occupied elsewhere, so there is Paul now and there is Lucy and Simon and his two companions with their imaginary names – each of them staring at Paul because he has called out. 'Sorry!' Although he isn't sorry. Quite the reverse.

Simon ambles over, 'No, *I'm* sorry. This is *crazy*. He's *never* this late. It's… he never doesn't come out, but he never leaves it this late, so I don't know, mate. Don't think badly of him.'

'I don't.'

'Don't think badly of magic.'

'Oh, I don't.' Paul thinking of nothing but that chain: broad links, dull and heavy, dragged into the air, driven upwards by pure will and then compelled to disappear: a whole building of human beings casting them away and the magician there to hold their wish, find it, touch it out and show proof of what they were and could be.

Just a trick. And just that last tangible moment before you're free –

seeing that, for once seeing that. And if you can see it, then it can be and nothing left to hold you back. 'I don't think badly of it. Really. I had a good time. Thanks.'

Just a trick. But I could see it, see myself.

Now you see it.

Yes.

'You going home? It's past two.'

'Is it?' Paul's watch agreeing that suddenly it is past two and on the way to three. 'Oh. Might as well hang on a while longer, though – d'you think?'

Simon takes a pound coin and folds it into his hand and out and back and melts it somewhere between his fingers. 'Yeah, might as well.' He shrugs. 'Come and join us, guys.' He beckons his friends. 'The smug one's Barry and the miserable one's Gareth – his mum's Welsh.'

Gareth wanders towards them, avoiding Lucy, 'She *wants* to be Welsh. That's different.' And Barry follows, nodding.

The four of them slouch together in a huddle – they shift and cough.

'When he *does* come out...' Gareth tugs his moustache.

Barry reaches round and tugs it, too, 'You mean *if*.'

'When he *does* come out, we should all just ignore him – like we're expecting someone else.'

They grin.

'No, but that would be rude, though.' Paul's sentence fading as he starts to feel inept – spoiling the joke. 'I mean, if we're his friends...' But then softly the men – Paul included – begin to grin in the way that friends do, before they get to trick their friends.

It's colder and the sky seems to rest down against them: attentive, but wearying.

Paul understands the magician isn't coming. He also understands it doesn't matter any more. They won't leave: Simon, Barry, Gareth, Lucy – they'll stand here and he'll stand with them – they're all going nowhere. Together.

But that's fine, I'm just fine now. I know why I'm waiting for him: The Great Man – I'm absolutely sure of that. I know exactly what I'll ask him, what I need him to make me do.

Robert Shearman

George Clooney's Moustache

I tried writing this on toilet paper but it's hard writing on toilet paper because the paper's so thin it breaks. And you can put some sheets together to make it thicker but that's not much better and you have to write so slowly to keep it from breaking that by the time you reach the end of the sentence you forgot how it started and you forget what it was you wanted to say anyway, and anyway you get through a lot of paper like that. XXXXXXXX **He** caught me, I knew he would, he's smart like that, I was taking so long in the bathroom that he began to bang on the door asking if I was all right and I said I was all right, and I flushed, but he said if I didn't open the door he'd break it down and so I did. I should have flushed away my writing first while I was at it but I just didn't have time to think and he picked it up and he read it and I thought he'd get angry because a lot of it was about him, well all of it really. But XXXXXXXX **he** didn't say anything bad and he said if I wanted to write he'd get me some proper paper if it meant that much to me. And a pencil too, not a sharp one, he'd seen a film once about how a sharp pencil could be used as a weapon and stuck into someone's neck and that was funny because I think I've seen that film too but I couldn't remember what it was called, neither of us could, we laughed about that. And I told him I'd never do that to myself, I'm scared of blood, and he looked a bit shifty and said he'd been more worried I'd do it to him actually, and I hadn't even thought of that and said I wouldn't, we laughed about that. So XXXXXXXX **he** gave me this pad and this pencil. And told me I could copy out what I'd written on the toilet paper if I liked. But I didn't want to, he'd been so nice about the whole thing and what I'd said on the toilet paper wasn't very kind. I didn't want to write anything for a while, I didn't know what to say any more, and he'd ask me sometimes about it over dinner, have you started writing yet, but he said it nicely, it wasn't a nag and didn't come out sarky. And so eventually I thought I'd better write something after he'd gone to all that trouble, and so I did, and this is it.

Over breakfast he read what I wrote last night. He said it was very good, but that some of the grammar needed a little work, that it wasn't always easy to read, and I asked about my handwriting, and he said that was good, and about my spelling, and he said that was good too, it was just the grammar, I could do with a few more full stops. So I'm going to do that. When I remember. I'll try. He said he'd have to change just one thing, and he crossed out a few words with a pen, and handed it back. And he'd crossed out all the times I'd used his name, he'd put 'he' instead, he said that he should never have let me know his name in the first place that was a mistake. So I could carry on writing, but no more names. And I said could I use another name instead, it'd get a bit much calling him 'he' all the time, and he said that was all right. And George told me that he was glad I enjoyed the pad and the pencil, that they'd been a present. And that I'd get more presents, so long as I behaved, so long as I did what I was told. I told George I would and he was so pleased. He asked what I was going to write next and I couldn't think what, and he said I should write about what I know. But I don't want to write about my life before, if you're reading this you probably know it already, it's probably not much different from yours. So I'm going to describe where I am. I don't like descriptive bits, I'd rather tell stories, but here goes. There are three rooms. (Actually there are more than three rooms, but I only get to go in three of them. There's the kitchen, but I'm not allowed in there because it's full of sharp things, George keeps it locked with the bolt he took from the bathroom. And there's the room which has the front door in it, I don't go there.) But there are my three. There's the sitting room which is where we eat our breakfast and our dinner and it's got a television in it and George watches the news a lot, and sometimes he watches other things too, sitcoms I think because I hear laughter and it isn't George's. Then there's the bathroom, but you know about that, it's only different now because he took the lock off. And then there's the bedroom which is where I am now, I spend most of my time here. George keeps it locked but he lets me out when I need to, when it's time for breakfast or dinner or when I need the bathroom. The walls are a bit old and have wallpaper on which is a bit old and when I get bored I can count the stripes but I don't need to be bored now because I have the pad and the pencil and I can use them instead. And that's enough for tonight and I'm going to sleep now, night night.

He asked me why I'd named him George. But he wasn't angry, he was smiling. Puzzled though. And I told him it was because he looked a bit like George Clooney. And he laughed and said he did not, and I said he did too, and I laughed as well. And actually I suppose he doesn't look much like George Clooney, not really, what I mean is that George Clooney has nice eyes and my George has nice eyes just like his, and you know how George Clooney has got a sort of square jaw, well my George has nothing like that but it's a nice jaw anyway. And the real George Clooney doesn't have a moustache the way my George Clooney does but still never mind. So if you're the police and you're out there looking for him then they're not that alike really, to be honest there's no point going after George Clooney. And George said that I was right, he did watch sitcoms, he couldn't only watch the news it'd do his head in. He was sorry if it disturbed me, he could turn the volume down if I liked, and I said that was okay, I liked to hear the laughter. And he said that if I was very good that could be another present, he'd let me watch a sitcom some time, not now but soon. I thanked him for that. And he said it was very odd there was nothing on the news yet, it'd been over a week now, you'd have thought there would be something. I said I didn't know, maybe they were keeping it a secret, and he said it just didn't make sense. Then he told me he'd wash up breakfast and he put me back in my room. And a bit later he came back and said why not, we'd watch a sitcom that night, he'd come and get me when one was on. I'd been very good and I deserved a present. (And I think he liked the fact I'd called him George.) And it's funny, I suppose I'm writing this for George now. I thought at first it was for Daddy, or Paul, or Jessie, although Jessie couldn't read it she's only two, but Paul could read it to her, he's a really good dad like that. But this is for George now, isn't it? Hello George. You really do look like George Clooney, I was being silly before, except for the moustache. And George came and got me and took me into the sitting room, he had the lights off and there was only the light from the TV screen, it was like going to the cinema! And I said that, do you remember, and you laughed, and we sat down on the couch and watched *Friends*. And it was an episode I'd seen before but that was okay, I pretended it was new and laughed anyway, I didn't want to hurt George's feelings. Although of course you've just read this, George, you know that now, sorry. Sorry. It was a great evening, a bit like a first date, and I hope we can do it again soon.

I'm in love with George Clooney! I am. I'm shaking as I write this, can you tell, I hope my handwriting isn't too wobbly, but I'm so relieved too. Just to let it out. I love you, George. Let me tell you why I love him. I love his body, no not like that. I love his eyes. I love his teeth. I love his neck. I love his nose. I love his face, it's a kind face, and I know George has had to do some bad things, I know that's why I'm here, but you can tell from his face he doesn't really want to, and there are some people out there who don't do bad things but their faces aren't kind and you can tell they'd like to do bad things but can't get round to it and I think that's worse somehow. It's a nice face and I love the way it smiles. I love his arms. I love his chest. I love his stomach. I love his hands. I love the way he's got bits of hair growing on his hands. I love his legs, I haven't seen much of his legs yet, but it's February and it's cold and I can't wait for summer when it gets hot and he'll get into his shorts. I love his hair, I want to run my fingers through it, I bet it tastes like butterscotch. I don't just love his body. I love his voice. I love his smell, it's a nice smell, I can't work out what it is yet I'll come back. I love the way he cuts up all my food for me in the kitchen. I love the way when he locks me in my room he smiles first and says good night and then he turns the key quite slowly so that it feels like he doesn't want to say goodbye yet. I love the way last night we watched *Friends* again and it was a better episode this time, Chandler and Joey were funny and it didn't have the monkey in it. And George didn't laugh at it, and nor did I, we let the TV do the laughing work for us. And after *Friends* George turned over and we watched the weather and then a documentary about plastic surgery, I don't know how people can go through that. And there was a late film and George said did I feel like staying up for it? And I said yes because it was nice just sitting there with him and being close to him and smelling him and I bet his hair tastes like butterscotch. And during the film George leaned over and he kissed me and he said sorry sorry was he being too forward and I said no he wasn't and he gave me that smile I love and took my hand in his hand with all the hairs on it. And he took me to his bedroom. And I thought it'd be like mine with all the old stripy wallpaper but it wasn't, there were silks and rugs and mirrors on the ceiling and a big four-poster bed. And he put me on the bed and it was the softest bed I'd ever felt and the sheets were like velvet they were like butterscotch. And we made love right there and then he was gentle but not too gentle and he was rough but not too much, he was in me and through me and George was all around me and all about me and there was nothing but George. And then he kissed me on the lips gentle and rough and that was the nicest thing of all and told me I was the best he'd ever had and that was a nice thing to hear because he is George Clooney after all. And then he took me back to my bedroom and said goodnight and did that slow key thing and I wrote all this. I love you, George. I'd marry you if I weren't married already.

I remember what he smells like. It's sweat. But a nice sweat, I love it.

George is a bit cross with me and making me write this. He wants me to say that what I wrote last night wasn't true. Well, some of it's true, watching *Friends* was true and it didn't have the monkey in it is true and the plastic surgery documentary is true. But nothing about the sex. George wants me to point that out. He said he'd be in enough trouble as it is for what he'd done without lies, and I said the sex was very loving and he said he didn't think the police would see it that way. So sorry I made that part up. And he wants me to say I made up the bit about being in love with him too. So sorry I made that up. (But I didn't, it's true, I love George Clooney.) And he said what was this about August, it'd all be over long before then, it should be over by now, why wasn't there anything on the news about it? And that he thought I should take out my pad and my pencil and write a letter to Paul or to Daddy and say what George wanted. He'd written one but they'd just ignored it, from me they'd know it was real and he meant business. And I said no. He looked surprised. So was I. I couldn't imagine saying no to George Clooney. But this pad and this pencil are for writing to George, these are love letters to him only. I'm not going to write to my husband with them, that would be cheap and nasty. And George got cross again and said that if I didn't write the letter he'd punish me, I wouldn't be allowed to watch TV any more and I said good, that plastic surgery thing was horrible it had given me nightmares, doing things to their breasts and to their lips, I don't know how people can go through that. And he promised if I wrote the letter he'd buy me some butterscotch, he thought I might like that, and I said I'd write it if I got the butterscotch first and he thought about it and then said yes. So I'm locked in my room again and he's at the supermarket and I'm having a nice dessert tonight and I'm meant to be writing the letter now but I'm writing this instead and I'm telling you now I won't write the letter even so. I don't love Paul any more, I love George. When George took me I wanted Paul at first, and Jessie, and Daddy, but if they wanted me they'd have come and got me by now, they wouldn't have let this happen. They don't deserve me the way George does. And I'll try and eat all the butterscotch before George reads this or he'll know I was breaking my promise and take the butterscotch away, sorry George sorry. But what we have, George, is good and pure, and I can't let you spoil that, George, I'm doing this for you, George, it's for you, George. When I think of what I wrote about you at first on that toilet paper it makes me ashamed. Hurtful things. I'll never do anything to hurt you again.

I've been a very naughty girl, and I'm sorry, properly sorry this time not like last time. And George was quite right to be angry and do what he did, and to be fair he only hit me the once and that was to get me to shut up. It's not entirely my fault, though, I'm not trying to get out of it, but I'd never have thought of the pencil if he hadn't put the idea in my head in the first place. But then George points out that I must have been writing with the side of the pencil, trying to sharpen it to a point, I must have been planning it quite on purpose, so I don't know what to think. After I stuck the pencil in his throat I didn't wait around, he was making a strange squealing noise I didn't like at all, and there was blood everywhere. Besides I was trying to escape. I rushed for the front door and I think that's where I made my big mistake, because it's in a room I hadn't seen before, I'd arrived with that blindfold on, and I wasted too much time looking around and taking it in. Then I remembered that George was behind me, I could hear the squealing closer, and I got the chain off the door and got to turn the key but didn't get to do the bolts before he reached me. And I suppose if I hadn't been distracted by that new wallpaper and stopped to count the stripes I might have got outside. As I say he only hit me the once and he didn't break the skin, and I think that was fair because I'd certainly broken his there was blood everywhere I don't like blood. And we didn't watch *Friends* for days, and he didn't let me have my pad and my pencil either, not for days. But the pencil hadn't been that sharp, I hadn't killed him or anything, and George is such a kind man he forgave me in the end. He gave me back my pad, as you can see, and he gave me back my pencil, but he makes sure that I only write when he's there to watch, but I like that better, it's nice to have his company. And we were watching the news tonight and something lovely happened, it said that Paul was dead. Paul was dead, and so was Jessie, and so was Daddy, and it was okay, it was all quite painless, they wouldn't have felt a thing. This meant I was a free woman I said, and George turned to me and smiled and said that was all he was waiting for, and he took out a ring. Diamonds I think yes, and he got on his knees and proposed and of course I said yes. We went to his room and made love again, and it was even better this time now we were engaged, it was official and everything. And I told him I was sorry I had tried to run away. And he said it was okay, and he kissed me, and told me that if I ever tried anything like that again with the pencil he'd be forced to kill me. And then he held me in his arms, all night long his arms around me, never leaving me, except for the bit in the middle I got up to write this.

George has started smoking. He'd stopped years ago he said, but he's been feeling tense. He looks tense too. And at night I can hear him walking and making the floorboards creak, I don't think he's sleeping much. I wasn't sure at first how I felt about the smoking. Daddy used to smoke, but stopped when they made it bad for you, and Paul doesn't smoke, and Jessie doesn't smoke, and I don't think Paul and I would have let her anyway. But I don't know, I think I like it with George. It makes him look rugged. He's asking me why no one's reported my disappearance, don't my family want me back? And I said that Paul probably knew I wasn't in love with him any more and was doing the decent thing. That didn't make him any less tense, not one bit. I asked him if I could cook dinner for him to help him unwind, and he looked at me a bit strangely then sort of shrugged and said why not. It was lovely to see the kitchen, all the saucepans and spoons and knives and sieves, all silver and gleaming, it quite took my breath away. He wouldn't let me do any of the sharp stuff, but it was nice us doing the meal together and I made him my specialty. We ate our beans and chips in the sitting room and I think George enjoyed it as much as I did. Afterwards he lit a cigarette and I asked if I could have one, a little shyly actually. And he said he'd nearly finished the packet, he needed them, but he'd get some more tomorrow, a lot more, I could have one of those. And I told him they made him look rugged. And that I loved him so much, I loved his hands and his teeth and his neck, I loved his arms, all I didn't love was his moustache, George Clooney didn't have a moustache, the real George Clooney, it spoiled the effect, it spoiled everything. He didn't say anything for a while, just sat there and smoked. I asked him if he was all right. And he said he was just working out what to do now. What should he do now? And I told him not to worry, I'd take care of the washing-up for once. And I did.

I'm worried about George. He's behaving very oddly. He hardly said a word when he let me out for breakfast, and he didn't touch his Rice Krispies. He smoked the last of his cigarettes, then said he was going out to buy some more, and locked me in my room. When he let me out for lunch I told him he'd promised me I could have a cigarette today, and he didn't say anything for a while, then handed me the packet. He lit it for me. I'd never smoked before and it was pretty horrid but I worked out it wasn't quite so bad if you don't put it in your mouth. I asked him if I looked rugged and he said he didn't know, so I asked if he could take me to the bathroom so I could look in the mirror, and we went and looked and I don't think I looked especially rugged, not like George does. But then I'm not sure I want to look rugged, so long as one of us is rugged that's all right with me, I asked George if he could do the rugged stuff on his own and he said sure. I told him that when we had a baby we'd see how it went, if it were a Jessie we wouldn't let it smoke, but we would if it were a Jimmy, he could be rugged like his father, we'd start him young, we'd start him right away. I asked him when he thought we could get to work on that, the whole baby idea. He didn't say anything for a while again and then said he needed to go out. I asked him why and he said he needed some cigarettes. I pointed out he'd only just bought some and then asked if he was getting extra in for Jimmy and he said yes that was it. He took off in the car so quickly it didn't dawn on me for a while he'd forgotten to lock me in my room. That was very exciting. I could go to the bathroom when I liked, I could turn on the TV and watch whatever I wanted, there was nothing good on though. I even opened the door to his bedroom, I hadn't been inside and my heart was pounding, I was so excited, and it was everything I hoped it would be, it had the silks and the mirrors and the four-poster bed, I couldn't wait for George to come home with his cigarettes so we could start making babies there. And eventually it occurred to me I could open the front door if I wanted to, and that the bolts weren't drawn and the chain wasn't on, I could get outside if I wanted to. Get some fresh air maybe. But I didn't want to. Not really. It wouldn't smell of George out there. I wanted George. I want George. I hope he's back soon. He's been gone hours, I hope he hasn't got lost. If he's not home soon he'll miss *Friends* and his beans and chips are getting cold.

George woke me up with a shout. He didn't scream of course, George Clooney wouldn't scream, but it was a definite shout. I went to see if he was all right. He seemed very upset. He told me that he'd been in Belgium. I said that was nice, what had Belgium been like and he said he didn't give a shit about Belgium, Belgium was just as far as his car had taken him before he needed to sleep for the night. It was impossible, how could he be back here? I said that maybe he'd only been pretending to be in Belgium, I did that sometimes, when I got bored I made up stories and sometimes they seemed almost real. Though, as far as I could recall, never stories about Belgium. And why was I still here, he asked, didn't I realise it was over, he'd set me free? and he shouted a bit. He went to the front door and opened it and told me that I could go, what was I waiting for? It was over. And I hadn't wanted to go outside yesterday when George was gone, I certainly didn't see the point now he was here. And I told him that wasn't how love worked, you couldn't just open someone's heart and close it again when you'd had enough, I would always be waiting for him, I was his life now, there was no escape. He told me to leave and I said I wouldn't. He called me a stupid bitch and I forgave him, I forgive you George I know you're very tense right now, but I'm not sure you should be encouraged, I may have to punish you for that. He went to the kitchen, came back with a knife, kept on jabbing at me with it. He said he didn't want to hurt me, he'd never wanted to hurt me, had he? He hadn't hurt me, not much? I agreed, and said that it was his very tenderness that had captured my love, his very distinctive rugged tenderness. I'll kill you, George said I'll kill you if I have to, and I told him that Paul had killed me once, or maybe he'd just tried to kill me, it was so long ago this was before we had Jessie and became a proper family and Paul realised he loved me after all and George would feel the same when we had a proper family George just you wait and see, and then George killed me.

George Clooney screamed. I thought that was disappointing. I do hope he doesn't disappoint me again. I poured him his breakfast cereal but he wasn't hungry. He told me that this time he'd nearly made it to America, after he'd killed me he'd locked my body in the bedroom then gone straight to the airport then caught the next flight out, he'd only shut his eyes for a little nap and here he was again. He was very upset by this and I felt very sorry for him. He asked to be freed. Please let me go, he said. I'd let Paul go, hadn't I? But Paul was a special case, I said, how many times do you get gazumped in your affections by George Clooney? I couldn't just stop loving George, I told him, it wasn't like a tap, it was real this love it wouldn't be denied. But if he did everything I told him to, I'd do my very best, I promised, I'd harden my heart to him, I'd try to get bored of him and let my passion for him die. What did he have to do, he asked. Convince me that you love me, I said. That you live for me, that you live only for me, you won't try to run again, will you George, that isn't love, but I'll lock you in your room anyway from now on, I know how hard it can be sometimes to do the right thing and listen to what your heart wants. Love me blindly love me desperately love me entirely love me without end or hope of end. And maybe I'll get bored of your love, what's more boring than that? And finish your breakfast. I'd made him his breakfast, the least he could do was to finish it. He ate his Krispies, and then I poured him a second bowl, and then a third, and then more, I could have made him eat those Krispies all day but then I got bored, you see George, I can get bored, there's hope for you yet. Then I kissed him, hard on the lips. I told him he was allowed to respond. I loved him, I said.

I loved his hands and I loved his eyes and I loved his teeth but the only thing I didn't love was his moustache. In fact I disliked it. In fact I hated it. In fact the very sight of it made me want to hurt him. George Clooney didn't have a moustache, my George would be better off without one, my George would be safer. And he said he'd shave it off right away, and I said no, I couldn't trust him with sharp objects, not any more. I'd have to shave it off for him. I fetched a knife from the kitchen. He asked for shaving cream and I said there was no need for that and he began to cry and I told him that he had to keep still he mustn't flinch, if he kept still and didn't flinch I wouldn't cut him, but he was crying so much he flinched so I did cut him, I took off his upper lip. I don't like blood, I'm scared of blood, but sacrifices have to be made. He looked a bit funny now without a lip but at least he was also without a moustache, it's not such a bad trade-off. And now I told him I wanted us to make love, I wanted to have butterscotch love. I wanted him inside me, not one scrap of him could get away, and to make the point I took the gobbet of flesh that had been his lip and popped it in my mouth and swallowed it down. And he threw up, and I'm sure I don't know why, I was the one who had eaten the disgusting thing. We had sex, and it wasn't as good as I remembered it, and I made allowances I knew he was scared and confused, and bleeding quite badly actually – but it was all right, I closed my eyes and I pictured the four-poster bed and the mirrors and even a fountain, why not, a little fountain in the corner, and I smelled him and he smelled of sweat but it was nice, it was a good sweat really, I love it.

I'm not convinced yet but he's at least trying hard. The effort he puts in is quite touching. I cut up his food for him and he always looks so grateful and says please and thank you, and I keep his hands tied for the meal so I have to feed him every single mouthful and he always remembers what I told him and to smile after each bite. If I'm stricter with him than he was, it's just because I love him more than he did me, I see that now, but he'll learn, there's so much time to learn. Sometimes I'll let him out of his room when *Friends* is on, though he hasn't actually watched one yet, I keep the blindfold on, he doesn't mind, he's lucky, the best bit is hearing the audience laugh and wondering why. And I light him cigarettes and let him puff away, he looks rugged like that, and I don't let him hold the cigarette because it might burn him, and I suppose that having it fed to him like a baby cuts down a little on the ruggedness but I can pretend I'm good at pretending I'm so good at it. Sometimes I get him to smoke a whole pack in one go to see if he'll be sick, and sometimes he is. And at other times we'll make love. And when he's not busy with the eating and the smoking and the sex he's got a job to keep him occupied. He sits in his bedroom and writes me letters. Just to let me know what he feels for me, to show me I'm his one and only. This is his latest:

I love
you

and they're getting better, I don't accept them unless they're neat and tidy. I haven't given him a pad yet, and I'm not sure I ever will. Writing on toilet paper is slow work, but it makes you really think about what you want to say. And you have to be careful, because toilet paper breaks so very easily.

Graham Mort

The Lesson

The old man sits on the steps of the white-painted church smoking his first cigarette of the day. His wife has been sick. She can't stand the smell of tobacco smoke in the house any more. Slow light flickers over the surface of the harbour. The blue-and-yellow-painted fishing boats are motionless, hardly moving because the sea is hardly moving. There is still a faint image of last night's moon settling beyond hills of ochre rock with their stubble of pines. The sky is pale, the air thickening under the rising sun. The old man smokes, occasionally tugging at the peak of his faded denim cap. The sun heats the town, soaking into the terracotta roofs, raising a stink of rotting fish.

A boy comes along the narrow street carrying a long loaf of bread under his arm. He wears a blue-and-white-striped tee-shirt, khaki shorts and sandals. The old man watches the boy's smooth brown legs go by, noticing the dimple of paler skin behind his knees. It could have been himself sixty-odd years ago.

A large dog comes out from the butcher's yard, pulling its chain, and the boy stops to stroke its mangy coat. The dog is old and useless. Joaquim should have put it down years ago. But he was soft, for a butcher. The boy skips on and the old man lets his eyes rest on the sea again, narrowing them against its glare. His father and brothers had all been fishermen, but he'd never trusted the sea. And he'd made sure he never had to, working in the quarry, blasting back the hillside to make new roads. He'd kept his feet on the land, never even learned to swim. He dips his head then spits in the direction of the dog that still tugs at its chain.

The last apartments to be built in the town are perched on the hillside behind the church, set on platforms cut out from the rock. The new road leads the way and the apartments follow. Now families from Barcelona come out for weekends in Japanese four-by-fours that are too big for the old streets. They live life to a different rhythm, staying up all night to party in the new night clubs and discos along the bay, then lying in bed all morning, squandering the first cool of the day. They're rich and they know nothing of struggle – not as he has known it.

The old man takes a last drag of the cigarette and pinches it out between his thumb and finger. A lifetime working with stone has calloused them so that he doesn't even feel the heat. He stands up slowly, stiff from sitting so long on cold stone. He pushes back the denim cap to scratch his temple. When he lifts the lid of the waste bin to throw in the spent cigarette there's a stink of mackerel heads and sardines. Everything decays quickly here; everything is consumed by the sun.

The next day, the old man takes up the same position, easing himself onto the church steps. He thinks of the statue of Christ they've erected inside, that sly smile playing across his bronze face. In his day, they'd smashed the faces of plaster saints with their rifle butts. But no one talks about that time now, even though there'd been fighting all the way from here to Figuères. No one would talk about it, and maybe that was for the best. Even the street signs are in Catalan, since Franco died. When the Republic had been crushed and the foreign volunteers gone home, he and his comrades had got out, running over the border into France. Only when things had eased had they drifted back, one by one to their villages. Or they never returned. Those that did, like him, found work and kept their heads down. They kept silence like a vow. His brothers had stayed with the sea, always, but he'd been different, felt and seen something else in the life he wanted. He'd always hankered for land – a piece of his own land. But that had never been.

The roofs of the town are made of ridged clay tiles and from his vantage point at the church they fall away downhill in rows to the quayside. The old man lights up his one cigarette of the day, watching swifts flicker out from under the eaves on scimitar wings. They're feeding on invisible insect swarms and he hears their young chittering with hunger. He found one dead in the street once, its feathers iridescent, its legs stumpy and wasted. That was the only time the swifts touched down. When they fell, too exhausted to fly on, and died where they lay. He'd heard that they even made love in the air. Their whole lives were spent on the wing between

Spain and Africa.

He thought of Lisa, that first time, before the fighting. The little stone barn in the valley that led down to vineyards above the next bay. Her eyes wide, the black dress almost hiding her in the gloom. And the heat, the sudden blush of sweat as he touched her. Touched her breasts and buried his face in her hair. The way she'd pushed him away then pulled him into her fiercely, biting his shoulder and tearing at his shirt. Now their daughters were married and had moved away to the city. Lisa has grown old, troubled by angina, hobbling down to the shops on her arthritic hip. But she won't let him help her prepare meals or clean the house, even though he wants to. It isn't his place. It hurts him to think that the girl he loved has grown old. He'd wanted to die first, for her to live forever. Forever young. Maybe she would. Maybe that's what the priests – those liars – meant by heaven.

The boy comes along the street, wearing the same clothes, carrying a bottle of Vichy water and a loaf of bread. The dog paddles out on its short length of chain and the boy holds out his hand to be licked. He pats the dog's head and the dog nuzzles him. Strange. Nobody had made much of that dog for years, and now here's this boy stroking it. Making a fuss. Pablo, Joaquim the butcher's dog: grown fat and decrepit on scraps. Not a bad life for a dog. The old man watches the boy walk away with jerky, impulsive steps, the way a young lamb or calf walks. The boy is distracted for a moment by a swallow, looking up and shading his eyes at its steel-blue flash from under the eaves. The old man catches his eye and smiles. For a moment the boy seems confused, then he too smiles and walks on.

The next day, the same. But the old man calls across to the boy in Catalan as he goes by.

'Good morning dog-boy!'

The boy looks startled, raising a hand to scratch his nose, almost dropping the loaf. He replies in Castilian. A city boy. His parents are probably loaded.

'Buenos días!'

The old man grins and points to the dog that still gazes after the boy in the street. He speaks in the boy's own language.

'You've made a friend for life there boy! Old Pedro's never had so much fuss made of him.'

The boy shrugs, drawing up his shoulders, a fluid gesture of defiance. 'He's just an old dog. It's OK.'

He says it in a matter-of-fact manner, looks directly into his eyes, and the old man rocks back uneasily under his gaze. It's as if the boy lives in a world where all things are equal. An old dog, an old man, what's the difference? The boy walks on, holding his shoulders just a little higher.

The next day the old man waits but the boy doesn't come. He smokes two cigarettes, for once, tugs at his cap, watches the dog wander out on its leash and sniff at the passers-by. But the boy is nowhere to be seen. The sea glitters. The town heats up like iron in a forge. Swifts scream over the rooftops and a hawk appears briefly, hovering over the scrubland above the town. The boy doesn't come and the old man sits in the reek of fish, watching the sea, thinking of Christ's mocking smile in the cool darkness of the church behind him.

He goes back home and sits in the shady kitchen of their house, watching Lisa prepare the lunch. She's making tomato bread and there's a strong scent of basil and raw garlic. Lisa puts the dish down on the table and watches him slyly.

'You're quiet today. Have the seagulls taken out your soul in the night?'

'Not the seagulls.'

She turns away, rubbing garlic over the flat loaf.

'It was you, my sweet.'

The old man speaks hoarsely, his voice thickened by the garlic, by his wife's sudden alertness to him.

'You tore my mind away and threw it to the sea!'

He rises and kisses her behind the ear where her grey hair is pinned into a bun. Lisa grins, her laughter rusty as an old key turning.

'That'll be the day old man. The day I stop your dreams!'

But he's already half-absent, examining his fingers spread out on the tabletop. All that banter! It's just words. He throws them out like ashes from a volcano. And they don't amount to much in the end. Just ashes, where there'd once been fire.

They eat lunch slowly, sipping the weak red wine he's brought from the bodega. The sea seethes beyond slatted shutters, closed against the sun. A breeze billows in the net curtains, as if an invisible intruder is at the window. Then he takes a siesta, sleeping beside his wife as sun bakes the town.

The next day the boy is there, as usual, trotting along the street to where the dog hangs out its tongue. The old man greets him with narrowed eyes. Bright shears of sun flicker over the bay.

'*Hola!*'

The boy looks up from patting the dog. A string of saliva hangs from its muzzle, swaying and gleaming in the sun.

'*Hola.*'

The boy is already almost past him.

'Hey, what's the big hurry?'

The old man pinches out the cigarette stub and the boy comes to a halt, watching wide-eyed.

'Doesn't that hurt?'

'Hurt?'

The old man laughs, rubbing at his stubble.

'I've got hands like iron, boy. Feel them!'

He holds out his hands and the boy touched his fingertips.

'What happened to them?'

'What happened to my hands? Why work, boy, work!'

He scuffles his feet in the rope espadrilles and fixes the boy with a hard stare.

'I wasn't much older than you when I started work at the quarry. See those villas up there?'

He gestures behind the church and the boy shades his eyes to where the white apartments glare.

'I helped cut those out of the hillside. My God, in my time I must have lifted a mountain and put it down again!'

The boy clutches the loaf, anxious to leave. But he's an inquisitive boy.

'How did you get it out?'

'How? Dynamite and sweat! Phoof!'

The old man blows out his breath and explodes his palms together.

'Dynamite, then picks and shovels and bare hands.'

The boy nods and walks on, no longer curious.

'*Adiós!*'

'*Adiós*, dog-boy!'

The old man watches him go. Heat shimmers on the hills and blue shadows bloom under juniper bushes and clumps of prickly pear.

Dynamite. First they drilled a line of holes at the cliff edge and then dropped in the charges, packing them so that the explosion would force the rock outward. Then the fuses were laid and the red flags raised. When the switch was thrown a line of dust jumped at the sky and then a whole slab of the limestone would shear away, hanging for a moment as if it had abandoned God's time to fall into human time. Into its fever of change. Then the report of the explosion would bound over the bay, echoing back from the mountains and the walls of the ruined monastery opposite.

The old man feels in his pocket for a match. They should have dealt with the fascists in the same way. Those bastards. They should have dynamited them off the land. But his brothers had been fishermen, not interested in politics. They understood only the sea, the way it tugged at their nets. The way the sun rose from it, then fell back into it each day. The way it drew its shoals towards their boat each night to feed them or half-feed them. The way it kept them in poverty. The old man strolls down to the harbour, smoking and greeting people as he goes. He's smoking too much these days.

Joaquim's daughter goes by on her moped waving at him with her bare arm, her bathing costume rolled up in a towel between her legs. There are at least three fascists he knows of in the town. Not just people who'd believed, but paid-up fascists who'd carried a gun. They'd kicked over the traces pretty quickly when Franco died. Then Juan Carlos had come back. What a joke! It'd taken a socialist government to give them a king! But he's too old to heat up those grudges now.

He goes into a bar and orders pastis, knocking it back in one jerk of his arm. The peasants had always been unreliable. Treacherous. Never trust a peasant. A communist schoolteacher from Montpellier had told him that when they'd gone on the run. He could still speak good French after those years over the border. He'd sent Lisa money from his job there, labouring on the roads. Somehow she'd made ends meet, raised their first daughter and waited for his return. And she's still waiting. Waiting for him to come back to her. An exile can come home, but he can never return. The old man has a child by a woman in France that Lisa knows nothing about. *Françoise*. Another daughter. A baby girl with creamy skin, chubby hands and dimpled knees. He remembers coils of blonde hair. But he hasn't seen her in over fifty years. These things happen. In wartime anything can happen. He wonders if she has kids of her own by now. Grandchildren. Unlike Lisa, she has never aged. And he knows that's a lie, too.

The pastis has cleared the old man's head. He walks out of the village to the headland where the tourists are crowded onto the pebble beach. He walks slowly now, careful of the youngsters on mopeds who race up the street. When they'd played here as kids there had been hardly any visitors. Then the villagers had grown wine, hewn stone, harvested the sea. And no one in the outside world had really cared. Now the new roads he'd helped to build had opened up the whole coastline. There was a new marina, yachts, a sailing club for the smart set from Barcelona. People in the town made money, whereas in the old days they'd just got by, or starved.

Here on a promontory of rock there's a diving board set up so that swimmers can launch themselves into the sea. The beach is full of tourists: mothers with pale, stretchmarked flesh, fathers barking at their kids, beautiful suntanned girls who preen in the water, calling to young men who swim around them, vying for their attention. Further out, there are snorkellers, their masked faces pressed in the water, staring down into the depths of the sea. He notices the boy climbing the iron ladder. Six steps. He stands for a moment, water streaming from his brown skin. Then he dives in, clean as a harpoon.

For a few seconds the sea gulps him. Then his head emerges, metres away, black as basalt in the blue-green water. The old man watches without being seen. The boy's body is fluid, like water itself, responding to whatever catches his interest as he sculls around. Then he dives back under. Soon he's lost amongst the heads of other swimmers. The old man walks home for lunch. By now half the town is frying sardines and the scent of hot fish comes down from open windows. As he passes the dog it pads out to sniff him, but he waves it away.

The next day is Sunday and the old man keeps away from the church. Instead, he takes his cigarette down to the quayside and chats to Ramon, his last remaining brother. They stand, gazing out to sea, to the ruined monastery on the mountain across the bay. The foothills opposite are covered in collapsing terraces that peter out as the hillsides steepen. All that land had been under vines or olives when they'd been boys. The war had put paid to that. The French had made their wine too cheap. It was hard to get decent local wine now. Hard to get decent anything – chorizo, cheese, game. It was all going to the bad.

'It's this government fleecing the poor, those whores!'

Ramon smiles and sighs.

'No matter, there's enough good wine to see us out!'

'See us out? And they will, those bastards!'

Ramon had always been the same. Passive, easy-going, simple in all these matters. He'd never even asked his brother about his years in exile, but greeted him on his return as if he'd just returned from a night out in the next village. The old man says nothing more. What's the point? He gazes out to where the vines are growing wild on the hillsides, to where the boy is trailing a stick at the water's edge, electrifying a fringe of silver light, as if a shoal of sardines is leaping at his heels.

That night the old man sits in silence, watching some nonsense on the television, hardly answering his wife's questions as she sits fanning herself in the heat.

On Monday morning, he's back in his usual position at the church. The boy is late, hurrying along, hardly finding time to pat the dog. He returns the old man's greeting politely, and seems to suppress a smile. Later in the morning, he's there in the little bay, flipping from the diving board and breaking the surface of the sea, which mirrors a blank, hot sky. The old man watches from the shade of the taverna with an iced lemonade in his hand. When he gets home for lunch he sits down to the anchovies his wife has prepared, eating without a word. She leans over him, trying to get a clue to his mood, but there's no smell of drink on him. Just the faint impression of sweat, sunlight, and tobacco, as always. She touches his neck where the white hairs grow, white and unruly. But he says nothing, staring from the dark centres of his eyes that have turned the colour of plums.

The day passes slowly, as all days do now. That night the old man dreams of the olive grove near Cadaqués where he'd shot a man in the fighting. It had all happened so quickly. He'd hardly meant to do it. The enemy had appeared suddenly, a grey uniform between the trees. He raised the rifle then felt it kick at his shoulder. The man's blood left a damson stain on the soil when they dragged him away by the heels. And he hadn't died at once. He'd woken to call for his mother, begging them to hold his hand, then gurgling and drowning in his own blood. It'd taken a whole day. They sat him in the shade of a rock and he'd died at sunset. A boy just like they were. A dark-skinned kid from the south. Whispering things they couldn't make out. They'd waited until he died, then buried him: covering his face with stones, dust filming his eyes where they stared towards home.

The old man wakes up shuddering and goes to the window, pushing the shutters open a crack. The dawn is coming up behind the town, staining the hillside opposite with apricot light. The bay lies calmed, like a turquoise stone sawn in half. The air is restless, as if there might be a storm. Leaves rustle on the fig tree beside the house. To his own amazement, the old man crosses himself. He hasn't done that since he was a child. Maybe the dream had brought that on. The war wasn't something you could talk about. How could you tell your wife such things? Perhaps Lisa had guessed, though she hadn't asked what her husband had done. Not a word when he'd come home and fallen into his long silence. It was the history of their land: blood and silence in each handful of earth.

That day the old man goes to the church early and smokes two cigarettes, pulling at his cap, watching gangs of swifts scream across the rooftops. The boy is also early and has time for the dog, which barks, excitedly at his approach. The boy crouches with the new loaf under his arm, pats the dog's head, speaks a few words of affection, then rises to find his path blocked. The old man has made up his mind. He speaks first.

'*Hola!*'

'*Hola.*'

The boy scuffles his feet.

'It's a fine day. Going to be hot!'

'Yes.'

The old man speaks awkwardly, gruffer than he wants to be. There's a silence and the boy scuffs his heel.

'Could I ask you a favour, boy?'

The boy considers carefully.

'A favour?'

The old man sits down on the steps and the boy sits next to him as if invited.

'See that out there?'

The boy shades his eyes and scans the sea, imagining something in particular will catch his eye.

'What?'

'The sea! You know, my father and brothers were all fishermen, my grandfather too and *his* father. The sea goes back in my family like blood goes back.'

He touched the boy's arm.

'Like blood. You get it? They said we had salt blood!'

'Yes...'

The boy is doubtful, clutching the loaf of bread, picking at the crust.

'But like I told you, boy, I broke with the sea. I worked the land, dug out all this damned rock. To tell you the truth – and, God knows, why should I? – I was afraid of it.'

He pauses. The boy's sandals draw little circles in the dust.

'And worse, I never learned to swim.'

'You can't swim?'

The boy is incredulous. Surely everyone could swim? He'd been able to swim almost at the same time that he could walk.

'Never learned to. Always had an excuse to get out of the damned water.'

He pauses for a second to laugh.

'And never missed it until now. Not until I saw you jumping off that diving board.'

Again the hoarse laugh, like a motor trying to start.

'I'm too old for diving, boy, but I have a favour to ask. Just one.'

The boy listens and nods, then hurries off clutching the loaf with a new kind of step. He seems taller, or heavier. There is more gravity in his step, yet he is a small boy in a striped T shirt taking a loaf home to his parents.

In the Mediterranean summer, all things decay. The dead are buried quickly, though without haste. Refuse rots overnight. Here, on the Costa Brava, the town council have it collected each morning. The bins are emptied and even the imported sand on the beach is swept clean to please the tourists. The refuse workers wear white overalls, tipping the green bins into their wagon. Two slim young men in peaked caps and blue uniforms empty the smaller waste bins along the waterfront with a kind of elegant ease, one tipping the bin, the other holding a refuse sack beneath it. The old man smoking on the church steps is a familiar sight. The fact that he holds a plastic carrier bag excites no curiosity. An old dog stares after him with mournful eyes, absent-mindedly wandering to the length of its chain. The sea lurches in dull shades of grey. The mountains smoulder under cloud, the monastery appearing and disappearing in mist. Dark-skinned men in yellow waterproofs and red bandanas unload crates of fish from a trawler in the harbour. This is a new day, no different from yesterday or tomorrow. The sun is rising, strengthening to a glare, burnishing the sky to a blinding pane of light.

In a few weeks it will be autumn. The bars will shutter up and only the hardiest tourists – stray Frenchmen, German hikers, hippies from Barcelona – will brave the gusts that shriek off the sea to jostle the yachts in the new marina, rattling steel cables against their masts. A wind for each season and each wind had a name. Autumn brings the Tramuntana. A harsh, dry wind that hurls over the mountains and onto the bay, shaking the almond trees. Then winter, the season of storms. After that? Well, who knows? It didn't do to look too far ahead these days.

A boy comes along the street with his shoulder bag and stops in front of the old man. They exchange a few words, the boy trailing one foot in the dust. Then they set off together, walking down to the main street that runs parallel with the sea, following its curve to the small cove where a few early swimmers are gathered. The old man's walk is stiff and stately, the boy manages to restrain his eagerness and keep in step with him. The sun is still hazy and the sea is still grey, like the hull of a naval ship. A few yachts make their way out to sea, tilting white sails. The red hills beyond are splashed with dark green pine trees.

The old man and the boy reach the beach and then walk to its furthest point where shingle slopes easily into the water, where there are rocks to hold onto and the open sea seems far away. When they have changed into their shorts, the boy goes first, beckoning to the old man who has not entered the sea since he was a child. His muscles are slack; the flesh on his chest and upper arms is loose and covered in white hair. But there is still some wiriness in his body, there is still strength in the limbs that have carried a rifle and dug out the earth and smashed and lifted rock for most of his life. The boy's skin is smooth and brown, perfected by the sun.

They enter the water slowly, feeling warm air on their naked shoulders, the sea cool on their legs. The boy watches the old man, expecting him to be afraid. But the old man is remembering the darkness of a barn in the next valley, the scented heat, the way Lisa's body had shuddered under him, her hair stuck to his face with sweat. Now he enters the sea. He splashes water onto his face and it is salty like the taste of anchovies or a soldier's sweat. He feels the water begin to buoy him up, remembers the shocked eyes of a dying boy under the olive trees near Cadaqués. The way the soldier had appeared in his sights then stumbled as if he'd tripped over a stone. He'd looked down into that white face and felt only relief. Relief that it was not his own life pouring away like dregs. Briefly, he thinks of the little girl he left in France. *Françoise*. A woman now. But that secret pain is long dulled. He looks at the boy.

'Now?'

'Yes, now! Come on!'

The boy is already afloat, kicking like a little frog with his brown legs. The old man dips his face into the sea and takes his first stroke, kicking off from the shingle where the boy has led him. Mist is lifting from the hills across the bay. The white buildings of Llançà across the bay seem to be falling into and rising from the sea. He can see the hairpin bends of the road with their steel barriers. At home Lisa is fanning herself with a newspaper in the shuttered kitchen, the old dog is waiting, the fish van is threading its way through the streets, honking as the women gather. After this, he'll take the boy for lemonade, have a small cognac for himself, and they'll talk about how things are and about how things used to be.

The old man feels the boy's hand slip away from his. He takes a second stroke, embracing the sea and everything in it: the fish and the rocks and the sunken salt-encrusted hulks that lie where the light cannot reach. He spits out seawater and is not afraid. No, what he feels in his belly is not fear, not exactly. And if he becomes afraid as the water deepens, then it will pass, as everything passes here under the white stare of the sun.

Helen Simpson

Diary of an Interesting Year

12th February 2040

My thirtieth birthday. G gave me this little spiral-backed notebook and a biro. It's a good present, hardly any rust on the spiral and no water damage to the paper. I'm going to start a diary. I'll keep my handwriting tiny to make the paper go further.

15th February 2040

G is really getting me down. He's in his element. They should carve it on his tombstone – 'I Was Right.'

23rd February 2040

Glad we don't live in London. The Hatchwells have got cousins staying with them, they trekked up from Peckham (three days). Went round this afternoon and they were saying the thing that finally drove them out was the sewage system – when the drains packed up it overflowed everywhere. They said the smell was unbelievable, the pavements were swimming in it, and of course the hospitals are down so there's nothing to be done about the cholera. Didn't get too close to them in case they were carrying it. They lost their two sons like that last year.

'You see,' G said to me on the way home, 'capitalism cared more about its children as accessories and demonstrations of earning power than for their future.'

'Oh shut up,' I said.

2nd March 2040

Can't sleep. I'm writing this instead of staring at the ceiling. There's a mosquito in the room, I can hear it whining close to my ear. Very humid, air like filthy soup, plus we're supposed to wear our face masks in bed too but I was running with sweat so I ripped mine off just now. Got up and looked at myself in the mirror on the landing – ribs like a fence, hair in greasy rat's tails. Yesterday the rats in the kitchen were busy gnawing away at the breadbin, they didn't even look up when I came in.

6th March 2040

Another quarrel with G. OK, yes, he was right, but why crow about it? That's what you get when you marry your tutor from Uni – wall-to-wall pontificating from an older man. 'I saw it coming, any fool could see it coming especially after the Big Melt,' he brags. 'Thresholds crossed, cascade effect, hopelessly optimistic to assume we had till 2060, blahdy blahdy blah, the plutonomy as lemming, democracy's massive own goal.' No wonder we haven't got any friends.

He cheered when rationing came in. He's the one that volunteered first as car share warden for our road; one piddling little Peugeot for the entire road. He gets a real kick out of the camaraderie round the stand-pipe.

– I'll swap my big tin of chickpeas for your little tin of sardines.

– No, no, my sardines are protein.

– Chickpeas are protein too, plus they fill you up more. Anyway, I thought you still had some tuna.

– No, I swapped that with Astrid Huggins for a tin of tomato soup.

Really sick of bartering, but hard to know how to earn money since the Internet went down. 'Also, money's no use unless you've got shedloads of it,' as I said to him in bed last night, 'the top layer hanging on inside their plastic bubbles of filtered air while the rest of us shuffle about with goitres and tumours and bits of old sheet tied over our mouths. Plus, we're soaking wet the whole time. We've given up on umbrellas, we just go round permanently drenched.' I only stopped ranting when I heard a snore and clocked he was asleep.

8th April 2040

Boring morning washing out rags. No wood for hot water, so had to use ashes and lye again. Hands very sore even though I put plastic bags over them. Did the face masks first, then the rags from my period. Took forever. At least I haven't got to do nappies like Lexi or Esme, that would send me right over the edge.

27th April 2040
Just back from Maia's. Seven months. She's very frightened. I don't blame her. She tried to make me promise I'd take care of the baby if anything happens to her. I havered (mostly at the thought of coming between her and that throwback Martin – she'd got a new black eye, I didn't ask). I suppose there's no harm in promising if it makes her feel better. After all, it wouldn't exactly be taking on a responsibility – I give a new baby three months max in these conditions. Diarrhoea, basically.

14th May 2040
Can't sleep. Bites itching, trying not to scratch. Heavy thumps and squeaks just above, in the ceiling. Think of something nice. Soap and hot water. Fresh air. Condoms! Sick of being permanently on knife edge re pregnancy. Start again. Wandering round a supermarket – warm, gorgeously lit – corridors of open fridges full of tiger prawns and fillet steak. Gliding off down the fast lane in a sports car, stopping to fill up with thirty litres of petrol. Online, booking tickets for *The Mousetrap*, click, ordering a crate of wine, click, a holiday home, click, a pair of patent leather boots, click, a gap year, click. I go to iTunes and download *The Marriage of Figaro*, then I chat face-to-face in real time with G's parents in Sydney. No, don't think about what happened to them. Horrible. Go to sleep.

21st May 2040
Another row with G. He blew my second candle out, he said one was enough. It wasn't though, I couldn't see to read any more. He drives me mad, it's like living with a policeman. It always was, even before the Collapse. 'The Earth has enough for everyone's need, but not for everyone's greed' was his favourite. Nobody likes being labelled greedy. I called him Killjoy and he didn't like that. 'Every one of us takes about twenty-five thousand breaths a day,' he told me. 'Each breath removes oxygen from the atmosphere and replaces it with carbon dioxide.' Well, pardon me for breathing! What was I supposed to do – turn into a tree?

6th June 2040
Went round to the Lumleys for the news last night. Whole road there squashed into front room, straining to listen to radio – batteries very low

(no new ones in the last govt delivery). Big news though – compulsory billeting imminent. The Shorthouses were up in arms, Kai shouting and red in the face, Lexi in tears. 'You work all your life', etc, etc. What planet is he on. None of us too keen, but nothing to be done about it. When we got back, G checked our stash of tins under the bedroom floorboards. A big rat shot out and I screamed my head off. G held me till I stopped crying then we had sex. Woke in the night and prayed not to be pregnant, though God knows who I was praying to.

12th June 2040
Visited Maia this afternoon. She was in bed, her legs have swollen up like balloons. On at me again to promise about the baby and this time I said yes. She said Astrid Huggins was going to help her when it started – Astrid was a nurse once, apparently, not really the hands-on sort but better than nothing. Nobody else in the road will have a clue what to do now we can't google it. 'All I remember from old films is that you're supposed to boil a kettle,' I said. We started to laugh, we got a bit hysterical. Knuckledragger Martin put his head round the door and growled at us to shut it.

1st July 2040
First billet arrived today by army truck. We've got a Spanish group of eight including one old lady, her daughter and twin toddler grandsons (all pretty feral), plus four unsmiling men of fighting age. A bit much since we only have two bedrooms. G and I tried to show them round but they ignored us, the grandmother bagged our bedroom straight off. We're under the kitchen table tonight. I might try to sleep on top of it because of the rats. We couldn't think of anything to say – the only Spanish we could remember was *Muchas gracias*, and as G said, we're certainly not saying *that*.

2nd July 2040
Fell off the table in my sleep. Bashed my elbow. Covered in bruises.

3rd July 2040
G depressed. The four Spaniards are bigger than him, and he's worried that the biggest one, Miguel, has his eye on me (with reason, I have to say).

4th July 2040

G depressed. The grandmother found our tins under the floorboards and all but danced a flamenco. Miguel punched G when he tried to reclaim a tin of sardines and since then his nose won't stop bleeding.

6th July 2040

Last night under the table G came up with a plan. He thinks we should head north. Now this lot are in the flat and a new group from Tehran promised next week, we might as well cut and run. Scotland's heaving, everyone else has already had the same idea, so he thinks we should get on one of the ferries to Stavanger then aim for Russia.

'I don't know,' I said. 'Where would we stay?'

'I've got the pop-up tent packed in a rucksack behind the shed,' he said, 'plus our sleeping bags and my wind-up radio.'

'Camping in the mud,' I said.

'Look on the bright side,' he said. 'We have a huge mortgage and we're just going to walk away from it.'

'Oh shut up,' I said.

17th July 2040

Maia died yesterday. It was horrible. The baby got stuck two weeks ago, it died inside her. Astrid Huggins was useless, she didn't have a clue. Martin started waving his Swiss Army knife around on the second day and yelling about a Caesarean, he had to be dragged off her. He's round at ours now drinking the last of our precious brandy with the Spaniards. That's it. We've got to go. Now, says G. Yes.

1st August 2040

Somewhere in Shropshire, or possibly Cheshire. We're staying off the beaten track. Heavy rain. This notebook's pages have gone all wavy. At least biro doesn't run. I'm lying inside the tent now, G is out foraging. We got away in the middle of the night. G slung our two rucksacks across the bike. We took turns to wheel it, then on the fourth morning we woke up and looked outside the tent flap and it was gone even though we'd covered it with leaves the night before.

'Could be worse,' said G, 'we could have had our throats cut while we slept.'

'Oh shut up,' I said.

3rd August 2040
Rivers and streams all toxic – fertilisers, typhoid etc. So, we're following G's DIY system. Dip billycan into stream or river. Add three drops of bleach. Boil up on camping stove with T-shirt stretched over billycan. Only moisture squeezed from the T-shirt is safe to drink; nothing else. 'You're joking,' I said, when G first showed me how to do this. But no.

9th August 2040
Radio news in muddy sleeping bags – skeleton govt obviously struggling, they keep playing the Enigma Variations. Last night they announced the end of fuel for civilian use and the compulsory disabling of all remaining civilian cars. As from now we must all stay at home, they said, and not travel without permission. There's talk of martial law. We're going cross-country as much as possible – less chance of being arrested or mugged – trying to cover ten miles a day but the weather slows us down. Torrential rain, often horizontal in gusting winds.

16th August 2040
Rare dry afternoon. Black lace clouds over yellow sky. Brown grass, frowsty grey mould, fungal frills. Dead trees come crashing down without warning – one nearly got us today, it made us jump. G was hoping we'd find stuff growing in the fields, but all the farmland round here is surrounded by razor wire and armed guards. He says he knows how to grow vegetables from his allotment days, but so what. They take too long. We're hungry now, we can't wait till March for some old carrots to get ripe.

22nd August 2040
G broke a front crown cracking a beechnut, there's a black hole and he whistles when he talks. 'Damsons, blackberries, young green nettles for soup,' he said at the start of all this, smacking his lips. He's not so keen now. No damsons or blackberries, of course – only chickweed and ivy.

He's just caught a lame squirrel, so I suppose I'll have to do something with it. No creatures left except squirrels, rats and pigeons, unless you count the insects. The news says they're full of protein, you're meant to grind them into a paste, but so far we haven't been able to face that.

24th August 2040
We met a pig this morning. It was a bit thin for a pig, and it didn't look well. G said, 'Quick! We've got to kill it.'

'Why?' I said. 'How?'

'With a knife,' he said. 'Bacon. Sausages.'

I pointed out that even if we managed to stab it to death with our old kitchen knife, which looked unlikely, we wouldn't be able just to open it up and find bacon and sausages inside.

'Milk, then!' said G wildly. 'It's a mammal, isn't it?'

Meanwhile the pig walked off.

25th August 2040
Ravenous. We've both got streaming colds. Jumping with fleas, itching like crazy. Weeping sores on hands and faces – unfortunate side effects from cloud seeding, the news says. What with all this and his toothache (back molar, swollen jaw) and the malaria, G is in a bad way.

27th August 2040
Found a dead hedgehog. Tried to peel off its spines and barbecue it over the last briquette. Disgusting. Both sick as dogs. Why did I used to moan about the barter system? Foraging is MUCH MUCH worse.

29th August 2040
Dreamt of Maia and the Swiss Army knife and woke up crying. G held me in his shaky arms and talked about Russia, how it's the new land of milk and honey since the Big Melt. 'Some really good farming opportunities opening up in Siberia,' he said through chattering teeth.

'We're like in the Three Sisters,' I said, '"If only we could get to Moscow." Do you remember that production at the National? We walked by the river afterwards, we stood and listened to Big Ben chime midnight.'

Hugged each other and carried on like this until sleep came.

31st August 2040
G woke up crying. I held him and hushed him and asked what was the matter. 'I wish I had a gun,' he said.

15th September 2040

Can't believe this notebook was still at the bottom of the rucksack. And the biro. Murderer wasn't interested in them. He's turned everything else inside out (including me). G didn't have a gun. This one has a gun.

19th September 2040

M speaks another language. Norwegian? Dutch? Croatian? We can't talk, so he hits me instead. He smells like an abandoned fridge, his breath stinks of rot. What he does to me is horrible. I don't want to think about it, I won't think about it. There's a tent and cooking stuff on the ground, but half the time we're up a tree with the gun. There's a big plank platform and a tarpaulin roped to the branches above. At night he pulls the rope ladder up after us. It's quite high, you can see for miles. He uses the platform for storing stuff he brings back from his mugging expeditions. I'm surrounded by tins of baked beans.

3rd October 2040

M can't seem to get through the day without at least two blow jobs. I'm always sick afterwards (sometimes during).

8th October 2040

M beat me up yesterday. I'd tried to escape. I shan't do that again, he's too fast.

14th October 2040

If we run out of beans I think he might kill me for food. There were warnings about it on the news a while back. This one wouldn't think twice. I'm just meat on legs to him. He bit me all over last night, hard. I'm covered in bite marks. I was literally licking my wounds afterwards when I remembered how nice the taste of blood is, how I miss it. Strength. Calves' liver for iron. How I haven't had a period for ages. When that thought popped out I missed a beat. Then my blood ran cold.

15th October 2040

Wasn't it juniper berries they used to use? As in gin? Even if it was I wouldn't know what they looked like, I only remember mint and basil. I can't be pregnant. I won't be pregnant.

17th October 2040
Very sick after drinking rank juice off random stewed herbs. Nothing else, though, worse luck.

20th October 2040
Can't sleep. Dreamed of G, I was moving against him, it started to go up a little way so I thought he wasn't really dead. Dreadful waking to find M there instead.

23rd October 2040
Can't sleep. Very bruised and scratched after today. They used to throw themselves downstairs to get rid of it. The trouble is, the gravel pit just wasn't deep enough, plus the bramble bushes kept breaking my fall. There was some sort of body down there too, seething with white vermin. Maybe it was a goat or a pig or something, but I don't think it was. I keep thinking it might have been G.

31st October 2040
This baby will be the death of me. Would. Let's make that a conditional. 'Would', not 'will'.

7th November 2040
It's all over. I'm still here. Too tired to

8th November 2040
Slept for hours. Stronger. I've got all the food and drink, and the gun. There's still some shouting from down there but it's weaker now. I think he's almost finished.

9th November 2040
Slept for hours. Fever gone. Baked beans for breakfast. More groans started up just now. Never mind. I can wait.

10th November 2040
It's over. I got stuck into his bottle of vodka, it was the demon drink that saved me. He was out mugging – left me up the tree as usual – I drank just enough to raise my courage. Nothing else had worked so I thought I'd get

him to beat me up. When he came back and saw me waving the bottle he was beside himself. I pretended to be drunker than I was and I lay down on the wooden platform with my arms round my head while he got the boot in. It worked. Not right away, but that night.

Meanwhile M decided he fancied a drink himself, and very soon he'd polished off the rest of it – more than three-quarters of a bottle. He was singing and sobbing and carrying on, out of his tree with alcohol, and then, when he was standing pissing off the side of the platform, I crept along and gave him a gigantic shove and he really was out of his tree. Crash.

13th November 2040
I've wrapped your remains in my good blue shirt; sorry I couldn't let you stay on board, but there's no future now for any baby above ground. I'm the end of the line!

This is the last page of my thirtieth birthday present. When I've finished it I'll wrap the notebook up in six plastic bags, sealing each one with duct tape against the rain, then I'll bury it in a hole on top of the blue shirt. I don't know why as I'm not mad enough to think anybody will ever read it. After that I'm going to buckle on this rucksack of provisions and head north with my gun. Wish me luck. Last line: good luck, good luck, good luck, good luck, good luck.

Tom Vowler

There Are New Birthdays Now

Mary called up that his coffee was going cold, that he should leave before the roads snarled up. He opened the boys' door, allowing the room's scent to grace him for a moment before going downstairs.

'Did you sleep at all?' his wife said.

'A little. Did they get off alright?'

'Of course.'

'And they know you're picking them up if I'm late back?'

'Yes.'

'And they know to wait inside?'

'Ben…'

'Sorry.'

'You should have some food before the drive. I made a flask.'

He wanted the car to be older and smaller. It reeked of family. Of a secure, contented nuclear family, which he supposed they were. Stopping at a service station he detached the child seats, placing them out of sight in the boot. She might not even see the car but doing it brought comfort.

After they'd separated he still saw his first wife regularly. Meetings with police, a counsellor they saw together before finding their own. There'd also been contact whenever something went wrong in her life. Small things: a burst pipe, which he went round to fix; some problem neighbours. Other times he'd just be summoned and they'd sit there in swollen silence until he felt able to leave. But when he told her he'd met someone, there was nothing. Certain dates would bring silent phone calls, which he assumed were her, while Mary laughed them off as wrong numbers. It was when their cat went missing that they decided to move. No reference to anything, no accusations, just that a clean start away from it all would be good. Barely anyone was told: family, a few friends. They scuttled away, unnoticed.

When the calls began again two weeks ago, he supposed she'd found them. Wasn't difficult these days, personal details strewn across the internet if you knew where to look. And then a letter, oddly warm, asking to meet. Her address was different, he saw. (It surprised him she stayed in the house as long as she did.) He considered ignoring it, or sending a polite reply without Mary knowing. But they'd said at the start: no secrets.

The letter hadn't asked for a response, offering instead a place and time to meet, a coffee shop near their old address. He couldn't place it, guessing one of the old bookshops had perished. You can't miss it, she assured him. The postscript said she knew he'd come.

'What do you think she wants?' Mary had asked.

'I don't know.'

'Surely anything could have been said in the letter.'

'It's probably nothing.'

'Why now, after all this time? Why that day?'

He paused. 'It would have been her birthday.' The tense confused Mary for a moment, before her face softened and she came and sat next to him, taking his hand.

'I didn't think. Which one?'

He looked upwards, calculating. 'Sixteenth.'

The birth of the boys had almost expunged the date from his mind, to the extent that he'd often notice it only once it had passed. For the first couple of years he and Jan had acknowledged the day, making a cake they never ate, perusing photo albums until it became too painful. But there were new birthdays now. For him, at least.

'Will you go?' Mary had asked.

'Yes.'

The roundabout confused him; it hadn't been there before. Traffic was now sent alongside the river through what had been wasteland. Nothing remained of the gorse that had been searched so meticulously, the line of men and women on their hands and knees striking him as absurd now. They found nothing, save a child's shoe that wasn't hers.

The letter had said that she still didn't drive, that if he could come to her it would be better. Public transport could have taken her anywhere of course, somewhere benign, but she wanted him to return and he had no desire to negotiate.

Driving along the High Street he wondered whether people would be familiar. It had been eight years but he knew the faces in small towns changed little. He welcomed the anonymity of the car and hoped the coffee shop would be quiet; it had been so long since he'd been recognised by strangers and he cared little for it. Occasionally a journalist picked up the story on an anniversary or when something similar happened elsewhere – they were still worthy of a feature if not news. It's why he took Mary's name when they married, to stop the double takes when you filled in a form or introduced yourself. And it wasn't fair on the boys to be labelled. To have a surname that was ghostly.

At first there'd been nothing but sympathy, attempts to share the grief. How could this have happened? they said. But then slowly, when nothing was found and time bellowed with the absence of news, the glare turned inwards, towards them. Disapproval appeared on faces. Questions reverberated from pockets of gossiping neighbours. How could they be so careless? Had they been drinking? Blame began to shift from some unseen stranger towards them. People needed their object of hate to have substance. Perhaps they even had something to do with it, the subtext.

He parked in a quiet terraced street, found a meter and put money in for two hours, wondering if this was too much or too little.

It was right where she said, a trendy frontage boasting exotic teas and organic juices. He was grateful the door didn't have a bell or rattle on opening. A few people were scattered about, their sum proving neither busy nor quiet. He weaved through them, avoiding eye contact, and ordered a latte. A cursory sweep showed no sign of her, no singly-occupied tables, so he sat in the corner seat.

It occurred to him to turn his phone off and as he did someone approached from the side.

'Hello, Ben.' His ex-wife stood there, bottle of beer in hand.

'Jan. I didn't see you when I came in.'

'Nipped out for a smoke. Can you believe we have to huddle round outside these days, like some underclass?'

'I gave up,' he said.

She sat down opposite him, moving the menu to one side. 'Let's have a good look at you,' she said, sitting back.

He'd been anxious their conversation would not be private, but there appeared enough space and background music between them and the nearest occupied table.

Ben's first thought was how she'd aged, how she looked ten, maybe more, years older than Mary, despite being younger by a year.

'How are you, Jan?'

'I'm alright. You look well. How's what's her name?'

'Mary.'

'Such a pretty name, I always thought. You did well.'

'She's good. How about you, did you ever…?'

'Ha. Take a look, Ben. The years haven't exactly been kind.' If this was an invitation to be contrary, he didn't take it.

Her hair – flecked with grey, its lustre gone – was drawn back tightly so that the blanched skin gave her face a cold leanness. Her features appeared taut, as if gripping the anguish that had penetrated them; even a forced smile drew attention to the perennial grief around it. Ben had kept no photographs when they moved, not of Jan anyway, and he found it hard to conjure up an image of the woman he'd once loved.

'Life been kind to you, Ben?'

'I'm OK.'

'Nothing much changes here. Same old, same old.'

He thought of something to say, telling himself it was bound to be awkward.

'Dad died last year,' Jan continued.

'I'm sorry.'

'The stress didn't help, they said. And the fags.'

'Your mother still…?'

'She'll go on forever. Longer than us, I reckon. Yours?'

'Good, yeah, they're good.'

A silence gathered, Jan's unblinking eyes fixed on his.

'Are you going to have another drink?' he asked.

He'd barely sat back down when Jan said: 'You had any more, then?' Her words should have been absurd absent of context, yet he understood.

'Children?'

'No, heart attacks. Course children.'

He looked down, trying to formulate a response.

'It's okay,' she said. 'I don't mind.'

Looking up, he nodded. 'Two,' he said, before quickly adding: 'Boys.'

'How old?'

'Three and five.'

She stared at him expectantly, as if he hadn't finished. 'Do they have names?'

'Max. Max and Peter.'

'Got any pictures?'

'No,' he lied.

'Bet they look just like their father.' He swilled the last of his coffee around, watching keenly the frothy patterns it made. 'Do you still think about her, Ben?'

'Of course.'

'She's still alive, you know.'

'Jan...'

'Ask me how I know.'

'How?' he said, wearily.

'A mother does. I'd know if something happened to her. No, she'll be meeting a boy tonight somewhere, in some hot place, a birthday dinner. He'll be shy, not pushy. He'll offer to pay but she won't let him, so they go halves. It's her first real date. Just getting into boys she is. Won't hand it to them on a plate.'

Ben thought it pointless to say that, were she alive, she'd have a new birthday now. A date plucked from the air, maybe a year or more wrong. That was the best scenario, that whoever took her did so out of a yearning emptiness, to replace a loss of their own. That somehow she'd been taken out of the country and had given love to another couple. The police had always maintained this was unlikely.

'Why did you want to meet, Jan?'

'I thought we could go for a walk.'

As a child Ben had always lost things: dinner money, inhalers, a watch his parents had bought him. He remembered not quite believing his eyes at first, thinking that Jan had brought her in even though he knew she hadn't. Or that the hydrangeas were obscuring his view, even though it was late autumn and both were near bare. There was a bird, a song thrush maybe, where she should have been, alertly hopping around her doll as it foraged. The police kept asking how long the gap was between seeing her and not, but it was impossible to say. Five, six minutes. No more than ten. One of them, the older of the two, smiled warmly while his colleague remained impassive as he took notes. These roles changed little over the weeks and months, especially when difficult questions, as they called them, had to be put. There was just a bird, Ben kept saying.

He knew immediately where they were going. He could have refused, chosen not to indulge her, but part of him, the piece lured by atonement, drove him on.

'For years,' Jan said, 'before I moved, I'd look out a window and see someone taking pictures. Not just press: ordinary people, like tourists, wanting to see the garden, the house, as if it was a pilgrimage or something.'

'I don't remember that.'

'You went straight back to work, hid in your office.'

'It seemed better to get on with things. I felt powerless at home.'

They crossed West Park Road, heading past the two pubs he hadn't gone in again. The streets were quiet; occasional passers-by made him lower his head. He noticed Jan held hers high, sucking hard on a cigarette.

'A young couple bought it. He ran his own business, I think he said. Can't remember about her. They knew of course, you could tell. I made tea as they were shown around and I could feel their tension as they walked about in silence upstairs. It's nice to think someone else is using it.'

'The house?'

'Her room. It was empty for so long. Rooms need people in them.'

'How do you know it's not empty now?'

'I watched them. They had a daughter; she'll be five, no six. Lovely fair hair…'

'Christ, Jan.'

'I know, it's strange, isn't it? Given what happened. You remember the bus stop by the alleyway? You can stand there and see right up the garden and nobody thinks anything of it. It's where they would have watched from.'

There had been no witnesses. Nobody saw a thing but it was assumed the person or people went up the alley, perhaps a car with its engine running waiting on Eliot Road.

As they neared the house Ben expected a terror to grip him, but in some sense he felt like one of the tourists, taking a macabre peek at the scene of the crime, as if it had happened to someone else.

'You over the other side of town now, I see,' he said.

'I would have stayed but the mortgage...'

'Why would you want to stay?'

'For when she comes back. How would she know where to go?'

They rounded the corner and he could see the driveway. Jan led them to the bus stop where fortunately nobody was waiting.

'What if a bus comes?'

'We wave it on.'

As they got there Ben looked along the alley. Litter-strewn, occasional graffiti, it seemed the epitome of commonplace, yet it was a portal to another world. He scoured the banal fascias of the houses in each direction. All those windows and front gardens. All those families. How had nobody seen anything?

He noticed there was a car in the drive.

'Oh, they'll be in,' Jan said. 'He works from home now; she finishes at one.'

'We should go.'

'One of them walks to school at ten past three.'

'Jan, please.'

'If it's raining she drives. Lazy really, given the distance.'

'They'll see us looking.'

'I would have walked, if, you know...'

'I'm going, Jan.'

'They've redecorated her room. It's violet now. New lampshade, too.'

He forced himself to look up at the front of their old house. It looked both the same and different. The sash windows now plastic. The silver birch gone. But still the same.

'You'd think they'd have put a fence up or something,' said Jan. 'You know, case lightning strikes twice.'

For a moment he was aware of the sound of Jan's words but not their meaning. His shirt, sodden with sweat, clung to his back. He thought he might be sick.

'We always left her in the garden for a few minutes,' he heard himself saying. 'People did.'

'I like what they've done with the beds. We always neglected the front.'

'No way it was more than ten minutes.'

'They fixed those loose tiles, too. Look.'

'You could have checked from an upstairs window. You knew she was outside as well.'

'Come on, Ben. You knew I was busy. You were watching her.'

He looked at Jan. For all her torment she spoke with a calmness that suggested insanity. Not the frenzied madness of that time, when she'd scream and scratch and spit at him. But a cold detachment from reality, a sort of dementia. She was right though: he'd known she was busy.

'Are you crying, Ben? Don't cry, it's her birthday.'

Driving back he tried to keep out thoughts of his daughter. Unlike Jan, Ben's image of her never aged, never grew up; she remained frozen in time, a face on a hundred posters. For most, he thought, death is cruel in its haste, rarely warning of its arrival, certainty its only compensation. But death revealed itself to them in episodes, and then never fully. It would linger above them, festering for days and weeks, its presence threatening to engulf them, before vanishing, swept away by ephemeral hope. The sightings all came to nothing though, and in the end he'd chosen to welcome its return.

And now he preferred to think of that time as a novel he'd read. You had to put things in boxes.

Mary smiled through the living room window as he pulled into the drive, the diffuse light behind her giving his wife an ethereal, haloed quality. She had been his saviour at a time when he sought life's ordinariness, when mundanity was sacred. He thought of how he'd entered her life with such a public narrative: like everyone else she'd followed the story on television, in the papers, from the appeals and press conferences. It was baggage and yet he brought nothing tangible – no maintenance orders, no access disputes, no weekend visits. There was nothing that bound him to his first marriage other than the power of an event.

Years passed before Mary had broached the subject of a family, her patience with him as profound as her belief in his innocence. 'There's no rush,' she'd said. At times she would quietly point out when his obsessive desire to protect the boys, to cocoon them, became overzealous, damaging.

He pictured Jan standing at the bus stop year after year, watching happiness play out in others, a new life seemingly beyond her. Her reaction on hearing about the boys was so understated that he considered if somehow she had known. Perhaps their old house wasn't the only place she watched. He would talk to Mary about moving again. Further away this time.

He'd hugged Jan as they parted and she'd held on longer than him, for a moment belying her blithe tone. He had never asked her forgiveness and now never would.

'What do you want?' he'd said, wondering if today was an end of it.

'A family, Ben. Same as you, that's all.'

He opened the front door and called up to the boys that he was home.

Tessa Hadley

Married Love

Lottie announced that she was getting married.

This was at the breakfast table at her parents' house one weekend. The kitchen in that house was upstairs, its windows overlooking the garden below. It was a tall, thin, old house, comfortably untidy, worn to fit the shape of the family. The summer morning was rainy, so all the lights were on, the atmosphere close and dreamy, perfumed with toast and coffee.

–Whatever for? Lottie's mother Hattie said, and carried on reading her book. She was an English teacher, but she read crime novels at weekends: this one was about a detective in Venice.

Lottie was nineteen, but she looked more like thirteen or fourteen. She was just over five feet tall, with a tight little figure and a barrel chest; she insisted on wearing the same glasses with thick black frames that she had chosen years earlier, and her hair, the colour of washed–out straw, was pulled into pigtails.

Everyone happened to be at home that weekend, even Lottie's older brother Rufus and her sister Em, who had both moved away.

–Have you got a boyfriend at last? Em asked.

Lottie was always pale, with milky translucent skin behind a ghostly arc of freckles across her snub nose, but she seemed to be even whiter than usual that morning, blue veins standing out at her temples; she clenched her hands on either side of the place mat in front of her. They were improbable hands for a violinist: pink and plump, with short blunt fingers and bitten cuticles.

–You're not taking me seriously! she cried.

A squall of rain urged against the steamed-up window panes, the kettle boiled, toast sprang from the toaster for no one in particular. Vaguely, they all looked at her, thinking their own thoughts. Lottie emanated intensity; her personality was like a demon trapped inside a space too small. Even as a baby she had been preternaturally perceptive and judgemental. Her talent for the violin, when it was discovered, had seemed an explanation for her surplus strength, or a solution to it; she had begun on an instrument so tiny that it looked like a Christmas-tree decoration. Now she was living with her parents while she studied for her music degree at the university.

–Why ever would you want to get married? Hattie said reasonably. – Dad and I have never felt the need.

–I'm not like you, Lottie said.

This was one of her battle cries.

–Of course, you're not like anybody, sweetheart. You're just yourself.

–For a start, I happen to have religious beliefs. I believe that marriage is a holy sacrament.

–No, you don't, Rufus said. –You've never said anything about them before.

–So when, exactly, are you getting married? Em asked sceptically. –And who to?

–How could I possibly know yet when? That's exactly what I want to talk to you about. I want to sort out a date. I want you all to be there. I want it to be a proper wedding. With a dress and everything. And bridesmaids, probably.

–So you have got a boyfriend! Em said.

Em was gracefully loose-jointed, with her mother's hooded, poetic eyes; she worked in the toxicology department of the city hospital.

–My husband, he's going to be.

Hattie put down her book and her coffee mug in concern. –Poppet, you're so young. There's no hurry about the marrying part. Of course, you can have a proper wedding one day if that's what you want, but there's no need to rush into anything.

Sullen white dents appeared in Lottie's cheeks where her jaw was set. –You forget that I have a whole life of my own now, as an adult, outside of this house, about which you know nothing, absolutely nothing. You don't warn Emily not to rush into anything.

–To be fair, Em said, –I'm not the one who just said I was getting married.

–Have we met him? Hattie asked. –Is he on your course?

–Is it the one with the stammer in your string quartet? asked Noah, Lottie's younger brother, who was still at school. –Tristan?

–How could you think I'd want to marry Tristan?

–Personally, I'd warn against anyone in a string quartet, Rufus said.

–Shut up, Rufus. It isn't anything to do with Tristan.

–So what's his name, then? Noah persisted.

Duncan, the children's father, arrived from his morning ritual with the *Guardian* in the bathroom upstairs. He was shorter than Hattie, stocky, densely and neatly made, with a wrinkled, ugly, interesting head; she was vague and languid, elegant, beginning to be faded. He taught special-needs kids at a local comprehensive, though not the same one where Hattie taught. –What is whose name? Alarm took flight in Hattie. –Lottie, darling, you're not pregnant, are you?

–I just don't believe this family, Lottie wailed. –There's something horrible about the way your minds work.

–Because if you're pregnant we can deal with that. It doesn't mean that you have to get married.

–Is she pregnant? Duncan asked.

–Of course I'm not.

–She says she's going to get married.

–Whatever for?

–Also that she has religious beliefs, all of a sudden.

This seemed to bother Rufus more than the marrying. He was an ironic pragmatist; he worked as a research analyst for the Cabinet Office.

–The reason, Lottie said, –is that I've met someone quite different from anyone I've ever known before, different from any of you. He's a great man. He's touched my life, and transformed it. I'm lucky he even noticed I exist.

She had a gift of vehemence, the occasional lightning flash of vision so strong that it revealed to others, for a moment, the world as it was from her perspective.

–And who is he? Em asked her, almost shyly.

–I'm not going to tell you now, Lottie said. –Not after this. Not yet.

–When you say 'great man', her father considered, –I get the feeling that you're not talking about one of your fellow students.

Hattie saw what he meant, after gaping at him for half a second. –One of your teachers! Is it? Lottie, blinking behind her glasses, turned her round white face toward her mother, precarious, defiant.

–Does this teacher know that you feel this way about him?

–You seriously think I'm making it all up? I told you, he loves me. He's going to marry me.

Duncan wondered if it wasn't Edgar Lennox. –He's some kind of High Anglican, isn't he? I believe he writes religious music.

–And so? Lottie challenged. –If it was him?

–Oh, no! Hattie stood up out of her chair, uncharacteristically guttural, almost growling. That's out of the question. Edgar Lennox. That's just not thinkable, in any way, shape, or form.

–I hate it when you use that phrase, Lottie shouted, standing up, too. –Way, shape, or form. It's so idiotic. It's exactly the sort of thing you would say. It just goes to show your mediocrity.

–Let's try to talk about this calmly, Duncan said.

Edgar Lennox was old enough to be Lottie's grandfather. Forty years older than she was, Hattie shrieked; later, it turned out to be more like forty-five. His already being married, to his second wife, was only a minor difficulty compared with this. Duncan and Hattie had met him twice: once when they went to the university open day with Lottie, and once before that, at a private view of paintings by one of Hattie's friends. He had seemed at the time Hattie's ideal of an elderly creative artist: tall, very thin, with a shock of upstanding white hair, a face whose hollows seemed to have been carved out by suffering, tanned skin as soft as leather, a charcoal-grey linen shirt.

–When you say he's touched your life, could we be quite specific about this? Duncan said. –Has he actually, in the ordinary, non-transcendent sense of the word, touched you?

Em protested in disgust. –Dad, you can't ask her that!

Em had been crying; her eyelids were swollen and puffy, and her face was blotched. Hattie's and Lottie's eyes were hot and dry.

Hattie turned on him. –How can you put it like that? How could you make it into one of your clever remarks?

–If you're asking, Lottie said, –whether we've consummated our relationship, then, yes, of course we have. What do you think we are? We're lovers.

–Naturally, I'm making a formal complaint to the university, Hattie said. –He'll lose his job. There's no question about that.

–That'll be sensible, won't it? Em said. –Then if they are married he won't be able to support her.

–You're sure she isn't making all this up? Rufus suggested.

–Think what you like, Lottie said. –You'll soon know.

She sat with her mouth primly shut, shining with a tragic light. Beyond the kitchen windows, veils of rain drove sideways into the sodden skirts of the horse chestnut tree, darkening the pink flowers. Hattie said that the whole thing reminded her of when she was at art college, and a friend of hers had heard suddenly that her sister was on the point of entering a convent, a closed order that allowed no contact with family or friends.

–We all piled onto a train and went up to Leeds together on the spur of the moment, six or seven of us who were close then, and met this sister in a tea shop, and tried to convince her of everything in the world that was worth staying for.

–Don't be ridiculous, Mum. I'm not going into a convent.

–Did it work? Noah asked. –Did you convince her?

Hattie frowned and pressed her knuckles to her forehead. –I can't remember whether she went into the convent or not in the end. Perhaps she did. I can only remember the tea shop, and after that a pub, and trying to think of all the things we couldn't bear to leave behind, and getting gradually drunker and drunker.

–This isn't the same thing, Duncan said firmly. –And we aren't at anything like that stage yet, anyway.

Lottie stared at them in genuine bewilderment. –I don't understand you all, she said. –How can you not want for me what I want?

Noah saw his parents leave the house late in the evening. His bedroom was in the attic, he was sitting on the sill of his little casement window, his feet in the lead-lined gutter that ran like a trough the length of the Georgian terrace, looking down over the stone parapet into the street, four storeys below. Though it was strictly forbidden, he had liked to sit this way ever since he was given this bedroom when he was eight; he used to fit into the small space perfectly, but now he had to squeeze, and his knees were jack-knifed up in front of his face. Rain was sluicing down the slate roof into the gutter. In the light of the street lamps, the road shone black; parked cars were plastered with wet leaves from the beeches and horse chestnuts in the muddy triangle of public garden opposite. His mother's high heels scraped fiercely in the empty street as she crossed to the car: she must have dressed up in her teaching clothes for the occasion. She was hanging on tightly to the strap of the bag slung over her shoulder. She and Duncan dithered around the car under the half-globes of their umbrellas, probably quarrelling about who should drive; they seemed as small as dolls from where he watched. He supposed they were going to try to find Edgar Lennox at his house; they had been calling him on the phone all day, without getting through. It was strange to think of the two households, more or less unknown to each other before tonight, connected by this drama, awake in the city when everyone else was getting ready for sleep.

Hours later – he wasn't sure how many hours, as he'd fallen asleep at his desk while revising for the geography G.C.S.E. exam he had on Monday morning – Noah woke to the sound of his mother's voice in the house again. She sounded like she did when she'd had too much wine at parties: rash and loud, extravagantly righteous. He went out to listen, leaning over the banister and sliding noiselessly down, a few steps at a time. The steep and narrow staircase, the core of the skinny house, drew sound upward. Above his head, an ancient skylight as wide as the stairwell rattled under the rain, leaking into a strategically placed bucket. His parents and Rufus and Em were crowded at the foot of the stairs, in the hallway's jumble of boots and bikes and baskets, junk mail, umbrellas dripping on the grey and white tiles. His mother still had her fawn mac on.

–I thought he'd be ashamed, she was saying, –if I told him that Lottie was marrying him because she thinks he's a great man. But it was obvious that he thinks he is one, too.

–Is he one? Rufus asked.

–Don't be ridiculous. What would he be doing teaching in a second–rate music department at a provincial university?

–I thought you said the department was something wonderful.

–That was before this.

–He does some film and television work if he can get it, Duncan said. All fairly high-toned. And he writes for the cathedral choir. Anyway, greatness wouldn't necessarily make him any better, as far as Lottie's concerned.

–He said that he could see how it must look from our point of view, from what he called 'any ordinary perspective'.

144

–How dare he think we're ordinary? Em raged.

–He said that the erotic drive was a creative force he felt he had to submit to.

–Oh, yuck! Hideous!

–Hattie, he didn't say that, exactly.

–And what was his wife like? Was she there? What's her name?

–Valerie. Val, he calls her. She was frosty. She said, 'Whatever happens, I keep this house,' as if that were something we were after. The house wasn't what you'd expect, anyway, not arty: stuffy and old-fashioned. I should think the wife's about my age, but she's let herself go – grey ponytail, no make-up, one of those girlish dowdy skirts with an elastic waistband.

–She was fierce, Duncan said. –I'd have been frightened of her, in his shoes.

–She wouldn't sit down; she stood up with her back against the wall, as if she were mounting guard over something. All she said was that Lottie would soon learn. They have a son, about the same age as Noah.

–Did she know about it all already?

–She hadn't known for long – he'd just told her. She'd been crying.

–We walked in on it all. We were the aftershock.

–Where is Lottie, anyway?

–It has to run its course, Duncan said. –We're not in a position to prevent anything.

–It can't be allowed to run its course, Duncan! What if they actually went through with this crazy wedding?

He groaned consolingly. –She's an adult – she's nineteen. Worse things happen at sea.

Noah turned and saw that Lottie was standing in her nightdress on the stairs just behind him. She put her finger to her lips; her eyes behind her glasses were black pits. She was shaken with waves of violent trembling, gripping the bannister to steady herself, probably because she had swallowed too many of the caffeine tablets she claimed she was addicted to; and no doubt also because she was exalted and frightened at her ability to raise this storm in adult lives. Noah felt a familiar irritation with her exaggerations, mixed with protectiveness. He and Lottie had grown up very close, adrift from the rest of the family in their bedrooms in the attic. He knew how passionately she succumbed to the roles she dreamed up for herself. She won't be able to get out of this one, he thought. She can't stop now.

The wedding was held in a registry office, with a blessing at a church afterwards; Edgar insisted on the Elizabethan prayer book and the Authorized Version of the Bible. He composed, for the occasion, a setting for Spenser's 'Epithalamion' and one of his students sang it at the reception, which was in a sixteenth-century manor house with a famous garden that belonged to the university. Hattie refused to have anything to do with it all; she shut herself in at home with her detective novels. Noah drank a lot and befriended Edgar's son, Harold, who had floppy pale hair and a choral scholarship at a cathedral school; he jumped like a shot bird if anyone spoke to him unexpectedly.

Emily said that Lottie's white suit looked like a child's nurse outfit – all it needed was a sewn-on red cross. Lottie was wearing contact lenses, and without her glasses her face seemed weakly, blandly expectant. A white flower fastened behind her ear slid gradually down her cheek during the course of the afternoon until it was bobbing against her chin. She clung to Edgar with uncharacteristic little movements, touching at his hand with her fingertips, dropping her forehead to rest against his upper arm while he spoke, or throwing back her head to gaze into his face.

–It won't last, Duncan reassured his other children.

To Edgar's credit, he seemed sheepish under the family's scrutiny, and did his best to jolly Lottie along, circulating with her arm tucked into his, playing the gentle public man, distinguished in his extreme thinness, his suit made out of some kind of rough grey silk. You would have picked him out in any gathering as subtle and thoughtful and well informed. But there weren't really quite enough people at the reception to make it feel like a success: the atmosphere was constrained; the sun never came out from behind a mottled thick lid of cloud. After the drink ran out and the students had melted away, too much dispiriting white hair seemed to show up in the knots of guests remaining, like snow in the flower beds. Duncan overheard someone, sotto voce, refer to the newlyweds as 'Little Nell and her grandfather'.

Valerie phoned Lottie a week or so after the wedding to ask whether she knew that Edgar had tried the same thing the year before with the student who had sung at the reception, a tall beautiful black girl with a career ahead of her: she'd had the sense to tell him where to go. –To fuck off, Valerie enjoyed enunciating precisely, as if she hadn't often used that word. Everyone knew about this because Valerie had also telephoned Hattie. When Hattie asked Lottie about it, Lottie only made one of her horrible new gestures, folding her hands together and letting her head droop, smiling secretively into her lap. –It's all right, Mum, she said. –He tells me everything. We don't have secrets. Soraya is an exceptional, gifted young woman. I love her, too.

Hattie hated the way every opinion Lottie offered now seemed to come from both of them: we like this, we always do that, we don't like this. They didn't like supermarkets; they didn't like Muzak in restaurants; they didn't like television costume dramas. As Duncan put it, they generally found that the modern world came out disappointingly below their expectations. Hattie said that she wasn't ready to have Edgar in her house yet.

The university agreed that it was acceptable for Lottie to continue with her studies, as long as she didn't take any of Edgar's classes; but of course he carried on working with her on her violin playing. Her old energy seemed to be directed inward now; she glowed with the promise of her future. She grew paler than ever, and wore her hair loose, and bought silky indeterminate dresses at charity shops. Hattie saw her unexpectedly from behind once and thought for a moment that her own daughter was a stranger, a stumpy little child playing on the streets in clothes from a dressing-up box. Edgar and Lottie were renting a flat not far from Hattie and Duncan: tiny, with an awful galley kitchen and the landlord's furniture, but filled with music. Edgar had to pay about half his salary to Valerie to cover his share of the mortgage on the house and the part of Harold's schooling that wasn't paid for by the scholarship, so he and Lottie were pretty hard up, but at first they carried this off, too, as if it were a sign of something rare and fine.

–God knows what they eat, Hattie said. –Lottie doesn't know how to boil an egg. Probably Edgar doesn't know how to boil one, either. I'll bet he's had women running round him all his life.

Noah reported that they often had Chinese takeaway.

Then Lottie began to have babies. Familiarity had just started to silt up around the whole improbable idea of her and Edgar as a couple – high-minded, humourless, poignant in their unworldliness – when everything jolted onto this new track. Three diminutive girls arrived in quick succession, and life at Lottie and Edgar's, which had seemed to drift with eighteenth-century underwater slowness, snapped into noisy, earthy and chaotic contemporaneity. Lottie in pregnancy was as swollen as a beach ball; afterwards she never recovered her neat boxy little figure, or that dreamily submissive phase of her personality. She became bossy, busy, cross; she abandoned her degree. She chopped off her hair with her own scissors, and mostly wore baggy tracksuit bottoms and T-shirts. Their tiny flat was submerged under packs of disposable nappies, cots, toys, washing, nursing bras and breast pads, a playpen, books on babies, books for babies. The tenant below them left in disgust, and they moved downstairs for the sake of the extra bedroom. As soon as the girls could toddle, they trashed Edgar's expensive audio equipment. He had to spend more and more time in his room at the university, anyway – he couldn't afford to turn down any commissions. Now Lottie spoke with emotion only about her children and about money.

The girls were all christened, but Lottie was more managerial than rapt during the ceremonies: Had everyone turned up who had promised? (Rufus wouldn't.) Was Noah capturing the important moments on his video camera? Why was Harold in a mood? With the fervour of a convert to practicality, she planned her days and steered through them. Duncan taught her to drive and she bought a battered old Ford Granada, unsubtle as a tank, and fitted it with child seats, ferrying the girls around from nursery to swimming to birthday parties to baby gym. She was impatient if anyone tried to turn the conversation around to art or music, unless it was Tiny Tots ballet. She seemed to be carrying around, under the surface of her intolerant contempt for idleness, a burning unexpressed message about her used-up youth, her put-aside talent.

–She ought to be abashed, Hattie said once. –We warned her. Instead, she seems to be angry with us.

Hattie had been longing for early retirement but she decided against it, fearing that the empty days might only fill up with grandchildren. She believed that in the mirror she could see the signs in her face – like threads drawn tight – of the strain of those extra years of teaching she had not wanted.

–Poor old Lottie, Duncan said.

–Lottie isn't old. Poor Edgar.

At weekends, Duncan sometimes came home to find Edgar taking refuge at his kitchen table, drinking tea while the children made scones or collages with Hattie. Edgar didn't do badly with them, considering, but it could take him three quarters of an hour to get all three little girls stuffed into coats and mittens and boots and pushchairs, ready to go. Physically, he was rather meticulous and pedantic. If Lottie was with him, she would push his fine long fingers brusquely aside and take over the zipping and buttoning. –Here, let me do it, she'd snap. To his credit, Edgar didn't seem to resent the intrusion of the babies into his life, or even to be wiped out by them, exactly: he gave himself over to their existence with a kind of bemused wonder. He drew himself down to their level, noticing everything they noticed, becoming involved in their childish chatter and speculation as Lottie didn't have time to be. They adored him – they ran to cling to his legs whenever their mummy was cross. Edgar's appearance was diminished, though, from what it had once been: his white hair had thinned and was cut shorter and lay down more tamely on his head; his clothes were the ordinary dull things anyone could buy in a supermarket. Hattie realised with surprise that it must have been Valerie who was behind the charcoal-grey linen shirts, the silk suits, the whole production of Edgar as exceptional and distinguished.

When Emily got pregnant with her first child, Lottie's youngest was nine months old and Charis, her eldest, was five. Lottie dumped black bags of used baby things on Emily one evening without warning. –Chuck them out if you don't want them, she said. –I've got no more use for them. I've had my tubes tied.

After he finished his degree, Noah went to London and found work intermittently as an assistant cameraman on small film projects. He dropped in at Lottie's whenever he came home, and they fell easily into their old companionable closeness. She fed him whatever awful mush she had cooked for tea. He was useful for swinging his nieces about and throwing them in the air, all the rough play that Edgar had to be careful of. Often, Edgar wasn't there; Noah assumed that he was working in his room at the university.

One summer evening, Noah was lying on his back on the floor in Lottie's front room. Two floor-length sash windows opened from this room onto a wrought-iron balcony; Lottie had made Edgar fix bars across, to stop the girls from getting out there. A warm incense of balsam poplar mingled with petrol fumes breathed from the street. They had drunk the bottle of wine that Noah had brought with their teatime mush; while they were giving the girls a bath, Lottie had produced triumphantly from the back of a cupboard a sticky bottle half full of Bacardi that nobody liked, and now they were drinking that, mixed with blackcurrant cordial because that was all she had. –We'll be horribly, pinkly sick, Lottie predicted. The girls were asleep at last. While Noah lay supine, Lottie crawled round him on her hands and knees, grunting with the effort, putting away in primary-coloured plastic boxes the primary-coloured toys that were strewn like strange manna all around the carpet.

–I'm grey, she complained. –My life's so grey.

–When does Edgar get back from work?

–Don't be thick, Noah. Ed's retired. The university couldn't keep on employing him forever. He's seventy-two this year. Why d'you think I've been going on to you about how hard up we are?

–Where is he, then?

–At Valerie's, I expect.

Noah opened his eyes in surprise, angling his head up from the floor to get a look at her. –Oh!

–That's where he usually is.

–Is that all right?

–Why shouldn't he? When we've been paying half the mortgage for all these years – at least that's finished at last, thank Christ. There's a room there where he can work; it's impossible here. And we don't have space for a piano. He still likes to write at a piano, before he puts it on the computer.

–So they get on OK, him and Valerie?

–She brings him coffee and plates of sandwiches while he's working. She unplugs the phone in the hall, in case it disturbs him. He plays things to her. I expect that sometimes while he's in the throes of composition he forgets he doesn't live there any more, in that quiet house.

–Mum said the house was old-fashioned.

–It is old-fashioned. Full of antiques, from Valerie's mother, but Valerie wouldn't know how to show them off. Valerie doesn't have a showing-off bone in her body. She's all complications. She's a gifted cellist, apparently, but she can't play in public.

–I suppose you've got to know her.

Lottie aimed bricks at a box. –Not in the face-to-face sense. Occasionally she and I do have to talk, about Harold's allowance or whatever.

–He doesn't still have an allowance?

–Not after we had the talk. On my wedding night, I tell you, it was like Bartók's *Bluebeard's Castle*. My metaphorical wedding night – I don't actually mean that one night in particular. Behind the first door, the torture chamber; behind the second door, a lake of tears, and so on. Behind the last door were his other wives, alive and well. Well, the first one isn't exactly alive, but I could tell you all about her.

–I'd forgotten there was a first one.

–Danish, actress, had problems with her abusive father, drank.

–He goes on about them?

–Not really. They're just his life – they crop up, as you can imagine. There's a lot of life behind him to crop up. Don't forget, once Valerie was the one he ran away with.

–I'd never thought of it like that.

–Were the babies my revenge? Poor Ed, I've nearly killed him.

Lottie lay down on the floor, head to toe with Noah, holding her glass on the soft mound of her stomach, tilting the viscous red drink backward and forward as she breathed.

–Do you know what I did the other week? I was so angry about something – can't remember what – that I drove up to the recycling depot with the babies in the back of the car to throw my violin into the skip for miscellaneous household waste.

Noah sat upright. –The one Mum and Dad bought for you? Didn't that cost loads of money? Thousands?

–I didn't actually do it. I looked down into the skip and got the violin out of the case to throw, and then I put it away again. Apart from anything else, I told myself, I could always sell it. And it's possible I might want to start again, when this is over. But probably I won't, ever.

–Is Edgar any good? Noah demanded drunkenly, suddenly aggressive. I mean, is his music really, actually any good?

–Noah, how can you ask that? You're not allowed to ask that.

Although Lottie protested, the question seemed intimately known to her, as if she had thrown herself too often against its closed door. –How can I judge? I can't tell. I think he's good. He's writing something at the moment, for strings. It'll get a premiere at the Festival. It's something new, different. Actually, I think it might be lovely.

Just then they heard Edgar's deliberate slow step on the stairs, his key in the door to the flat.

–He pretends this new piece is for me. But I know it's not about me.

Edgar stood squinting at them from the doorway, getting used to the light; his khaki hooded waterproof and stooped shoulders gave him, incongruously, the toughened, bemused aura of an explorer returned. Noah imagined how infantile he and Lottie must look, lying on the floor among the toys with their bright-red drinks, and how uninteresting youth must sometimes seem.

–We're finishing up that Bacardi, Ed, Lottie said, enunciating too carefully. –Do you want some?

Edgar's eyes these days had retreated behind his jutting cheekbones and sprouting eyebrows; something suave had gone out of his manner. He said that he would rather have a hot drink. Forgetfully he waited, as if he expected Lottie to jump up and make it for him. When he remembered after a moment, and went into the kitchen to do it himself, he didn't imply the least reproach; he was merely absorbed, as if his thoughts were elsewhere. Noah saw how hungrily from where she lay Lottie followed the ordinary kitchen music – the crescendo of the kettle, the chatter of crockery, the punctuation of cupboard doors, the chiming of the spoon in the cup – as if she might hear in it something that was meant for her.

Sarah Hall

Vuotjärvi

She stood on the pontoon and watched him swim out. His head above
the lake surface grew smaller and more distant. After a while he turned
and looked to the shore. His face was white and featureless. It eclipsed
as he turned away again and continued swimming. The water was sorrel-
coloured, with ruddy patches where the sun lit its depth. When they'd
arrived they had knelt on the wooden structure and examined cupped
handfuls, trying to discern what its suspension of particles or dye might
be. Peat perhaps. Some kind of mineral. The rich silt of the lakebed.
Evergreens lined the edge of the glinting mass. Beyond was a vast
Scandinavian sky that had, for the duration of their stay, failed to shed
its light completely at night. The humidity had surprised them, this far
north. The air was glutinous. The meadow grass and the barks glistened.
Locals complained that it was the worst year ever for mosquitoes. Spring
conditions had suited the larvae. They were everywhere now, whining in
the air, their legs floating long and dusty behind them. In the outhouse
there was no escaping. They seemed to rise invisibly from the walls, from
the chaff and sawdust covering the silage container below the hole. She
had rows of bites along her ankle bones, legs and arms. Each bite was
raised into a welt, but was not itchy.

Though there was electricity at the cottage, they had been carrying
buckets of the orange water up to wash plates and cups. A natural well was
being directed to the house, they had been informed, but the plumbing
was not yet complete. Two other cottages were tucked into the strong
greenery along the shoreline, painted red, shingled, their plots impeccable.
There was a pleasing folk-art look about them. Their inhabitants had not
been seen much. Wood smoke curled from the sauna sheds in the early
evening. The second night, while they'd been standing at the water's edge
observing the start of a vague, ineffectual sunset, two forms had exited
the nearest shed, made their way along a scythed path, and entered the

lake. She had waved to them. The Finnish neighbours had waved back, then swum round a pin-covered promontory, out of sight. There was a correctness here, a sensual formality, which she liked very much. *You must always take your shoes off inside*, the friend whose cousin had lent the cottage had said to them. *It's a particular thing.* Since arriving they had worn no shoes at all. Nor much clothing. The grass around the cottage had been softened by a rainstorm. She had woken during the first night to the purring of rain on the cottage roof.

Under the feet, against the tambour of pontoon planks, the lake slapped and knocked. He was three hundred years out or so. She could see that he was swimming breaststroke. His feet and hands barely broke the surface. He did not turn round again and his movements were slow and regular. His head grew smaller. He had decided to swim to an island in the middle of the lake and back again. It was perhaps a mile and a half together. He was a strong swimmer and she was not concerned. At home he went a long way up the rivers. She did not want to join him. She liked swimming, but not any great distance. She was happy to float on her back, her head submerged, listening to the somatic echo. Or she would crouch and unfold in the water, crouch and unfold. Or look down at her hands – two moon-white creatures in the rippling copper.

The lake was deep, but it was not cold. They had already rowed out in the little boat belonging to the cottage and dropped anchor and gone in where the shadows were expansive, the bottom no more than a black imagining. The temperature seemed almost indistinguishable from that of her blood, a degree or two cooler. He had held her waist as they kicked their legs, bringing her gently to him. His shoulders under the surface looked stained, tones of surgical disinfectant. His face was wet. There was a taste of iron when they kissed. Suddenly she had become breathless, from exertion, from the eroticism of their bodies drifting together, the memory of that morning's lovemaking, on their sides, discovering the fit of him behind her, that she should lean away slightly and tip her pelvis as if pouring water from it. That feeling of rapture, of flood, like being suspended.

Her fears had begun to coalesce. The lake depth was unknown and the pressure against her limbs was a trick: it felt no greater than in the shallows. Underneath was vestigial territory. Rotting vegetation. Benthic silence. The scale of her body in this place was terribly wrong. Something was reaching up, pulling down. Urgency to get out made her kick away to the boat, haul against the side and scramble over its rim. Once inside she had rested her head on the oarlock, breathing away the panic, amazed by the direness of the impulse. *Are you OK?* he'd called. *Oh God, for some reason I thought I should feel imperilled, and then I did,* she said. *What an idiot. Look at you. Calm as anything in there.* He acted out a frantic drowning, and she laughed.

She had rowed the boat back to the cottage while he lay against the prow and sunbathed, getting used to the rotation of the long thin oars, the lunge and drag. Soon the vessel began to skim through the water, and was easier to steer. They'd beached the boat, pulling it high up into the trees and looping the rope around a trunk, taking the bung out so the hull wouldn't fill if it rained again. Then they'd walked through the meadow to the cottage, through blooms of airborne pollen and ferrying insects, their shoulders sunburnt, hungry, in no rush to eat. The midday sky was an immense shale. When she lifted her arm her skin smelled of the lake, almost sexual, eel-like. All she had been able to think about was having him move behind her again, fractionally, his hand on her hip, until it was too much, or not enough, and he had to turn her against the bed, rest his weight on her, take hold of her neck, her hair, move harder.

A eucalypt scent. Pine resin. Spruce. The reeds behind her rustled. A breeze combed the lake surface, left it smooth for a moment, then came again. The pontoon rose and sank, instinctively, like a diaphragm. The pages of the book he had left next to his sunglasses and camera flickered. She picked it up. It was a speculative text about humanity's chances of extinction within the century. All the ways it might happen. Plague. Bio-terror. Asteroid impact. *Finland is the right place to read a book like this,* he'd joked as he began it on the plane. *They're such great survivalists. There's some kind of seed bank here, just in case we mess everything up. I think that's in Norway,* she had said. They had read dreadful sections out to each other over the last few days. *The twelve-day incubation period for smallpox means it could spread globally before an epidemic is declared, or contained. Aerosolising sarin is the terrorist's main challenge.* Most unpredictable were the colliders, the superviruses, strangelets. Dark matter.

She rocked up on her toes and strained to see his head, which was now a tiny brown spot, difficult to identify between the onshore waves. He must be two thirds of the way to the island. Soon she would see him climb the rocky shirt in front of the huddle of trees, and stand upright. Even at this distance, even minute, she would surely see him, once he was out. Her eyesight was good. He was tall. And he was naked. His pale form would contrast with the dark green hub of the island. He would probably rest for a time then set off back. She put the book down, under the camera.

He had decided to make the swim after they'd taken a sauna. The sauna hut was traditional in design, beautifully crafted. He'd prepared it, checked the tank, cleared away the old ashes and built a new fire under the stones, as instructed by the cousin. They had waited for the heat to intensify, then lain on the benches in the cedary fug, listening to the interior wood panelling click and creak. The heat was so dense they were immobilised, robbed of energy. They became soaked with perspiration, reaching out to touch each other with extreme effort. Finally, the situation felt forced, the environment unendurable. They bathed in the lake afterwards, and emerged refreshed. *Then he said he would try for the island. I think it'll take about forty-five minutes, or an hour. Photograph me coming back victorious.*

She could no longer see him in the water so she kept her eyes on the spot where she thought he would probably get out. The foliage mossed together the more she looked. Birds circled over the lake. A bird was calling nearby, within the forest, the notes hollow and looping, a song that did not seem diurnal. Now that she could no longer see him it was hard to remain focused. Her mind wandered. She thought about his sounds of arousal, surprise and relief as the soft obstruction yielded, finding a way inside, acute pleasure in those wet recurring motions, the stunned intervals. They were now experts in the act, which was a series of steady, humid acts. He was becoming more vocal. He would speak to her of what he desired. His assertions, his voice, worked her as if she were being touched. The world before and after was incredibly vivid.

The bird in the forest let up. The fluttering in her chest stopped.

She thought about the blue Arabia crockery they had seen in the antique market by the quay in Helsinki. The city's Russian architecture: the Uspenski cathedral with its golden domes and the sentinelled railway station. The quiet Finnish underlay, restraint and elegance, design that would always oppose corruption. Helsinki was attractive, a clean blend of modern and historic. It lacked people. The drive to the cottage had taken six hours, the arboreal view varying only slightly once outside the city. Road signs were impossible. It was a language so unexported the pronunciation could not even be guessed. It sounded similar to and was possibly rooted in the oldest human language, a cross-continental language, she had read. There were sixty thousand lakes. Theirs was called Vuotjärvi. It was situated between two bigger lakes, towards the dialect of Savo. The GPS unit had led them off the motorway, down minor roads, then along seventeen kilometres of gravel track, past glimmers of water, almost to their destination. The lane to the cottage was overgrown, its entrance easily missed. They had found the place by calling the owner on her mobile phone, hearing her real voice behind the froth of bushes, and walking towards it. Anna Sutela was delighted to meet them and to lend the cottage. It was older than most of the lake cottages. The previous owner had seen a wolf in the garden. She had prepared a salad for their supper and would eat with them before driving back to Kuopio.

He had been gone forty-five minutes, probably more. The lake had a dark tint to its edges, underneath the tree line. There were small white bars at its centre where the wind was freer. Or a current was moving, flowing between the two larger lakes. Time had seemed irrelevant, their circadian rhythms were gone, yesterday they had eaten at midnight, but it was now definitely evening. She searched the little island for his intrusive shape. Perhaps he had arrived and was walking its circumference. If he was still swimming there it meant the exercise was not as easy as anticipated. If he was still swimming there he would need more stamina.

The sky and the lake transferred tropical yellow patches between each other. Such eerie empty beauty. She began to feel a little uncomfortable. She should have been watching more carefully, consistently. That was really her only duty. She strained her eyes. There was no sign of him. There was no point calling his name, the distance was too great, and the neighbouring Finns might hear and think her disturbance improper. She stepped to the edge of the pontoon, as if those few extra inches might provide enough clarity to locate him. The wooden structure sank slightly and water lapped across her toes. She stepped back, turned, walked off the pontoon and made her way round the little beach above where the boat was moored. She began to unknot the line tied around the tree trunk.

The sensible thing was to row out. Not because she imagined he was in trouble, just in case. He might be struggling. He might have cramp and be treading water, or be floating in the recovery position. Perhaps he was sitting on the island, tired, having underestimated. Or he might already be swimming back to the cottage and she could accompany him, companionably, encourage him if he was flagging, make sure he was really all right and not in any jeopardy. She should have rowed alongside him from the beginning, not because she thought he wouldn't make it, she did think he would make it, but because the boat would be a handy back-up, eroding none of his achievement, simply ensuring the safety of the swim. Why hadn't she gone? Why hadn't she acted more responsibly? She had been too blasé about the whole thing. The possibility of disaster had not really occurred to her, not in a valid way, a way to make her officiously oversee the exercise. Suppose he was in difficulty, now, beyond her field of vision, somewhere in the water.

She tugged at the mooring. He had knotted the rope earlier that day. The knot looked slack but seemed very stiff and loosened out of its synthetic coils and links only a millimetre or two. Her fingers felt too weak for the operation. This was not supposed to be the hard part. The hard part would be moving the boat from its position up the bank where they had dragged it together down onto the beach and into the lake. She became frustrated and began to yank at both ends of the line, without regard for its undoing. A horrible feeling was trickling into her. A sense that she fought, uselessly, he was vanishing. *Fucking thing. Come on.* A small, aggravated cry left her. She stopped for a moment and took hold of herself. She looked at the inelaborate shape in her hands. Then she pushed the standing end of the cord through the tuck. The knot released, and the plastic length buzzed as she pulled it loose. She slid the rope from the trunk and threw it into the boat.

The boat was moulded fibreglass rather than wood, but it had still felt very heavy when they'd moved it out of the water before. She was uncertain about managing now, alone, even in reverse, with a downslope. She had not put on shoes. Her shoes were in the porch of the cottage, on the other side of the meadow, too far away and timewasting to retrieve. She tried not to notice how vulnerable her feet felt. She had on a thin cotton shirt, bikini bottoms. She took a breath, leaned against the prow of the boat and pushed. Her feet dug into the ground. Plush earth, twigs and thistles, pebbles where the bank became beach. The vessel resisted, shunted forward a notch of two, then stuck. She pushed again, got traction, gathered momentum. The boat ground across the stony apron of the beach and slid into the water. The first time she had launched a boat. The first stage in a successful rescue, a solo rescue. Already a positive retrospective was forming in her mind. How it might later be told. She felt a source of energy packed within herself. And adrenalin, like a lit taper.

She lifted an oar, steadied it, fitted the metal ball on its underside into the oarlock, then did the same on the other side. She waded the boat out to thigh level, climbed in, took her position on the seat and pulled with her right arm to turn the boat. She remembered the action. Now it was easy. Now it was simply speed, how fast she could row. She turned and looked at the island, imagined her trajectory, began to pull on the oars. The oars, charming and narrow and traditional when they had tested the boat initially, now seemed impractical. She worked her shoulders hard, exaggerating the strokes, improving them. The water was uniform. Though the boat seemed not to be moving locally she was in fact passing new sections of shore, passing the cottage of the neighbouring Finns and noticing, because of the new angle, their electric-green lawn and jetty with bathing steps, passing the promontory, its congestion of trees, its rocks stepping down towards the glistening surface, passing away from the land. Then she was in open water.

She kept pulling hard. Her grip on the oars was firm. Tenderness to her palm, which would mean blisters. She leaned forward, pushed back. She was making good time. It was not very long since she had lost sight of him. The oarlocks rotated. The paddles washed. She pushed away the image of a sallow indistinct form drifting under the surface. She would find him. He would be stranded on the island. He would be pleased to see her. Or, if he was in difficulty in the water, the sight of the boat would sustain him; she would arrive and help him in. She would give him her dry shirt to put on. She would kneel in the hull in front of him and hold him. She would tell him that she was in love with him, because she had not yet told him this, though she had wanted to for weeks, though he must see it, mustn't he, whenever she came alive under him, pushing him back so she could see his eyes in that driven, other state, their concentrated pleading look, or when she suffered that peculiar tearful euphoria in climax, with its physical gain, its fear and foreknowledge of loss. *This is all I want. I can't be without it.*

Her strokes became heavier. Her technique was slipping, or she was tired from rowing earlier. It sounded as if the lake was splashing up against the prow more and more. She would have to break, so that she could never recover and realign. She slackened the tight grasp of her hands, flexed her fingers. She turned around to look for him again. Inside the boat was a pool of rusty water.

For a moment she did not understand. A leak. There was a leak. *Shit.* How had it gone unnoticed? Had the bottom been punctured when the boat was moved, either up or down the bank? In the centre of the hull was a small black eye. A small black hole. *No.* In the rush to launch she had not fitted the bung. It was still in the small locker by the pontoon. It was her fault that the vessel was not watertight. *Or, most likely, it will be an unforeseen event, manufactured under the auspices of technological advancement, which finishes humanity.* She let go of the oars and shunted forward on the seat. She cast her eyes around the boat. Rope. The little three-pronged anchor. A sponge. There was nothing with which to bail. She could take off her shirt; stuff it into the hole. But she knew that would fail. The cotton would balloon. The twist of fabric would slip out. She was about half a mile into the lake.

Everything was so quiet.

Suddenly she knew how it would all play out. The boat would continue to take on water and would lug down as she tried to row back, its debilitation unstoppable, and then it would submerse. She would make it to the shore, because she could swim well enough, but it would be ugly and ungraceful, it would involve swallowing water and choking because of the desperation. The rescue would be aborted. He would never make it back. Though she would pick her way along the green shoreline to the Finns as quickly as she could, and bang insanely on their door, and beg to use their boat, and listen as they spoke to the emergency services in their pure, impenetrable language, they would not find him or his body. He would be lost. She would be complicit. She would not ever love in this way again.

She heard herself whimpering. The scenery passed out of focus. Her fear was bifurcating; she could feel the fibrous separation in her chest, the intimate tearing, so uncomfortable she could hardly bear it. Then, without any pain, she sealed, and the fear was singular again, for herself only.

She looked out over the water, and thought, just for a second, that she might see him swimming casually along, close enough to come and help her. If he converted his easy breaststroke into a craw he could get to her before the boat took on too much water. His presence would somehow ameliorate the crisis. Alone, her chances would be worse. She stood up and the boat rocked. A small oblique tide rolled against her ankle, and withdrew. *Where are you? Please.* She scanned the water. The lake was empty. It was full of the night-resistant sky. She sat down and the seiche came again across her feet. The pool settled. It was four or five inches deep. Something else was in it. That colour. And though she felt overwhelmed by the foreign character of this place, by not understanding its substance, the instinct to fight against it was immediate and furious. A desire that tasted bloody in her mouth. She reached for one oar and then the other. She searched the shore and at first could not differentiate between the tiny cottages. Which was it? Which? The first red-roofed one. With the separate outhouse and sauna. And the little beach. And the meadow that had been left wild, where there had once been a wolf. She turned the boat with her right arm, and began to pull heavily in that direction. *In winter,* Anna Sutela had said to them, *there are twenty hours of darkness. The snow reaches the cottage roof. We do not come here.*

Zoe Lambert

These Words Are No More Than a Story About a Woman on a Bus

The woman heading towards you is old. You're not sure how old. You don't spend long guessing. Old will do. You watch warily as she makes for the seat next to you at the back of the bus. She's wearing a beige anorak. From a distance it looks respectable. Up close the coat is stained, the cuffs are grimy, and inside the collar is streaked and grey. She sits down and you shift slightly, placing your briefcase on your knee. You open it and flick through the letters and bills you picked up from the mailbox. But it's too early to contemplate bills, so you roll yourself a cigarette for the walk to the office and wonder where you left your antihistamines. The woman is watching you and your briefcase, so you close it carefully and glance outside. The bus is caught in traffic on Candle Road. It's shuddering and shunting round the bollards.

They threw letters from the trains, she says, as if you were mid-conversation.

Deportees would push their notes through high, thin windows.

What? You mumble. Sorry?

Letters, she says. She begins to cough. Her coughs are harsh and wracking. She wipes her mouth with a stained handkerchief. She grasps your hand, her fingers digging into your palm. You try to free your hand from the scaly feel of her skin. You notice her hands are scarred, the skin stretched shiny and tight. Old scars. You worry about your personal space. She doesn't understand this; her knees press against your suit trousers, her breath is sharp and bitter on your cheek.

On her courier trips, she says, she'd find the notes, frozen and crisp by the train tracks. Sometimes wet with blurred ink scrawls. She'd leave them on the verges, like paper gravestones, with pebbles on the corners. Her father travelled on one of those trains. But she never found a note.

Where's this? you ask, loosening your tie.

Lithuania.

You think of Eurovision. Or is that Latvia? You draw a blank.

Her name, she says, is Elena Vidugirytė. She frowns at the ceiling as if she is picking a story from the air. Jonas Zemaitas, she says. Jonas Zemaitas.

She will tell you about Jonas.

You're not sure you want to know about Jonas. Or why she is telling you. Perhaps you should get off the bus to escape her, but your hangover plus hayfever won't let you stand. You rub your eyes and grunt.

This is all she needs.

Jonas, she says, was the commander of the Southern Partisan District. She met him when she joined the partisans with her brother, Jurgis. They volunteered after their father, the Mayor of Ukmerge, was deported, after they were moved from their villa to a tiny cottage on the edge of the town.

But it's the end she remembers, she says. The end.

The last time she saw Jonas she was delivering a message to his group in the forests near to Ukmerge. She was a messenger, a courier, between the groups of partisans in the area.

She remembers, she says, that the only noise was the rain on the leaves and the soft crunch of her boots on the forest floor. Around her the trees were tall and spindly, with a canopy of leaves, leaving the grass yellowing and patchy underneath. She remembers climbing over a fallen branch. She clutched her skirt. It was sodden and heavy and water trickled down her neck. She was so wet she wanted to cry.

She should have been used to creeping through the forest at night. But she wasn't. The darkness scared her; one of the strange, jagged shadows beyond the glow of her lamp could be a *velnias* with their riddles and their tricks. Or worse, Russians. They searched the woods for the partisans with their dogs and their lamps and informers' lies. They were picking off the partisans in ambushes. A week before, three in Jonas' division had been captured and taken to the prison in Vilnius.

Elena tucked in her scarf. She wanted to be by the fire with her mother, a glass of vodka and some fried bread. Her mother had begged her not to do this. Jorgis' decision she had not questioned, but Elena's she couldn't understand. It left her alone at night, sleepless and praying with a small illegal cross.

By day, Elena and her mother weaved for the collective. The former weavers, women who now had authority, examined and criticised their work. They'd throw their cloths on the floor of the cottage and wipe their boots on the weave of bourgeois wives. They'd grip and squeeze Elena's hands and denounce them as not the hands of workers.

Her mother would retell the old myths as they weaved, especially the tricks *laumes* would play on women like that. *Laumes* loved weaving, but when they were mistaken for bourgeois wives, they'd cast a spell on the spiteful women's thread, so it continually unravelled. Every cloth the women touched fell apart.

You find yourself half listening, even though passengers are glancing over and raising their eyebrows at the woman's loud accent. You can feel the beginnings of a headache and the itch in your eyes is unbearable. You give in and rub.

Don't rub, she says.

On each trip she had to go a different route. That night she skirted round the mounds of unmarked graves. The soil was still fresh and she'd heard the dead had dug the pits themselves. Then she followed the stream north-east to where Jonas and his group were camped. The note almost hummed in her pocket, the words heavy and resonant against her hip. She was not supposed to read it. Not supposed to know. But she had. She always did. In case it said something about Jonas or Jurgis. And this one did.

She could hear barking in the distance. Barking meant Russians and their dogs. But it was far away. She stopped and listened. There were voices. What was that? *'Pasmikst, pakabakst?'*

She was shaking, but it was them of course. They weren't far. She followed the voices till she saw the lights of their cigarettes and the low-burning lamp.

Elena came out shyly, and stood on the edge of the clearing. *'Labas.'*

'Labas. Did you bring any *cepelinai?'* Jonas asked, approaching her.

'Just bread. Sorry. And some ham.'

Last time she had hugged him. This time he didn't wait. He was already under the tent with Feliksas and Pranuté. They were wet and bedraggled in their patched overcoats, with pustules and sores on their faces. They barely said hello. Elena saw that the second tent, where the others had been, was empty. The roof had collapsed on one side and was covered by yellowing leaves. Underneath a puddle had formed and four stones had been placed there, like graves.

'Come over, then. Get under here.'

She walked round the puddle in the middle of the clearing.

'You could fish in that,' she said and crouched next to Jonas. She handed him the message and the bread and ham. They bit into the small loaves, barely chewing large mouthfuls. She watched Jonas read and eat at the same time. Then he focused on the bread. His face was streaked with dirt, yellow decay edged his teeth, and his knuckles were cracked and sore. His hands were shaking. His hands always fluttered and fidgeted, touching his forehead and his neck. The few times they had walked into the bushes together, she'd stroked his neck till he was calm.

Jonas read the note again, and tucked it into his coat pocket. She watched to see his reaction, but he just looked cold and tired. She edged nearer and took his hand.

'Are you alright?'

'Yes.' He freed his hand and scratched a weeping bite on his wrist.

Before, she thought, they would have been married by now. She tried to imagine him indoors, sitting at a table, the stove burning, and in another room, a neatly-made bed. She tried to picture him standing by the fire in the old villa. She couldn't. In her mind, he drifted out of the window and floated into the woods, as if he were a *laumiukas*.

She knew that he grew up in a village south of Vilnius and that he'd graduated from the Kavnas Military School just before the war. In an old military photo he'd shown her, he had close-cut blonde hair, a smooth shaved chin and a wide open smile. She'd asked if she could keep the photo, but he said no. It was too risky.

They had met seven times. That was all. She'd sewn special epaulettes for his coat. He loved them. She'd brought him as much food as she could, sometimes taking from her mother's larder or saving him the meat from her plate. On her missions, she wasn't supposed to dawdle, but immediately return with the message. Jonas would walk with her for a little of the way. But after a few minutes he'd become fretful and want to get back to the others.

Elena wondered if he thought of her when she was not there, or if she disappeared from his mind, like a *laume* at the end of a tale.

The last time they met, they'd argued. Usually, she stayed quiet. That night, she couldn't. Jonas had said that the Lithuanian government had just given into the Russians. It had been weak. They'd tried to bargain, but were tricked and either sent to Siberia or shot. That was no loss; they'd done nothing for Lithuania. And everyone knows not to bargain with devils. Elena thought it was more complicated than that. Things always were. She'd said this and he'd sneered. That was the talk of conspirators, he said. Things were never so complicated as not having a choice. Capitulate or fight. They should have fought. There was always a choice. He was angry. She didn't know how someone could stay so angry all the time.

'Not always,' she said. She was thinking of her father, locking himself in the mayor's office till they came for him.

'Women,' he said. 'That's a woman talking.'

'Do you have a reply?' she asked as he fingered the note. Jonas nodded and scribbled, sealing it in an envelope.

'You should get back. You must be tired,' he said.

'Yes. I should.' She crouched, as if to stand. 'Goodbye then,' she said and then more loudly, as if pointing something out. 'Goodbye, Jonas.'

She walked across the clearing. He was leaving. He had to take the regiment further south, to group with other divisions near Vilnius. It was out of her area. Too far for her to walk. Leaving, like that. No goodbye, nothing. As if she were nothing. She was angry then. 'Jonas?' she said, even though the others looked up.

'What?'

'When will I see you?'

'I don't know.'

'You were going to go? Just like that? Without saying anything?'

'Why? Have you read the message?'

'No, I…'

He turned away. 'You should go,' he said.

She grabbed her lamp and ran into the woods. He didn't follow, even though she looked behind to see if he would. She walked, holding the lamp in front of her, its pool of light flickering. It was darker here, the foliage thicker. She wasn't sure where she was. Perhaps she should go back towards the clearing and retrace her steps home in the other direction, past the stream. Then she saw that she was at the stream. How did she get here? It was shallow with stones. She could cross. But the bank was muddy. She slipped on the verge, her lamp shattering and her hands deep in the mud. She lay there. The sound of the water trickling was soothing in the dark. Further along – she wasn't sure in which direction – the stream was wide and nearly still. On a bright day, the sun would shoot through the leaves and branches, the trees casting dark shadows on the water.

She didn't know whether to go back or follow the stream. She pulled herself out of the mud and wiped her hands on her skirt. She wanted to return to the clearing, but there was nothing to be said. Tomorrow, she'd continue weaving with her mother and again the day after that. She'd carry on delivering messages but Jonas would be gone. The message. She slid the note out of the envelope. She tried to read the words but they were blurred. His hands had been shaking and the scrawl said nothing. She folded it in the envelope and carefully put it in her pocket.

She heard barking, far off. She listened and eventually she heard guns. She heard voices, shouts and more shots. She should run, get away, hide. Perhaps they'd look for her as well. But her legs were weak. She huddled against a tree, her knees to her chest, shivering.

How had the Russians found them? The others could have talked. There had been rumours about the prison in Vilnius. Stories of a room where they made you stand naked on a small ledge above a floor of ice. But she didn't believe they would talk. She held onto the tree trunk, her cheek pressed against the smooth, wet bark. From somewhere she could smell smoke.

Later, she got up slowly, and feeling her way, she walked back to the clearing. The clearing was not hard to find. It was lit by a dimming fire where the tent used to be. Footprints and tracks scoured the mud. All the equipment, the bowls, the blankets had been dragged into the fire.

She didn't get home till morning. Her mother had not slept. She was waiting in the kitchen, pacing up and down. She bandaged Elena's hands and gave her a large vodka. You will have to go, she said. You will have to leave.

The bus shudders and stops. You grab the seat in front of you. She grasps

168

your forearm, her fingers crinkling your sleeve. Passengers are staring out of the windows, muttering to each other and rubbing at the glass. The driver seems to have disappeared. You worry vaguely about being late for work. She uprights herself and examines her scarred hands, turning them in front of her.

She can see Jonas, she says, coughing. She can always see him, even now, crouched in the tent, biting into the hard loaf, his hands fidgety, unsure. And later when she dragged him from the fire and laid him on the ground in the clearing, the epaulettes she'd sewn were black and burnt.

You try not to stare at her hands. You shift in your seat. Clear your throat. Glance down the bus. Some of the passengers are queuing to get off. Through the window, you watch them trailing, one after the other, past the school railings, to the bus stop at the end of the road.

You turn to her, clasping your briefcase, ready to leave. You're not sure what to do with this story, or what to say to Elena, the old woman sitting beside you on the bus.

Kevin Barry

Wifey Redux

This is the story of a happy marriage but before you throw up and turn the page let me say that it will end with my face pressed hard into the cold metal of the Volvo's bonnet, my hands cuffed behind my back, and my rights droned into my ear – this will occur in the car park of a big-box retail unit on the Naas Road in Dublin.

We were teenage sweethearts, Saoirse and I. She was exquisite, and seventeen; I was a couple of years older. She was blonde and wispily slight with a delicate, bone-china complexion. Her green eyes were depthless pools – I'm sorry, but this is a love story – and I drowned in them. She had amazing tits, too, small but textbook, perfectly cuppable, and an outstanding arse. I mean literally an outstanding arse. Lasciviously draw in the air, while letting your tongue loll and eyes roll, the abrupt curve of a perfect, flab-free butt cheek: she had a pair of those. It was shelved, the kind of arse my father used to say (in wry and manly sidemouthing) you could settle a mug of tea on. Also, she had a raunchy laugh and unwavering taste and she understood me. In retrospect, with the due modesty of middle age, I accept there wasn't that much to understand. I was a moderately poetical kid, and moderately rebellious, but diligent in my studies all the same, and three months out of college I had a comfortable nook secured in the civil service. We got married when Saoirse was twenty-one and I was twenty-three. That seems impossibly young now but this was the late eighties. And we made a picture – I was a gorgeous kid myself. A Matt Dillon type, people used to say, which dates me. But your dates can work out, and we were historically lucky in the property market. We bought a fabulous old terrace house with a view to the seafront in Dun Laoghaire. We could lie in bed and watch the ships roll out across Dublin Bay, all lighted and melancholy in the night. We'd lie amid the flicker of candles and feast on each other. We couldn't believe our luck.

We had bought the place for a song. Some old dear had died in it, and it had granny odours, so it took a while to strip back the flock wallpaper and tan-coloured linoleum, but it was a perfect dream that we unpeeled. The high ceilings, the bay windows, the palm tree set in the front garden: haughty Edwardiana. We did it up with the sweat of our love and frequently broke off from our DIY tasks to fuck each other histrionically (it felt like we were running a race) on the stripped floorboards. The house rose 35 percent in value the year after we bought it. It has since octupled in value.

Those early years of our marriage were perfect bliss. Together, we made a game out of life – everything was an adventure; even getting the tyres filled, even doing the groceries. We laughed a lot. We tiddled each other in the frozen foods aisle. We bit each other lustfully in the back row of the pictures at the late show, Saturdays. We made ironical play of our perfect marriage. She called me 'Hubby' and I called her 'Wifey'. I can see her under a single sheet, with her bare, brown legs showing, and coyly in the morning she calls to me as I dress:

'Hubby? Don't go just yet… Wifey needs… attendance.'

'Oh but Wifey, it's past eight already and…'

'What's the wush, Hubby?'

Saoirse could not (and cannot) pronounce the letter 'R' – a rabbit was a wabbit – which made her even more cute and bonkable.

I rose steadily in the civil service. I was pretty much unsackable, unless I whipped out a rifle in the canteen or raped somebody in the photocopier room. Hubby went to work, and Wifey stayed at home, but we were absolutely an equal partnership. Together, in slow-mo, we jogged the dewy, early-morning park. Our equity by the month swelled, the figures rolling ever upwards with gay abandon. The electricity of our enraptured smiles – ! ! – could have powered the National fucking Grid. Things just couldn't get any better, and they did.

In the third year of our marriage, a girl-child was born to us. Our darling we named Ellie, and she was a marvel. She was the living image of her beautiful mother, and I was doubly in love – I pushed her stroller along the breezy promenade, the Holyhead ferry hooted, and my heart soared with the black-backed gulls. Ellie slept eight hours a night from day one. Never so much as a teething pain. A perfect, placid child, and mantelpiece-pretty. We were so lucky I came to fear some unspeakable tragedy, some deft disintegration. But the seasons as they unrolled in south County Dublin were distinct and lovely, and each had its scheduled joys – the Easter eggs, the buckets and spades, the Halloween masks, the lovely tinsel schmaltz of Crimbo. Hubby, Wifey, Baby Ellie – heaven had come down and settled all about us.

If, over the subsequent years, the weight of devotion between Saoirse and I ever so fractionally diminished – and I mean *tinily* – this, too, I felt, was healthy. We probably needed to pull back, just a tad, from the obsessive quality of our love for each other. This minuscule diminishing was evident, perhaps, in the faint sardonic note that entered our conversation. Say when I came home from work in the evening, and she said:

'Well, *Hubby*?'

With that kind of dry-up note at the end of a sentence, that sarcastic stress? And I would answer in kind:

'Well, *Wifey*?'

Of course the century turned, and early middle age slugged into the picture, and our arses dropped. Happens. And sure, I began to thicken a little around the waist. And yes, unavoidably, the impromptu fucking tends to die off a bit when you've a kid in the house. But we were happy still, just a little more calmly so, and I repeat that this is the story of a happy, happy marriage. (Pounds table twice for emphasis.)

Not that I didn't linger sometimes in memory. How could I not? I mean Saoirse, when she was seventeen, was... erotic perfection. I could never desire anyone more than I did Saoirse back then. It was painful, almost, that I had wanted her so badly, and it had felt sinful, almost (I was brought up Catholic), to be able to sate my lust for her, at will, whenever I wanted, in whatever manner I wanted, and for so many ecstatic years.

I'm not saying she hasn't aged well. She remains an extremely handsome woman. She has what my mother used to call an excellent hold of herself. Certainly, there is a little weight on her now, and that would have seemed unimaginable on those svelte, fawnish, teenage limbs, but as I have said, I'm no Twiggy myself these days. We like creamy pasta dishes flecked with lobster bits. We like ludicrously expensive chocolate. The kind with chilli bits baked in and a lavender dusting. And yes, occasionally, in the small hours, I suffer from... weeping jags. As the ships roll out remorselessly across Dublin Bay. And fine, let's get it all out there, let's – Saoirse has developed a Pinot Grigio habit that would knock a fucking horse.

But we are happy. We love each other. And we are dealing.

Because we married so young, however, and because we had our beautiful Ellie so early in life, we have that strange sensation of still being closely attuned to the operatics of the teenage world even now as our daughter has entered it. It's almost as if we never left it ourselves, and we know all the old steps of the dance still as Ellie pelts through that skittle sequence of drugs, music, fashion, melancholia, suicidal ideation and, well, sex.

The difficult central fact of this thing: Ellie is now seventeen years old and everything about her is a taunt to man. The hair, the colouring, the build. Her sidelong glance, and the hoarseness of her laugh, and the particular way she pokes the tip of her tongue from the corner of her mouth in sardonic dismissal, and the hammy, poppy-eyed stare that translates as:

'Are you for *weal*?'

No, she can't say her Rs either. And she wears half-nothing. Hot pants, ripped tights, belly tops, and she has piercings all over. A slash of crimson lippy. Thigh-high boots.

Now understand that this is not about to get weird and fucked up but I need to point out that she is identical to Saoirse at that age. I am just being brutally honest here. And I would plead that the situation is not unusual. It's just one of those things you're supposed to keep shtum about. Horribly often, our beautiful, perfect daughters emerge into a perfect facsimile of how our beautiful, desirable wives had been, back then, when they were young. And slim. And sober. There is a horrid poignancy to it. And to even put this stuff down on paper looks wrong. There are certain people (hello, Dr Murtagh!) who would see this and think: your man is bad again. So I should just get to the story of how the trouble started. And, of course, it concerns my hatred for the boys who flock around my beautiful daughter.

Oh, trust me. Every hank of hair and hormones with the price of a lip ring in the borough of Dun Laoghaire has been panting after our Ellie. But she flicked them all away, one after the other, nothing lasted for more than an innocent date or two. Not until young and burly Aodhan McAdam showed up on the scene.

Even saying the horrible, smug, hiccupy syllables of that fucker's name makes me retch. He wasn't her usual type, so immediately I was worried. The usual type – so far as it had been established – was black-clad, pale-skinned, basically depressed-looking, given to eyeliner and guitar cases, Columbine types, sniper material, little runts in duster coats, addicted to their antihistamine inhalers, self-harmers, yadda yadda, but basically innocent. I knew by the way she carried herself that she did not succumb to them. A father can tell – although this is another of the facts you're supposed to keep shtum about. But then – hear the brush and rattle of doom's timpani drums – enter Aodhan McAdam. 'How ya doin' boss-man?'

This, quickly, became his ritual greeting when I answered the door, evenings, and found him in his trackpants and Abercrombie & Fitch polo shirt on the chequered tiles of our porch. He typically accompanied the greeting with a pally little punch on my upper arm and a big, toothy grin. He was seventeen, six two, with blonde, floppy hair, and about eight million quids' worth of dental work. Looked like he'd been raised on prime beef and full-fat milk. Handsome as a movie star and so easy in his skin. One of those horrible, mid-Atlantic twangs – these kids don't even sound fucking Irish any more – and broad as a jeep; I had no doubt he could beat the shit out of me. Which meant that I would have to surprise him.

I knew after the first two weeks that they were fucking. It was the way she carried herself – she was little-girl no more. And what did her mother do about this? She went and fetched another bottle of Pinot Grigio from the fridge.

'Saoirse, we need to talk about what's going on back there?'

Wrong, I know, you're supposed to leave these things be. But I couldn't… I couldn't *not* bring it up. It was poisoning me.

Saoirse and I were in the front den. We keep the bigger TV in there, and the coffee table we commissioned from the Artisans with Aids programme, and a retro fifties couch in a burnt-orange shade that our shapes have settled into – unpleasantly, it makes it look like we have arses the size of boulders – and stacks upon stacks of DVDs climb the walls, just about every box set yet issued.

'I suppose you know,' I said, 'that they're, well… you *know*.'

'Don't,' Saoirse said.

I sighed and left the den. The way it worked, Ellie had the use of the sitting room down at the back of the ground floor; no teenager wants to sit with her parents. She'd had a decorator in – it was got up in like a purple-and-black scheme – and she had a really fabulous Eames couch we'd got at auction for her sixteenth, and I went down there to check on Aodhan and herself. The shade was down, and they were watching some hip-hop crap on satellite, and they were under a duvet. This was a summer evening.

'Yo, Popsicle,' Ellie said.

'Hey,' Aodhan McAdam said, and leered at me.

I unleashed the coldest look I could summon and tried to say something and felt like I had a mouthful of marbles. I went back to the front den. I settled into the massive arse shape on my side of the couch.

'Do you realise,' I said, 'that they're under a duvet back there?'

'Mmm-hmm?'

Saoirse was watching a *Wire* episode with crew commentary and was nose deep in a bucket-sized glass of Pinot Grigio. She drank it ice cold – I could see the splinters of frozen crystals in there.

'I mean what the fuck are they doing under a duvet? It's July!'

She turned to me, and smiled benignly.

'I think we can pwesume,' she said, 'that she's jackin' him off.'

'Lovely,' I said.

'Ellie's seventeen,' she said. 'The fuck do you think she's doing?'

'That *fucking* little McAdam bastard…'

'Not so little,' Saoirse said. 'And actually he's kinda hot?'

You're supposed to just deal. But my brain would not stop whirring. I lay there that night in bed, and I was under siege. Random images came at me which I will not describe. I was nauseous. I knew it was a natural thing. I knew there was no stopping it. And as the morning surfaced on the bay, I tried to accept it. But I got out of the bed and I felt like I'd fought a war. I thought, maybe it's better that he's a rugby type rather than one of the sniper types. At least maybe he's healthier.

That evening, after work, as I took my walk along the prom, with the cold sea oblivious, I saw them: the rugby boys. They hang out by a particular strip of green down there, sitting around the rain shelter, or tossing a ball about, and chortling all the time, chortling, with their big shiteater grins and testosterone. They all have the floppy hair, the polo shirts in soft pastels, the Canterbury trackpants, the mid-Atlantic twangs. Aodhan McAdam was among them, and he saw me, and grinned, and he made a pair of pistols with his fingers and fired them at me.

Ka-pow, he mouthed.

Ha-ha, I grinned back.

He was no doubt giving the rest of the scrum a full account about what went on beneath the duvet. Of course he was! And later he was back for more. Bell rings about ten: orthodontic beam on porch. In fact, he appeared to have pretty much moved into the house. Every night now he was among us.

'Babes!' she squealed, and she raced down the hallway, and leapt onto him, and right there – right in front of me! – he cupped her butt cheek.

Now often, between box-set episodes, Saoirse and I hang in the kitchen – it's maybe our fave space, and it's tricked out with as much cutesy, old-timey shit as a soul could reasonably stomach. The Aga. The stoneware pots from Puglia. The St. Brigid's Cross made out of actual, west of Ireland reeds for an ethnic-type touch. We snack hard and we just, like, sway with the kitchen vibe? But now Ellie and Aodhan were invading. Eighteen times a night they were out of the back room and attacking the fridge. Saoirse just smiled, fondly, as they ploughed into the hummus, the olives, the flatbreads, the cold cuts, the blue cheese, the Ben 'n' Jerry's, the lavender-dusted chocolate from Fallon & Byrne. I watched the motherfucker from the island counter – the way he wolfed the stuff down was unreal.

'Do they feed you at your own place at all, Aodhan?' I said, wryly.

He chortled, and he took out a six-pack of Petit Filous yoghurts, and he made for the couch-and-duvet in my back room. He mock punched me in the gut as he passed by.

'This ol' boy's runnin' on heavy fuel,' he said, and he mussed my hair, or what's left of it.

Later, in the den, I turned to Saoirse:

'He's treating me like a bitch,' I said.

She was freezeframing bits of *The Wire* that featured the gay killer Omar because she had a thing for him. She had lately been waking in the night and crying out his name.

'So what are you going to do about it?' she said.

'I know they're fucking,' I said. 'I can just… smell it?'

'You need to talk to Doctor Murtagh about this,' she said.

'Meaning?'

'Meaning cognitive fucking thewapy,' she said. 'Meaning medication time. Meaning this is looking like a bweakdown-type thing again?'

All over the house, I felt like I could hear him... chomping? You know sometimes, in a plane, when your ears are weird, and they flip out the food trays, and you chew, and you can hear the jaw motions of your own mastication in a loud, amped, massively unpleasant way? It was like I was hearing that all over the house–

Aodhan!

Chomping!

Also, he was using the downstairs loo, under the stairs, and of course he pissed like a prize stallion. Saoirse thought it was all marvellous, and she talked increasingly about how hot she thought he was, as hot almost as Omar. We're talking a lunk but angelically pretty – like a beefy choirboy that could mangle a bear? Fucking hideous.

Then summer thickened and there was a heat wave. We garden, and we have a terrific deck – done out with all this Tunisian shit we bought off the lepers in Zarzis – overlooking the back lawn. During the heat wave, Aodhan and Ellie took over the deck space. I watched from the kitchen – I was deveining some king prawns while Saoirse expertly pestled a coriander-seed-and-lime-zest marinade. Ellie lay face down on the lounger, in a string bikini, and he sat on the lounger's edge, and with his big sausagey fingers he untied the top of the bikini, and pushed the straps gently back. Then he shook the lotion bottle, rubbed a squirt of it onto his palms, and began to massage it in, super slow, like some fucking porno set-up. Through the open window I heard her throaty little moans, and I saw the way she turned to him, adoringly, and he bent down and whispered to her, and she squealed.

'Next thing,' I said to Saoirse, 'they're actually going to have it off in front of us.'

'What is she, a nun?'

'I've had enough of this,' I said.

I flung the prawns into the Belfast sink and I stormed out of the house. I bought cigarettes for the first time in six months and lit one right there on the forecourt of the Topaz. I smoked, and I took off along the prom. I passed the rugby boys' rain shelter, and it was deserted, and I saw that there was an amount of graffiti scrawled around the back wall of the shelter. I went to have a closer look.

Nicknames, stuff about schools rugby rivals, so-and-so loves such-and-such, or so-and-so loves???, but then, prominently, this:

B-L-O! And P! That they had used my surname's initial for emphasis, the P of my dead father's Prendergast! I went and power-walked the length of the pier and back three times. A glorious summer evening, and busy on the pier, with friends and neighbours all about – but I just ignored them all; I pelted up and down, with my arms swinging, and I ground my teeth, and I cried a little (a lot), and I smoked the pack.

I could see the neighbours thinking:

Is he not great again?

Later, in the den:

Aodhan had gone home, and I could hear the *thunk, shlank, whumpf* of her music from upstairs, and Saoirse had gone into her keeping-an-eye-on-me mode; she was all concerned and hand-holdy now.

'I think we can pwesume, hon,' she said, 'that he didn't, like, white it himself?'

'A gentleman!' I said. 'But even so he's been mouthing off, hasn't he? And it doesn't bother you at all that she's…'

I couldn't finish it.

'She's seventeen, Jonathan.'

'I say we front her.'

'This is nuts. And say what? That she shouldn't be giving blow jobs?'

'Please, Saoirse…'

'I was giving blow jobs at seventeen.'

'Congratulations.'

'As you well know.'

'But I wasn't mouthing off about it, was I? I was keeping it to myself!'

'Just leave it, Jonathan…'

Again that night I hardly slept. I developed this incessant buzzing sound in my head. It sounded like I had a broken strip light in there. More images came at me, and you can picture exactly what they were:

Ellie, descending.

And big Aodhan McAdam – ! – grinning.

The next morning I went to her room. Fuck it, I was going to be strong. There was going to be a conversation about Respect. For herself, for her home, for her parents. For duvets. I knocked, crisply, twice, and I pushed in the door, and I could feel that my forehead was taut with self-righteousness (or whatever), and I found her in a sobbing mess on the bed.

Suicidal!

Ellie's tears nuke my innards.

'Oh, babycakes!' I wailed. 'What is it!'

I threw myself on the bed. So much for the Respect conversation. Aodhan, it turned out, had taken his oral gratification and skedaddled. It was so over.

She was inconsolable. We had the worst Saturday morning of all time in our house. Which is saying a great deal. She was between rage and tears and when she is upset she behaves appallingly, my angel. It started right off, at breakfast:

A sunny Saturday, heaven-sent, in pj's – it should have been perfection. Saoirse was sitting at the island counter, trembling, as she ate pinhead porridge with acai fruit and counted off the hours till she could start glugging back the ice-cold Pinot Grigio. I was scraping an anti-death spread the colour of Van Gogh's sunflowers onto a piece of nine-grain artisanal toast. Ellie was vexing between flushes of crimson rage and sobbing fits and making a sound like a lung-diseased porpoise.

'Oh please, Ell?' I said. 'It's only been, like…'

'Eleven weeks!' she cried. 'Eleven weeks of my fucking life I gave that dickwad!'

'Look, baby, I know it doesn't seem like it now? But you'll get over this and it might work out for the best and…'

And maybe the blow-job rep will start to fade, I didn't say.

'What's this?' she said.

She held a box of muesli in her hand.

'It's a box of muesli,' I said.

'No it is not,' she said.

Admittedly, it was an own-brand line from a mid-range supermarket – a rare anomaly.

'Ah, Ellie, it's fine, look, it's actually quite tasty…'

She turned the box upside down and emptied the muesli onto the limestone flags that had cost peasants their dignity to hump over from County Clare.

'This is not *actual* ceweal,' she said. 'This is, like, twibute ceweal?'

She began with her bare feet to slowly crush the muesli into the flagstones. Deliberately grinding up and down, with a steady rhythm to her step, like a French yokel mashing grapes, or a chick on a Stairmaster set to a high gradient.

'I want him back,' she said.

'Ah, look, Ellie, I mean…'

'I want Aodhan back.'

She came across the flags and caught me by the pj's lapels.

'And I want him back today!'

I fell to my knees and hugged her waist.

'But this is madness!' I cried.

Generally speaking, in the run of a life, when you find yourself using the expression –

'But this is madness!'

– you can take it that things are not going to quickly improve. It was half ten in the morning but Saoirse didn't give a toss any more and she went to the fridge and took the cork from a half-drunk bottle of Pinot Grigio. With her teeth.

So! The next development!

I was sent to have a heart-to-heart with Aodhan McAdam. He had, of course, switched his phone off – they are by seventeen experts in avoidance tactics. And Ellie could not and would not lower her dignity by going to find him herself. And Saoirse hadn't left the house in eleven months, except for Vida Pura™ blood transfusions, Dakota hotstone treatments, and Beach Body Bootcamp (abandoned). So it was down to me. I was to find out his mood, his motives, his intentions. Essentially, I was to win him back. Saoirse was as intent on getting him back as Ellie. He was male youth, after all, and she liked having that stuff around the house.

It turned out that McAdam worked a Saturday job. Oh right, I thought, so he's going with the humble shit – a Saturday job! He worked at this DIY warehouse on the Naas Road. I got in the Volvo and rolled. I played a motivational CD. N'gutha Ba'al, the Zambian self-confidence guru, told me in his rich, honeyed timbre that I had a warrior's inner glow and the spirit of a cheetah. I cried a little (a lot) at this. I felt husky and brave and stout-hearted but the feeling was fleet as the light on the bay. Traffic was scant but scary. Cars edged out at the intersections in abrupt, skittery movements. Trucks loomed, and the sound of their exhausts was horrifyingly amplified. Pedestrians were straight out of a bad dream.

Everybody's hair looked odd. I drove through the south side of the city, tightened my grip on the wheel and tried to remember to breathe in the belly. The Volvo was grinding like an assassin as I pulled into the Do-It-Rite! car park. I tried to play the thing like I was an ordinary Joe, a Saturday-man just out on an errand, but I knew at once I wanted to climb up the store's signage and rip down that exclamation mark

!

from Do-It-Rite!

I stormed – stormed! – towards the entrance but that didn't work out, as the automatic doors did not register my presence as a human being. So I had to take a little step back and approach the doors again – but still they would not part – and I reversed three steps, four, and approached yet again, but still they would not part, and in my shame I raised my eyes to the heavens, and I saw that the letters of the Do-It-Rite! signage were so flimsily attached, with just brackets and screws, and this too was an outrage – the shoddiness of the fix. Then a Saturday-man approached and the doors glided open and I entered the store in the slipstream of his normalcy.

I hunted the aisles for Aodhan McAdam. They were shooting day-for-night in the vast warehouse space, it was luridly strip-lit, and I prowled by the paint racks, the guttering supplies, the mops and hinges, the masonry nails, the rat traps and the laminate flooring kits, and some cronky half-smothered yelps of rage escaped my throat as I walked, and every Saturday-man I passed did a double take on me. The place was the size of a half-dozen soccer pitches patchworked together, and the staff wore yellow dungaree cover-alls, so that they could be picked out for DIY advice, and eventually I saw up top of a set of cover-alls the blond, floppy hair, the megawatt grin and the powerful jaw muscles, those hideous chompers.

'Aodhan!'

The grin turned to me, and it was so enormous it dazzled his features to an indistinctness, I saw just that exclamation mark

!

from the Do-It-Rite! – but when he focused, the grin died, at once, right there.

'Jonathan?'

I went to him, and I smiled, and I took gently his elbow in my hand.

'Can we talk, Aodhan?'

'Sure, man, I mean…'

Now it is a rare enough occurrence in contemporary life that the occasion presents itself for truly felt speech. We are trapped – all of us – behind this glaring wash of irony. But in the quietest aisle of the Do-It-Rite! that Saturday – drylining accessories – as Aodhan McAdam and I squatted discreetly on our haunches, I spoke honestly, and powerfully, and from the heart.

'Listen,' I said, 'I know about the blow jobs. That's perfectly natural. I was getting blow jobs myself when I was seventeen. I wasn't broadcasting the fact, and I could *spell*, but I was…'

He tried to rise from his haunches, he tried to get away, but I had this strange animal strength (your eyebrows ascend, Dr Murtagh), and I kept his bony elbow clamped in my claw, and I lasered my eyes into his, and he was scared enough, I could see that.

I said:

'Ellie Prendergast, or should I say Ellie P, is the most beautiful girl in this city. She is an absolute fucking angel. If you hurt her, I will kill you. I'm telling you this now so you can give yourself a chance.'

I slapped him once across the face. It was a manic shot with plenty of sting to it. I told him of youth's fleeting nature. I told him he didn't realise how quickly all this would pass. I told him how it had been for me. I spoke of the darknesses that can so quickly seep between the cracks of a life. I told him of the images I had witnessed and voices I had heard. He began to cry in fear. I told him how my Wifey had been plagued by evil faeries in the night – oh it was all coming out! – and how my Ellie was to me a deity to be worshipped, and I would protect her with my life.

'I have Type 1 diabetes!' he sobbed. 'I can't deal with this shit!'

Oh but I laid it on with a motherfucking trowel. I brought him to the pits of despair and showed him around. My threats were veiled and made stranger by the serenity of my smile. I said I expected him on the porch at eight o'clock, in his trackpants and his Abercrombie & Fitch polo shirt. But before that he would have a job to do. We rose from our haunches and I caught the scruff of his neck and I led him along the aisles to the paint racks – Saturday-men watched, staff in yellow cover-alls watched, but no one approached us – and I showed him the white paint, how much of it there was and how cheap it was, and I explained I'd be pulling a spot check on the rain shelter at seven o'clock, sharp.

I let go of him then. I sucked up the last of my calm, and I said:

'Listen, Aodhan, we're doing a shopping run this afternoon... Can I fetch anything in particular? You two go for that barbecue salmon in the vac-packs, don't you?'

I left him ashen-faced and limp. I prowled the aisles some more and now these hot little barks of triumph came up as I walked. The Saturday-men avoided my eyes, and they scurried from my path, and I barked a little louder. As I'm here, I thought, why not pick up a couple of things?

So I bought an extendable ladder and a claw hammer.

The automatic doors registered my presence at once and I was let outside to the sun-kissed afternoon. I propped and extended the ladder against the front of the store and I climbed with the claw hammer hanging coolly in my grip. It took no more than a half-dozen wrenches to loose the exclamation mark

!

from the Do-It-Rite! and carefully I placed it under my arm – it was light as air – and I descended. I walked across the car park. I placed it carefully on the tarmac in front of the Volvo – my intention was to drive over it and smash it to pieces – but then I thought, no, that would be too quick. So I got down on my knees and I started to tap gently with the hammer at the blue plastic of the exclamation mark

!

until it began to crack here and there, and tiny shatter lines appeared, and these joined up, piece by piece, until the entire surface of the

!

had become a beautiful mosaic in the blue of the sign, like the trace of tiny backroads on an old map – marking out lost fields, lost kingdoms, a lost world – and I was serene as a bird riding the swells of morning air over those fields.

The squad car appeared.

Carys Bray

Everything a Parent Needs to Know

Helen's daughter hates her.

'I hate you.' The words shoot out of Jessica's gap-toothed mouth. Helen would like to duck, but she laughs. It's a laugh that is arrested and immediately charged with impersonation: a whimper in disguise.

Jessica is pressed into the corner, each hand resting on a cool tile wall. The shrieks of other children echo around the pool and the chlorine-fogged air. 'I liked Daddy best,' she fires. 'I wish…'

Helen is porcupined by these articulated arrows. Nothing in all she has read can help her. She feels like an actress who has learned the wrong lines. She has rehearsed *Mary Poppins*, only to find herself appearing in *Night, Mother*.

'Never back your child into a corner. Always provide a way out and allow your child to save face. Humiliation can be extremely damaging for children. Avoid public humiliation at all costs'.
(*Everything a Parent Needs to Know: Two Hundred Steps to Familial Bliss* by Denise Goody)

Helen kneels, aware that she appears to be begging.

She is begging. 'Come out of the corner. Don't stand there. Come and talk to me by the chairs.'

'No.'

'Well why don't you just get in the—'

'No.'

'If you just—'

'No.'

Helen fights another coil of laughter, this one cloaks tears. She is hot. The heavy, leisure-centre air is giving her a headache and the knees of her jeans are damp. She could roll them up, but she would rather have wet trousers than expose her raspberry-ripple legs. Jessica's head drops and Helen can see the knobble on the back of her neck through its almost transparent covering of pale skin and biro-fine veins.

'Look, Jess.' Helen gives herself eight out of ten for patience. 'Look. You said you wanted to wear Paul's old trunks. You said you didn't want to wear the swimsuit.'

It is essential to respect your child's autonomy. Allow your child to make decisions and accept consequences. She will thank you for it.
(*Parenting for Idiots!* by Jo Ann Humble)

Jessica moves her hands from the wall and clasps them tight in front of her. She has been drawing at school. There is felt tip on her fingers. Her drawings usually feature herself and Helen. Semi-circle heads grow straight out of boxy middles. Legs are pencil thin and overlong. Helen's face is often scribbled over. This is because it is usually raining or snowing in Jessica's pictures. It is nothing personal. Children don't really hate their parents. There are messages on the pictures. The messages are like tricks. Jessica recoils if Helen reads them incorrectly. Today's picture reads, *acisseʃ morf mum oT*.

Without the protection of a costume, Jessica seems shelled. Her torso is buttery soft and pale. Her fine, mousey hair is jumbled into a ponytail. Paul's old trunks are blue and red. Helen holds the pink goggles. A small child's voice snakes through the air: 'Is that a boy or a girl?'

The absolute, most important thing is to give a child a definite sense of who they are. Your child should feel comfortable with herself, happy in her own skin, certain of who she is.
(*A Happy Childhood, a Happy Life!* by Brenda Jolly)

'Jessica, if you don't go over there to your class right now, I will be very, very cross.' Helen's voice wibbles, undermining her reported crossness. Another laugh wings her throat and she clips it to stop the tears that are fluttering close behind. 'Look,' she tries. 'You said you didn't want to wear your swimming costume. You found the trunks. You wanted to wear them.' Jessica's toes flex and tense again. 'So I said you could, but I wanted to bring the costume too, just in case. And then you said that I never listen to you. So I left the costume at home.'

Jessica stares at her feet. They are rigid. Toes curled, like claws. The other parents are watching. Helen can feel their stares between her shoulder blades. They will think, look at that poor girl whose mother has made her come swimming dressed like a boy. They will notice the crack of Helen's bottom peeping out of the top of her jeans as she kneels in the damp patch. Helen would like to reach around and pull her knickers higher, but she can't remember what kind they are.

Jessica raises her head slightly and glares out from under her fringe. Helen extends a hand, a come-on-this-is-enough hand, a let's-be-friends hand, and Jessica flinches, as if she is expecting to be hit. As if she is used to it. As if she can count on it. She is cornered, cowering and half naked. A tantrum would be better. A tantrum would involve an eye-rolling, we're-all-in-this-together glance at the other parents. It could be deflected by a shrug, a smile, and a when-will-she-grow-out-of-this chat in the changing room afterwards. But Jessica doesn't do tantrums.

When all else fails, think a happy thought. Like Peter Pan and Wendy, you won't soar unless you are happy. Remember a happy moment and grasp it as tightly as you would grasp your sword if you were to come face to face with an unfriendly dragon (no offence to any friendly dragons out there!).

(*Give a little whistle: Disney solutions to parenting challenges* by Jo White)

Helen's happy thought is that Dave from her adult education class put his hand up last week to say that he had enjoyed doing The Whatsit of Alfred Prufrock. 'I relate to it,' he said. 'That stuff about walking in a room and wondering if people are looking at you. Getting it wrong and saying, "That's not what I meant." I thought it was all right, even though he's a bit of a tosser. He should eat the bloody peach and roll his trousers up if he wants to.'

Before Dave and his less appreciative classmates had made it down the echoing stairwell of the further education college, Helen's imagination had given him sole charge of an aged mother and a life full of noble sacrifice as a dutiful, loving son. His mother would be waiting for him when he got home, Helen thought. When she heard the front door open his mother would shout, 'Is that you, our Dave?' And Dave would call, 'Yes, our Mam.' Then he would make her a cup of tea and sit next to her on the sofa. They would talk about his childhood. About how she always did her best and how he was grateful. Then Dave's mum, who actually had a name by this stage in Helen's invention – Phyllis – would put her arm around Dave and say, 'You're a good lad, all I ever wanted was for you to be happy. Now get that little book out, and read me another one of those funny poems by that George Eliot.'

Jessica whispers something, inaudibly.

'Say it again.'

'I want to go home.'

'Is this because of the trunks? It's fine if it is. It just seems to me that in the car, before we got here, you didn't really want to come. So I'm wondering if it's just the trunks?'

Jessica shrugs twice in quick succession. There have been so many swimming lessons. But she can't manage a length without a float. She thrashes and hammers at the water, fighting her way to the deep end. Occasionally the float pops out of her hands and she soaks into the water. Helen's stomach clenches as she waits for the teacher to slide into the pool and retrieve Jessica. He's always quick.

But still…

Today in the car on the way to the pool Jessica had mumbled, 'I might need some help swimming.'

Followed by: 'Actually, I will need some help swimming.' After that: 'Because I might have forgotten how to swim.' And finally: 'I can't really swim.'

'That's why you're going, Jessica,' Helen had replied brightly. 'So you can learn how to swim.' It is vitally important to introduce children to as many new experiences as possible. Like puppies, children need to be socialised. Children will not be afraid if they have been socialised correctly. They will approach life with the *joie de vivre* of a puppy.

(*Like Dogs, Like Children: the new way to train your child* by Ben Ruff)

Helen stands. She gives up. Other parents drink too much, make promises they can't keep and hit their children. Helen gives up. Her feet have gone to sleep. They prickle as she walks toward the chairs where the other parents are sitting. Jessica follows several paces behind.

'Ah,' calls one of the parents. 'Ah, poor love.'

'Did you forget her costume?' another asks. 'Is that all they could find for you behind the desk?'

The changing rooms are quiet. Jessica puts her clothes back on ponderously. There is something heavy and cheerless in her, as if she was made for disappointment. She cultivates every hurt, every injury, and she wears them in the creases of her forehead, and in the tentativeness of her occasional embrace. Helen bends to help with her socks. Jessica's feet are soft and white, and her little toes curl like monkey nuts. Helen would like to kiss them.

'Remember when I was late for school in Reception Class, Mummy?'

'No.'

'Yes, you do. I couldn't find my cardigan, and you shouted at me, and I was crying when we got there.'

'No.'

'Well, I do.'

One day, Helen thinks, Jessica will sit on an orange, plastic chair in a designated room at a GP surgery and describe her horrendous childhood to a sympathetic counsellor. The trauma of attending swimming lessons wearing her older brother's trunks will equal her already misremembered recollections of the divorce. The counsellor will agree that her mother has ruined her life. This scene approaches with the inevitability of a speeding train.

'I'm sorry if I shouted at you when you were in Reception, Jess.'

'That's all right.' Jessica shrugs and examines the felt tip on her hands.

When they get home, Paul opens the door to them.

'You're early, Mum,' he says, caught red-handed with the Xbox controller. Fluff is growing on his upper lip and chin, but it cannot obscure the openness of his face.

'You obviously weren't expecting us.'

'How come you're back already?'

Helen relieves him of the controller as she explains.

'Doh!' He slaps his forehead. 'You muppet, Jess!'

'Remember the story of Thumper,' Helen says. 'If you can't say anything nice…'

'Lol.' He grins.

'I don't think that's actually a word.' She smiles back at him.

'Lolz,' he says.

'That doesn't sound like a word, either. Go and do your homework.'

'Rofl,' he calls over his shoulder as he walks up the stairs.

'I think those are actually initials, not words,' Helen says. 'You can't really pronounce them like words because the vowels aren't—'

'Chillax, Mum,' he calls as he closes his bedroom door.

Jessica picks at her dinner. Her reasons for not liking food include it being too yellow, too soft and too runny.

'Remember when it was May Day at nursery, Mummy?'

'No. Eat your dinner, please, Jess.'

'Remember when it was May Day and everyone came with a May Day hat with ribbons on, to dance around the May Pole?'

'Not really.'

'Except me, cos you forgot.'

Helen remembers.

Paul laughs. 'OMG, that's nothing,' he says with his mouth full. 'I remember once when Mum was an hour late picking me up from school because there was an accident on the coast road and she couldn't turn the car around or anything. She didn't have her mobile with her and no one knew where she was. Any more grub?'

Disappointment bounces off Paul like hail. He is amenable, unguarded, confiding. 'We did about boners in biology,' he said to her recently. 'Someone said that the Leaning Tower of Pisa is like a giant boner!' He laughed for a long time and eventually she had to join in. They stood in the kitchen together, giggling madly, until Jessica appeared in the doorway and drizzled sadness over the pair of them.

The mother-daughter bond is the strongest, most loving tie of all. Girls need a loving, committed, attentive mother.

With such a mother, what could possibly go wrong?!

(*All you need is love!* by Pauline McCartney)

At bedtime, Helen arms herself with fiction. 'How about this story, Jess?' she asks.

'No.'

'Or this one?'

'No.'

'How about you choose one yourself?'

'It's okay. We can have the one you wanted.'

'I was just making a suggestion, Jess. It's your choice. What would *you* like?'

'No, it's okay, we can have the one you wanted. I don't mind.'

'Well I was hoping you would pick one that you like, so it would be more fun for you.'

'I'm trying to be kind, Mummy.'

'Sorry.' Helen reads Jessica a story about a dog. He runs away from home and gets so dirty that his family don't recognise him. They don't believe it's him until he's been in the bath. Then everyone hugs, and they are all happy. 'That's a lovely story, isn't it?' Helen smiles.

'I wanted *Nobody Likes Me.*' Jessica shrugs in a way that is meant to suggest not minding and minding very much all at once. 'The one where the boy's mum is horrible to him and he hides under the bed and falls asleep and dreams about—'

Helen bends to kiss the soft skin of her cheek.

'Ouch.' Jessica rubs her face hard with the flat of her hand.

'Sorry. I love you, Jess. Goodnight.'

'Goodnight, Mummy.'

Jessica has arranged her cuddly animals so that they are lying with their heads on her pillow. There is a small corner left for her. She rolls onto her side to make more room for the creatures, allowing herself a tiny wrap of duvet. And then she is still.

Later, after Paul has gone to bed, Helen reads. Tonight she eschews help for happiness. She ignores the growing pile of hard-backed, hard-faced, hard-to-follow advice, and grasps her earlier happy thought.

It's dark outside when she falls asleep on the sofa, her head resting on the pages of a small poetry book. She dreams of Jessica's toes curled like claws, scuttling across the bottom of the swimming pool in the thick silence, oblivious to her poolside cries of, 'Time for you, and time for me, Jess.'

Adam Marek

The Stone Thrower

Hal was awakened by a brief expletive from one of the chickens outside. And then there was another, coupled with a dull thud. Out of bed, Hal stuck his head into the hoverfly graveyard between netting and pane to see that in the enclosure directly below the window, two of the chickens were dead.

And then a third fell. Right there as Hal watched. Something had shot down from the sky and smacked its head against the chicken wire, felling it with a squawk. A black pebble. The kind Maddy and his boys were collecting from the lake shore just yesterday, right outside the holiday house they'd fled to. Now, the other stones in the pen, the ones that had killed the first two chickens, were conspicuous beside them. Three stones, three dead chickens.

Hal followed the line of trajectory back, all the way across to the other side of the lake, where there was a person, a male, young. His white T-shirt was vivid against the dark wall of conifers behind as he curled his arm, winding himself up onto his back foot. He uncoiled with a co-ordinated swish that took in the whole of his body, terminating at his fingertips. The pebble he threw only became visible at the top of its arc, as it rounded against the brightening sky. Its descent was invisible, until it flared into being again, upon the head of chicken number four.

Now almost half the coop was killed.

These were not Hal's chickens, but while he rented the house by the lake they were his charges. Indignation took him outside in his pyjamas, stopping only to plunge his feet into the still-damp boots that waited by the porch door.

'Oi!' He yelled, with his hands cupped either side of his mouth. 'What the hell are you doing?' The other side of the lake was far, five minutes in a rowing boat or a ten-minute walk round the side, too far to think about chasing the kid off.

Again the boy cocked his arm back and threw. Hal retreated to the porch, imagining what havoc a pebble lobbed with such force might wreak on his skull.

Hal heard the whistle of the stone displacing air as it shot into the coop and struck the back of chicken number five. The remaining four hopped up against the wire, all in the same corner, as if once there had been a door there.

Hal's binoculars were hanging on one of the hooks in the porch, alongside musty raincoats and propped oars. His hands shook as he looked through them, jiggling the image of the boy in the lenses. Hal did not feel the same sense of invisibility that he felt when watching the redstarts and flycatchers in the woods behind the house. Instead, he felt an increased sense of vulnerability, as if he were physically closer to the boy, and therefore an easier target – if there were such a thing as an easier target to this demon who'd felled five chickens with five stones from an impossible distance. Impossible, because Hal had thrown stones from the shore himself, with his boys, on several occasions over the last week. There'd been no attempts to throw stones to the other side because it was inconceivably far. They'd thrown only for the pleasure of throwing.

The boy looked only a year or two older than Joseph, the eldest of his boys, maybe 11 or 12. He moved with a disquieting confidence for a child. His hair was long at the front, a blonde fringe that hung over his right eye, all the way to his mouth. He stooped again, and the range of his spine stood out all the way down his back.

When he stood and threw, the thrust of his arm, the coiling and uncoiling of energy in his form, was breathtaking. Here was art. Prodigious skill, and in his face an Olympian's focus. Not the snarl Hal had expected, the kind of wonky facial arrangement that the local yahoos presented when they goaded him from the bus shelter on his trips to the chemist. This boy looked like a good boy. He was clean, and were he in a playing field hurling baseballs, his fringe tucked inside a cap, he would be a magnet for admiration.

The sixth chicken fell.

'For God's sake will you stop!' he yelled from the porch. The force of the words drove spit from his lips. 'I have children in the house. I have a sick child. This isn't our house. These aren't my chickens.'

There were footsteps on the stairs, and then the inner door to the porch opened. It was Maddy in a pair of Hal's pyjamas.

'Get back upstairs!' Hal said. 'There's a crazy kid out here throwing stones.'

'Throwing stones?' Maddy came fully into the porch, rubbing the heel of her palm in her eye.

The seventh chicken was struck in such a way that a flurry of feathers sprang out from the point of impact on its lower back. Its last cluck was a wheeze.

Now the remaining two were hopping from one corner to the next, frantic, bobbing their heads forward, stepping round their fallen comrades.

'Don't go out there!' Maddy said as Hal flung open the door and bolted outside. Across the lake, the boy passed a pebble from right hand to left. Hal ran, and while he ran he threw his hands up into the air and called out 'Stop!' once again. But the boy did not stop.

'Get in here you idiot!' Maddy said, her head venturing no more than an inch or two outside. 'Have you called the police yet? I'm going to call the police.'

While Hal's fingers were on the latch of the coop, he saw the boy throw. Hal flicked the metal hook from the eye. The chicken wire bit into his fingers as he lifted the door to swing it open. He scampered back to the house and was at the porch door when he turned and saw the eighth chicken fall, twitching. One of its legs kicked a regular beat in the dirt. It managed maybe ten of these kicks before a second stone struck its head, making its legs buck up off the ground.

'Is the number for the police still the same on a mobile?' Maddy said.

The boys were on the stairs now, and Maddy yelled at them, 'Get back in your room! Keep away from the windows!' But her panic brought smiles to their faces, widened their eyes, quickened their footsteps.

Hal barked with exasperation at the last chicken, whose timid evacuation of the cage was happening one slow strut at a time. Hal's shouts did nothing but force blinks out of its dumb face.

Again the boy stooped.

Hal ran out, leaping from side to side, corralling the chicken into the corner where the coop butted up against the house. Inside, Maddy held the boys back with her outstretched leg while she translated this event into terse statements of fact for the emergency services operator.

The back of Hal's neck prickled, sensitive to the stone's accelerating descent. He raked his fingers through the soft dirt and flung a handful of powdered soil and tiny stones to the left of the chicken, causing her to flap and flee, stranding herself in the corner, head pushed up against the house. And it was here that Hal seized her, throwing the whole length of himself into the dirt.

With the chicken squeezed between his two palms, he rolled onto his back, pivoted on his backside and was up and out of the way just as the stone hit the spot where he'd been less than a second ago and bounced up against the whitewood panels of the house.

Inside the safety of the porch, the boys were amazed at the sight of a chicken alive indoors. Hal held it aloft, his pride immovable under the blizzard of Maddy's curses.

'Are the police on their way?' He asked.

'...Such a moron, thick as pig shit,' Maddy continued. 'Risking your life for a goddamned chicken. The boys and me alone in the house...'

'Who's out there Dad?' Joseph asked. 'Are the chickens really all dead?'

'All but this one,' Hal said, holding it up again. The chicken's neck was fully elongated, its head swivelling left and right, eyes rapid-blinking, camera shutters to take everything in. Hal looked out the window, at the boy across the lake, but only just glimpsed him walking away before the window exploded inwards.

The boys screamed. Something flashed across Hal's face. His whole world shattered into bright fragments. They were stunned by the sound of shards striking floor tiles. Hands and arms flew up protectively, backs turned away from the window. There was blood. And all the while, he held the chicken high, his arms maintaining their stalwart position against the chaos.

Only when all the glass had fallen, and the clatter was ended, could Hal comprehend the scene. The faces of Maddy and both boys were spattered with blood. He felt something well up on his eyebrow and drip down onto his cheekbone. The chicken was decapitated, still kicking between his hands. Its blood ran down his arms, gathering at his elbows.

They were each stranded in a sea of glass, Maddy ordering them not to move, she and the boys barefoot. Their walking boots were cups for long and wicked splinters. Outside, the boy was gone.

Jon McGregor

Wires

It was a sugar beet, presumably, since that was a sugar beet lorry in front of her and this thing turning in the air at something like sixty miles an hour had just fallen off it. It looked like a giant turnip, and was covered in mud, and basically looked more or less like whatever she would have imagined a sugar beet to look like if she'd given it any thought before now. Which she didn't think she had. It was totally filthy. They didn't make sugar out of that, did they? What did they do, grind it? Cook it?

Regardless, whatever, it was coming straight for her.

Meaning this was, what, one of those time-slows-down moments or something. Her life was presumably going to start flashing in front of her eyes right about now. She wondered why she hadn't screamed or anything. 'Oh,' seemed to be about as much as she'd managed. But in the time it had taken to say 'Oh' she'd apparently had the time to make a list of all the things she was having the time to think about, like, ie *Item One*, how she'd said 'Oh' without any panic or fear, and did that mean she was repressed or just calm or collected or what; *Item Two*, what would Marcus say when he found out, would he try and find someone to blame, such as herself for driving too close or even for driving on her own at all, or such as the lorry driver for overloading the lorry, or such as her, again, for not having joined the union like he'd told her to, like anyone was in a union these days, especially anyone with a part-time job who was still at uni and not actually all that bothered about pension rights or legal representation; *Item Three*, but she couldn't possibly be thinking all this in the time it was taking for the sugar beet to turn in the air and crash through the windscreen, if that's what it was going to do, and what then, meaning this must be like a neural-pathway illusion or something; *Item Four*, actually Marcus did go on sometimes, he did reckon himself, and how come she thought things like that about him so often, maybe she was being unfair, because they were good together, people had told her they were good

197

together, but basically she was confused and she didn't know where she stood; *Item Five*, a witty and deadpan way of mentioning this on her status update would be something like, Emily Wilkinson is sweet enough already thanks without a sugar beet in the face, although actually she wouldn't be able to put that, if that's what was actually going to happen, thinking about it logically; *Item Six*, although did she really even know what a neural pathway was, or was it just something she'd heard someone else talk about and decided to start saying?

Item Seven was just, basically, wtf.

Meanwhile: before she had time to do anything useful, like e.g swerve or brake or duck or throw her arms up in front of her face, the sugar beet smashed through the windscreen and thumped into the passenger seat beside her. There was a roar of cold air. And now she swerved, only now, once there was no need and it just made things more dangerous, into the middle lane and back again into the slow lane. It was totally instinctive, and totally useless, and basically made her think of her great-grandad saying God help us if there's a war on. She saw other people looking at her, or she thought she did, all shocked faces and big mouths; a woman pulling at her boyfriend's arm and pointing, a man swearing and reaching for his phone, another man in a blue van waving her over to the hard shoulder. But she might have imagined this, or invented it afterwards. Marcus was always saying that people didn't look at her as much as she thought they did. She never knew whether he meant this to reassure her or if he was saying she reckoned herself too much.

Anyway. Point being. Status update: Emily Wilkinson is still alive.

She pulled over to the hard shoulder and came to a stop. The blue van pulled over in front of her. She put her hazard lights on and listened to the clicking sound they made. When she looked up the people in the passing cars already had no idea what had happened. The drama was over. The traffic was back to full speed, the lorry was already miles down the road. She wondered if she was supposed to start crying. She didn't feel like crying.

Someone was standing next to the car. 'Bloody hell,' he said. He peered in at her through the hole in the windscreen. He looked like a mechanic or a breakdown man or something. He was wearing a waxed jacket with rips in the elbows, and jeans. He looked tired; his eyes were puffy and dark and his breathing was heavy. He rested his hand on the bonnet and leaned in closer. 'Bloody *hell*,' he said again, raising his voice against the traffic; 'you all right, love?' She smiled, and nodded, and shrugged, which was weird, which meant was she for some reason apologising for his concern? 'Bloody *hell*,' he said for a third time. 'You could have been killed.'

Thanks. Great. This was, what, news?

She looked down at the sugar beet, which was sitting on a heap of glass on the passenger seat beside her. The bits of glass were small and lumpy, like gravel. She noticed more bits of glass on the floor, and the dashboard, and spread across her lap. She noticed that her left arm was scratched, and that she was still holding on to the steering wheel, and that maybe she wasn't breathing quite as much as she should have been, although that happened whenever she thought about her breathing, it going wrong like that, too deep or too shallow or too quick, although that wasn't just her though, surely, it was one of those well-known paradoxes, like a Buddhist thing or something. Total mindlessness. Mindfulness. Just breathe.

'The police are on their way,' someone else said. She looked up and saw another man, a younger man in a sweatshirt and jeans, holding up a silver phone. 'I just called the police,' he said. 'They're on their way.' He seemed pleased to have a phone with him, the way he was holding it, like this was his first one or something. Which there was no way. His jeans had grass stains on the knees, and his boots were thick with mud.

'You called them, did you?' the older man asked. The younger man nodded, and put his phone in his pocket, and looked at her. She sat there, waiting for the two of them to catch up. Like: yes, a sugar beet had come through the windscreen; no, she wasn't hurt; yes, this other guy did phone the police. Any further questions? I can email you the notes? The younger man looked through the hole in the windscreen, and at the windscreen itself, and whistled. Actually whistled: this long descending note like the sound effect of a rock falling towards someone's head in an old film. What was that?

'You all right?' he asked her. 'You cut or anything? You in shock?' She shook her head. Not that she knew how she would know she was in shock. She was pretty sure one of the symptoms of being in shock would be not thinking you were in shock. Like with hypothermia, when you take off your clothes and roll around laughing in the snow. She'd read that somewhere. He looked at the sugar beet and whistled again. 'I mean,' he said, and now she didn't know if he was talking to her or to the other man; 'that could've been fatal, couldn't it?' The other man nodded and said something in agreement. They both looked at her again. 'You could have been killed,' the younger man said. It was good of him to clarify that for her. She wondered what she was supposed to say. They looked as if they were waiting for her to ask something, to ask for help in some way.

'Well. Thanks for stopping,' she said. They could probably go now, really, if they'd called the police. There was no need to wait. She thought she probably wanted them to go now.

'Oh no, it's nothing, don't be daft,' the older man said.

'Couldn't just leave you like that, could we?' the younger man said. He looked at her arm. 'You're bleeding,' he said. 'Look.' He pointed to the scratches on her arm, and she looked down at herself. She could see the blood, but she couldn't feel anything. There wasn't much of it. It could be someone else's, couldn't it? But there wasn't anyone else. It must be hers. But she couldn't feel anything. She looked back at the younger man.

'It's fine,' she said. 'It's nothing. Really. Thanks.'

'No, it might be though,' he said, 'it might get infected. You have to be careful with things like that. There's a first-aid box in the van. Hang on.' He turned and walked back to the van, a blue Transit with the name and number of a landscape gardening company painted across the back, and a little cartoon gardener with a speech bubble saying no job was too small. The doors were tied shut with a length of orange rope. The number plate was splattered with mud, but it looked like a K reg. K450 something, although she wasn't sure if that was 0 the number or O the letter. The older man turned and smiled at her, while they were waiting, and she supposed that was him trying to be reassuring but to be honest it looked a bit weird. Although he probably couldn't help it. He probably had some kind of condition. Like a degenerative eye condition, maybe? And then on top of that, which would be painful enough, he had to put up with people like her thinking he looked creepy when he was just trying to be nice. She smiled back; she didn't want him thinking she'd been thinking all that about him looking creepy or weird.

'Police will be here in a minute,' he said. She nodded. 'Lorry must have been overloaded,' he said. 'Driver's probably none the wiser even now.'

'No,' she said, glancing down at the sugar beet again. 'I suppose not.' The younger man came back, waving a green plastic first-aid box at her. He looked just as pleased as when he'd held up the phone. She wondered if he was on some sort of special supported apprenticeship or something, if he was a little bit learning challenged, and then she thought it was probably discriminatory of her to have even thought that and she tried to get the thought out of her mind. Only you can't get thoughts out of your mind just by trying; that was another one of those Buddhist things. She should just concentrate on not thinking about her breathing instead, she thought. Just, total mindlessness. Mindfulness. Just breathe.

He passed the first-aid box through the hole in the windscreen. His hands were stained with oil and mud, and as they touched hers they felt heavy and awkward. She put the box in her lap and opened it. She wondered what he wanted her to do. 'I don't know,' he said. 'I just thought. Has it got antiseptic cream in there?' She rummaged through the bandages and wipes and creams and scissors. And now what. She took out a wipe, dabbed at her arm, and closed the box. She handed it back to him, holding the bloody wipe in one hand.

'Thanks,' she said. 'I think I'll be okay now.' Was she talking too slowly? Patronising him? Or was she making reasonable allowances for his learning challenges? But he might not even be that. She was over-complicating the situation, probably. Which was another thing Marcus said to her sometimes, that she did that. She looked at him. He shrugged.

'Well, yeah,' he said. 'If you're sure. I just thought, you know.'

Status update: Emily Wilkinson regrets not having signed up for breakdown insurance.

'Thanks,' she said.

She'd chosen Hull because she'd thought it would sound interesting to say she was going to a provincial university. Or more exactly because she thought it would make her sound interesting to even say 'provincial university', which she didn't think anyone had said since about 1987 or some other time way before she was born. She wasn't even exactly sure what provincial meant. Was it just anywhere not London? That seemed pretty sweeping. That was where most people lived. Maybe it meant anywhere that wasn't London or Oxford or Cambridge, and that was still pretty sweeping. Whatever, people didn't seem to say it any more, which was why she'd been looking forward to saying it. Only it turned out that no one knew what she was talking about and they mostly thought she was saying provisional, which totally wasn't the same thing at all.

Anyway, though, that hadn't been the only reason she'd chosen Hull. Another reason was it was a long way from home. As in definitely too far to visit. Plus when she went on the open day she'd loved the way the river smelt of the sea, and obviously the bridge, which looked like something from a film, and also the silence you hit when you got to the edge of the town, and the way it didn't take long to get to the edge of town. And of course she'd liked the Larkin thing, except again it didn't seem like too many people were bothered about that. Or knew about it. Or knew how much it meant, if they did know about it. When she first got there she kept putting 'Emily Wilkinson is a bit chilly and smells of fish' on her status updates, but no one got the reference so she gave it up. Plus it made her look weird, obviously, even after she'd explained it in the comments.

She'd met Marcus in her second year, when he'd taught a module on 'The Literature of Marginal(ised) Places'. Which she'd enjoyed enough to actually go to at least half of the lectures rather than just download the notes. He had a way of explaining things like he properly wanted you to understand, instead of just wanting to show off or get through the class as quick as he could. There was something sort of generous about the way he talked, in class, and the way he listened to the students. Plus he was what it was difficult to think of a better word for than totally buff, and also had what she couldn't be more articulate than call a lovely mouth, and basically made her spend quite a lot of time not actively addressing the issues of appropriation inherent in a culturally privileged form such as literary fiction taking exclusion and marginality as its subject. Her friend Jenny had said she couldn't see it at all, as in the buffness and the lovely mouth rather than the inherent appropriation, but that had only made her think it was maybe something more along the lines of a genuine connection thing and not just some kind of stereotypical type of crush; and Jenny did at least agree that no way did it count as inappropriate if it was just a PhD student and not an actual lecturer. His last seminar had been on the Tasmanian novel, which it turned out there were quite a few of, and afterwards he'd kept her talking until the others had left and said were there any issues she wanted to discuss and actually did she want to go for a drink. To which her response had been, and that took you so long why?

There hadn't really been anyone before Marcus. Not since coming to university, anyway. There'd been a few things at parties, and she'd slept with one of her housemates a bunch of times, but nothing serious enough to make her change her relationship setting. With Marcus it had been different, almost immediately. He'd asked her out, like formally, and they'd had late-night conversations about their relationship and what relationships meant and even whether or not they were in love and how they would know and whether love could ever be defined without reference to the other. She didn't really know. She thought being in love probably didn't mean telling your girlfriend what she could wear when you went to the pub together, or asking her not to talk to certain people, or telling her she was the reason you couldn't finish your thesis.

They hadn't moved in together, but almost as soon as they'd started going out their possessions had begun drifting from one house to the other until it felt like they were just living together in two places. Sometimes when she woke up it took her a moment to remember which house she was in. It wasn't always a nice feeling. Which meant, what? She fully had no idea what it meant. Because she liked Marcus, she liked him a lot. She liked the conversations they had, which were smart and complicated and went on for hours. And she liked the way he looked at her when he wanted to do the things she'd been thinking about in class when she should have been thinking about discourses of liminality, when she'd been imagining saying he was welcome to cross her threshold any day. There was still all that. But there were other things. Things that made her uncomfortable, uncertain, things she was pretty sure weren't part of how a relationship was supposed to make you feel happy or good about yourself or whatever it was a relationship was supposed to make you feel.

She should be calling him now, and she wasn't. He'd want her to have called, when he heard. Something like this. He should be the first person she thought of calling. He'd think it was odd that she hadn't. He'd be hurt. She thought about calling Jenny instead, to tell her what had happened, or her supervisor, to tell her she'd be late getting back to the office. She should call someone, probably, but she couldn't really imagine having the words to explain it and she couldn't face having anyone else tell her she could have been killed and plus anyway she was totally fine, wasn't she? She looked down at the sugar beet again. Was that what that smell was? It wasn't a sugary smell at all. It was more like an earthy smell, like wet earth, like something rotting in the earth. She didn't see how they could get from that to a bowl of white sugar on a café table, or even to that sort of wet, boozy smell you got when you drove past the refinery, coming up the A1. Which come to think of it was probably where the lorry would have been heading. It would be, what, an hour's drive from here? Maybe she should go there and give them back their sugar beet, tell them what had happened. Complain, maybe.

The passenger door opened, and the older man leaned in towards her. 'You need to get out,' he said. It seemed a bit too directive, the way he said it. She didn't move. 'It's not safe, being on the hard shoulder like this,' he added. 'We should all be behind the barrier.' They'd been discussing this, had they? It looked like they'd been discussing something. The older man was already holding out his hand to help her across the passenger seat. She looked at the traffic, roaring and weaving and hurtling past, and she remembered hearing about incidents where people had been struck and killed on the hard shoulder, when they were changing a tyre, or going for a piss, or just stopping to help. She remembered her cousin once telling her about a school minibus which had driven into the back of a Highways Maintenance truck and burst into flames. Which meant they were right about this, did it, probably? She swung her feet over into the passenger's side, took the man's hand, and squeezed out onto the tarmac. It was an awkward manoeuvre, and she didn't think she'd completed it with much elegance or style. The younger man was already standing behind the barrier, and she clambered over to join him. She didn't do that very gracefully either. He started climbing up the embankment.

'Just in case,' he said, looking back at her. Meaning what, she wondered. 'Something could flip, couldn't it?' he said, and he did something with his hands which was presumably supposed to look like a vehicle striking a barrier and somersaulting across it. The older man caught her eye, and nodded, and she followed them both up the embankment, through the litter and the long grass.

It was much colder at the top. Sort of exposed. The wind was whipping away the sound of the traffic, making her feel further from the road than they really were. The two men looked awkward, as though maybe they were uncomfortable about the time this whole situation was taking. The younger man made the whistling noise again. She could barely hear it against the wind.

'You're lucky,' he said, nodding down towards her car. 'I mean, you know. You're lucky we stopped. You could have been killed.' She didn't know what to say to this. She nodded, and folded her arms against the cold. The older man arched his back, rubbing at his neck with both hands.

'They'll be here soon,' he said, and she nodded again, looking around.

Behind them, the ground sloped away towards a small woodland of what she thought might be hawthorn or rowan trees or something like that. The ones with the red berries. There were ragged strips of bin liners and carrier bags hanging from the branches, flapping in the wind. Past the trees, there was a warehouse, and an access road, and she noticed that the streetlights along the access road were coming on already. Beyond the access road, a few miles further away, there were some houses which she wasn't sure if they were some estate on the outskirts of Hull or some other town altogether. Hull was further than that, she was pretty sure. It was the other side of the estuary, and they were still south of the river. Almost certainly.

The older man started down the slope, towards the trees. 'I'm just going to, you know,' he said. 'While we're waiting.' She turned away, looking back at the road. She was getting colder now. She looked at her car, and at the blue van. They were both rocking gently in the slipstream of the passing traffic, their hazard lights blinking in sequence. She wondered if she felt like crying yet. She didn't think so. It still didn't seem like the right moment.

She would talk to Marcus at the weekend, she decided. He'd understand, when it came down to it. Once he gave her a chance to explain. She'd say something like although they'd been good together at times and she was still very fond of him she just couldn't see where things were going for them. She didn't like the way he made her feel about herself, sometimes. She needed some time to find out who she was and what she needed from a relationship. Something like that.

She'd tried it out with Jenny. Jenny had said it sounded about right. Jenny had said she thought Marcus was reasonable and would probably take it on board, although obviously he'd still be disappointed. That was how she talked sometimes, like she was a personal guidance counsellor or something, or an older and wiser cousin. Whereas in fact she was only like a year older, and had spent that year mostly in Thailand and Australia, which was her version of travelling the world and which she thought made her the total source of wisdom when in fact it made her the total source of knowing about youth hostels and full-moon parties and not even having heard of Philip fucking Larkin. And she was wrong about Marcus. It was way more likely he would shout at her when she told him. Or break something. It wouldn't be the first time. Everyone thought he was so reasonable. But she wasn't going to back down this time. She was certain of it, suddenly. Something like this, it made you think about things, about your priorities. She could say that to him, in fact. She could explain what had happened and that it had made her rethink a few things. Maybe she should call him now in fact, and tell him what had happened. So he'd already have the context when she talked about wanting to finish things. Maybe that would be sensible. She should do that. She wanted to do that, she realised. She wanted to hear his voice, and to know that he knew she was okay. Which meant what. She wanted him to know where she was. Her phone was still in her bag, in the car. She started to move down the embankment. The younger man grabbed her arm.

'You should stay up here,' he said. 'It's safer.' She looked at him, and at his hand on her arm. 'They'll be here in a minute,' he said.

'I just need to get my phone,' she said. 'I need to call someone. I'll be careful, thanks.' She tried to step away, but he held her back. 'Excuse me?' she said.

'You're probably in shock,' he said. 'You should be careful. Maybe you should sit down.'

'I'm okay, actually, thanks? I don't want to sit down?' She spoke clearly, looking him in the eye, raising her voice above the wind and the traffic. Plus raising her voice against maybe he was a bit deaf, as well as the learning-challenged thing. She wanted him to let go of her arm. She tried to pull away again, but his grip was too tight. She looked at him, like: what are you doing? He shook his head. He said something else, but she couldn't hear him. She didn't know if the wind had picked up or what was going on. He looked confused, as if he couldn't remember what he was supposed to be saying.

She glanced down the other side of the embankment, and saw the older man at the edge of the woodland. He was standing with his back to the trees, looking up at the two of them, his hands held tensely by his sides. What was he. He seemed to be trying to say something to the younger man. He seemed to be waiting for something. She tried to pull away. But what.

John Burnside

The Deer Larder

The first email arrived on Thursday evening, around 9 o'clock. I remember it quite clearly, because I had spent the day at the hospital, going from one department to the next, having various tests and X-rays done before ending up back in rheumatology, being examined by my usual doctor and a very tall, rather pretty student who hadn't quiet mastered the necessary air of professional detachment. The consultant was detached enough for them both, though. As usual. Which is not to say that she was lacking in any way – quite the contrary, in fact. No: as always, Elizabeth Marsh – my beautiful, shrewd, faintly glamourous doctor – displayed the reassuring mix of good humour, consideration and mild irony that made me thankful I had been assigned to a female specialist rather than a man. If there is one thing I cannot abide, it's the seriousness of male professionals.

Still, St Hubert's was a teaching hospital so, with the best will in the world, it was hard not to feel like the elephant man as she pointed out the various interesting features of my disease: the localised but fairly extreme psoriasis, the odd little pools of inflammation on the scan, the visibly damaged areas revealed by the X-rays, while the younger woman – whose dark hair and very blue eyes reminded me, each time our eyes met, of a girlfriend I'd had twenty years before – tried to seem unperturbed. Of course, I knew things had worsened since my last appointment, but I had tried not to think about it too much. Some of the pain was new, but I am a fairly old hand at this by now and I have been preparing myself for this slow fall into creaky middle age since my first bout of iritis back in the early 90s. I do my bit to keep the whole process civilised: I take an interest, I make light, I use the kind of language doctors like – which is to say, accurate and undramatic, the language of a detached observer, descriptive, neutral and, most important of all, entirely innocent of any pretence to clinical knowledge. Privately, I am fascinated by the way it all works – the body, the disease, the cause and effects, the observable phenomena, the management of pain and expectations. Still, I am always glad to get back home and be alone again – and that night was no different. Few pleasures equal the relief from locking the front door behind me, turning on the desk lamp and settling down to work. The relief, and the simple happiness.

The email arrived just as I was taking my first break. My routine is pretty consistent: I do a few pages – I write commercial film scripts, mostly for training and PR companies – then I get a pot of coffee going and check my emails. That night, it was the only item in my inbox, which was odd, because there are usually masses of minor tasks and requests to deal with. At first sight, I thought it was one of those joke mails that sometimes slip through the spam detector, as specimen of those random fragments of surreal narrative that people send out by the thousand to complete strangers – presumably for some reason known to them, though I have never been able figure out what that reason might be. My ISP is pretty good at filtering that kind of thing, but occasionally they get through – sad little narratives of trouble and desire, of achievement and loss, always starting in the middle of the story and never reaching anything so satisfying as an end. This seemed no different, in spite of the fact it was addressed to a specific individual, someone the sender seemed to know fairly well. But then, that might have been part of the game, part of the art, as it were.

On the other hand, this email might have ended up in my inbox because of a simple error – an address badly transcribed or mistyped after a long day's work, or a few too many glasses of wine. For some reason, I didn't delete the message right away, so I can quote it in full:

Dear Monique

Well, here I am on the island, sitting in my little study with a nice glass of – guess what? – and hammering away at the Maupassant book. Finally. Got heaps done already and I have only been here four days. I've got to 'La Maison Tellier' and I still can't get over how wonderful it is – how wonderful, and how terrifying when you think of what's to come and how this book foreshadows it all.

It's beautiful here, on this side of the island. This morning started out grey and drizzly, but by mid-afternoon it had cleared and now, in this soft, slightly pastel early evening light, it's completely still, the kind of stillness where

everything seems more vivid and, at the same time, more convincing. From
the window, all I can see is the flat expanse of the water, still as mercury,
and the white hull of a sailing boat moored just opposite the jetty by our one
and only shop. It's preternaturally serene, utterly calm and almost silent – yet
it's changing all the time. Something is always shifting. The light, the colours,
the reflections. In the evenings, the water can be periwinkle blue for half an
hour or so before it darkens, smooth, though not in a hard way, but with a
strange surface tension, a strange perturbability to it. Like quicksilver – yes, like
quicksilver, always about to change, always on the point of shifting and, at the
same time, so very smooth, so very still.

You would love it here. And I meant what I said in my last email – you
really are welcome any time. It is easy enough to get here – just let me know
and I will pick you up at the ferry. I promise I won't make a big thing of it and
I'm not asking you to change your mind. Honestly. I just think it's silly for us
not to be friends, don't you think?
Love
Martin

That was all. It wasn't particularly interesting, it was even slightly
embarrassing, to have been given such an unexpected glimpse of
Martin's sad love life. Obviously, Monique had recently dumped him,
probably for someone a little less wet and, despite those assurances to the
contrary, his rhapsodies about the island were intended to get back, on
any terms, if only for a few intense and awkward days. Then, of course,
the arguments would begin again – I knew that scenario well enough,
after all – and there would be tears, *his* probably, before the week was out.
No: there was nothing very interesting about this little love story and, to
be honest, the only thing that caught my attention was the mention of
the Maupassant. It wasn't six months since I had written a script, for an
educational production company, about Maupassant and Poe, and I'd
been captivated by the beauty of the man's work – a beauty that seemed
to me unbearably poignant, considering how painful and squalid his life
had been. Of course if I'd been more attentive that first night, I would
have seen the reference to Maupassant – that mad syphilitic who wrote
one or two of the most horrifying stories in the entire European tradition
– as an obvious clue, a pointer to the game that was about to played. And
for as long as I could manage it, I convinced myself that what happened

next really was a game, a diversion, like so many other diversions that one finds out there in the cold reaches of cyberspace, where nothing is as it seems and everything from the latest atrocities in Gaza and Chad to the antics of *Big Brother*, has the quality and status of a diversion.

But I wasn't paying attention – on the contrary. I was thinking about the side effects of the new drugs I had just been prescribed, about my diminishing skills as a touch-typist – my fingers had already started to warp into strange shapes over the keyboard – and, most of all, I was thinking about happiness, and about how much time remained before the solitude I had worked so hard to attain was transformed from a joy into a burden by the vagaries of my far-from-rare disease.

For the next several days I had no commitments – which meant I could stay in the flat and work as and when I liked, breaking off for coffee and a tuna sandwich, or an old movie on DVD, before returning to my desk for one of those *small* revelations that makes everything magical. When I say small revelations, I'm not being overly modest: I don't entertain big ideas, not these days anyway, and I have no illusions about my supposed talents. I just take what somebody else gives me – a defined project, with clear limits and constraints – and I try to light it up, somehow, like a medieval copyist illuminating his given text. Maybe I wanted something else when I first started out, but nowadays, this is enough. I work according to my own schedule and, occasionally, I create something that shines – shines, yes, even if it's only for a few moments in a mostly workaday piece. This is as much as I am allowed by the job I have chosen to do, but it turns out to be more than enough and, even now, when my body has started to betray me in all manner of subtle, yet utterly persuasive ways, I can still be surprised by the happiness I feel when I lock myself away and get to work, knowing that I won't be interrupted. Sometimes I want to kick myself for not having arrived at this place sooner – because it took me a ridiculously long while to realise that happiness was a much simpler proposition than I had first imagined. Growing up, we think it's going to be some big event: love at first sight, say, or a brilliant career; glittering prizes; a perfect wife; beautiful, gifted children. I have none of these things, but I am comfortable and I do work that, more often than not, I enjoy, work that leaves room in my day-to-day existence for the unglamorous, apparently negligible events that, cumulatively, add up to a more or less happy life. That's why there are no novels, or plays, or Hollywood movies about happiness. It's too ordinary, and it's too slow.

The second email, followed almost immediately by the third, came three days after the first and together, they betrayed a change in mood. That didn't surprise me – it would have been foolish of Monique to accept Martin's invitation, or even to take it seriously – but I was a little annoyed that the mistake, if it was a mistake, had been repeated. I was also somewhat embarrassed by the tone of the messages – there was an ugly desperation to them that made me a little queasy – and I deleted them immediately. I guessed that Martin had been drunk when he wrote them and I was fairly certain that he would wake the next morning feeling more than a little shamefaced. I even expected to receive an apology, sooner rather than later – and I was surprised again when it didn't come the very next day.

The one thing that didn't occur to me was to reply to Martin and inform him of his mistake – and, looking back, I don't know why I didn't do exactly that. Maybe I was embarrassed for myself, as well as for him. Maybe it was all too close to the bone, too much of a reminder of my own lover's folly. I didn't need any reminder of the old days– of the lovely and self-deceived time before I came to understand that wonderful remark of Maurois (a man who knew a thing or two about romantic love), a remark that has been taped to the wall next to my computer for years now:

LE BONHEUR EST UNE FLEUR QU' IL NE FAUT PAS *CUEILLIR*

I think, at the time, I even considered emailing those words to my mysterious correspondent, with a simple explanation of what had happened – but I didn't. If I had, I could have put this matter by and forgotten it – a choice that, for the basest of reasons, was no longer possible after the fourth email arrived, two days later, on a clear green evening when the city was winding up the business of the day and switching its lights on, one by one, silver and cherry red and gold, for the night to come.

It began abruptly: no greeting, no reference to the earlier emails, no attempt at the preamble. It assumed something it had no business to assume – or so it seemed until it occurred to me again that this was a piece of artifice, a device to draw me into the story. Or not to me, exactly – I was quite certain that I had not been targeted, as such – but the reader. Because, surely this was a fiction. Surely this was a literary game, a diversion that someone out there had devised for his own reasons – Martin, not Martin, it hardly mattered. Anybody can be anybody in cyberspace, after all – a fact that, on reflection, seems to me quite appalling now. It's all flimflam, it's all a con. I've always disliked the telephone because I can't see the other person's face – yet for years I was happy to conduct my business almost entirely by email, where I couldn't even hear a voice, or know if it was a man or a woman, a friend or a foe, even a person or a program that I was dealing with.

I'm not sure how to tell this, the email began. *You're going to think I'm crazy, or maybe you'll just put it down to too little sleep and my usual overactive imagination – and it's true, I haven't been sleeping, I've hardly slept at all since I got here in fact, but what I am about to tell you isn't some hallucination and it certainly didn't spring from my overactive mind. In fact, it didn't come from anywhere. It was just – there. It's been there all along; I just didn't see it till now.*

If you remember I said I was going to go for a long walk to clear my head – I didn't remember this, of course, because he hadn't said anything of the kind.

and that's where I was today, all day, walking on the old trail that runs clear across the island, up through the hills and over to the west side. The trail was made by some old one-legged patriarch from the late nineteenth century – he'd ride back and forth with his retinue all around him, surveying his domain, or stalking the deer, or whatever it was they did back then, and his people would keep it in order, or eight or so miles of it, from the eastern shore to the high pass through the hills and then down, past waterfalls and huge, tumbled rocks to this beautiful, lonely beach on the western side. On that side, there are no roads, so the only way to get to that beach is on foot, via this old track, which is mostly just a trail through the peat now, though there are still places where you find stone walkways and sometimes there will be an old culvert, with water running under your feet, or you'll find a couple of stepping stones in a shallow burn, buried in the water that can be tobacco dark with the peat or cool and clear as the cream of the well. Only sometimes, though. The rest of the time – when the burn is deep, say, or where the old track has crumbled away – it's all about wading through waist-high water, or slopping across wet peat and rushes or, worst of all, fighting your way through chest-high bracken, not knowing what's in there with you, waiting to strike at your ankles or leaping unnoticed into your clothes and hair. Midges, ticks, something the local folk call keds – and who knows what else. Let's just say it's not idyll. Still, for a while I was glad I'd made the effort. It was good to be out in the air, good to be out in the open, away from the house, with its frightful, yet strangely appealing shadows.

Anyhow, I got across fine and I stood a long time on the beach, communing with whatever was out there – I'm not going to say Nature, because it wasn't that, or not in the usual sense. Of course, I thought of you, and I wished you were with me. I stood awhile and looked out across the water and thought my thoughts. Then, just as I started to think about heading back, it started to rain. Nothing much, at first, just a slow, sweet smirr, more mist than rain really. Scotch mist, or something like it. It wasn't that bad and, to be honest, the ground was so wet underfoot, the paths streaming with cold water and the peat so thick and spongy, it was barely a step up from the bog, so a little bit more wet wasn't going to make that much of a difference.

Well, that's what I thought to begin with. By the time I got back up onto the hill, though it was pouring down, thick, heavy rain bouncing off my face and hands – I'd not thought to bring gloves, and my hands were suddenly freezing – so I could hardly see where I was going. The only thing for it was to put my head down and plod on, following the path where it led and trusting that I wouldn't go astray – and, of course, that was exactly what I did. I had a map, but it was useless out and, anyway, by the time I'd realised how far off-track I'd gone, it was sodden through. So I just kept going, trying to remember landmarks I had seen on my way over and keeping the big hill to my right. The fairy hill, they call it, but I don't think they're thinking about the fairies in children's books. I wasn't too worried, not to begin with at least. Mostly I was just annoyed with myself for not being better prepared. But I was OK, in spite of everything. I was trying to see it as an adventure, and I was thinking about getting back to the house and getting into a nice hot bath with a big tumbler of whisky and some music on the radio.

When I first caught sight of the girl, I didn't believe she was real. I thought it was a mirage, or maybe some kind of Brocken spectre, one of those tricks of the light or the gloaming that hill walkers tell you about. I mean, what else could I think? One moment, I was alone and then, suddenly, she was there, walking beside me, step for step, through the wet peat. She had her head down – she didn't look at me, not once – but she knew I was there. She knew I was there from the first – and that was why her head was down, because I was there. She didn't want to look at me, she was desperately trying to pretend I wasn't there – and it came to me, why I cannot begin to think, but it came to me that she was frightened. I frightened her. And, God knows, she frightened me too – but what frightened me most, at that moment was her fear. Because, at that moment, as we walked in step through the driving rain, I felt like a monster, or an apparition. That's how I still feel, now that I'm back, and neither the bath nor the whisky – not one, but four, maybe five big glasses of the stuff – can change that fact.

I don't know how long she was there, beside me. It felt like ages but it probably wasn't and then, just as suddenly as she had come, she had gone, and I was alone again, trudging home in the rain, though at that very moment when I noticed she wasn't with me any more, I saw something – a configuration of rocks, a dark, kidney-shaped lochan in the middle distance – that told me I wasn't far from the car park where I had started out that morning, and I pressed on, trying to tell myself that it had all been a trick of the weather, a hallucination and nothing more, born out of fatigue and confusion. An hour later, I was behind the wheel of the car: sodden, frozen, caked in mud and peat, but safe.

But here's the thing. I'm back, and I'm warm and I'm all alone behind a locked door – but I'm not safe at all, and I'm not alone, even if there's nobody here with me. And I know it sounds crazy, but I can't helping thinking that something I should have left behind out there on the moor has come indoors and is hidden in the house somewhere, waiting to materialise. I'm not talking about a ghost, or some fairy creature from the old stories – I'm not even talking about that girl, I'm just – I don't know—

I know this sounds crazy, but please believe me when I say it's real. I'm not imagining it, it's here – It's here right now, somewhere at the edge of my vision, just outside the door or in a far corner of the house, and it's not something I can give a name to, but it's there and it has something to do with that girl. It's not like some ghost in a film, and it's not threatening or sinister, or not exactly. If anything, it's something more abstract than that, some disembodied current of fear or apprehension or

And that was where the message ended. In mid-sentence, just like that. Maybe he had hit the send button by accident, maybe he'd just given up trying to express what he couldn't put into words and, maybe, just maybe, something terrible had happened. Something that might bring Monique to his aid, and so begin the inevitable process of reconciliation.

And then again, maybe – and as soon as the thought occurred to me, I was immediately certain that I had guessed the truth – maybe this was all part of the game: a cliffhanger in a to-be-continued serial novel, designed to keep me – Martin/Not-Martin's anonymous reader – in suspense till the next instalment arrived.

I thought again of the Maupassant reference in the first message, and I had to smile. It was, quite clearly, a literary divertissement, a modern-day Horla story for the virtual world – and where better to accommodate Maupassant's terrifying sliver of nothingness than in cyberspace – and no doubt it would run and run. And I have to admit, this thought came as something of a relief. I had started to dislike poor lovesick Martin in his island hideaway. He certainly struck me as someone who had no business writing a biography of Maupassant. In fact, the very idea offended me. Now that I knew he was only a character, a literary invention, I could relax. That's how it is when you have attained the fragile, or perhaps I should say provisional condition of happiness – there are so many minor events, so many possible defects to the texture of existence that place it in jeopardy. Considered in that light, it's not so hard to see why, having broken his finger, Diogenes committed suicide: a moment's happiness is enough, if it is held uncontaminated in the tide of events, but it has to be perfect. It has to be incorruptible.

I fully expected another email the nest morning and I was surprised when nothing out of the ordinary showed up in my inbox. But then, I told myself, perhaps that was part of the game too. Perhaps my correspondent was savouring the fact that, as a storyteller, he had all the time in the world.

Whatever the reason, the next email didn't appear until four days had passed and, when it did, it was darker, and more conventional in approach. It even reminded me of those nineteenth-century stories I had read so closely when I'd worked on the Maupassant piece, beautiful, subtle stories where the first glimmers of existentialism began to shine through the fabric of the everyday – and I recalled the pleasure I had taken in that double nostalgia, first for the monochrome, coffee- and tobacco-scented nothingness-haunts-being mood of the 50s, and then, going back in time, for the damp, musty folds of bourgeois dread that prefigured it.

The email was four pages long: oddly formal, suffused with a sense of inevitable doom, it was more than a little overdone, but it had its moments nevertheless. The best passage came when Martin – I saw him, now, as something of a dandy, a displaced *fin de siècle* poet sitting at a computer screen in an office somewhere, making up stories for an unknown reader in the off hours – described his second encounter with the girl he'd met on the moor:

You remember I told you about the odd little hut behind the house

– I didn't remember, of course, but that was of no consequence –

and how I couldn't figure out what it was. It turns out that it's a deer larder, which is to say, a place where they used to hang the carcasses of the deer when they brought them in off the moor. It's louvred all the way round, so the wind blows through the slats and dries the meat – I looked this up in a book, and it really is fascinating how it works, how the wind blows through and the meat dries slowly. They say it's much better than a cold store, but nobody's allowed to use them any more, because of health and safety regulations—

Anyway, the next morning after my walk on the moor, I had this sudden, almost frantic urge to see inside – only it was locked and it took me a long time to find the key. I had to search and search and then finally I found it in a drawer in the kitchen, under a pile of rags. I don't know why it was so important to me, but it was – I had to see what it was like, I just had to.

Anyway, I finally unlocked the door and I stepped inside. Nobody had been in there for years, everything was covered in dust and cobwebs, and there wasn't much to see, just a few hooks hanging from a beam and a heap of old sacking. It had a dirt floor, and it smelled of earth and damp and, behind it all, a subtle trace of something in a far corner, something almost sweet, like iron, or rust. There was no light of course, and even though it was only ten or twelve feet deep, I couldn't see into the far corner – or rather, I couldn't see clearly, though I could make out a shape, some solid object, maybe a table, set against the back wall and, on it, something that I couldn't see at all, probably just more sacking, or some other junk. There was no reason to investigate further – it was just an old shed, really – but I couldn't let it go, just like that. Something was there, and I had to know what it was.

I moved forward, slowly, careful of the dark, not at all sure what I expected to find, but I knew I would find something. About halfway across as I came within reach of the table – and that was what it was, a long, narrow table, about three feet off the ground – I saw that what I had taken for a heap of rags was actually a body, not a deer, but a person and then, slowly, with a sudden sense of total horror, as if I had caught myself in the commission of some vicious and perverse crime, I saw that it was the girl, the one I had seen on the moor, and I realised that she was watching me – that she had, in fact, been watching me since I first entered the room. And, though she didn't say anything, though she didn't cry out or even move from where she was lying, I could see that she was terrified. I wanted to say something, I wanted to reassure her, but I knew it was hopeless. Anything I said would be a lie – I don't know how I knew this but I did, I knew it as surely as I have ever known anything – whatever I said would be a lie and I knew, immediately, that she was right to be afraid. Because I really was the monster she thought I was. I really was her worst nightmare, in the flesh—

The email broke off then, and the story wasn't taken up for several days. Of course, I thought this wasn't altogether fair and it annoyed me to think that, having got me hooked, my correspondent was growing tired of his story. Then again, perhaps he had just run out of ideas. Certainly I detected, in the final email, the wish for an ending, a sense that the time had come to move on – and I suppose I regretted the loss of this regular diversion. When it did come, that last message was short, and more than a little unsatisfactory. It had a cursory, almost telegrammatic quality – an air, not so much of haste, as of exhausted resignation:

Still here. I didn't know why you don't answer. I never wanted—
Well it's too late now. It's here. She is here, with me, I think forever. Can you imagine that? Forever? I couldn't have done, before, now I can. In fact, now I can't imagine anything else.
lol
Martin

And that was where it ended. I waited a few days, to see if there would be more, then I forgot about it. I got a big, rather interesting project to work on, and I went on a special diet. The new drugs were more effective than I had expected and, all in all, life carried on as usual. I didn't think about Martin again but, once, or maybe twice at most, I dreamed about the deer larder and that terrified girl, lying silent in the darkness, and when I woke, I had to congratulate my former correspondent on having gotten to me, if only for a moment.

That, it would appear, was the end of Martin's story, but mine remained open – no longer told, yet still unfinished – until a certain Thursday evening, exactly three months later. I know this to be the case because I had just returned from my appointment at the hospital and, in those days, my appointments were on a three-monthly schedule. I didn't get back from town till quite late and I was feeling a little low – winter was drawing in and my hands were worse than usual – but I set to work as soon as I'd had a bite to eat and got warmed up. I had a new project to work on, something a little out of the ordinary. Something into which I was pretty sure I could work the odd small miracle and I was determined to make the most of that.

I stumbled across the story while I was on the trail of something else. That's how it happens, more often than not: the stuff that stops you dead in your tracks, the little snippets of information or narrative that seem suddenly important – those vivid, beautiful or frightening discoveries that seem life-changing – come when you're surfing the Web, looking for something far more pedestrian, or even banal. As it happens, the trail I had been following, for some time, bore almost no relation to my research topic and, when I came upon that final decisive story, I read it, at first, with only passing interest. Passing interest, idle curiosity even – and then, after a line or two, a growing sense of horror. It wasn't a long article, just a quirky news item, one of those stranger-than-fiction pieces that you only ever half believe but can't put out of your mind for days afterwards. Usually, such pieces have an obvious whiff of exaggeration or invention about them – it's not that they are out-and-out lies, it's just that they are so loosely based on the known facts that they might as well be fictions. Not this one, though. This one was true, more or less. I knew that even before I knew what I was reading.

As I say, it wasn't a long piece, and it was quite badly put together, wordy and rambling and stylistically weak. Real cub-reporter stuff. In short, it told the story of a man who had been found, naked and alone and quite obviously mad, squatting on a raised beach on the isle of Jura. Someone had seen him from a ferry boat and called the police; subsequently, the man, who could not or would not speak and appeared not to have eaten or slept for some time, was taken to a hospital on the mainland, where he was later identified as Martin Crisp, a university lecturer from Reading, who had been renting a house on the island over the summer. The piece concluded with two quotes, the first, from a local man, who said that Mr Crisp had been touched by the fairies, and it would be a long time before he ever came right, the second, from one of the hospital staff, who said that Mr Crisp was still unable to speak but, though it was obvious that something terrible had happened to this man, there was no clinical reason for his condition. When asked to elaborate further, the doctor – whose name, by what seemed to me a chilling coincidence, was Elizabeth Marsh – remarked that she had never before had a case quite like this one. 'It's not that Mr Crisp *can't* talk,' she said – and I pictured my own Dr Marsh saying this – 'But it seems to me that he's said what he wanted to say and now he's waiting for his answer.'

Rachel Trezise

Hard As Nails

My tabard was covered in cat's hair, black needles thread through the pink cotton on the bust and the skirt and the collar. I didn't realise until I was at the end of Trinity Road and struggling to untangle my iPod wires. There was something in the herbal hand lotion at the salon that acted like catnip. Sooty went nuts for it. If I didn't hang my tabard in the wardrobe he'd roll all over it like a slug dipped in salt. Last night was yoga class: I'd thrown my uniform in a rushed heap on the bathroom floor and my mother, sick of cleaning up after me, left it there. I gave up on the iPod, ripping the buds out of my ears and stuffing it into my work bag. I was nervous already. I'd woken to a letter from the new nail salon in Pontypridd, inviting me for an interview in a week's time. I'd sent my CV on a whim, after a bad week at Hard as Nails. Joanna wasn't paying me enough in the first place, and then she'd confiscated my tips. Now I was petrified about her finding out about my trying to leave.

It was eight forty-five as I rounded the corner onto the high street, a Friday in the middle of August. The sky was curdled, the town damp-smelling. Seren had opened up. She was sitting in the backroom eating cereal, the bowl balanced between her knees. I went straight to the desk, cutting strips of Sellotape with which to prise the cat hair from my overall.

Joanna came in a little after nine, her sixteen-year-old son, Conan, in tow. He was wearing his stainless steel colander on his head, the kind that has two small handles on either side, the names of food pressed out of the sides to act as drainage: salad, pasta, fruit. He called it his 'Britney helmet'. He reckoned he could communicate spiritually with Britney Spears while he was wearing it. Conan had a mental age of eleven but a memory like a camera. He'd remember things he'd heard on the telly and repeat them for months on end. 'Pain in the arse kid,' Joanna said, sending him to the armchair. 'Babysitter's let me down again.' She went to the fridge. As she opened it Seren froze, the spoon in her hand suspended in front of her

O-shaped mouth. 'I knew it,' Joanna barked. 'No milk.' She slammed the door closed, the bottles of wine inside shaking. 'I'll go,' said Seren. She dropped her spoon into the dish, the milk splashing. 'I'll go. It's my fault.'

Joanna eyeballed her miserably. 'No, I will,' she said. 'You'll take too long. Put the kettle on.' Joanna turned and headed for the entrance, picking up her handbag on her way out. For a time the room was still, filled with the echo of the door chime. 'What's Britney saying today, Conan?' Seren asked, taking her spoon up. Conan tapped the colander with his knuckle. 'She's saying,' he said, pausing momentarily for effect, 'that our brains can only develop from loving relationships. She's saying that cruelly-treated children grow into cruel adults who crave a lot of attention.' Seren nodded absently, slipping a spoonful of her breakfast sludge past her glossy lips. The smell of it was fresh, citrus-like. 'What is that?' I asked her. Seren was a fifteen-year-old chain-smoker. She only ate breakfast when it was doughnuts from ASDA or muffins from Maccy D's. 'Tangerine,' she said, chewing as she spoke.

'In milk?'

'Yeah.' There was a disturbance then, coming from outside, Joanna's voice crackling. We got up and stumbled to the front of the shop, all three of us hanging out of the door. Joanna had Mrs Winterbottom pinned against the pebbledashed wall of the bank, the tips of their noses almost touching. 'How many years?' Joanna was shouting into Mrs Winterbottom's face, slapping the wall next to her as she uttered each word, breast heaving with rage.

'Oh, don't get so het up,' Mrs Winterbottom said, trying to wriggle out of the acquisition. 'I told you. My daughter gave me a voucher. Under normal circumstances I would have come to you. You know that, Jo.' Joanna'd caught Mrs Winterbottom leaving the rival nail salon on the opposite side of the street. 'How many years?' she repeated, words peppered with spittle. The optician was out at his door now too, fiddling with the lapels of his white coat.

'Two years, Joanna. Only two years you've been here.'

'Well, two years and no more,' Joanna spluttered. 'You're banned from Hard as Nails now, forever, and it's your stupid fucking daughter's fault. You want to go to American Nails? You're welcome. Piss on your own fireworks, why don't you?' She turned around, coming towards us. I couldn't help flinching as she approached: I knew that's what I had coming if she found out about my interview, worse probably. She'd butcher me. 'What are you all looking at?' she said. 'Inside! Come on!' She clapped her hands, dispersing us. 'That's it,' she said, when we were all in, the door chimes clanging. 'I've had as much as I can take. No appointments for next week so we'll shut up shop, book a self-catering cheapy, Benidorm, Alicante, wherever.'

It had been a funny time in Tonypandy since the centenary of the riots the previous year. There'd been a march through the town to mark it and the council had unveiled a statue in the car park – the Lady with the Lamp, a woman in a brown dress, the lamp balanced on her head. From a distance it looked like she was drinking a yard of ale. Afterwards everyone had congregated outside the supermarket to watch a laser show, gloved hands curled around cans of lager. Joanna was so drunk she got the heel of her best shoe caught in the gutter and had to limp home, sliding everywhere on the ice. It was a Sunday night. The salon was closed the following day. When we came back on Tuesday the boarded-up jeweller shop across the road had reopened as a nail salon. There were signboards painted with big American flags, and a neon sign in the window. Joanna had been apoplectic. She stood on the doorstep, glaring, her keys bunched in her hand, their metal ridges cutting into the skin of her palm. 'What the fucking fuck?' she muttered to herself. 'What the fucking, fuck, fuck?' Seren made coffee and tried to hand her a mug. Joanna waved it away, eyes glazed. 'Right!' she said after half an hour. She opened the till and prised out forty pounds, forcing the money into Seren's hand. 'Get over there and ask them for a Hot Mitts manicure. Let's see what we're up against.'

Seren was out of the door more quickly than angels can fly, pausing to light a cigarette on the pavement. I had to call her back. 'Take your tabard off, Ser,' I said. 'They'll see the name of our salon on it.' She unpopped her buttons, shrugged out of her overall, and swapped it for her hoodie.

'Remember everything,' Joanna said. 'And for God's sake don't give them a bloody tip.' Joanna went back to the window to watch Seren cross the street.

'Do you think they're really American?' I asked her from the desk.

'Don't be stupid, Kayla,' she answered. 'They'll be from Maerdy, or the other valley.' I hadn't meant the technicians, but the manicures. In America they filed nails to a point; in Europe you file them square. I'd learned these things on my Beauty GNVQ. I was properly qualified, unlike Seren, whom Joanna had taken on as a favour to her cousin, Seren's mother, before Seren had sat her CSE's. Joanna was tidying her workstation, arranging the nail polish colours in alphabetical order. She moved her container full of emery boards an inch across the surface of the desk and stared at it sombrely for a moment. Then she moved it again, to the other side. She muttered something to herself before sliding it back to its original position. Our first customer arrived and I busied myself making coffee and warming towels, until Seren came back, her head swollen with the secret information, eyes watery with glee.

'Where the hell have you been?' said Joanna. 'It doesn't take that long.'

Seren stood in the middle of the salon, enjoying the attention. 'Chinks,' she spat.

'What?' Joanna curled her hair behind her ears, as if its presence in front of them had caused her to mishear the word.

'Chinks,' Seren said. 'Six of 'em, just sitting there, masks over their faces to stop the dust going in their mouths. They don't talk. They don't say anything. They give you a menu to choose from. You point at what you want and they do it. Probably they can't speak English. Don't smile or nothing.'

'They don't ask you where you're going on holiday?'

'They don't ask you anything. Like getting your nails done in a morgue.' She dropped her change on the desk in front of me. It was a good manicure; the beige-pink polish smooth and shiny, the cuticles pushed back even. Joanna didn't ask to see the manicure. Because the manicurists in American Nails were foreign she thought we were home and dry. Even when most of our Christmas business went awry she expected things to get back to normal in the New Year. It was only at the beginning of February when it still hadn't picked up that she started asking around: where did they come from? Were they illegals? Who was managing the place? Some said they were the wives of the chefs at the new all-you-could-eat Chinese buffet up the valley. Others thought they were illegals, slave labour trafficked by the Triads. Rumours about the manager snowballed. One day he was a twenty-four-year-old with a Hummer and a spider web tattoo on his neck. The next day he was nineteen, the Hummer morphed into a Porsche Panamera, the tattoo crept up onto his cheek.

'Nothing new,' my grancha said, when I told him the story over

Sunday lunch at the carvery. 'The Chinese used to be crawling over one another like crabs in a pot here back. It was the laundries then. They ran the laundries, see.'

It wasn't the first time Joanna had attacked an old customer for switching allegiances. She'd poured a bottle of Bacardi Breezer over Susan Prosser in the NUM club when she'd spotted a receipt from American Nails scrunched up in the bottom of her handbag. It wasn't the first time we'd been on holiday together either. We'd been to Ibiza for a week in March. Basically Joanna took us for company. She didn't have any friends of her own – the woman could start an argument in an empty toilet cubicle. She paid for the flights, the accommodation, our food, drinks, everything, then when we got back she started taking thirty per cent out of our wages to cover it all.

It was early on a Friday evening when we arrived at our apartment in the centre of Benidorm, the day I would have had my interview in Pontypridd. I'd rung the salon manager a few days earlier and told her I wouldn't be able to make it. She refused to cancel the appointment outright. She was impressed with my CV, she said. She'd rearranged it for the following week. We dropped our cases and walked a few blocks east, to a Scottish pub Joanna'd heard about. 'There's a Welsh bar here too,' Seren said as we took our table on the balcony. 'I saw an advert in the reception.'

'Can't go there,' Joanna said, removing her sunglasses and studying the laminated menu. 'I'm banned. Since 1987.' She stared intently at the list of dishes, offering no further explanation. 'Hola!' she shrieked as the waitress approached. 'Scampi and chips times three, and three pints of Buckfast.' She fanned herself with the menu before handing it to the waitress. 'Is that all?' the waitress asked.

'Yep,' Joanna said. 'Maybe some bread and butter.'

I'd wanted to order the Caesar salad. 'I don't like fish,' I said, pins and needles of panic pricking the backs of my legs. 'Yes you do,' Joanna said. 'Anyway, it's scampi. It's not real fish.' The waitress came back with three large glasses of a burgundy-coloured drink. 'Taste it,' Joanna said taking a glass from the tray and passing it to me. It was sweet and viscous, like Calpol. 'Nice,' I said, appeasing her. I thought about ordering a glass of water to go with it but the waitress was already rushing off to another table, the moment passed. Our food came quickly and we unwrapped our cutlery, setting the paper serviettes aside. 'We'll have a quiet one tonight,' Joanna said munching on a chip, 'plenty of time to go mad later, maybe a few drinks in one of the bars on the seafront.' Seren and I exchanged a look. We knew Joanna didn't do quiet.

'Agreed?' Joanna snapped.

'Yes,' Seren whimpered.

Joanna glowered at me.

'Of course,' I said. 'Fine.'

Back at the apartment Joanna poured a large slug of the vodka she'd bought at the airport into a mug from the kitchen cupboard. She emptied her suitcase onto her bed, locating her hair straighteners. 'Chuck us your adaptor,' she said to me. 'I've forgotten mine.' While she was waiting for the plates to heat up she went out onto the balcony where Seren was smoking a cigarette, hand shielding her eyes from the red lozenge sun.

'What's the matter with you?' Joanna asked her. 'Chop chop. We're wasting valuable drinking time hanging around here. Get your glad rags on.' I cringed at the 'glad rags', phrase, the kind of maxim my grancha might have used; but Joanna was forty-one, I suppose it had to be expected. She leaned on the balcony railing, her back to the sea view.

'I don't really feel like it, Jo,' Seren mumbled, flicking ash off her cigarette.

'What d'you mean you don't feel like it?' Joanna said. I stepped closer to the patio door, listening for Seren's answer, a can of deodorant tight in my grip. Seren was silent. 'What else are you going to do?' Joanna asked her, her nose wrinkled with disdain.

'Let me lie down for an hour,' Seren said. 'I've got a bit of indigestion. It was that Buckfast stuff, it must have been. I'll be OK later. I'll follow you down.' She stubbed her cigarette out in the ashtray.

'Indigestion?' Joanna said, voice popping with incredulity. 'Bloody sixteen you are, not sixty-one. You're on holiday, Ser.' Seren got up out of her chair and walked limply into the bedroom, ignoring my presence behind the door. She sat back on her bed, her arm crossed over her stomach. Joanna followed her into the bedroom.

'Please, Auntie Jo,' Seren said, before Joanna could speak. 'I'll be OK if you leave me alone for half an hour.'

'PMT you've got, or something,' Joanna said. There was a hot flash of resentment in Seren's eyes, but she didn't pursue the argument. She turned onto her side, drawing her knees up into a foetal position.

'Just me and you then, kid,' Joanna said taking the deodorant out of my hand. She lifted her top and sprayed her armpits, the room clotting with its sweet vanilla scent. We walked down to the seafront and into Acropolis, a small bar cluttered with nautical paraphernalia; fishing nets and rubber sharks. It was lit with a drooping string of Christmas lights tacked to the upper wall. We sat at the bar, Joanna ordering a jug of Sangria for us. She proceeded to pour it, filling her own glass to the top, leaving mine only half full. 'What d'you think's the matter with Madam?' she asked me, the rim of her glass pressed to her face.

I shrugged non-committally. 'She said she had indigestion.'

Joanna screwed her eyes up, as if in disagreement, but said nothing. A group of English boys in their mid-twenties ambled in, their hair cropped close to their skulls, wearing chequered shirts of varying colours and designs. 'Here we go,' Joanna said out of the side of her mouth as the men crowded around us, queuing for drinks. While the one next to her was getting served, Joanna reached around, scratching her neck, strategically elbowing him in the ribs. 'Oh sorry sunshine,' she said turning to face him, and then, eyeing him up and down, 'Well, you're a pretty boy, aren't you? Fancy me bumping into someone as handsome as you.'

It was one in the morning by the time I managed to sneak away. Joanna had made a makeshift dance floor out of the corridor between the gents and the kitchen. She was gyrating to a rap song with her English boy quarry, arching her back, rubbing her haunches against his pelvis, his knobbly workman's hand pressed on the black lycra skirt clung to her hips. I slipped out of the door and began the walk back to the apartment, the clicking sound of grasshoppers lining my route, the bass in the music diluting. All at once I could taste the rusty wine I'd been drinking and the salt blown up from the beach. As I neared our building I heard Joanna calling. Glancing over my shoulder I saw her waddling up the concrete road, her shoes in her hands. I pretended I hadn't. I went into the building hoping that she'd turn back.

The door to the apartment wasn't locked and as I crossed the threshold I felt the atmosphere thicken, the light breeze from outdoors disappeared. The apartment smelled of sweating feet. 'Seren?' Her bed was empty, the covers pulled back. There was a light from under the bathroom door, a thin yellow sliver reflecting on the linoleum in the hall. Seren was crouched in the wheel position at the base of the shower, her legs pulled up, her glossy pedicure reflecting the bare bulb, her naked vagina in full view. 'Seren?' I asked, expecting her to cover herself. She exhaled noisily through her nose. I still couldn't see her face. 'Seren?' I said, stepping closer. I couldn't help staring at her, the way her labia minora resembled a mouth turned onto its side, and then, between the lips, something solid: an orange quarter, peel side facing out. A baby's head. She was crowning.

'Jesus!' I said, my voice a shock to myself.

'Grr-rrr.' Seren growled and ground her teeth. The baby's head was protruding, moving further and further out of her body, its eyes closed; skin buff-coloured and waxy, like cheap soap. There was a sprinkling of dark fuzz, a Mohican-like band marking the centre of its head. I was kneeling on the bathmat in time to see the body slide clean out. It landed with a smack on the base of the shower tray, its torso the colour of thistle and speckled with blood. The bungee cord landed on its stomach, coiling around itself. I reached out to touch it, then pulled back again before I could. I was too squeamish to touch raw chicken. At home my mother teased me, chasing me around the kitchen with the headless body, its flesh daubed with butter and thyme, ready for the oven.

'Seren?' I said, out of habit now as much as anything else.

'Is it out?' she asked me, her voice tired but full of hope.

'Yeah it's out. I don't know if it's alive.' Seren began to tread backwards, away from the baby, squatting down at the edge of the shower tray. I saw her face for the first time, red and exhausted; broken blood vessels in the whites of her eyes. 'I'll call an ambulance,' I said, the idea a revelation. I knew the emergency number was 112. I'd had to use it in Ibiza when Joanna got into a bar fight. My mobile was like water in my palms. I dropped it twice in a row, the plastic clattering on the bathroom tiles.

'Ambulance please,' I said to the Spanish-speaking voice in the receiver. I could hear the alcohol in my words but I was sober now. The call was over by the time Joanna appeared. She seemed to crash into the room, holding onto the lip of the sink to steady herself. 'Well,' she said, about to launch into some anecdote, when she noticed the tiny body in the shower tray. 'Is that a baby?' she said, matter-of-fact, squinting against the harsh light. 'And where the fuck did you get your toes done? We haven't even got that colour. Cosmic latte. It's still on order.'

'I've called an ambulance,' I said. In no time Joanna had left the room and then returned with a pair of scissors from the kitchen drawer, her fingernails thrust through the plastic handle. She stooped at the base of the shower reaching for the bloodied cord. 'Don't,' Seren said. 'Don't touch me.'

'Don't touch her,' I repeated robotically.

Joanna ignored us, the cord gripped in her hand. With one swift cut she sliced it in half. She picked the baby up, holding it to her midrib, the scissors left on the bathmat. 'Why didn't you tell us, Ser?' she said. 'Why didn't you say anything?' Slowly she began to back away from the shower. She stood in the middle of the bathroom, gently rocking the baby. 'You don't know how lucky you are,' she said, her voice a murmur, an unusual purr. 'What I wouldn't have done for a perfect little baby like this. What did I get, huh? Developmentally disabled, no bloody cure.' She turned the baby in her arms, looking at its face.

'Give him to Seren,' I said.

Joanna looked blankly at Seren, still crouched in the shower tray. 'I had my tubes tied,' she said. 'After Conan. I couldn't risk that again.'

'The ambulance is on its way,' I said. 'Give the baby to Seren, Jo.'

Joanna didn't seem to hear anything I said. Perhaps I wasn't talking at all. 'You don't want a baby, do you?' she asked Seren, as if she was asking her if she wanted a thump. 'Sixteen, you are. Your mother'll do her nut.' She was still rocking the baby, holding its midget hand in her fingers.

'It's Cai's,' Seren said, a squeak from inside the shower cubicle.

We looked at Seren, her head pressed into her hands. 'Who?' Joanna said.

'Cai,' Seren said. 'The manager from American Nails.' And then, a little more forcefully, 'It's my baby, Jo. Give it to me.' She held her arms out for the baby.

Joanna stepped back. 'Come on, Seren,' she said. 'You don't want a baby, do you?' She swung around to face the door and began walking purposefully towards it, her bare feet producing a sharp ripping sound with each step she took.

'Come back, Jo,' I shouted at her. 'Give it to Seren.' I was in the hall following her before I realised I'd moved. Joanna had slipped out, the front door left open. I stepped out into the corridor. I could hear her, halfway down the stairs.

'Don't leave me,' Seren called, her voice pulling me back.

I went to the patio door, my face squashed against the glass, watching as Joanna staggered toward the beach, the baby still bundled against her chest.

The ambulance took Seren to the clinic. Two policemen drove me to the police station. They sat me down on a wooden chair in an empty room and asked me questions in Spanglish about Joanna and her whereabouts. 'She went to the beach,' I told them, repeating myself until all I could hear was my blood beating against the sides of my skull, my tongue so dry I couldn't shape it around words. Later they locked me alone in a cell, a thin scratchy blanket, like a potato sack, in my hand. I twisted around on the mattress, trying to get comfortable, feeling every metal spring. I fell into a hypnotic doze, encountering short bursts of dream in one part of my brain, a cold, hazy reality in the other. At one point I was sure I heard Joanna's voice echoing in the corridor outside. 'Mental impairments,' she was shrieking, over and over again. 'Mental impairments, American Nails. Mental impairments, American Nails.'

When I woke a policeman and a plain-clothed woman with ginger hair were standing in the doorway to the cell. I could see a ration of daylight through the air vent underneath the sink. 'Kayla?' the woman said. 'I'm a representative from the British Embassy.' She had a thick Birmingham accent and freckles on her cleavage. 'I've come to help you, alright?' She drove me to our apartment in the town centre and walked me into the building. The front door was sealed with yellow policia tape. I stopped, gawking at it. 'It's OK,' she said. 'We're just going to collect your things. We've got permission.' She took the key from my hand and opened the door, peeling the tape and ducking underneath it. The sweating feet odour had gone, replaced with aloe vera; the potted cacti and flora from the balcony. 'Which suitcase is yours?' Together we threw my possessions into my pink wheelie suitcase, my flip-flops, my underwear, my clunky adaptor plug. Joanna's hair straighteners were still on the bed, opened to a V shape.

'Some of my toiletries are in the bathroom,' I said, hoping the woman would fetch them for me. I didn't want to see the blood stains, or the scissors on the bathmat. 'Go on then, bab,' she said with a thin smile.

'You'll have to go. I won't know what belongs to you, what belongs to Seren.' She pronounced Seren with an extra E, serene. She didn't mention Jo. The shower was hidden behind a white plastic sheet, another strip of police tape securing it. I took my can of deodorant and bottle of CK One from the shelf above the sink and went back to the common room area.

'Are you ready to go to the airport?' the woman asked. 'There's a flight to Gatwick leaving in three and a half hours.' I nodded. 'And you're sure you have funds to pay for it?' I had three hundred pounds credit left on the card I'd used for my GNVQ course.

My mother was waiting at the terminal building in London. She hugged me too tightly. We didn't speak until we arrived at Leigh Delamere Services two hours later. 'Seren's still at the clinic,' she said while we waited in the queue at the till. 'Retained placenta. She didn't pass the afterbirth. But they'll see to that. She'll be alright. Joanna they've arrested for infanticide.'

'Infanticide?' I asked, opening my purse and realising I only had Euros. 'Murder,' she said, 'of a baby. I knew something wasn't right about that woman. I knew it was only a matter of time.'

I zipped my purse closed. 'I don't think she killed the baby,' I said.

'Shh,' my mother said. We were getting closer to the cashier. Speaking without moving her lips she said, 'you'll get a chance to tell your side of the story. They'll call you back to Benidorm for the trial, worst luck.' She paid for our things and we sat down in the food court. I peeled the cellophane back on my pre-prepared sandwich. My mother reached across the table, patting at my wrist.

'I'm not ill,' I said. My stomach was rumbling. I stuffed the corner of my sandwich into my mouth, the mayonnaise cool and slick on my tongue. I retched suddenly, dropping the sandwich. The chunk I'd bitten off I spat into my paper napkin. Roast chicken. I couldn't get that picture of Seren out of my mind's eye: her body flipped backward on the shower tray, red, raw and opened; the baby between her feet. Seren's creamy, milk-coloured toenails. 'But I'm not hungry,' I said, pushing the sandwich and its packaging away. 'You need to build yourself up nice and strong,' my mother said. 'You've got that interview in Pontypridd in a few days. It's a trauma you've been through, you don't know it yet.'

But I did. I didn't want to go anywhere near a nail salon again.

Madeleine D'Arcy

The Fox and the Placenta

Marilyn sighs. 'I used to be such a fun-time girl.'

Unlike Monroe, this Marilyn is not a blonde. Her hair is russet red and curly and right now her fun-time girl-self is hampered by the fact that she's nine months pregnant. She's sitting Humpty-Dumpty style on a green corduroy beanbag, watching Richard and Judy on the telly.

'I'm going out to get a better hose for the birthing pool,' says Brendan in his soft Derry accent. 'Will I get you a wee cake or something while I'm out?'

'Yes, please,' says Marilyn. Her sweet tooth has gone demented since the second trimester.

'Can I have some Clarnico Iced Caramels – you know the ones I mean? They're pink and white with toffee inside.'

'I think so.'

'If you see any, will you buy me a packet?'

'I will. Now ring me if you get a twinge – I'll come straight back.'

'Okay. I hope I won't have any more of those fake ones though. All pain, no gain. I'm fed up with them. What are they called again?'

'Braxton Hicks,' he says.

Top marks. He's read Miriam what's-her-name's *Parent and Child* book from cover to cover as if fatherhood is some kind of weird A level. As if he's definitely the father. She's told him there's a chance he's not. He seems so sure it's his though.

'I think I'll go to bed for a while,' she says. 'I just can't get comfortable on this.' It's a huge struggle to half roll, half grapple her way out of the beanbag and onto her hands and knees. From this position she grabs the top rail of the birthing pool and hauls herself upright.

'Is this pool supposed to be full?' she says.

'No, no… I'll empty it before I go. I was just assessing the time it took to fill.'

'Thanks so much, Brendan. I really appreciate it. Gosh, I'm exhausted. Those bleeding foxes were howling again last night and between them and this,' she indicates her huge frontal bump, 'I didn't get a wink of sleep.'

She shoves her feet into her Birkenstocks and makes a slow journey to the bedroom. A pair of red patent high-heeled shoes from the January sales sit unworn on the shelf. She looks at them, sadly, before hauling herself onto the bed.

Nine months ago, everything was different.

Brendan was just her friend. Not a bit like her ex-boyfriend, Sam the love rat. As her friend Laura pointed out, Sam was mean and egotistical and Marilyn's better off without him.

'Brendan's much nicer,' said Laura. 'He's mad about you. But you can't resist bastards, that's your problem.'

'I'm not stupid,' protested Marilyn. 'I know Brendan's great. I've always loved him – as a friend, I mean.'

'Admit it, you can't allow yourself to fall for him because he's such a nice bloke.'

'It's just… he's not a hunter-forager-gatherer-you-Tarzan-me-Jane geezer, is he?'

'You'll never learn,' sighed Laura.

Nine months ago, Marilyn was at a loose end, still mourning the end of her relationship with Sam, when she found herself crying on Brendan's shoulder after an alcohol-fuelled night out. Every cliché in the book applies to the situation that followed. Herself a mess, Brendan declaring himself to be in love with her; throes of drunken passion, then waking with a fearsome hangover on a grey January morning, trying to remember what had happened. And Brendan lying there beside her in bed, like a fond dog. He, of course, remembered everything.

'I'll phone you later,' said Brendan, happily, at about midday. 'I've got to do some work but I'll ring you at six, okay?'

Sam called round that lunchtime to say he'd made a terrible mistake. Marilyn was only just out of the shower. As she pointed out to Laura afterwards, it's all very entertaining on TV but not when it happens to you.

'I was vulnerable,' she said. 'You'd be surprised how confusing things can be, especially when you have that hangover lust going on.'

When Sam left, having rid himself of 10cc (the sperm, not the 80s band), she knew she'd made a terrible mistake.

At 6 p.m. sharp, the phone rang.

'Hi,' Brendan spoke shyly. 'Are you okay?'

'Yeah. Why wouldn't I be?'

'Would you like to come out for dinner tonight?'

'Well,' she thought for a moment. 'Dinner? Where?'

'Well, I've booked Le Petit Prince. It's a new French-Moroccan place.'

'Oh.'

'But I can book somewhere else... whatever you like.'

'Oh no. That's... fine. What time?'

He arrived with flowers and paid for dinner, though she earned as much money as he did, if not more, and suggested more than once they should go Dutch. Good old Brendan. She wished she'd never been taken in, that last time, by Sam.

Marilyn lies back, bolstered by every pillow in the house, eyes closed, listening to the soothing music of Deep Forest. She feels like an overblown balloon, ready to explode. She breathes in and out just like the yoga teacher at the Natural Centre for Birth and Rebirthing has taught her. She tries to soften each part of her body from the tips of her fingers and the top of her scalp right down to the soles of her feet. The 'Corpse Pose' it's called. Not such a nice thought. When you're pregnant, you want everything to be fertile and alive, not dead. There's another name for it too, Sumatra, something like that. No, Sumatra's a volcano, isn't it? The Corpse Pose. Funny the way she's practically devouring murder mysteries while waiting for the baby. Weird, that. Sam would have scorned such lowly literature... Sam's lying low for a while. His reaction to the little problem she's given him has not been great... The mystery of the double dads... Nothing like this happens in Agatha Christie books... Dead bodies in libraries... Caribbean mysteries...

A dog begins to bark outside. Maybe it's one of the foxes, but the foxes usually emerge only at dusk and their bark is almost a whine. Long rangy dog-like beasts, they're more like wolves than foxes.

More barking. She's determined to relax. *I'm going to sodding well relax if it kills me.* But she's distracted... Brendan has a cute face, like a friendly terrier. Sam is a wilder fox type, tough, skinny, cynical. Behind the Victorian houses that form the lines of the Haringey Ladder, the foxes look more grey than red as they slouch in the shadows between street lamps. They're red foxes nonetheless. Mr Singh from Number Five has told her there are no grey foxes in England, that grey foxes live in North America. Maybe the London foxes have crossbred with stray dogs. Now there are hordes of them, packs that come out when daylight turns to night. They roam through back gardens, foraging in people's dustbins, skulking near the kebab shop on Green Lanes, making forays on greaseproof paper packages, licking polystyrene trays outside the chipper. In her darkest nights Marilyn dreams of werewolves leaping for her throat, but most of the time she dreams of nothing.

Now she hears the key clicking in the front door. Someone shuffles in. There's the flapping of paper bags and footsteps going back in the direction of the kitchen. She fancies a cup of tea but it takes a while to manoeuvre herself out of bed. She stands up eventually and makes her way slowly downstairs.

Brendan's put the kettle on.

'Hi,' he says. 'How're you feeling?'

'Alright. Bored.'

'Will I make tea?'

'Yes, please.'

'I'd be back ages ago only I met Mr Singh – you know him – the old man in Number Five. He was in a chatty mood, told me they're selling dustbins in Wood Green Shopping Centre with a sign above them saying "Fox-proof". He's just bought one.'

'What does "Fox-proof" mean?'

'There's a special locking mechanism, apparently. He says the foxes are using teamwork to knock over the normal bins, even the big ones. I thought your bin had blown over in the wind, but Mr Singh says it's the foxes.'

'Did you get cake?'

'Not *just* cake.' He shakes a packet of Clarnico Iced Caramels in front of her.

'Great. I'll be like a mountain after the baby's born, but what the hell.'

She can't wait to get her teeth into a pink Iced Caramel. As she chews, she wonders if this means the baby will be a girl. She's always wanted a little baby, though not quite like this.

Everything happens so fast.

'I think it's not a false alarm this time,' says Marilyn.

Brendan times the contractions, rings the Home Birth Team and fills the birthing pool at record-breaking speed with the new improved hose he bought earlier.

Marilyn's waters break in the birthing pool. She can't bear to stay in it a second longer. The midwife from Derry arrives to run the show and chats to Brendan about their favourite pubs in Magherafelt, while he covers the carpet with the towelling material he's bought.

'You're doing great, Marilyn,' says the midwife. 'Wonderful! You're five centimetres dilated already.'

The midwife from China arrives to administer rescue remedy and tiny homeopathic tablets to everyone, especially Brendan. The midwife from Derry thinks Brendan should have some brandy as well, so he does.

Marilyn walks naked in cowboy mode around the room. She stops and groans sometimes and seems unaware of company.

'I'll sing,' Brendan says. He begins to sing 'I'm Coming Out' by Pink, but his voice is badly off key.

'Shut up!' screams Marilyn and she shrieks for the TENS machine but soon she's too busy to bother with it. She holds Brendan's hand until he moans. The midwife from Derry tells Brendan he should have a break so he leaves the room to gulp more brandy in the kitchen, but he's back within minutes.

Marilyn is hanging off the radiator in the front room, then she's half lying, half squatting, on the floor.

'We've got to shout this baby out,' says the midwife from Derry to the midwife from China. 'Brendan, you support her on this side. Ling, will you hold her on the other? I'll stay in front.'

All four of them shout and count and breathe and yell 'PUSH!' when the midwife from Derry says 'Now'. Marilyn shouts loudest and the baby comes out. There is an enormous and blessed silence.

Brendan holds the baby for a moment before the midwife from Derry lays the child on Marilyn's breast. Marilyn looks at her baby and astounds herself by falling into a new kind of love. The baby makes its first mewling cry and somebody remembers to ask what sex it is.

Then the midwife from Derry tends to Marilyn and gives her an injection so the placenta will come out faster, and the midwife from China checks the baby (it's a boy) and the placenta comes out and Marilyn yelps while the midwife from China stitches her up and the midwife from Derry says, 'You won't remember half of this, you know,' and Brendan says, '*I* will. I'll never forget it. You were *wonderful*, Marilyn. You were amazing. You were mighty. You were an *Amazon*. I love you so much...'

It's ten hours since the baby was born. Marilyn lies back, eyes closed, determined to relax. The... what is it again? The Corpse Pose. Sumatra. Something like that.

The painkillers are beginning to wear off. Her stitches feel itchy and uncomfortable.

A dog barks. 'Oh God,' she groans quietly. 'Shut up.' More high-pitched whining and some clanking and banging noises out back. The sound of something falling. Brendan cursing.

The baby in the Moses basket beside her begins to cry. Marilyn wants to cry too. What on earth is she going to do? This tiny scrap of a thing needs a decent mother – one that knows how to breastfeed – one that knows who the father is.

Terrible noises out back. Is that Brendan roaring? More whines and clattering sounds.

She picks up the crying baby as if he's a Ming vase, careful to support his neck. She does everything in slow motion.

'Oh my poor sweet thing,' she says.

The baby stops crying and looks up at her with blind newborn eyes. She walks round the room with the child, talking gently.

'What's wrong with you? Why don't you go to sleep like a good little boy?'

She carries the baby downstairs. It's painful to walk. As she enters the kitchen she feels a cold breeze. The back door is open and rain is pouring down outside. Before she has a chance to close it, Brendan comes stalking in. He looks like a wild man, wet and sweaty at the same time. The knees of his jeans and the front of his sweater are muddy, as if he's been dragged through a swamp.

'Jesus!' he says. He's holding her biggest cooking pot. 'The fucking foxes knocked over the dustbin and one of them tried to make off with the placenta.'

'What?'

Brendan kicks the back door shut.

'It's okay, I got it back.' He holds out the cooking pot. It's filled with a huge fleshy thing that looks rank.

'Ugh, that's disgusting.'

'Nah. It's just natural. Don't worry, I'll give it a rinse. The thing is…'

'Oh God, why did you…?'

'Well, you were wrecked after giving birth so I didn't want to bother you. The midwife said some people like to bury the placenta in the garden and plant a tree.'

'Crikey, was all that inside *me*?'

'Yeah. So anyway… I wrapped it in a few bin bags and I put it in the dustbin before the midwife left. I was a bit dazed myself so I figured it would be alright there for a while.'

'And…?'

'Well, just now I heard the bin go over, so I ran out. There was a whole gang of foxes out there and one of them had the bag in his mouth.'

'What?'

'So I had to grapple with the fucker. Jesus, was I scared or what… I looked him in the eye and I swear to God he wanted that placenta as much as I did. We knocked over your garden bench, but it's okay, I can fix that… Anyway, the rubbish bags tore and the placenta fell on the ground so I had to grab it before he had a chance to run off with it. It's grand though. There's only a couple of bite marks.'

'I don't even *want* the thing,' she says. 'I can't bear to look at it… It's so… revolting.' Marilyn sees disappointment in his face. 'Are you okay?' she adds.

'Grand. One of the foxes isn't so good, though.'

'Why?'

'I knocked him out. He's stretched out flat on the grass at the moment. I might have to call a vet.'

He beams at her as she shakes with laughter.

'No way I was letting some thieving fox go off with *your* placenta, kid,' he grins at the baby.

'Oh, oh, oh, my stitches,' she says. She's on the verge of wetting herself and it hurts to laugh so she stops.

'Gosh,' she says. 'You Tarzan, me Jane.'

'All part of the service.'

She stares at Brendan. There's a tough, lean, wild determination about him now. She looks down at the baby in her arms to see if there's a resemblance but the baby's just a small alien with a strange conical head. There's only a tiny bit of hair on it and it's red like hers; he's a little red fox. But the mouth, the mouth... surely that's Brendan's upper lip?

'You know,' she says. 'We have to arrange a paternity test as soon as we can.'

'I know that. I didn't want to talk about it though. Not till I had to.'

In the silence that follows, Marilyn remembers the moment after giving birth, when Brendan said he loved her. She thinks how easy, how nice, how convenient it would be if she could just tell him that she loves him too. She realises that's what she wants to say.

Marilyn looks through the back window. The rain has stopped now, and the sun is setting in an orange-red glow beyond the row of houses in the street behind hers. The sky is dark, almost purple, and she can barely see the shadows of the rooftops. No stars can be seen but she makes a wish anyhow.

'Brendan,' she says. 'Thank you for being so good to me. I can't think how you've put up with all this...'

'It's been difficult,' says Brendan. 'But you didn't lie, Marilyn. You're honest. And brave.'

Marilyn feels weak and teary. 'You're brave too.'

Brendan takes off his muddy sweater and throws it on the floor, before putting his arms gently around Marilyn and the baby.

'So,' he says. 'What are we going to call the baby?'

Marilyn closes her eyes and relaxes, and when she opens them again, she sees a fox walking wearily across the garden, disappearing into the night.

Carys Davies

The Redemption of Galen Pike

They'd all seen Sheriff Nye bringing Pike into town: the two shapes snaking down the path off the mountain through the patches of melting snow and over the green showing beneath, each of them growing bigger as they moved across the rocky pasture and came down into North Street to the jailhouse – Nye on his horse, the tall gaunt figure of Galen Pike following behind on the rope.

The current Piper City jailhouse was a low cramped brick building containing a single square cell, Piper City being at this time, in spite of the pretensions of its name, a small and thinly populated town of a hundred and ninety-three souls in the foothills of the Colorado mountains. Aside from the cell, there was a scrubby yard behind, where the hangings took place, a front office with a table, a chair and a broom; a hook on the wall where the cell keys hung from a thick ring; a small stove where Knapp the jailer warmed his coffee and cooked his pancakes in the morning.

For years, Walter Haig's sister Patience had been visiting the felons who found themselves incarcerated for any length of time in the Piper City jail. Mostly they were outsiders – drifters and vagrants drawn to the place by the occasional but persistent rumours of gold – and whenever one came along, Patience visited him.

Galen Pike's crime revolted Patience more than she could say, and on her way to the jailhouse to meet him for the first time, she told herself she wouldn't think of it; walking past the closed bank, the shuttered front of the general store, the locked-up haberdasher's, the drawn blinds of the dentist, she averted her gaze.

She would do what she always did with the felons; she would bring Galen Pike something to eat and drink, she would sit with him and talk to him and keep him company in the days that he had left. She would not recite scripture, or lecture him about the Commandments or the deadly sins, and she would only read to him if he desired it – a psalm or a prayer or a few selected verses she thought might be helpful to someone in his situation but that was all.

She was a thin, plain woman, Patience Haig.

Straight brown hair scraped back from her forehead so severely that there was a small bald patch where the hair was divided in the centre. It was tied behind in a long dry braid. Her face, too, was long and narrow, her features small and unremarkable, except for her nose which was damaged and lopsided, the right nostril squashed and flattened against the bridge. She wore black flat-heeled boots and a grey dress with long sleeves and a capacious square collar. She was thirty-six years old.

If the preparation of the heart is taken seriously the right words will come. As she walked, Patience silently repeated the advice Abigail Warner had given her when she'd passed on to Patience the responsibility of visiting the jail. Patience was always a little nervous before meeting a new prisoner for the first time, and as she came to the end of Franklin Street and turned the corner into North, she reminded herself that the old woman's advice had always stood her in good stead: if she thought about how lonely it would be – how bleak and frightening and uncomfortable – to be shut up in a twelve-foot box far from home without company or kindness, then whatever the awfulness of the crime that had been committed, she always found that she was able, with the help of her basket of biscuits and strawberry cordial, to establish a calm and companionable atmosphere in the grim little room. Almost always, she had found the men happy to see her.

'Good morning, Mr Pike,' she said, stepping through the barred door and hearing it clang behind her.

Galen Pike loosened the phlegm in his scrawny throat, blew out his hollow cheeks and hawked on the ground.

'I have warm biscuits,' continued Patience, setting her basket on the narrow table between them, 'and strawberry cordial.'

Pike looked her slowly up and down. He looked at her flat-heeled tightly-laced boots, her grey long-sleeved dress and scraped-back hair and asked her, in a nasty smoke-cracked drawl, if she was a preacher.

'No,' said Patience, 'I am your friend.'

Pike burst out laughing.

He bared his yellow teeth and threw back his mane of filthy black hair and observed that if she was his friend she'd have brought him something a little stronger than strawberry cordial to drink.

If she was his friend, he said, lowering his voice and pushing his vicious ravenous-looking face close to hers and rocking forward on the straight-backed chair to which he was trussed with rope and a heavy chain, she'd have used her little white hand to slip the key to his cell off its hook on her way in and popped it in her pretty Red Riding Hood basket instead of leaving it out there on the goddamn wall with that fat pancake-scoffing fucker of a jailer.

Patience blinked and took a breath and replied crisply that he should know very well she couldn't do the second thing, and she certainly wouldn't do the first because she didn't believe anyone needed anything stronger than strawberry cordial to refresh themselves on a warm day.

She removed the clean white cloth that covered the biscuits. The cloth was damp from the steam and she used it to wipe the surface of the greasy little table which was spotted and streaked with thick unidentifiable stains, and poured out three inches of cordial into the pewter mug she'd brought from home that belonged to her brother Walter.

She told Galen Pike that she would sit with him; that she would come every morning between now and Wednesday unless he told her not to, and on Wednesday she would come too, to be with him then also, if he desired it. In the meantime, if he wanted to, he could unburden himself about what he had done, she would not judge him. Or they could talk about other things, or if he liked she would read to him, or they might sit in silence if he preferred. She didn't mind in the least, she said, if they sat in silence, she was used to silence, she liked it almost more than speaking.

Pike looked at her, frowning and wrinkling his big hooked nose, as if he was trying to figure out whether he'd been sent a mad person. When he didn't make any reply to what she'd said, Patience settled herself in the chair opposite him and took out her knitting and for half an hour neither she nor Galen Pike spoke a word, until Pike, irritated perhaps by the prolonged quiet or the rapid clickety-clack of her wooden needles, leaned across the table with the top half of his scrawny body and twisted his face up close to hers like before and asked, what was a dried-up old lady like her doing knitting a baby's bootie?

Patience coloured at the insult but ignored it and told Pike that she and the other women from the Franklin Street Friends' Meeting House were preparing a supply of clothing for Piper City's new hostel for unwed mothers. A lot of girls, she said, ended up coming this way, dragging themselves along the Boulder Road, looking for somewhere to lay their head.

Pike slouched against the back of his chair. He twisted his grimy-fingered hands which were fastened together in a complicated knot and roped tightly, one on top of the other, across his lap.

'Unwed mothers?' he said in a leering unpleasant way. 'Where is all that then?'

'Nowhere at present,' Patience replied, looking up from her work, 'but when it opens it will be here on North Street. The application is with the mayor.'

When Patience Haig wasn't visiting the occasional residents of the Piper City jail, she was fighting the town's Republican mayor, Byron Lym.

Over the years, she and her brother Walter and the other Friends from the Franklin Street Meeting House had joined forces with the pastor and congregation of the Episcopalian church and a number of other Piper City residents to press for certain improvements in the town: a new roof for the dilapidated schoolhouse; a road out to Piet Larsen's so they could get a cart out there from time to time and bring the old man into town so he could feel a bit of life about him; a library; a small fever hospital; a hostel on North Street for unwed mothers.

So far, Lym had blocked or sabotaged each and every one of the projects. He'd said no to the new roof for the school, no to Piet Larson's road, no to the library, no to the hospital and a few days from now, they would find out if he was going to say no to the hostel too.

'He is a difficult man, the mayor,' said Patience, but Pike wasn't listening, he was looking out through the cell's tiny window at the maroon peaks of the mountains and when, at the end of an hour, he had asked no more questions about the hostel or anything else, or shown any desire at all to enter into any kind of conversation, Patience put her needles together and placed the finished bootie in her basket and told him that she would come again in the morning if he'd like her to.

Pike yawned and without turning his eyes from the window told her to suit herself, it was all the same to him whether she came or not. In another week he would be dead and that would be that.

Over the next three days, Patience visited Galen Pike every morning.

She brought fresh biscuits and cordial and asked Pike if he wished to talk, or have her read to him. When he didn't reply she took out her knitting and they sat together in silence.

On the fifth morning, a Sunday, Patience arrived a little later than usual, apologising as she stepped in past Knapp when he unlocked, and then locked, the barred door behind her; she'd been at Meeting for Worship, she said, and there'd been a great quantity of notices afterwards, mostly on the subject of the hostel, as the mayor had indicated he'd be making his decision shortly, possibly as early as tomorrow.

Pike yawned and spat on the floor and said he didn't give a shit where she'd been or what she'd been doing and the only thing he wanted to know was how she'd got that pretty nose.

Knapp, in his office, peeped out from behind his newspaper. He'd never known any of the men to be so unmannerly to Miss Haig. He craned his neck a little farther to see if anything interesting would happen now, if Patience Haig would put Pike in his place, or maybe get up and walk out and leave him to rot in there by hisself for the last three days of his life like he deserved.

'I fell off a gate, Mr Pike,' said Patience. 'When I was nine.'

'Ain't that a shame,' said Pike in his nasty drawl, and Knapp kept his eye on Patience, but all she said was that it was quite all right she'd got used to it a long time ago and didn't notice it unless people remarked on it, which in her experience they never did unless they meant to be rude or unkind, and after that the two of them settled into their customary silence.

Patience took out her knitting.

In his office Knapp folded up the newspaper and began heating his coffee and cooking his pancakes. The fat in his skillet began to pop and smoke and then he poured in the batter and when the first pancake was cooked he slid it onto a plate and then he cooked another and another and when he had a pile of half a dozen he drew his chair up to his table and began to eat. Every so often he looked up and over into the cell where Patience Haig and Galen Pike sat together, as if he was still hoping for some significant event or exchange of words, something he might tell his wife about on Wednesday when he was done keeping an eye on Pike and could go home. It was creepy, he thought, as he munched on his pancakes and gulped his coffee, the way the fellow was so scrawny and thin.

'*QUIT SNOOPING!*' yelled Pike all of a sudden into the silence, opening his mouth wide in a big yellow-toothed snarl that made Knapp jump like a frightened squirrel and drop his fork.

'Jesus Christ,' growled Pike. 'Nosy fat curly-tailed fuckin' hog.'

He turned to Patience. 'What all d'y'all do then? At the worship meeting?'

Patience laid down her knitting and explained that there were nineteen members of the Piper City Friends' Meeting, including herself and her brother Walter, and on Sunday mornings they gathered together at the Franklin Street Meeting House where they sat on two rows of benches arranged around a small central table.

'What about the preacher?'

'No preacher,' said Patience. Instead, they abided in silence and sought the light of God within themselves and no one spoke out loud unless the spirit moved them.

'What light of God?' said Galen Pike.

'The light of God that shines in every man,' said Patience.

On the following day Byron Lym summoned Patience Haig and the pastor of the Episcopalian church and a handful of the other Piper City residents who supported the creation of the hostel for unwed mothers and told them they couldn't have it.

Afterwards, walking home, Patience passed Mayor Lym's big yellow house with its screened-in porch and its magical square of mown green lawn and its herbaceous borders and its sweeping driveway of twinkling smooth-rolled macadam out in front. She passed the schoolhouse with its perished square of flapping tarpaulin tethered to the beams of the broken roof; she passed the plot of unused ground next to the lumber yard where they'd hoped to build the library; the empty warehouse that could so easily be converted into a fever hospital; and by the time she reached Franklin Street she felt so low, so crushed and despondent and depressed, that she didn't go to the jail at all that day to visit Galen Pike.

She ate lunch with her brother Walter and let loose a tirade against the mayor. 'Byron Lym has no interest in the unfortunate people of this world,' she said, speaking quickly and breathlessly. Boiling fury and exasperated irritation bordering on despair made her burst out: 'He is selfish and corrupt and bad for the town.'

Walter served the macaroni cheese and Patience sat without eating, fuming.

Byron Lym had won every election in Piper City for fifteen years. The margin was narrow, but on election day, the Republican vote always seemed to win out: there were enough people in Piper City who didn't seem to mind Byron Lym stealing their taxes and spending them on himself, as long as he kept them low.

'It's wrong, Walter,' she declared, 'the way that man manages to hold onto those votes. It's like a greedy child with a handful of sticky candies and it shouldn't be allowed when there's not one ounce of goodness in him, not one single solitary drop.'

Walter raised his eyebrows and looked at his sister with his mild smile. 'No light of God, sister?'

Patience threw her napkin at him across the table. 'Don't tease me Walter. Doubtless it is there in some dark silk-lined pocket of his embroidered waistcoat but if it is he keeps it well hidden.'

When they'd finished eating she asked her brother to please excuse her, she was going out for some air and for an hour Walter could hear her out on the porch glider, rocking furiously back and forth, the rusty rings creaking and tugging in the porch roof as if they might pull the whole thing down at any moment.

In his cell, Pike sat with the rope cutting into his wrists, the chain grinding against his hips every time he shifted himself in the chair. He looked around at the bare brick walls and the thick bars, at Knapp reading his newspaper or hunched over his skillet or dragging the twigs of his old broom across the office floor.

He closed his eyes and sat listening to the rustle of the aspen trees outside, and from time to time he turned his head and looked out through the tiny window at the maroon peaks of the mountains.

Eleven o'clock had come and gone, then twelve and the woman in the grey dress with the lopsided nose had not appeared. Three o'clock, four, still no sign, and Galen Pike discovered that he missed her.

He missed the gentle tapping of her knitting needles, the soft reedy tooting of the stale air of his cell as it went in and out of her squashed nostril. He realised that from the moment he woke up in the mornings, he was listening for her quick light step in the street outside. From the moment Knapp pushed his oatmeal through the bars and reached in for his potty, he was looking over at the office door and waiting for it to open. She was the only person in the world who did not recoil from him in disgust. In the courthouse people had held themselves against the wall, gawping at his dirty black hair and straggly vagabond's beard, shaking their heads as if they had seen the devil. This one, with her neat hair and her long plain face and her flat polished shoes, sat there straight and stiff and looked him in the eye. He felt bad about calling her an old lady and being rude about her nose. He missed the way she gathered the silence of his cell about her like something warm that did not exclude him from it. He'd even come to enjoy the strawberry cordial.

Slowly, inch by careful inch, and with the greatest difficulty, he began working his hands loose from the tight coils of the rope.

'Forgive me, Mr Pike,' said Patience when she came in the morning.

She would have come yesterday, she said, but the mayor had turned down their application for the hostel. He said it would be 'a blister in the eye of any visitor to Piper City and an affront to the respectability of its inhabitants'. Afterwards her spirits had been so low she'd gone straight home. 'My company would have been very poor I'm afraid, Mr Pike, even for someone who makes as few demands on it as you.'

Pike wished Knapp wasn't there. He hated the way the fat jailer spied on them. 'Ain't that a shame,' he said, his voice low, hoarse.

'Yes.'

Suddenly there were tears in Patience Haig's eyes. Her plain narrow face looked even longer than ever, pulled down by the twitching corners of her thin mouth.

Pike studied her. He didn't know what to say.

Knapp had edged closer, attracted no doubt by the soft sound of Patience Haig crying. When Pike saw him he jumped up with his chair on his back and shook his chains and roared and rushed towards the bars like a gorilla, sending the terrified Knapp scurrying back to his stove on the far side of his little office. When Pike returned to the table he found Patience laughing quietly.

'He's like the winged lion in the Book of Revelation,' she said, blowing her nose. 'Full of eyes before, behind and within.'

'Ain't that the truth.'

Patience sniffed and dried her cheeks with a half-made bootie. She straightened her long dry braid and squared her bony shoulders.

'Well,' she said. 'Enough of my disappointments, Mr Pike. How are you today?'

Pike wanted to tell her he'd missed her yesterday when she hadn't come.

'I'm okay', he said.

'That's good,' said Patience.

'I have something for you,' said Galen Pike, laying his hand upon the table. He had made it, he said, to brighten her frock.

It was a kind of rosette, or flower, woven from what appeared to be loose threads from the rope that had been twined about his hands, which Patience saw now was no longer there. Four rough stringy petals; at the centre a button from his putrid blood-soaked shirt. Patience held it for a moment in the palm of her hand. The rough petals scraped her skin. She wondered if Pike meant it as a romantic gesture of some sort.

If the preparation of the heart is taken seriously the right words will come.

'Thank you, Mr Pike,' she said gently. Thank you but she couldn't accept it, she was against adornment, material decoration.

She placed the flower back in the hollow of his cupped hand. His dirty fingers closed around it.

'You hate me.'

'No.'

Knapp held his breath. He watched Pike turn the rope flower over in his hand and shake his head, the foul matted tangle of snakes and rat-tails, and heard him tell Patience Haig she was wrong about the light of God being in every man. He didn't have it. It had passed him by. Where he was, was dark and swampy and bad.

'Nonsense,' said Patience.

It was true, said Pike, looking out through the tiny window at the maroon-coloured peaks beyond. Since his mother died he'd done all manner of wicked things. Since she passed away, years and years and years ago, there'd been no one to tell him how to behave; no one in the world he'd wanted to please, whose good opinion mattered at all. If he'd wanted to do something, he'd gone ahead and done it. He looked at Patience. What was her name? he asked.

'Patience,' she said. 'Patience Haig.'

'You remind me, a little, Miss Haig, of my mother.'

Knapp's beady eyes moved from Galen Pike to the thin Quaker lady in her drab frock. It was hard to tell from her expression if she enjoyed this comparison with Pike's mother. Her face showed no emotion, her long braid lay neatly down her back, her hands folded in her lap.

'I am afraid of the hangman, Miss Haig,' said Galen Pike.

He touched his hand to his throat. Would she shave him, in the morning? And cut his hair? Would she bring him a clean shirt so he wouldn't look so dirty and overgrown when they came for him in the morning? That is, he added with an awkward kind of grimace, if she didn't disapprove too much of him being anxious about his appearance.

Patience looked at her hands. Of course she would shave him, she said softly. If he thought it would help.

And then, because she wanted very much to lighten the heaviness of the moment, she smiled, and said she hoped she wouldn't make too much of a mess of it; she'd watched her brother Walter shaving a few times but had no experience herself. Pike said he was sure it would be all right. He trusted her not to hurt him.

When she'd finished shaving him the next morning, and given him Walter's clean shirt to put on instead of his stinking one, Patience asked him if he wanted her to read something. The twenty-third Psalm was beautiful, she said. It would give him strength, she was sure. Pike said all he wanted was for her to go with him. For ten minutes more they sat quietly. There was the sound of Knapp's broom moving across the floor of his little office, outside in the yard the rustle of the aspen trees, and then Knapp came with the key, and Sheriff Nye and two of his men, and Dr Harriman and the hangman from Boulder.

Nye unlocked the chain around Pike's waist and untied the remaining rope that fastened his legs to the chair, and took him by the arm.

In the yard he asked him if he had any last words and in a strong voice Pike said he wanted to thank Miss Patience Haig for the tasty biscuits and the cordial and the clean shirt and the shave but most of all he wanted to thank her for her sweet quiet company. She was the best and kindest person he had ever known. He had not deserved her but he was grateful and he wished he had something to give her, some small remembrance or lasting token of appreciation to show his gratitude, but he had nothing and all he could hope was that if she ever thought of him after he was dead, it would not be badly.

It was hard to tell, Knapp said later to his wife, what effect this short speech of Pike's had on Patience Haig, but when the burlap bag came smartly down over Pike's black eyes and repulsive ravenous features and the floor opened beneath his feet, he was certain Miss Haig struggled with her famous composure; that behind the rough snap of the cloth and the clatter of the scaffold's wooden machinery, he heard a small high cry escape from her plain upright figure.

When it was over Patience asked Knapp if she might sit for while in the empty cell. She looked for the rope flower but it wasn't there. Knapp must have spirited it away, or perhaps Pike had taken it with him.

It seemed an eternity since he'd first wandered into town. There'd still been snow on the ground, though the worst of the winter had been over. For months before there'd been talk of a little gold to the south, and she remembered seeing the four Piper City men heading off on their expedition to look for it, Pike making the fifth as bag carrier and general dogsbody, loaded up with cooking pots and shovels, dynamite, fuel, picks.

She walked slowly away from the jailhouse, trying to empty her mind of everything that had happened since the four Piper City men had failed to return and their horrible fate had been discovered. She tried to empty her mind of the quiet hours she'd spent with Galen Pike at the jail, of Byron Lym's crushing rejection of her latest project, of the terrible hanging. She had never felt so miserable in her entire life. She turned out of North Street into Franklin, past the shuttered front of the general store, the closed bank, the locked-up haberdasher's, the drawn blinds of the dentist. She paused before the heavy pine doors of the bank. On the brass knocker someone had tied an evergreen wreath with a thick black ribbon. *Poor Mr Shrigley, she thought. Poor Mr Palgrave. Poor Damon Archer and Dawson Mew.*

She walked on a little way and then she stopped and turned and looked back at the silent premises of the four dead men.

It had not occurred to her before.

'Oh dear Lord,' she whispered, thinking of Byron Lym's stubborn but wafer-thin majority at the polls.

In Piper City everyone knew how everyone else voted and if Patience's memory served her and she was not mistaken, there'd been forty-eight Republican voters at the last election, and since then Galen Pike had eaten four of them. It was doubtful Lym could succeed next time without them.

Patience turned on her heel.

She squared her bony shoulders and tucked her basket into the crook of her arm.

Quickened her step along Franklin Street towards home.

Ran up the steps onto the porch and in through the screen door, to tell Walter the news.

Kirsty Gunn

The Scenario

At a dinner party a few weeks ago I saw my old friend Clare Revell and we immediately fell into a conversation about words and feelings. The night before I had watched the film *Melancholia* by Lars Von Trier and I told Clare that I had been irritated by its 'lack of rigour' – is the expression I used, that old line, meaning, in this case, I said to her, the way the film seemed pulled together, affecting as it may have been but pulled together out of many different bits and pieces, using movie stars, particular kinds of characters, film homages and so on, to make it seem important, and all of those moments given gravitas and unity by the same few bars from Wagner's *Tristan and Isolde* – the famous few, at that – played over and over and over again.

'But I don't agree at all,' said Clare – I think that is how the conversation kicked off proper: *I don't agree at all.* 'Why shouldn't a story be made of bits and pieces?' she said. 'And what do you mean by "lack of rigour" anyway? That's just a fancy way of saying someone doesn't do things according to the way you do them, that you don't like their approach. I felt *Melancholia* was a great film, actually—'

'You *felt*?' I said. 'What's the point of you telling me what you *felt*? I want to know what it is about the film that made you have that response – of a "feeling" towards it. I want you to give me a reason why it's great – not just some old "feeling".'

Clare laughed then, showing her gums in that pretty, sexy way that I think Tolstoy used when he drew an image of the little princess in *War and Peace* and described her in terms of that particular physical configuration, 'she had a short upper lip and showed her teeth very sweetly when she smiled,' he writes. I've always found those kinds of smiles pretty and sexy – surprising somehow – and fun. Blame it on that dear old Russian if you want to. Then Clare took off her jersey and settled into her seat, because this was the discussion beginning fully now; we'd just laid out the opening of things and now we could fully get into the subject and its ideas.

I looked over at my husband in the corner of the room, and then at the other guests. They were all happily talking and engaged. Clearly no one was going to notice or mind if Clare and I got deep into some private, esoteric conversation about feeling and reason that, in a way, didn't belong at a party like this – a cocktail party, really, but with a buffet and music that might lend itself later to dancing – that would shut everyone else out, like a portcullis coming down, 'No Entry', our fancy kind of talk. I had a sip of my wine, and Clare began.

'There's something I want to tell you about,' she said, 'that happened to me years ago when I was still a student. I was reading semantics and philosopy as you know, and it was all Roland Barthes and Irigaray and Deleuze and Guattari. Books like *Language and the Text* – do you know that book?'

I shook my head. I knew of the book but I hadn't read it, and Clare went on to describe it in brief, 'all about signs and the signified' she said, and told me how important it had been to her, that particular title, as a young woman, when she was learning who she was, who she was to be. She'd been thinking about all of this, she said, because she'd just finished reading the new novel by Jeffrey Eugenides, and that book began with a character reading an inspirational book by Barthes, *A Lover's Discourse*. In fact, that information was 'the way in' to Eugenides' novel, she told me, which she had also loved. In fact, she said, she'd even written an email to Jeffrey Eugenides telling him how much she'd enjoyed his latest work, and he'd 'pinged an email straight back', telling her how delighted he was that she'd liked it.

'And all because of a book by Barthes being at the beginning of it,' Clare said. 'Reminding me of a whole period of my life.'

The story, proper – I've used that phrase before, I know – as she started to tell me (we'd both topped up our glasses of wine by now and were fully and cozily settled, like two cats, is how I thought of it, into our chairs – though my husband told me much later that night, before we went to bed, that throughout the entire period of the evening, while we'd all been having those pre-dinner drinks, I'd in fact been sitting in the most vulgar way possible, with my legs wide open so that everyone could see right up my skirt) began all those years ago when Clare was a young woman at the LSE and studying semiotics with a woman who I will call X, who is a leader in her field, the author of seminal texts about meaning and perception, language and the body, 'high, high theory' as Clare put it. 'These were impenetrable books,' she said, 'that I desperately wanted to read and understand because I fancied her rotten.' She stopped for a second, then laughed out loud. 'For me,' she said, 'the books, the reading... It was all about sex and love and feelings and wanting her to fancy me and not the world of words, of ideas, at all!' She laughed again, showing her teeth. 'I just wanted to kiss her! Nothing to do with books! And I felt like a fraud because I was supposed to be understanding all this theory and learning from it. Signs and the Signified. I was supposed to be her student and she my tutor – and I felt like a charlatan, an imposter, because really it wasn't about what she was teaching me. It was about bodies and sex.'

'Wow,' I said. She'd given such a clear definition of things. *Writing and the Body* – that was a book that I'd read and found very influential at university, myself, by Gabriel Josipovici, and it covered the same kind of ground. 'I see exactly why you're telling me this off the back of what we said about *Melancholia*,' I said. I think I said that then. Because we were having, Clare and I, that particular delicious feeling you sometimes get when talking with someone, about the conversation actually being about several things at once – the primary subject having been about that film, and how it had caused both of us to express quite opposing views, and then this other very different, narratively-oriented conversation that had come out of that, all about bodies versus language and what had happened to Clare with a glamorous older woman when she was a student. And what had happened? I was interested, you see, in finding out more on that subject of whether or not the feelings that coursed through any response to anything, whether a film by Lars Von Trier or the story Clare was presenting now, might have value and be of interest.

I was sitting there, as my husband told me later, with my legs wide open and thinking about that – while all the time holding fast to all my ideals about the real artist being someone with a unifying vision, the kind of person, in other words, who wouldn't need to rely on the famous bits from *Tristan and Isolde* – the bits that everybody loves anyhow – to make the audience believe that what had been created was meaningful and somehow righteous, in the aesthetic sense, well made and fit for purpose, beautiful that way.

And there was Clare, just the opposite, who'd told me on a previous occasion that – and she was adamant that she was not being post-modern at all – she always cried in the bit of the film of *Mary Poppins* when the old crippled woman comes out into the twilight and Mary Poppins sings *Feed the Birds* to her. So yes. We were different, she and I. We were different, alright, and I was intrigued, I was coming to realise, over the course of our discussion, by the rigidity of my own views that seemed so dull, somehow, me sitting there in my black tights and my high-heeled black shoes, my short black skirt – what a trip! – next to this free and open-minded intellectual with her pink gums and white teeth and a story to tell... That had a river in it, she went on, and a bridge, and the cold air of midwinter on her exposed skin, on her throat and face and, when her shirt was unbuttoned, on her breasts, a story braced with coldness, December in London, a chill wind coming off the Thames, the 'freezing' and 'exciting' qualities of the day.

For there she was in the story, too, wild and free. Fancying the pants off this extraordinary-sounding older woman and – 'What was she like?' I kept asking Clare. 'Like, physically? Tall? Fair?'

'Oh, yeah, all of that,' said Clare, right back. 'She was amazing,' and she kept returning to that phrase of how much she fancied her: 'I fancied her rotten,' she repeated.

For that reason, I never got a real portrait of X for the purpose of writing this, something I would have liked, actually, to have been able to create a portrait of that woman in the Henry James way of showing character that is not the Tolstoy way but more uptight and detailing all the moral qualities of a person before you get anything of the physical, like you always get with Tolstoy straight away, the physical, you read about that first. Instead I'm left just with that 'tall' and 'fair' of my own here – enough to make X a Walkyrie, I suppose, to keep the Wagner theme live, more a daughter of the god Wotan than an earthly Isolde – and Clare said she was having classes with this woman every week and loving the classes, of course, just sucking in every single thing about signs and signifiers, and going off and doing all the reading in between, reading that Barthes book and Lacan and Foucault and everyone, and all because she was in love with this person, X, and this was the only way, through reading the books X had read and had written about, those many texts of hers, Clare could get close.

'Finally,' Clare said, 'after all this, after all the tutorials and the flirtation – because I knew she was flirting with me, using the books, her *texts*, to flirt with me – so, finally…' And this is what I thought Clare said… 'We had a day together.'

Finally we had a day together.

As I say, that is what I thought she said. The next part of the story depends upon me writing it like that – faithfully, but with a sense of drama, of narrative fulfillment – in the way I heard Clare say it, that 'Finally' performing its trick, you see. 'Finally we had a day together.'

Clare knows she looked great that day. She was wearing a leather jacket and a shirt that she loved. 'It was from Flip' – I know I've got that part exact. 'And it was beautiful, beautiful cotton,' she said. When I asked her more details about that later – when we went on to talk about the importance of the feel of the clothes you wear on top of your body, that first layer of clothing and how that makes you feel when you are with someone you fancy, how you remember every detail – she said it was a pale blue shirt with a thin, thin yellow stripe, 'a fine stripe', Clare said, putting her thumb and forefinger together to show how very fine it was. 'It was quite preppy—'

'A Connecticut shirt,' I interpreted. 'Like the boys wear there, on the Eastern Seaboard.'

'Yes,' Clare said. 'And it was made of, as I said, this beautiful cotton and I know I looked great in that shirt. I knew I looked just great.'

So, and again I say it, *Finally*, there she was. Dressed as she was – and it was 'illegal'. Clare kept using that word. 'It was illegal,' she said. For them to be having this day together, time out, a whole day, first having lunch, somewhere in Soho and then walking around London, the two of them, in term time, and on their own… And they'd ended up on Westminster Bridge kissing – with the air cold, it was freezing on Clare's exposed skin, from where this woman had unbuttoned her shirt right there on the Bridge, had unbuttoned that pale blue-and-yellow-stripe cotton beneath her leather jacket in order to touch her breasts as they kissed. December and a thin cold wind was blowing across the Thames and there they were, these two women, a young woman in a leather jacket and a rather gorgeous sounding boy's shirt and a sophisticated and should I write splendid older woman? (I want her to be splendid, so keep it in), a beautiful tall older woman, her teacher. Yes, 'tall' and 'fair', and they were kissing, they couldn't stop and X had put her hand inside the boy's shirt, 'and she groped me, she was groping me!' Clare said.

She took a handful of the soya nuts she'd been eating and crunched them all down. I saw the flash of those wild and lovely pink gums, those white teeth. She laughed, and I did. We both laughed.

'So you see what I mean?' Clare said. 'It was illegal! For me to be with my teacher this way, for her to be doing that. She was my teacher and I was loving it, kissing her and being kissed, being felt up. I was in love with her, I wanted to run off with her... And all of this happening on Westminster Bridge in the cold, in December, we were kissing, it was wild, and then suddenly she pulled back.' Clare said. 'She pulled away from me and asked me "Do you read *Feminist Review*?"'

'What?' I said. And then, 'Wow.'

'I know,' Clare said. '"Do you read '*Feminist Review*?"'

'I don't even know *Feminist Review*?' I said. 'I mean. I've never read it. I've heard of it but—'

'I know,' Clare said again, back to me. 'And I hadn't read it either – but I wasn't going to tell her that...'

'So,' I said. 'What did you do?

'Well I went, *Yeah*', Clare said. 'I said, "Yeah, a bit. I know *Feminist Review*."'

'And—'

'Then she said to me – and remember the cold air, it was on my face, on my skin, my shirt was still unbuttoned, my jacket was open to the December air—'

'And the river flowing beneath you...' I said.

'Sure, the river. And it was cold. It was bloody cold, and a second ago we'd been kissing and she'd been feeling me up, and then – get this, okay? This is the part of the story I've been wanting to get to – she said to me, after I'd said that, yes, I knew *Feminist Review*, she said that, well, could this be a scenario?'

'Hah!' I said.

'I know!' Clare replied.

'Because what does that even mean, right?' I said.

'I thought the same thing! What is that, a scenario?'

Clare grabbed another handful of the soya nuts and chewed and crunched and swallowed them so quickly it was as though ravenous hordes were chasing her.

'Well I think it has a capital letter, for a start,' I said. 'But I don't know... What it is. Do you know now?'

'I think so,' said Clare. 'But on the other hand, maybe not.'

'Well it's not like saying "Affair", is it?' I answered. 'Though "Affair" most certainly has a capital letter as well. But it's not like that, is it? Scenario?'

'But neither is it just a situation,' Clare added.

'No,' I agreed. 'It's not that. It's not just a situation. It's definitely something that's—'

'A Scenario. Exactly,' Clare said. 'It's what was happening – right there, at that minute. It was her way of saying – what? That this could be the reality for the two of us? To be together? That it could be this big deal—'

'Or also,' I said, 'a way of saying that what was going on was nothing at all.'

'Yeah!' Clare grinned, then she gave out a quick laugh. 'Weird, eh?' she said. 'To use that word when all that time I was feeling so much. You know, the cold, the kissing. My shirt unbuttoned. Feelings you see. It's what we were talking about before. And then this word came down – in the midst of all the feelings—'

'It came between the two of you,' I said.

What I was thinking, that moment, as Clare was crunching nuts and talking about all of this, was that 'Scenario' was a word all right. A word that that glamorous woman had used, knowingly, wisely and slyly, a word she'd used on purpose – whether or not it had come out of the pages of *Feminist Review* – she was using it for her own purpose, that word, to stand, meaningfully and solidly between herself and this young woman she was kissing and fondling. It was a word she carefully, mindfully inserted between herself and Clare, between her hands and the opened shirt, the bare breasts, the cold, shivery skin.

Scenario.

'Like, what is that, right?' Clare said to me.

I was sitting there, my husband said, as I wrote earlier, with my legs akimbo, wide open, like an old lady or a man sits, and I wasn't wearing trousers but a short, short black skirt.

'Scenario,' I said.

'What did it all add up to?' My husband asked me, later that same night. We were having a discussion about the evening; he'd met a really nice couple, he said. He was in television production, but interesting programmes, art and culture, and she was a painter. 'You'd have liked them,' he said. He wanted to invite them for supper sometime.

'I mean,' he said, 'where did your discussion with Clare lead you in the end?'

It was quite late. I was getting ready for bed.

'You sitting there with your legs wide open, like some old man, for Christ's sake,' he said. 'Your legs all over the place... Jesus, Mary.'

'It led nowhere at all,' I told him. After all, that wasn't the point of it. We were exploring the concept of language and feeling, the right of one over the other. We didn't have a conclusion to reach.

'Well, I thought it was a bit rude,' my husband said. 'A party, after all, and you two holed up in the corner talking in a way that seemed exclusive. You know, Mary,' he said. 'You two shut all the rest of us out.'

And he was right, when I look back on it. I'd been aware of it at the time, whether it was an okay thing to do, have this separate conversation while the party was going on, I wrote about that earlier, but had ignored the thought.

'She said: *Could this be a scenario?*' Clare said.

An invitation. And a dismissal.

'It was both those things,' I said.

'What?'

'By calling it a scenario,' I told Clare, 'while she was touching you. She was both inviting you to have an affair with her and denying the significance of what was going on at the same time. She was opening up the possibility of something happening, while closing down the likelihood of it ever occurring.'

'Like a discussion about semantics,' Clare said. 'Language and the body.'

'Exactly,' I said. 'The Scenario. It sounds like a short story. I'm going to write it all down.'

'Beginning with this party?' Clare said.

'Oh, don't do that,' my husband told me. 'Don't go turning all that into fiction. Bad enough that it happened, darling. You sitting there flapping your legs around... No thought for anyone else in the room.'

That's what he said, I told Clare weeks later, when the party was long over and the story was done. That my husband had said I'd had no thought for anyone else in the room.

'Except me,' Clare said.

'Except you,' I replied. 'The conversation we were having.'

'Was it a scenario then?' my husband had asked me. 'What happened? Did you figure that out at least?' I'd finished telling him about the party, what Clare and I had been talking about. It was late and I was undressing.

'Maybe,' I answered him. I pulled my T-shirt over my head and stood there naked.

'Maybe,' I said again, and then we went to bed.

China Miéville

The Dowager of Bees

I was inducted twenty-two years ago in the windowless basement room of a chic Montreal hotel. The door was small and said JANITOR outside. Inside, the room was gorgeous, full of lush gaming-related paintings and shelves of hardbound rule books. Four of us were sitting at a card table while two defeated young wallflowers watched, big-eyed and silent.

'What's a Willesden?' said Gil 'Sugarface' Sugar. He was elderly and, everyone said, paunchy but still punchy.

'Willesden,' I said. 'It's in London.'

He said, 'I'm not calling you the Willesden Kid.'

'It's an honour to play with you.'

'Get on with it,' said Denno Kane, a baby-faced dark-skinned polyglot renowned for Vingt-et-un but eager to put down money wherever there were cards.

Sugarface and Denno went way back, and they went there with the dour Welsh woman twice my age sitting opposite me. I'd met her in Detroit. She'd been taking a break after bankrupting a small city with a pair of sevens. She'd watched me clean up small-fry stockbrokers.

'Nice fingers,' she'd sneered: I did tricks when I dealt. 'I'm Joy. No surname.'

I pretty much shouted like a fanboy that I knew who she was. 'Let me play with you,' I said.

She'd laughed full of scorn but she liked my front. Now here I was, one of three designated hors-d'oeuvres and the only one left at the table still playing.

We'd nearly died of happiness when they told us to bring the packs. The other two spent a lot of money on theirs. I bought mine from a gas station around the corner. Sugarface didn't pass comment on the logo on their backs.

My co-rookies went out as fast as expected but, with luck I deserved not at all, I was keeping up. The big three didn't mind. I wasn't disrespectful. I wore my most expensive suit. Sugarface had on a tux without a tie, Joy a churchy dress. Denno wore a green T-shirt with sauce stains.

He won a big hand. 'How you doing?' he said.

'An honour to play with you,' I said.

The two Collateral Damage got up and very politely thanked everyone for their time as if anyone even gave a shit they were talking. They left.

'*O tempora, o mores,*' Joy said.

Denno swore in Russian, then Greek.

More rounds. I had a straight. Didn't raise too high. Joy to show. She was as good as they said: her face was flint.

'Well,' she said at last. Peered over the back of her cards and laid them slowly down.

Denno whistled. Sugarface gasped and sat back.

Two of Spades; Seven and Jack of Clubs; Eight of Diamonds; and a card I'd never seen before.

An image of an elderly woman done in black and bright yellow. She wore a fur coat, held a clutch, and a cigarette in a long holder. There were insects on her stole and by her face.

'Hell,' Sugarface said. 'God damn.'

'Full Hive,' said Joy. 'The Dowager of Bees.'

She took out a notebook and wrote something and handed it to Sugarface, who signed the page with a rueful nod and passed it to Denno. The shiny yellow card sat on the table with the reds and blacks. The woman was as stylised as all face cards, bordered and reversed beneath herself.

Denno passed me the paper. 'On the dotted,' he said.

'I don't get it,' I said. There was a moment.

'Oh ho,' said Sugarface keenly.

'What is this?' I said.

'Well, *mazel tov,*' said Denno.

'The others had to be gone, sure, right,' Sugarface said.

'OK, haze the newbie,' I said. 'That's cool.'

'Show some respect,' Denno said.

He went to the shelf and came back with a leather-bound edition of

Robert's Rules of Poker. He flicked through pages and held it open in front of me, pointing to the relevant section.

It was in a chapter entitled 'Hands that Include Hidden Suits'.

'Full Hive,' I read. 'Dowager of Bees + one black Jack + three number cards' values' totalling a prime number.' There was a lot more but he slammed it closed before I could read on.

'I've got that book,' I said, 'and I don't remember...'

'Trust me, it's going to beat whatever you've got,' he said as he put the volume back. I showed him my straight hesitantly.

'Please,' he said. 'You're physically hurting me.'

'Sign,' Sugarface said. 'You owe Joy a favour you don't want to do.'

'What favour?'

'You listening?' Denno said. 'One you don't want to do. Sign. You have a year and a day. Don't make her come asking.'

It didn't seem ridiculous. Everything felt very important. My ears were ringing. I looked at the card, the big stingered insects. Everyone watched me.

Joy's page said '1) D.o.B. Favour', and then the signatures. I signed.

Sugarface clapped. Joy nodded and took her notebook back. Denno poured me an expensive wine.

'Long time since I saw an induction,' Sugarface said.

He collected the cards. I watched the yellow lady with the gas station logo on her back fold in with the rest of them. He shuffled.

'Mine was in Moscow,' he said. ''66.'

'Your induction?' Denno said. 'Kinshasa, me. Eleven years ago.'

Joy said, 'Swansea Bridge Club.'

I said nothing. I got dealt three of a kind. I won a little money. I wasn't focusing any more. No one said anything else about the favour owed.

'Having a good time?' Sugarface said.

The card didn't show up again. I rubbed the deck between my fingers and it felt standard and cheap.

When we were done and packing up, I walked as nonchalantly as I could to the bookshelf and picked up those rules. I checked the contents page and the index for Dowager, Bees, Hidden Suits, Suits (Hidden). Nothing.

I realised that the others had stopped talking and were staring at me indulgently.

'Bless him,' Denno said.

'The round's finished,' Sugarface told me. 'You won't find anything now.'

He threw all three decks into the trash. I was still reading, looking through the lists of hands. There was nothing about a Full Hive.

'You're only inducted once,' Joy said. 'Buy yourself something nice.'

She waited in the doorway without complaining while I went to the bin and rummaged around in the cigarette ash and fished out every card and separated out the deck I'd bought.

It contained no Dowager of Bees. I did find extra cards: there were fifty-five, but two were Jokers, and one was instructions for Solitaire.

I made sure I had her address, and three hundred and forty-seven days later, I found Joy and did her a favour I didn't want to.

The second time I saw a hidden suit was in Manchester.

It was six years later. I wasn't a Poker top-ranker but I could hold my own, and besides, I'd diversified, could play you at Baccarat, Whist, Rummy, Bridge, Faro, Spoil Five Euchre, Chemin-de-Fer, Canasta, Uruguay Canasta, Panguingue, Snap. Pretty much anything. I'd find ways to bet on any of them too. I won my first car at Tarabish. It made me want to win more.

There was a GameFest (they called it) at the Corn Exchange. Mostly families checking out kids' stuff. The few professionals there were goofing around or accompanying friends. There were five of us in a little roomlet made with temporary walls in the corner of the hall. We were drunk and playing unlikely games for petty cash and giggles.

We were on Old Maid. That's the one where you start by removing one Queen, then deal the fifty-one and pass cards one hand to the next and get rid of pairs until everyone's out except some poor schmuck who's left holding just that last mismatched Queen, the Old Maid. They lose.

A civilian would say it was pure luck. No such thing.

We thought up a way to bet. Antes into a pot, which got distributed as people came out. Whoever had the Old Maid would end up losing double. It was a burning hot day and I remember a blaze of light came right down through a high window and made our table shine.

I was out, sitting back safe, having made my cash. People took cards from each other and discarded pairs triumphantly. Three people left. More passing. Pairs down. Two. A woman in her twenties with a strawberry-blonde bob and a leather jacket too battered not to be second-hand, facing down a plump, blinky, middle-aged guy in a corduroy jacket. We watched them swap and throw down cards, their faces set, and then someone gave a little cry and I frowned because the two of them were sitting back staring at each other, and each still held a single card.

'Did we mess up?' someone said. 'Did we miscount?'

The man turned his: the Queen of Spades. He was the Old Maid.

We all looked at the young woman. Her eyes were wide. She looked at me. The back of her card looked the same as all the others. I didn't feel drunk any more.

'Show,' I said.

She lowered it face up. Its background was dark flat grey. The design was of two rows of four links of metal picked out in white.

She swallowed. She said, 'Eight of Chains.'

Someone went to bar the door.

'What now?' her opponent said. He was terrified. 'I don't know what happens.'

'None of us do,' I said.

'Gin's my usual game, I don't… What's the *rule*?'

A tall guy to the young woman's right was leafing through a tatty paperback of *Hoyle's*. The fat man looked up a gaming site on his phone.

'I don't understand,' said a boy of about seventeen. 'What is that?'

By that time I knew that, definitionally, if he didn't, everyone else present did understand what was happening. If there's any, there's only ever one.

'You've been inducted,' I told him. 'Just watch and listen. Who else had it?' I said. 'At any point?'

The guy looking with the rulebook raised her hand. 'I got dealt it,' he said. 'She took it from me. Here we are.' He started to read. '"Old Maid: Rules for Hidden Suits." It's the what of Chains?'

I said, 'The Eight,' but the man with the Queen interrupted.

'Got it,' he said, squinting at his phone. He sagged with relief.

'I'm still the loser,' he said. 'I still lost.'

I could see the boy was about to complain that he didn't understand again and I showed him a warning finger.

The young woman licked her lips. 'There must be a forfeit, though,' she said. 'Even so.'

The big guy hesitated and nodded and passed her his phone. She read. The rest of us were too polite to ask but I caught the eye of the man with the rulebook and he gave me a tiny reassuring nod.

'OK,' the young woman said. She was tense but controlled. 'OK, that's not so bad.'

'Right?' her opponent said. 'It could be worse, right?'

'That's not so bad.'

We all breathed out. I picked up the cards and folded them back into the deck and shuffled. We all got silly as the tension eased. I made the cards spring from one hand to the other and dance about. People cheered.

'I don't understand,' the boy said. 'Can I see?' He held out his hand for the deck and I made the cards jump through the air to land right in front of him and everyone laughed, even the woman who'd ended up with the Chains.

'You can try,' I said. 'I wouldn't hold your breath, though.' He went through the deck and, of course, did not find the card. Without asking, he picked up the phone too, but the round was over and there was nothing about the hidden suits on the site, or on any site.

The young woman took a while to clear up her stuff and she kept looking at me. She wanted me to wait for her.

'You're really good at that stuff,' the big man said, making flickering fingers.

'Many hours,' I said. 'Sleight and magic.'

He glanced behind him. The woman was putting on her jacket. He lowered his voice.

'I almost didn't give her the phone,' he whispered. 'The Eight's not so bad. Which is good, because…'

I shook my head so he wouldn't tell me more.

'But if she'd seen what it said about the Nine,' he said, and shook his head. 'Or the Six. Or if she'd ended up with the Two of Scissors…!'

'She didn't,' I said. It was crass of him to talk this way. 'There's no percentage thinking about the might'ves.'

He left as the young woman approached. He gave me a friendly wave. As if I wasn't a hypocrite. As if all of us, all players, don't live in a dense forest of might'ves.

The kind of event for which I'd hoped when I was young and endlessly practising passes, turning cards around my fingers, didn't come. I couldn't have said what it was exactly anyway – some chimera, something epochal, valuable, ostentatious and secret.

I didn't cheat often or big enough to attract notice, my big wins I won straight, but occasionally, depending on the stakes, the game, my opponents, my finances, and whim, I'd twist my fingers according to muscle memory and take a trick that would otherwise have escaped me, withhold from my opponent some card I knew they needed.

If I was very drunk I might show Belinda a trick or two. She loved seeing them and I loved to see her look when I showed her. Sometimes I called her Chains. Sometimes she called me Bees.

She had more luck than me, and she bet higher, and she knew hands and odds and combinations better, but she lost more, too. We once worked out that our earnings were almost identical.

We went to Paris for the art. We went to Brazil and took pictures of the Jesus. We played Go Fish in Bucharest. We loved watching each other at the tables but didn't play against each other often because we knew we wouldn't hold back.

We'd swapped numbers that day in Manchester, but it was a few weeks later that she called, and her mood was good when she did, so I figured she'd got through the forfeit.

She didn't ask me if I ever cheated and I didn't volunteer any information and I never did it against her but she was too good a player not to suspect.

For the first year or so we didn't talk overmuch about the hidden suits, though we said enough to start to use those pet names, shyly. Every once in a long while she'd disappear for a day or two and come back tired and thoughtful. I knew it was the terms of the forfeit and I didn't say anything.

Once in Vegas a Canadian oncologist blithely told us there were hidden suits in the Baraja deck too. I was appalled by the conversation and we made our excuses.

I understand the interest in the Baraja, the Italian deck, the German with its other colours, the Ganjifa, and so on, but I was always a devotee of the standard modern Rouennais fifty-two. I loved the history that led to what we play with, the misprisions, the errors of copying that got us suicide Kings and one-eyed Jacks. I loved the innovation of the rotational symmetry that isn't a reflection. I loved the black and the red, against which the colours of the hidden suits are so stark – blue, grey, green, the white of Chains, the yellow of the Bees.

'I only saw one other,' Belinda told me once, carefully. 'The Nine of Teeth. But just for an instant.'

The difficulty is that it's bad form to talk about them brazenly, but once you're inducted it's also a good idea to learn as many rules for as many hands featuring as many cards in as many suits in as many games as you might ever play, just in case. And you can't exactly look them up most of the time.

No matter how proper you are, there are questions you'll end up hearing asked, or asking. What bird is it flying above the Detective of Scissors? Where's the missing link on the Nine of Chains? Why does the Ace of Ivy grow on bones?

You might feel you know these cards, whether you've seen them or not. 'We all end up getting to know certain cards pretty well, I guess,' Belinda said to me once. 'One way or another.' You might have a favourite.

The third time was Lublin.

We were playing Bourré in a deconsecrated church. I'd faced two of my opponents before, and had had a fist fight with one. Belinda and I were taking turns: she stood behind me with her hand on my shoulder. She could see my cards but no one else's.

I picked up my hand. Five cards. One of them I'd never seen before. One two three four blue smokestacks, protruding into blue sky, gushing stylised clouds of blue smoke.

I showed nothing. Belinda's hand twitched. I wasn't afraid anyone noticed but to me it was as if she screamed, *'Oh my God!'*

I went into my memory for whatever I had about the Four of Chimneys.

What it would do in combination with my other cards. I weighed up possibilities.

There was a lot of betting. I got tenser and tenser. When I eventually laid down my hand I cannot tell you how much I loved the sound of everyone's amazement. They were calculating the extra losses my win would mean for them, they were gasping with envy, they were stunned at the sight of the card.

No one asked what it was. Everyone present was a previous inductee. The only time that ever happened to me.

People passed me their chips and their extra chips. They wrote down their secrets for me. I wondered what I'd do with the horses and keys that were now mine. I hadn't only been dealt a hidden card; I'd played it well.

I'd told myself repeatedly that it was an instant's insanity to do what I did, something I can't explain. But then, I had been perfecting finger tricks for a long time.

As everyone relaxed and a heavy-faced ex-soldier picked up the deck and collected our hands, I laughed at some witticism and nodded and barely looked at him as I folded my cards and passed them. I don't know if Belinda's hand tightened again. I didn't fear that the dealer, or anyone else, would notice the fleeting fingertip motion by which I extracted the Four of Chimneys from my hand and slipped it into my cuff.

I didn't know if it would still be there when I got home. But I sat in my bathroom and rolled up my sleeve and there it was, waiting to be folded back into the deck so it could leave as it arrived.

'You're going to have a long wait,' I whispered.

Four chimneys, two by two, two facing up, two down, blowing smoke in strong dark blue and black lines.

I felt shy. I put it away.

'What a game,' was all Belinda or I ever said about that night. We carried on. We won more than we lost.

I kept the card in stiff clear plastic in my wallet. I didn't want to scuff it. Sometimes I'd take it out and glance at those block-print chimneys for a couple of seconds, until I got all anxious, as I did, and turned it over and looked for a lot longer at the back.

I've played with super-expensive decks as well as with the gas-station plastic. Pros aren't that precious; mostly we use the workhorse deck produced by Bicycle, as close as you can get to a default. It's had the same meaningless filigree on the back for years. You want choice? It comes in red or blue.

We'd been playing a red-backed Bicycle deck when I got dealt the Four of Chimneys.

I kept up my finger exercises. I listened for stories about the hidden cards. I maybe listened extra hard for stories about hands with Chimneys. I was never superstitious but I did develop one tick. I liked to hold the card against my skin. I liked to feel it pressed against me.

Before a big-pot game, I'd take my Four of Chimneys out of its little case – always with a thrill of excitement, surprise, regret and relief that it was still there – and slip it under a band on the inside of my right forearm behind my wrist, under my shirt, a kind of simple cuff holdout. It made me feel lucky, is how I thought about it.

Some freight shipping companies put aside a few cabins for paying customers. You can cross the Atlantic that way. We got word that one of them had set up a floating big-money game. Of course we booked passage. It was expensive, even though it wasn't as if we were tripping over pleasure-seekers or looking down from our deck onto a sculpted pool. It was a merchant ship: our view was a deck full of containers.

For two days we kept to ourselves. On the third day, before play, I was out under the sky and someone tapped me on the back.

'Kid.'

'Sugarface!'

I was astonished he was still alive. He looked almost exactly the same.

'Should have guessed I'd find you here,' he said. 'Been following your career.'

Belinda liked him a lot. He flirted with her and stayed on the right side of sleazy. He told her exaggerated stories of our first meeting. He showed her the face he said I'd worn when I saw the Dowager of Bees, not even hesitating to find out whether she'd been inducted before he told the story.

In the evening I tucked my card face down into its little band on my right wrist as usual and flicked it before covering it with my shirt and jacket. We gathered in the makeshift state room and sipped mojitos while the sun went down.

Seven players. I'd sat across from all but one before: it's not that big a world. Besides me and Belinda and Sugarface, there was a Maronite computer programmer I'd once beaten at Pig; a French publisher who'd partnered me during a devastating hand at Bridge; a South African judge known as the Cribbage Assassin; and the captain. He was a puffed-up little prick in a blue brocade shirt. He was new to all of us. We realised this whole gig was his brainchild, just so he could play big.

He named the game, of course. Texas Hold-'Em, of course. I rolled my eyes.

The Lebanese guy was weaker than I'd remembered. The judge was cautious but smart and hard to read. The publisher built up slowly with sneaky bets. Sugarface played exactly like I recalled.

Belinda was my main competition. We tore into each other. The captain could barely play at all but he didn't even realise. He preened. He barked at people that it was their deal, their bet, told them what they needed to win. We all pretty much hated him. His ship, his trip, his table were the only reasons we didn't tell him to go fuck himself.

I was playing well but Belinda was playing better. She beat me with two pairs. Furious, I made one of my cards spin over my knuckles. The programmer toasted me and the judge applauded. Belinda smiled kindly and took several thousand dollars off me with an offhand bluff.

Deep night and the sky was like a massive sheet of lead. We changed the cards. The captain took a new pack from a drawer and tossed them to Sugarface.

Bicycle cards. Red-backed. Sugarface opened the packet and dealt us our two hole cards.

Usually most serious players just keep them face down in front of them but that night I wanted to hold mine up like in a cowboy film. Pair of Threes. Good start.

We bet – we bet big – everyone stays in. Sugarface deals the flop: three community cards, face up. A Six, a Ten, Jack of Clubs. I have a good feeling, then a bad feeling, then a good feeling. Sugarface winks. This round of betting we lose Mr IT. I can read him easily and I'm not surprised.

Fourth shared card, the turn. Hi there, Charlemagne: the King of Hearts has been shy till now but there he is. There's some muttering and murmuring. Belinda is rock still while she calculates, even stiller than usual, so she's either in good shape or bad shape and I'm guessing good. The judge goes out. Publisher blows me a kiss and follows.

Sugarface makes us wait a long time, puffing out his cheeks. In the end he joins them.

It's me to bet, and as I consider and see the red backs of my opponents' hands, floating like unmanned boats into my head comes the name of a hand I've heard about over the years.

They call it a Boiler Room: a Ten; a Jack; a King; a Three; and the Four of Chimneys.

I start to consider what that would win me. What would be the takings from this table, not just in money. And I realise that I'm thinking with a sort of calm wonder, almost wryly, *Oh*, this *is what I've been waiting for.*

And as I'm thinking that, with my hands stock still to anyone watching, my fingers are snatching my no-longer-helpful spare Three and sending it to Hell via my sleeve, and coaxing my stolen card out from under its band, toward my cuff and fingertips, a clean sleight, bringing it back up and slipping it into position, all in a fraction of a second, all unseen.

Belinda's in, and the captain's in, of course, which I was banking on, and I don't care what piece of shit he's holding, he's not going to beat my hand – my winning hand – now. I'm ready.

The betting's done and Sugarface deals the river, the fifth shared card. It skitters down. The lights flicker and everyone's gasping and everything goes slow, because the last card out of the deck, the last card face up on the table, is a new colour.

It's the Four of Chimneys.

'Oh hell yes,' I hear Sugarface say. '*Mon Dieu*,' I hear, and 'Oh my God.'
    That's Belinda.

I stare at the blue in the red and black. A shared hidden card. Everyone can have a hidden card in their hand.

The boat pitches, and for a fraction of an instant I see the night beyond the windows and it's as if I hear a drone, as if someone's walking on the deck, someone tall and stiff and dignified in a deep coat, smoking, looking in at us with austere curiosity, with satisfaction.

I can hear the captain saying, 'What is this? What does this mean?' and Sugarface saying, 'Just keep quiet and watch, and show some respect; this is your induction,' and Belinda is staring right at me, her mouth open, her eyes wide.

My frantic little fingers are fumbling deeper in my sleeve than you'd think possible but I dropped that Three to nestle I don't know where against my skin, there's no retrieving it, and I can't swap it back in or its replacement back out again, and everyone can see I have two hole cards in my hand, just as I should.

And one of them's my Four of Chimneys, like the one on the table, and there's only ever one Four of Chimneys, if there's ever a Four of Chimneys at all.

Sugarface is looking at me and saying, 'What's the matter, Kid?' and he looks at Belinda and down at the table and at the back of my cards and up at me and his face falls and he says, 'Oh no, Kid, oh no, no, oh Kid, oh no,' and there's more sorrow and fear in his voice than I've ever heard.

'What is this?' the captain blathers. 'What is this card?' I go to fold but Sugarface takes hold of my wrist.

'Kid, I don't want to see what I think I'm going to see,' he says gently. 'Judge,' he says. 'Get the rulebook.' He starts to pull my hand down. 'I need you to look up "Hidden Suits",' he says.

Everyone is watching my descending cards but Belinda. She's staring at her own hand.

'I need you to look up "Cheating",' Sugarface says. 'I need you to look up "Sanctions".'

Belinda's cards twitch with a tiny instant motion of her fingers as with her free hand she grabs my wrist too. She's stronger than Sugarface. Pushes my cards back up.

'I call,' she says.

'We're mid-play,' he says.

She says, 'Look up a "Link Evens", Judge.'

Even the captain's silent while the judge turns pages. 'Two Four Six Eight Ten including a Chain,' she reads out. 'She can preemptive call with that. Nothing can beat it. Wins… any single object in the room she chooses.' She looks up.

'And everyone keep your paws off that prize,' Belinda says. She's staring at the hand in my hand. 'No looking, no touching, no turning. Just slide it to me face down.'

The judge looks at the cards on the table. 'If she has a Two and an Eight,' she says, 'she wins. But there's a winner's forfeit…'

'I have the Two of Hearts,' Belinda says. She sounds exhausted but she smiles at me. 'And I'm holding the Eight of Chains.'

Everyone sits up.

'Wait,' I manage to whisper. 'What's the forfeit?'

No one hears me. Belinda is lowering her cards to show them.

'I win,' Belinda says.

'What is it?' I try to say.

'I win, and I choose a card as my pot,' Belinda announces. She looks at what I'm holding as her own cards go down, picking a prize to remove from all scrutiny. She meets my eye and smiles. She could always read me. I know she'll choose the right one.

Jessie Greengrass

Scropton, Sudbury, Marchington, Uttoxeter

(after Johnson)

My parents were grocers. For twenty-five years they owned a shop with a green awning and crates of vegetables on the pavement outside, and they worked hard with only Sundays off to go to church, and even on Sundays they went through the accounts after lunch. On bank holidays and early-closing days when other people put on their best hats and went visiting my parents would check stock: sorting vegetables, pulling wilted cabbages and rotting carrots from the bottoms of sacks and setting them aside to be sold as swill. They could judge weight with their hands but they were not educated people and had little time for the things which interested me, for books or for numbers beyond imperial measures and the columns of pounds and shillings and pence. I was their only child, and I have never been sure if I was a source of pride to them or a disappointment, because it is true that I was clever, that I was quick with my mind, but the academic life that I have chosen could not possibly be the one they would have thought of for me, and there is no reason to say they would have judged it better. I showed no interest in the shop, ever: quite the reverse, or perhaps they wouldn't have sold it.

Two months after my eleventh birthday I passed the exam to go to the grammar school. There I found that the fathers of the other children were not shop- keepers. Instead they were men who rose each morning to walk up the hill to the station and take the train to city jobs. They worked in banks and offices, places whose interiors were unimaginable to me. They didn't have breakfast in their shirtsleeves before walking down the stairs to put the trays of apples out, or go next door for a pint of bitter in the evening while the dinner cooked. They drank wine from stemmed glasses. The mothers of the other children didn't work at all. They sat on committees and collected things for the Save the Children fund and their nails were coated with shellac, not dirt from the potato barrel. I loved my parents and I didn't want to hurt them, but I found in a moment of pre-adolescent revelation that I was ashamed of them; and because I was ashamed of them I found that I was ashamed also of myself, and this muddle made me sly. I told lies, or half lies. I said cruel things to my friends about my parents in order that there might seem to be a greater distance between us, and to my parents in turn I was sullen and I refused to speak about school or about the friends I had made there, other than to point out by mean comparison the respects in which their lives were superior to my own; and then afterwards I would be ashamed and my shame would make me angry and resentful: I felt that it was not my fault that I had been put into such an intolerable position.

Sometimes after school or in the holidays my parents would ask me to mind the shop for them. They had very little time to themselves, and I see now how nice it would have been for them if they had been able to go out together sometimes on a sunny afternoon, for a walk down through the fields past the church to the river; but the thought that my friends might see me in a grocer's apron twisting shut a paper bag of apricots or cherries appalled me. I considered it insensitive of my parents to ask, to not know how busy I was, how I had better things to do with my time than mind their shop for them. It is easy now to say that what hurt I inflicted with this attitude was not my fault, that I was a child: but I knew quite clearly how I wounded when I refused them, and so I am unable to escape with such glib sophistry the twisting hook. To my further shame I refused my parents in a way which was evasive, and perhaps it is for this reason that it still sits so ill with me, because I couldn't bring myself to tell the truth, which was that I thought their shop beneath me. Instead I told them that I had homework to do, that I needed to spend some time thinking about an essay or that I must go and see this friend or that friend who had a book that I must read; but the truth was not well hidden and it must have been obvious to them. I made my refusals in a lofty tone, as if to suggest that my parents couldn't possibly understand the sorts of pressures I was under when I had to write five hundred words on the repeal of the corn laws by Monday. Then I would put on the tweed jacket they had bought me and I would walk out of the shop, and in case someone I knew should see me I would try to look as though I had been thinking of buying something but had decided not to; and then because really there was nothing at all that I needed to do I would go and sit in the long grass beyond the boundary of the cricket pitch to watch the aeroplanes make white trails overhead.

After a while my parents stopped asking for my help, and when I was fourteen they sold the shop and, having been quite old already when I was born, retired to live by the sea. Shortly after that I won a scholarship to a boarding school and then my two lives could be quite separate. At school I didn't need to mention the grocer's shop but only the slightly more respectable address of my parents' new bungalow, avoiding any more direct enquiries regarding my home life with evasions that had become through practice habitual; and when I went to stay with my parents in the holidays there was no one I knew in the town and so I didn't need to feel ashamed of them and could go back to loving them simply; but by then it was too late.

If there is such a thing as original sin then I think that this is how it comes upon us, it settles over us in moments of carelessness, and this is why we are taught to act decently as children, to be good and to be polite, because not to do so is to court that instant when one becomes other than one wants to be. For years I had been unable to think of the school and the shop and the town except with pain because of the way my pride had prevented me from helping my parents when they asked for it. This small act of refusal became in retrospect the prism through which the rest of my life was split, laying bare the flaw at the heart of my character, the way that I am neither wholly kind nor wholly honest but at best half-good and in addition evasive, a wriggler-out of situations. Then one Friday evening some months ago I passed through a large railway interchange, and as I stood on the concourse waiting for my train to be called the announcer called instead the name of the town where the shop had been and the names of the towns that surrounded it and which I had not thought of for years. It was a summer evening and there was an end-of-term feeling, a feeling of devil-take-us, and suddenly I was filled with such a powerful desire to abandon my own journey and embark instead upon this other one that I began to move towards the platform; and perhaps I would have gone further still if it wasn't for the crowd of people between the newspaper stand and the flower stall who slowed me and gave me time to realise how futile such a journey would be, all of my ties to this place being after all ties to the past; but still the station names were so familiar and they had such associations. I could taste holidays when I heard them. I could hear the rattle of the old trains, I could smell the polish of the wooden carriage floors and the dusty fabric of the seats. I could feel the satisfying give of the elastic in the luggage racks when I slung my suitcase into them and how much of a struggle it was to fetch it down again. The thrill it was to walk past the smoking compartment to the buffet car.

Through the weeks that followed I was unable to rid myself of the idea of going back to the town, of seeing once more the market square and the shop and standing again in the streets which in memory still seemed so familiar. The faces of my parents, now long dead, hovered in front of me, and my shame at the condescension with which I had treated them felt fresh. I told myself that I could gain nothing from such a return, that it could not alleviate any shred of my guilt but only cause me further pain by showing clearly all the ways that things had changed but how the past itself could not be changed; but I was unable to make myself believe it. I found myself considering such a journey as one might a pilgrimage, its attendant discomforts a scouring; and then I was appalled, and told myself how foolish, how grandiose, to think in such a way about a day return on the East Midlands Railway and an afternoon's stroll about a market town. It was pointless anyway, I thought, to hope that such a journey might allow me in some way to escape the shame I felt over my behaviour towards my parents: a penance is not a penance that is undertaken for reprieve, and if I hoped for absolution it wouldn't come. Such an exercise could be on my part only a further kind of evasion, a small compounding of an existent sin. In this manner it went on and to every argument I was able to find a counter-argument; but still the thought of making the journey wouldn't leave me. It began to interfere with my work. I was unable to concentrate on other things; my mind drifted always back to the grocer's shop, and in the end this was why I went: not with any hope of gaining respite from the past, but only to alleviate such irritations in the present, and because I was tired of thinking about it, tired of the internal arguments, and would have relief at least from them.

I set the date of my journey for a Wednesday, because it was convenient, but travel in the middle of the week always makes me feel as though nothing good can come from it. I did not look forward to the day, and when it arrived I made my way to the station not with hope but with stoicism, as in the direction of a thing to be endured. It was both wet and cold, summer having, while I vacillated, given on to autumn, the fine days to a solid equinoctial grey. All through the morning rain slid down the windows of the intercity train and at the stations the wind blew it through the open doors in gusts. At Crewe I bought a cup of coffee and a sandwich which I didn't eat, and changed on to the branch line. My surroundings were by then familiar, but because this familiarity was not complete I found in it a further source of discomfort. Things were not as I remembered them. The fields, the hedgerows, were meaner than they had been presented to me in recollection, the colours more muted. They were neither pretty nor engaging and they were not that pastoral ideal in which, on Saturday afternoons, I thought my better self had sometimes played, but only working land, churned up to mud by the passage of machinery. I began to regret in earnest that I had come. Once again the arguments against my journey were rehearsed and seemed irrefutable, while those for it appeared both tenuous and coy. The things which had seemed from a distance to be so large – the figures of my parents and myself, the looping dramas in which we had been contained – seemed, the closer I got to my destination, ever more insignificant, until as we drew into the station I wondered if my past had the capacity to mean anything at all.

I had thought that I would visit on arrival those places which I best remembered: the school, the cricket pitch, the church, the fields where I had played and where my friends had played. Now, such an itinerary seemed trivial. These places had never in themselves meant much to me and would now mean even less; besides which I had no desire to see how it had all become so much diminished. I found that what I wanted, now that I was here, was only to stand once more in front of the grocer's shop, to see what parts of it might have endured and to see also if I could find there any trace of my parents, or of myself. I walked out of the station and down the hill towards the market, and as I went I looked at little, trying not to notice the places where terraced cottages had given way to cul-de-sacs or how three pubs had been knocked down. Although I remembered clearly the route the distances felt wrong, the turnings came in unexpected places; and I thought that it is strange how memory retains the structure of things and the details but so little in between. I felt as though I had on a new pair of glasses and through them the world appeared peculiar, bent out of shape, and I was no longer any judge of depth but must be careful where I put my feet. I felt as though, with each step, I might fall; and I would have turned around and gone straight home, were it not for how foolish I would have looked to myself afterwards.

The market square at the corner of which my parents' shop had stood was busy in spite of the rain. There had used to be a stall stacked with trays of eggs and above the eggs a row of plucked chickens strung up by their feet, and there had been a fish- monger selling halibut from a table piled with ice and a man who made his own sausages; but now it was all antiques and bric-a-brac, mirrors and candle- sticks and broken iron mangles. A woman in a wonky turban sat by a pile of rag rugs and I could, if I had wanted to, have purchased any number of hand-sewn cushions. Dodging through the middle I found that the building where our shop had been was still there, and although until that moment I hadn't thought that I minded, yet to see it was an overwhelming relief, and I knew that if it had been gone I would have been distraught. It was no longer a grocer's. The awning had been taken down and the shutters, and the old bottle-glass windows had been replaced, but up above it looked just the same, the dirty red brick and the tiled roof, the bay window where our sitting room had been. Now the shop sold children's clothes at what seemed to me to be remarkable prices. Through the new plate windows I could see racks of miniature Breton jumpers and bright yellow anoraks. I wondered if I should go in; unable to decide, I hovered on the pavement, getting in the way of people rushing from one dry place to another. After a few minutes it began to seem as if to go in now would be more peculiar than not to do so, and nor could I just walk away; besides which, I felt a kind of peace standing on the cobbles in the rain. I felt as though perhaps I had hit entirely by accident upon the only right thing I could have done, and so in the end it was all that I did: I stood outside the shop all afternoon while people jostled past me, and as I stood I thought of myself and of my parents, and of how we are all formed perhaps more by carelessness than by design.

My coat was a city coat, not meant for more than the rush from doorstep to bus stop, and soon I felt the rain soak through it to join the stream running downwards from my neck. I didn't have a hat, and my hair plastered itself to my skull. Annoyed by my continued obstruction of the pavement, shoppers muttered and tutted. Out of the corner of my eye I could see the bored stallholders, distracted from their work by the spectacle I made, gathering together to watch me. Inside the shop, a woman in a navy suit reached for the phone and I wondered if perhaps she was calling the police. Someone asked me without obvious compassion if I was all right, but not being quite sure one way or the other I offered no answer. I knew that people were laughing at me but the injury to my pride no longer caused me any pain; I found in my gathering humiliation a kind of joy, to see how little after all it mattered what people thought of me, and it saddened me that I had for so long felt myself to be governed by imagined opinions, I was sorry for it, and I was sorry too for the gap it had caused between me and my parents: I was sorry even though being sorry could do no good, even though it could bring about no reconciliation or reprieve, and I felt that for this brief spell, my regrets being not conditional on my pardon but genuine and deeply felt, I had been granted the charism of contrition. It occurred to me for the first time that my parents themselves had been as proud as I was, too proud to acknowledge my slights for what they were or to try to cross the distance which had grown steadily wider between my life and theirs. I thought that if they had been more humble then perhaps I also might have been, and things might have come out better for us, overall; and such a thought no longer seemed to be a way of eluding blame, but only a thing that was at once both true and sad, and past, and done.

I stood until the market had packed up and gone and until the light had begun to fade and the rain had slowed to a steady drizzle, and then I made my way back to the station. On the train I sat, dripping steadily, in a carriage empty except for myself and some schoolchildren who nudged one another and giggled at the sight of me, but their laughter no longer chafed. The train started and the announcer ticked the stations off, backwards now, and I thought that it was a relief to be returning home and to have the whole thing over with at last, although I wasn't sure if I meant by that the trip only or the worry or something else again, an arc that had drawn down finally to its long completion. I couldn't say if I was changed, apart from being wetter; I still felt myself to be overly fussy, to be half good, half stunted and half grown, given to settling on the easy route, but perhaps I had gained some measure of understanding; and I felt that regardless of whether anything was different because of it, still what I had done had been satisfactory, and I hoped too that it might in some way have been expiatory, and that I might have made amends; and perhaps after all I had been afforded some measure of absolution.

Biographies

Colm Tóibín is the author of eight novels, including *Brooklyn* and *Nora Webster*, and two collections of stories. His play *The Testament of Mary* was nominated for a Tony Award for best play in 2013. His work has been translated into more than thirty languages. He is a contributing editor at the *London Review of Books*. He is Irene and Sidney B. Silverman Professor of the Humanities at Columbia University.

Nicholas Royle is the author of *First Novel*, as well as six earlier novels, and a short story collection, *Mortality*. He has edited nineteen anthologies and is series editor of *Best British Short Stories* (Salt). A senior lecturer in creative writing at the Manchester Writing School at MMU, he also runs Nightjar Press and is an editor at Salt Publishing. His latest publication is *In Camera* (Negative Press London), with artist David Gledhill.

Neil Gaiman is the *New York Times* bestselling author of the novels *Neverwhere, Stardust, American Gods, Coraline, Anansi Boys, The Graveyard Book, Good Omens* (with Terry Pratchett), *The Ocean at the End of the Lane*, and *The Truth Is a Cave in the Black Mountains*; the Sandman series of graphic novels; and the story collections *Smoke and Mirrors, Fragile Things*, and *Trigger Warning*. He is the winner of numerous literary honours, including the Hugo, Bram Stoker, and World Fantasy awards, and the Newbery and Carnegie Medals. Originally from England, he now lives in the United States. He is Professor in the Arts at Bard College.

Tamar Yellin was born in Yorkshire and studied Hebrew and Arabic at Oxford. Her first novel, *The Genizah at the House of Shepher*, was a finalist for the Jewish Quarterly/H. H. Wingate Prize, winner of the Ribalow Prize for Literature and winner of the inaugural Sami Rohr Prize, an international award for emerging Jewish writers. Her short stories have appeared in numerous publications including *London Magazine, Stand* and *Best Short Stories*. Her collection, *Kafka in Brontëland*, won the Reform Judaism Prize for Literature and was longlisted for the Frank O'Connor International Short Story Award. Her latest book is *Tales of the Ten Lost Tribes*. She has a website at www.tamaryellin.com

Claire Keegan grew up in rural Ireland, studied Literature and Politics at Loyola University, New Orleans, and subsequently earned an MA at the University of Wales and an M.Phil at Trinity College, Dublin. Her debut, *Antarctica*, was a Los Angeles Times Book of the Year. The Observer called these stories: 'Among the finest recently written in English'. In 2007, *Walk the Blue Fields* was published to huge critical acclaim and went on to win many awards including The Edge Hill Prize. *Foster* (2010) won The Davy Byrnes Award, judged by Richard Ford: 'Keegan is a rarity – someone I will always want to read'. The story was subsequently published by Faber, published in The New Yorker and Best American Stories. Her stories have been translated into 14 languages.

Chris Beckett, since winning the Edge Hill Prize for 'The Turin Test', has published another collection of short stories, *The Peacock Cloak*, and has also published three novels, one of which (*Dark Eden*) won the Arthur C. Clarke award for 2012. All his published work to date, whether in the long or the short form, can, at least to some degree, be categorised as science fiction, but he is currently branching out in his short story writing and has plans to publish a third story collection (late 2016 or early 2017) which will include stories written in a range of styles and registers, but none of them SF. It will also be a new departure in that the stories will have been written especially for the collection. Chris Beckett is now a full-time writer. He lives in Cambridge.

Ali Smith was born in Inverness in 1962. She is the author of *Free Love and Other Stories, Like, Other Stories and Other Stories, Hotel World, The Whole Story and Other Stories, The Accidental, Girl Meets Boy, The First Person and Other Stories, There but for the, Artful, How to be both,* and *Public Library and other stories*. *Hotel World* was shortlisted for the Booker Prize and the Orange Prize and *The Accidental* was shortlisted for the Man Booker and the Orange Prize. *How to be both* won the Baileys Prize, the Goldsmiths Prize and the Costa Novel Award and was shortlisted for the Man Booker and the Folio Prize. Ali Smith lives in Cambridge and her next novel is forthcoming in 2016.

Jeremy Dyson was born in Leeds, Yorkshire. He is one of the creators of the BAFTA award-winning comedy *The League of Gentlemen* and co-writer of the acclaimed West End show *Ghost Stories*. He has served as script editor on a number of successful BBC programmes, such as *The Armstrong and Miller Show*. He has written a number of books, including *What Happens Now, Bright Darkness: Lost Art of the Supernatural Horror Film* and two short story collections, *Never Trust a Rabbit* and *The Cranes that Built the Cranes*, the latter of which won the Edge Hill Prize.

A.L. Kennedy was born in Dundee in 1965. She is the author of 17 books: 6 literary novels, 1 science fiction novel, 7 short story collections and 3 works of non-fiction. She is a Fellow of the Royal Society of Arts and a Fellow of the Royal Society of Literature. She was twice included in the Granta Best of Young British Novelists list. Her prose is published in a number of languages. She has won awards including the 2007 Costa Book Award and the Austrian State Prize for International Literature. She is also a dramatist for the stage, radio, TV and film. She is an essayist and regularly reads her work on BBC radio. She occasionally writes and performs one-person shows. She writes for a number of UK and overseas publications and for The Guardian Online.

Robert Shearman has written five short story collections, and between them they have won the World Fantasy Award, the Shirley Jackson Award, the Edge Hill Readers Prize, and three British Fantasy Awards. He began his career in the theatre, and was resident dramatist at the Northcott Theatre in Exeter, and regular writer for Alan Ayckbourn at the Stephen Joseph Theatre in Scarborough; his plays have won the Sunday Times Playwriting Award, the World Drama Trust Award, the inaugural Sophie Winter Memorial Prize, and the Guinness Award for Ingenuity in association with the Royal National Theatre. He is a regular writer for BBC Radio, and his own interactive drama series The Chain Gang has won two Sony Awards. But he is probably best known for his work on *Doctor Who*, bringing back the Daleks for the BAFTA winning first series in an episode nominated for a Hugo Award. He is very proud of his association with Edge Hill – they were the first body to recognise his debut book, and give him the confidence to adopt short stories as his favourite medium!

Graham Mort is Professor of Creative Writing and Transcultural Literature at Lancaster University. He has worked extensively in literature development in sub-Saharan Africa and is currently helping to develop new projects in Kurdistan and South Africa. *Visibility: New & Selected Poems,* appeared from Seren in 2007, when he was also winner of the Bridport short fiction prize. Graham's first book of stories, *Touch,* was published by Seren in 2010 and his latest book of poems, *Cusp,* in 2011. *Terroir,* a new collection of short fiction, appeared in 2015 and *Black Shiver Moss* (new poems) will follow from Seren in 2017.

Helen Simpson's sixth short story collection, *Cockfosters,* follows *Four Bare Legs in a Bed* (1990), *Dear George* (1995), *Hey Yeah Right Get a Life* (2000), *Constitutional* (2005) and *In-Flight Entertainment* (2010). *A Bunch of Fives: Selected Stories* (2012) includes five stories from each of her first five collections. She has received the Sunday Times Young Writer of the Year Award, the Somerset Maugham Award, the Hawthornden Prize and the E.M. Forster Award.

Tom Vowler is an award-winning novelist and short story writer living in south west England. His debut story collection, *The Method,* won the Scott Prize in 2010, while his novel *What Lies Within* received critical acclaim. He is editor of the literary journal *Short Fiction* and an associate lecturer in creative writing at Plymouth University, where he's just completed his PhD. His second novel, *That Dark Remembered Day,* was published in 2014. Represented by the Ed Victor Literary Agency, Tom's second collection of stories, *Dazzling the Gods,* is forthcoming in 2016. More at www.tomvowler.co.uk.

Tessa Hadley has written six novels - including *Accidents in the Home* and *The London Train* - and two collections of short stories. Her latest novel, *The Past,* was published by Jonathan Cape in September 2015. She publishes short stories regularly in the New Yorker, reviews for the Guardian and the London Review of Books, and is a Professor of Creative Writing at Bath Spa University; she was awarded a Windham Campbell prize for Fiction in 2016. She is married with three grown-up sons, and after living for thirty years in Cardiff, in 2011 she moved with her husband to live in London.

Sarah Hall was born in Cumbria in 1974. She is the author of four novels - *Haweswater, The Electric Michelangelo, The Carhullan Army* and *How to Paint a Dead Man* – and a collection of short stories, *The Beautiful Indifference*, which was shortlisted for the Frank O'Connor Prize and won the Edge Hill Prize. Sarah Hall is an honorary fellow of Aberystwyth University, and a fellow of the Civitella Ranieri Foundation (2007). She has judged a number of prestigious literary awards and prizes. She tutors for the Faber Academy, The Guardian, the Arvon Foundation, and has taught creative writing in a variety of establishments in the UK and abroad. She currently lives in Norwich, Norfolk.

Zoe Lambert is a writer based in Lancaster. She has published short stories in anthologies, and her first collection, *The War Tour*, came out in 2011, and was shortlisted for the Edge Hill Prize. She is currently working on a novel.

Kevin Barry is the author of the novels *Beatlebone* and *City Of Bohane* and the story collections *Dark Lies The Island* and *There Are Little Kingdoms*. In addition to the Edge Hill Prize, his awards include the IMPAC Dublin City Literary Award, the Goldsmith's Prize, the Sunday Times EFG Short Story Prize and the European Union Prize for Literature. His stories have appeared in the New Yorker and Granta and many other journals. His work has been translated into 16 languages. He also writes screenplays, plays and radio plays. He lives in County Sligo, Ireland.

Carys Bray's debut collection *Sweet Home* won the Scott Prize. Her first novel, *A Song for Issy Bradley*, was shortlisted for the Costa Book Awards and the Desmond Elliott Prize. It won the Author's Club Best First Novel Award and the Utah Book Award. Her second novel *The Museum of You* was recently published. Carys has an MA and PhD in Creative Writing from Edge Hill University. She lives in Southport with her husband and children. She is working on a third novel.

Adam Marek is the author of two short story collections: *Instruction Manual for Swallowing* and *The Stone Thrower*. He won the 2011 Arts Foundation Short Story Fellowship, and was shortlisted for the inaugural Sunday Times EFG Short Story Award. His stories have appeared on BBC Radio 4, and in many magazines and anthologies, including *Prospect* and *The Sunday Times*

Magazine, and *The Penguin Book of the British Short Story*. Visit Adam online at www.adammarek.co.uk.

Jon McGregor writes novels and short stories. His recent books include a short story collection, *This Isn't the Sort of Thing That Happens to Someone Like You*, and his third novel, *Even the Dogs*, which won the IMPAC Dublin Literature Award in 2012. He is a Professor of Creative Writing at the University of Nottingham, where he edits *The Letters Page*, a literary journal in letters. His new novel, *Reservoir 13*, will be published by 4th Estate in Spring 2017.

John Burnside teaches at the University of St Andrews. His poetry collections include *Feast Days* (1992), winner of the Geoffrey Faber Memorial Prize, *The Asylum Dance* (2000), winner of the Whitbread Poetry Award and *Black Cat Bone* (2011), which won both the Forward and the T. S. Eliot Prize. In 2011, he received the Petrarca Preis for poetry. His latest poetry collection is *All One Breath* (Jonathan Cape, 2014). His novels include *The Devil's Footprints* (2007), *Glister* (2008) and *A Summer of Drowning* (2011). He is also the author of a collection of short stories, *Burning Elvis* (2000), and three memoirs, *A Lie About My Father (2006)*, *Waking Up in Toytown* (2010) and *I Put A Spell On You* (2015). His most recent book is the story collection *Something Like Happy*.

Rachel Trezise grew up and still lives in the Rhondda Valley, South Wales. Her debut novel was *In and Out of the Goldfish Bowl*. Her debut short story collection, *Fresh Apples*, won the International Dylan Thomas Prize in 2006. Her story in this anthology, 'Hard as Nails', comes from her second short story collection *Cosmic Latte*. Her debut full length play, *Tonypandemonium*, was staged by National Theatre Wales in 2013 and published in Bloomsbury's *Contemporary Welsh Plays* in 2015. She has also written non-fiction. She's working on a new play and a new collection of short stories.

Madeleine D'Arcy was born in Ireland and later spent thirteen years in the UK. She worked as a criminal legal aid solicitor and as a legal editor in London before returning to Cork City with her husband and son. In 2010 she received the Hennessy First Fiction Award and the overall Hennessy

Award of New Irish Writer. Her debut collection of short fiction, *Waiting For The Bullet*, was published by Doire Press, Ireland, in 2014. She holds an MA in Creative Writing from University College Cork (2014, First Class Honours). For more information, please see her website: www.madeleinedarcy.com.

Carys Davies is the author of two collections of short stories, *Some New Ambush* and *The Redemption of Galen Pike*, which won the 2015 Frank O'Connor International Short Story Award and the 2015 Jerwood Fiction Uncovered Prize. She is also the recipient of the Royal Society of Literature's V.S. Pritchett Prize, the Society of Authors' Olive Cook Short Story Award, a Northern Writers' Award, and a 2016-2017 Cullman Fellowship at the New York Public Library. A collected edition of her stories recently came out in Australia and New Zealand, and *The Redemption of Galen Pike* will be published in 2017 in Canada, the United States, and Macedonia. Born in Wales, she lives in Lancaster.

Kirsty Gunn is the author of eight works of fiction including two collections of award winning short stories, a compendium of poetry, essays and fragments, and, most recently, *My Katherine Mansfield Project*. She is published in the UK by Faber and in over twelve countries and languages throughout the world. She has a Chair in Creative Writing at the University of Dundee where she created and directs the programme of Writing Study and Practice, and was winner of The Edge Hill Prize for *Infidelities* in 2015. She is married with two daughters and lives in London and Scotland.

China Miéville lives and works in London. He is three-time winner of the prestigious Arthur C. Clarke Award and has also won the British Fantasy Award twice. *The City & The City*, an existential thriller, was received critical acclaim and drew comparison with the works of Kafka and Orwell and Philip K. Dick. His third collection of short stories is *Three Moments of an Explosion*.

Jessie Greengrass was born in 1982. She studied philosophy in Cambridge and London, where she now lives with her partner and child. Jessie is a founder member of the Brautigan Free Press, and has appeared on London Fields Radio's Page One talking about the work of Dorothy L Sayers.

Credits

Acknowledgements

On behalf of myself and Dr James Byrne, Co-Director of Edge Hill University Press, I'd like to thank:

...the good people of Corporate Communications, our funders, at Edge Hill University – especially Roy Bayfield, Stephanie Cully and Natalie McRae for their support and practical help
...the good people of Freight Books, especially my old sparring partner Adrian Searle, also Robbie Guillory, Laura Waddell and Fiona Brownlee, who made this book beautiful and guided us through
...the good people of the Department of English, History & Creative Writing, especially Prof. Mike Bradshaw for his unflinching support
...the good people of the Creative Writing team at Edge Hill, who helped bring the Press into being, many of whom have also contributed to the Short Story Prize over the years in various roles – Billy Cowan, Philippa Holloway, Prof. Robert Sheppard, Dr Kim Wiltshire and Dr Peter Wright
...Ailsa Cox, founder of the Prize
...those who played an important role in the development of the Prize – Professor Alastair McCulloch, Katherine Straker, Mark Flinn, Professor Rhiannon Evans, Angela Samata, and Prize interns Wendy Gillett and Christine Riaz
...and most of all, a huge thank you to the dedicated Edge Hill University Press interns, without whom this book would still just be an idea: John Rutter, Sarah Billington, Liam McMahon, Laura Tickle, Harriet Hirshman, Abbie Conran and Harry Draper. May you all go on to leave us far behind. (But come back to visit sometimes)
...and thank you, John Cater, for the green light.

Rodge Glass
Ormskirk, Lancashire, 2016